TALENT
FOR
DECEPTION

MARIANNE DIMMICK

Rutledge Books, Inc.   Danbury, CT

This is a work of fiction. To the author's knowledge, Hid'n Oaks, Minnesota, doesn't exist and all persons contained in the story are fictitious, with the exception of the actors, songwriters, singers and professional athletes mentioned.

Copyright© 2002 by Marianne Dimmick

ALL RIGHTS RESERVED
Rutledge Books, Inc.
107 Mill Plain Road, Danbury, CT, 06811
1-800-278-8533
www.rutledgebooks.com

Manufactured in the United States of America

Cataloging in Publication Data
Dimmick, Marianne
     Talent For Deception

          ISBN: 1-58244-228-2

          1. Fiction

Library of Congress Control Number: 2002109577

CHAPTER ONE

HID'N OAKS LAKE, MINNESOTA
MAY 1951

ALTHOUGH IT WASN'T ABOUT TO MAKE PEOPLE THINK OF HID'N OAKS AS A tropical paradise, the town did have an unusually mild winter—for Minnesota. Total inches of snow amounted to a scant twenty inches, with one snowstorm accounting for twelve of the twenty. The days below zero were also unusual, a measly total of four.

On this twenty-first day of May, after three weeks of stifling hot, August-like weather, people were convinced that winter and the chilly nip of spring were memories. Summer was here and it was staying. Some people were already grumbling about the heat, saying that Mother Nature had some kind of deep-seated grudge against the town.

It was nine-thirty by the time Karen was able to slip out the back door to take advantage of the weather and go for what was becoming her evening swim. As she walked down the brick path to the lake, she couldn't help but smile to herself, thinking about what a silly baby she used to be. Up to the time she was twelve years old she refused to swim in water that wasn't as clear as glass. If she couldn't see bottom, she didn't go in the lake, afraid some gigantic snapping turtle or one of those ugly gar fish was just waiting for the chance to chomp off her toes or stab her to death. She was a mere child then—after all, it was five years ago. She was a married woman now. Mrs.

Talent for Deception

Paul Dmitri. Only she didn't feel like she was married. Not with her husband fighting in Korea, in what they kept referring to as a "conflict." She prayed every night that he would be home by Thanksgiving to celebrate their first year anniversary.

Humming to herself, taking two steps at a time, she continued down the path, passing under the canopy the oak trees provided. As soon as she realized she was humming "I'll Be Seeing You" she stopped. It was the song that was playing on the radio the day Paul left for Korea. At the time, he said it was a good omen. Maybe so, but hearing it by herself only made her feel like crying. She missed him more than she could bear.

She tossed her towel on the bench, slipped out of her robe, and laid it over the towel. Her hands automatically smoothed down her bathing suit. She liked the way the new Jantzen fit. It was perfect. No sag at all. She was glad she had bought the black one, it set off the deep tan she already had a head start on. By the end of May, she'd be as dark as a Brazil nut.

An owl hooted from its perch somewhere behind her. She walked to the end of the pier and looked out across the lake, first to the left and then to the right. It sure didn't look anything like the aerial map her father-in-law had hanging on the wall in his den. On the map, the lake looked like an oversized, lop-sided whale with a bad case of mumps.

She loved living with her in-laws, glad that her parents moved to Hawaii. Mike didn't treat her like she was a dumb child or preach to her about swimming alone at night. She couldn't count the times her parents harped about cramps and how people drowned when they got one. Cramps were something old, out-of-shape people had to worry about. She was young and an excellent swimmer. Mike knew it and he at least gave her credit for having enough sense to know her own limits. Of course, he didn't know that for the past three nights she'd been swimming over to Sunset

Bay. Tonight her plan had been to swim across the wider part of the lake. But it was five miles there and back. Sunset Bay was two: enough for tonight.

The lake was so beautiful at night. Peaceful. Like a huge pool of ink with splashes of moonlight on top of it. Starting with Memorial Day, it would change, with the yearly invasion of vacationers who whizzed back and forth all day in their motorboats and kids screaming and splashing water all over the place. Like clockwork, the summer residents would roll in, leaving their winter lives behind, and settle in until Labor Day when they packed up and went back to their other lives. Every year it got more crowded than the year before. Seemed like every summer nine hundred residents played host to nine million strangers, although she did have to admit that some of them were interesting to watch and talk to.

Leaning forward, her toes curled over the edge of the pier, she was all set to dive in, then hesitated, reluctant to spoil the calm beauty with the ripples her dive would make. All it took was one gentle, teasing breeze to brush across her shoulders for her not to care. She dove in and, before she lost momentum, turned up toward the surface. Immediately upon surfacing she let out an involuntary gasp. The water was cooler than it was last night. She pulled her sleek body forward into a smooth, easy Australian Crawl.

Her arms dipped in and out of the water with a smooth, knifelike precision while her feet kicked in a soundless rhythm beneath the surface. She was a strong swimmer, but she had never been concerned with speed—she didn't want to be Johnny Weissmuller. She wanted to be compared to Esther Williams: graceful, like it was all so effortless.

As she got closer to her turnaround point, she realized the temperature must have gone down, and steam was doing a lazy sort of dance as it rose out of the water. The bank was less than a hundred feet away. She needed five minutes to rest before heading back home.

On the bank, standing behind an oak tree, a man watched her, patiently measuring her progress with a cold excitement. He wasn't sure at first it was her. If it was, this was the fourth time she'd been out this week for a late night swim. He waited, hoping she'd swim all the way to his side of the lake. Like she had the last three nights.

Treading water, her feet feeling for the bottom, she sighed when they touched some rocks. Once she got to shallow water, she stood and looked behind her and saw fog drifting across the lake. Five minutes wasn't going to make that much difference.

She stepped up onto the bank and shook her hair free of excess water, then plopped down on propped elbows. Her heart was already slowing down. Two more minutes and she'd have her breath back and be able to head back before the fog got too thick.

He moved away from the tree, carefully edging his way toward her. He was six feet away from her when a twig snapped under his foot. She jumped up, instinctively turning toward the sound. She recognized Carl immediately and felt foolish for being frightened, hoping he couldn't tell in the moonlight that she was blushing.

Carl Anderson was not a very friendly man, but he surely wasn't someone to be afraid of. In fact, she always thought he was sort of ruggedly good-looking, like they said in movie magazines about stars who weren't exactly handsome, but weren't homely either. She hoped he didn't mind her trespassing. Regardless of it being vacant land, it was still his property.

She stood up. "Oh, hello, Mr. Anderson. You startled me."

When he didn't answer she became more embarrassed. To make things worse, she was getting an uneasy feeling in her stomach and an alarm was ticking inside her head, urging her to follow her instincts and go back into the water. She tried to think of how she could leave gracefully without offending him. She couldn't just jump in the water without a word. But he wasn't saying anything either, and it was making her feel uncomfortable. Of all the possible things that could pop into her head, all she could think of was that expression she always thought was so funny. It wasn't so funny now, it really did feel like her heart had jumped right up into her throat. She couldn't move. She was afraid to do or say anything, so she did what she usually did when she was uncertain, she smiled. But she could tell it wasn't her normal smile, and a nervous laugh died in her throat.

He moved so fast she didn't have time to react. He seized her wrist, and yanked her to him. The impact of her 110-pound body slamming into his solid frame knocked the wind out of her. Before she could get it back, he had his hand over her mouth and was pushing her back down to the ground.

A flash of pain shot up her arms as her elbows hit the ground and she let out a small moan, not quite comprehending what was really happening, and thinking how odd it was that Carl didn't seem to be the least bit sorry about hurting her. He had her arms pinned under her with one hand, and his other hand was covering her mouth. She was willing, ready now to scream but knew it would be too muffled for anyone to hear. He pulled his other hand out from under her and she heard the sound of a zipper. She tried to wiggle away from him and he removed his hand from her face and slapped her.

"Mr. Anderson—*please, please* don't—"

"Hold still! And shut your yap. You make one sound and I'll kill you. You unnerstan' me?"

The snarl in his voice made her cringe. Never in her life had anyone spoken to her in such a harsh manner.

"If you open your mouth again, I'll kill you and bury you right here." He tore away her swimsuit. Again she struggled, trying to get

5

free, but he was too strong. He pinned her body down with his, then grabbed her by the throat. "You think I'm kiddin'? If you do, you better start prayin'." Praying is exactly what she was doing.

He yanked up his zipper and stared down at her lying at his feet, watching her trying to cover herself up with her arms. Her eyes were closed tight.

Her tears burned her temples as they rolled into her hair. She began to tremble and bit her lip so hard it bled. She didn't notice. She had no concept of how much time had passed. Was it only minutes ago—or hours—she had prayed for someone to appear, find them and rescue her? Now it made her ill to think someone might see them, see her like this. She began praying no one would find them. No man, except Paul and Dr. Grant, had ever seen her naked. "Oh, God." She began sobbing.

He leaned forward and whispered, "Shut up. And you better keep quiet about this. Keep it our little secret." He let out a raspy chuckle that made her skin crawl. It made her feel like throwing up to think that she thought he was ruggedly handsome. He was worse than an animal. Animals had feelings. She closed her eyes and lay as still as she could.

From somewhere not too far away she heard what sounded like splashing and slowly opened her eyes, afraid he was still standing over her. He wasn't. She wanted to get up and run into the water but forced herself to stay as still as possible until she was sure he was gone. A few seconds later, she saw him in the moonlight. He was naked. He had his clothes over his shoulder and was walking away. She realized he must have washed himself off. As soon as he was out of sight, she made a frantic search for her bathing suit. What she found was not going to cover her, but she grabbed it up anyway.

As a precaution, she took one quick look around her to make sure he was really gone, then ran into the water. She stumbled on some rocks, bent down to pick up two of them and tied the Jantzen around them, then threw the rocks out as far as she could.

The fog was spreading rapidly. It wasn't going to take long for it to get so thick and high it would be impossible to tell if she was heading in the right direction. She didn't give a tinker's damn about being graceful, she wanted to get across the lake, away from here. She shot forward and started to swim with as much power as her aching arms and legs could give. The more her body protested, the harder she pumped them. She was afraid her pelvis might be crushed and her vagina would never heal itself together. She switched over on her back, trying to pull herself along without using her lower body, but it was too slow. She had to get home. She turned over again and swam as hard as she could, knowing she had to get across before the fog got heavier and blocked everything out. If it did, she'd never find her way back.

She started to cry when she looked up and saw a halo of light straight ahead of her, like a lighthouse beacon guiding her home. It was the patio light that was the Dmitri symbol of hospitality, always on from dusk to dawn.

The pier posts couldn't have been more comforting if they were human. She embraced them as if they were, clinging to them so tightly that her arms grew numb. The drop in the temperature had been considerable and brought out an army of goose bumps on her arms and shoulders. It was only when she started to choke that she realized the sobbing sounds she heard were coming out of her. She covered her mouth with one hand, using her other hand to pull herself along the pier to shallow water. She stepped out of the water and hurried into the boathouse.

Not wanting to turn on a light, she groped around in the dark for a bar of soap. Her fingers touched something round. She dug her fingernails into it and with relief felt the softness cake up inside her nails.

When she started to scrub herself, she realized how sore she was,

7

the upper part of her body was full of bruises. As much as it hurt, she refused to ease up, she wanted the smell of him off of her. Wanted to be clean. When she was satisfied she was free of his smell, she rinsed herself off and climbed back onto the pier. Without drying herself off, she put on her robe. When she looked up at the patio light again, what she saw shrank her sense of security. It was no longer a symbol of hospitality, it had become an accusing spotlight waiting to expose her shame. Her heart was pounding so hard she was afraid it was going to burst right through her sore rib cage.

The thought made her stomach retch and without warning bile shot up and out of her throat and into her towel. She threw the towel on the ground by the picnic table. Tomorrow, first thing in the morning, she'd come down and wash it out. She ran over to the path.

It took all her strength to get back up the hill. When she reached the corner of the house, she leaned against it, waiting for the pain and nausea to pass. She started to shiver. It was impossible for her to stay out here all night. Somehow she had to get up the steps and into her room before she was too sore to move or she passed out.

Trying not to make any noise, she turned the doorknob and edged her way into the kitchen. Once she was all the way in, she locked the door carefully and tiptoed quickly across the kitchen floor, speeding past her father-in-law's bedroom door without stopping to say good night. She raced up the stairs to her bedroom and locked the door, then hurried into her bathroom. Looking in the mirror, she saw someone strange looking back at her. She knew she would never be the same. Her life would never be the same. She turned on the shower and stepped into the tub.

The steam in the bathroom was thicker than the fog on the lake by the time she turned off the water. Her skin was almost fuchsia. After she gently toweled herself dry, she splashed the vanilla cologne Paul had given her for Christmas over her neck and shoulders. She pulled on a pair of her husband's pajamas, climbed into bed, and

8

cried into his pillow.

When she had no more tears left, she tried closing her eyes, hoping sleep would come quickly and carry her off on a magic carpet to a place where she could erase her memory. She hoped she would find that what had just happened was nothing more than a bad dream. But when she closed her eyes she was confronted with flashbacks of Carl. Images of him jumped out at her and pulled her back to all the different places she had seen him over the last few years. The hardware store where she had caught him staring, in the drugstore, at the gas station and walking down main street. It wasn't unusual for people to stare at her. She was used to it. Now she knew it was different with Carl and asked herself how she could have been so dense. All this time she had taken it for granted Carl was just admiring her, or that he was just thinking about something, or waiting for her to say hello so he could say hello back. But he wasn't waiting for her to say hello, or admiring her. He was thinking about raping her.

There was no one she knew who had been raped. Who would tell? She never would. She'd die of shame. She was never going to understand why God let it happen to her. She had been a good girl all her life. Obeyed her parents, did what they told her to…most of the time. The really important stuff, like all the never-dos they drummed into her head. Never to raise her voice or sass her elders. Never do anything to make them ashamed of her. Never to be too forward, or dress or act like some common floozy. They told her to always act like a lady, to always mind her manners. What they forgot to tell her was that there were people who didn't deserve to be treated with respect. Why didn't they ever take the time to warn her about that?

She didn't care if God struck her dead, she wished Carl were dead. How could it be sinful to wish someone or something evil was gone? Wishing wasn't like praying. Even if it were, she didn't care.

She rolled over on her side, making a pledge never to tell a soul about tonight. If anyone found out, she'd die. Kill herself. Her body relaxed and she began to imagine herself floating on a plump, cottony white cloud that was going to take her further and further away from tonight. To some safe place, a haven where there were only good, happy memories to relive and wonderful times were yet to be. Where she and Paul would live happily ever after.

CHAPTER TWO

MIKE DMITRI WAS SITTING UP IN BED, ANNOYED THAT HE WAS STILL AWAKE and puzzled by the way Karen had sneaked into the house earlier. There was no other way to put it. He never heard the door click open, but he had heard it lock. Karen knew in this house, doors were never locked. She must have seen his light was still on, his door was cracked at least an inch, he saw her robe whiz past his door. It wasn't like Karen not to stick her head in to say good night. There was no reason for her to feel she had to sneak in the house like some half-assed burglar.

Well, there was no reason for him not to admit he was relieved she hadn't stuck her head in. He was in no mood for chit-chat tonight anyway. Not after going at it with Dina. The girl was too headstrong. At twenty, she was as pig-headed as her grandfather had been at forty. He hated to think what she was going to be like at forty. The day she was born he saw it, knew she was going to turn out to be a Cossack. His daughter had always been a challenge, which he wanted her to be, but not all the time. She could be intolerably wearing. There were times, like tonight, he wished she was more like her mother: pleasant, flexible. Instead, she was more like him. It was the price parents paid when they overplayed setting an example.

Tonight he was in no mood to acknowledge their likenesses. He was still angry with her for overstepping her bounds. He hadn't said it to her because she would have reminded him that he was the one who taught her and Paul they had to set their own limits. But that wasn't the issue. Dina had had to be reminded she was temporarily in charge of everything down at the yard but he was still head of this family and capable of making his own decisions. He didn't need her permission to lend Carl $100,000 to build a resort. In another week, he'd be able to get rid of the walker and be ready to put in eight, nine hours in at the yard. He'd be running things down there again and the Cossack could go back to college and get her law degree. With luck, by that time, she'd be married to Jake Tanner and *he* could deal with her—if the slowpoke ever got around to asking her.

He glanced over at the clock behind his late wife's picture on the nightstand. Midnight. Too late for warm milk. What he wanted was a shot of brandy, but alcohol kept him awake. His insomnia was doing a dandy job of that without the liquor, thanks to Dina.

It wasn't only the to-do with Dina that had kept him awake. Sleep had been hard to track down for quite a while now. It was the nightmares, the terrible images of Paul lying in some Korean ditch, dying all alone, that kept him awake. It was odd that he never doubted Jake Tanner would make it back home. But when it came to his son Paul, there was a sense of foreboding that haunted him, that made him think he'd never see his son again.

His eyelids were getting heavy, a good sign that he was at last tired enough to get some decent sleep, now that his girls were home safe, tucked in their beds, and all was well in his house at least. He looked over at Helen's picture again and grinned, thinking if she were alive, she'd be giving him the raspberries about what an old mother hen he was. Helen had never seen any point in worrying—she'd often said you could either do something about a problem or not.

He yawned, reached over to pick up Helen's picture, kissed his finger and touched her lips with it. "We made it through another day,

Rainbow. Good night." He put her back on the nightstand and turned out the light.

On the other side of the lake, Carl Anderson sat on his porch steps with his legs stretched out in front of him. His thumb was hooked around the first belt loop of his Levis, his fingers stroked the cowboy busting a bronc on his belt buckle. There was a half-smoked cigarillo dangling from his lips. He took a long drag, illuminating a face that was hard-boned and red from the sun. His cheeks were hollow, his nose had been broken twice and was slightly crooked. There was a smile on his lips but it lacked warmth, and his brown eyes looked like humor would be wasted on them. He ran his hand over his still damp, dark brown hair and sniffed for any telltale female odors he hadn't rinsed off in the lake. He didn't smell any.

He took another long drag and held up his wrist to check his watch. It was 12:30. He flicked the cigarillo onto the driveway, while his eyes looked over toward the black outline across the lake. The fog didn't stop him and he didn't need daylight or binoculars to see the Dmitri Place. He knew the spot by heart. Outside, inside, upside, downside. It was him Mike came to when he needed kitchen cabinets and his bathrooms remodeled.

He swore under his breath. The Dmitri Place. Everybody called it "the Dmitri Place," like it was some goddamn monument or church for crissakes. Old biddies in town carried on about the velvety, carpet-like lawn and the lovely French windows. All they were was doors with small panes of glass in 'em. He didn't deny the place was built solidly of fieldstone and oak. And it had a good-sized kitchen he wouldn't mind having.

Mike and Helen's room was right off the kitchen, the bitch's room right above theirs.

He stood up and stretched. The movement made a board creak beneath him. Goddamn boards. Whole place was going to hell. But

13

he wasn't gonna worry 'bout it much longer. Not anymore, now that he had the $100,000 to build his resort. He was gonna tear down this shack and build a private residence in back of the resort for him and Marth. He pulled the check out of his pocket and stared at it, reassuring himself it was real. He put it back.

Seventeen damn long years he'd been dreaming about having his own resort, ever since him and Charlie worked construction in the Catskills, turning farmhouses into hotels, and also that place they built for that ex-bootlegger. That was where he first got the idea of having his own resort. Who knows what might have been, if he had not gotten stupid? Well, water under the bridge. He got away from there just in time. No one around here knew he was there except Charlie, and he wasn't about to tell anyone. Not even Marth knew. And never would.

It was dumb what he'd done tonight. He had to lay off the boilermakers, or at least cut down a few. Soon he'd be important in this town and he couldn't afford taking dumb risks, screwin' up his plans. Not that he had to worry about her opening her yap. She'd be too scared to open her mouth.

Tomorrow he'd put the check in the bank, buy all the materials on his list and maybe order some suits. Soon as the resort was built, no more overalls and tee shirts. Businessmen wore suits and ties. And white shirts and their shoes were always shined. He took the check out of his pocket and fondled it.

After his resort was finished, it was gonna make the Dmitri Place look like a turd shack. Everything was gonna be oak—the lodge, the cabins and, in time, the restaurant. None of this crummy clapboard crap like some of the places he worked on in the Catskills. And this dump he was livin' in now, with lousy, squeaky boards. Anderson's Resort was gonna be a damn gold mine. He'd be richer than old Mike ever dreamed of being.

Yessir, a goddamn gold mine. Even his rumpot buddies over at the Fisherman's Bar and Grill who smirked every time he talked about his resort, hadn't smirked tonight after he waved the check in their faces. Impressed the hell out of the damn rummies. He bought four rounds of boilermakers and they were plastered to the damn gills, while he was just getting started. He could handle ten, twelve boilermakers, maybe more.

Which was a hell of a lot more than the great Mike Dmitri could do. Only drink ole Mike ever could handle was highballs, and only four at that. Highballs! Sissy drinks. Nowadays, all the old Russki drank was juice. Straight.

Mike Dmitri, the big ladies' man. What a crock. He was sick of listening to the brown noses who ran off at the mouth saying Mike was such a prince of a guy. But he kept his opinions to himself. Kept his trap shut. Mike sure as hell wasn't no prince in his home. Helen'd been the one who ruled his roost. She led the great Mike Dmitri around by his nose, like he was a puppet. No one could say that about Carl Anderson. He wasn't giving up his balls for no woman. Everyone knew who was king in his castle.

Whenever he looked back on it, it was hard to believe he'd worked for Mike for thirteen back-busting years. For thirteen damn long, hard years he'd stuck it out, busted his ass for Mike Dmitri. He started in 1937 when he was twenty years old. He jacked until Mike found out he was a carpenter by trade. Didn't take long for Mike to see he was the best, a master carpenter. He'd even told Carl in front of everyone it was a sorry waste of his time to be sawing down trees instead of making things out of the wood. Mike made him master carpenter. He was top dog in Dmitri Construction. When construction slowed down, he worked in the yard and the quarry. He didn't gripe about any job he was asked to do. He did them all.

December 7, 1941 changed a lot of things for him. Not that he was so dumb as to say it out loud, but when the Japs bombed Pearl, they did him a favor. He was glad when a bum eardrum and flat feet kept him out of the war. He didn't want to risk getting his ass shot off for nobody, except to save himself. But lucky for him, Mike's good buddy, Phil Tanner, couldn't wait to enlist the Monday after Pearl. And the great Mike Dmitri had to come running to him, ask him to be his foreman. Yeah, until Phil got back.

Who'd've thought that old geezer would actually make it back? Not him.

He reached in his pocket for another cigarillo, feeling the check before he pulled one out of the box and stuck it in his mouth and lit it, thinking about how things just seemed to turn out wrong for him. Wrong place, wrong time. But he never cried the blues about how things never came easy for him. No man alive or dead could say Carl Anderson was afraid of hard work. No one heard him gripe about it when Phil came back and took his job away from him. He just sat back and waited. First Helen Dmitri croaked, then Mike had a stroke, the kid got hitched and shipped off to Korea. Everyone expected him to get Phil's job and Phil would move into the office. That's the way it was supposed to happen. But no, someone had to take a royal dump on him. That wisenheimer college brat of Mike's came back and took over the office. Dina Dmitri was like a thistle up his ass from the first day she started hanging around the lumberyard. He called her the what-zis, why-do kid. Snot-nosed punk had a way of asking questions like she was giving him the third degree. "What's this?" "What's that?" "Why do you do this?"

Had to be two years ago when she came prancing into the yard to take charge. Sashaying around like the queen bee. He remembered it good because it was the same day he quit. Thinking about it still ate at him. Dina, the queen bee, sitting behind Mike's desk, and him having to stand in front of her like some kid called on the carpet. He hated having to look at her, hated having her know he hated it. She had a way of looking at him, made him feel like a cockroach or something. Made him feel like he had to wipe spit off his face. Unconsciously, he brushed the side of his face.

Soon people were going to see Carl Anderson was nobody's fool. Not then, not now. He always did what he said he'd do. He hadn't been sitting on his can doing nothing. He kept his eyes and ears open, he knew after the war was over, people would be buying cars, getting away from the cities and taking vacations at lakes. He wanted to pay off his debts first before borrowing the money for the resort. Between this dump and the five acres he'd bought from Mike, he still owed close to $20,000.

He figured he had time. There were a few residents who rented out dinky cabins and some cottages for years but no one talked about building a resort. Until that jabber-jaw realtor shot off his mouth about how nice it would be if Hid'n Oaks had one. It nearly gave him a stroke.

He knew time had run out. He had to make his move right away and start building before someone else beat him to it.

It fried him having to go to Mike for the dough. That old Mike Dmitri was the only one willing and able to lend him $100,000. And for as much as he hated the idea of Mike being his partner until the loan was paid up, it didn't seem so bad now. Being partners didn't make him feel like he had kissed Mike's ass for the money.

If people knew Mike was charging him way below the bank rate, that he never quibbled about interest at all, they wouldn't give him so much credit for being such a sharp businessman like they did. Not that he expected Mike to hand him the damn money on some damn silver platter, but Mike did have his dough handed to him by his Uncle Walter. Mike's uncle was the one who busted his ass workin' as a lumberjack and walker. It was Walter who started the sawmill and the yard. Mike's big contribution was to come up with the construction idea.

Talk about timing! Today the damn Dmitri name was all over town. The sawmill, the lumberyard, the construction company and the stone quarry. Just today Mike said he was planning on building a furniture shop for his kid when he got back from Korea. Wouldn't surprise him if they named the whole damn town "Dmitri."

The squeaking of the screen door opening and closing, followed by the creaking of the boards told him he was about to be joined by his wife, Martha. She walked over to the swing and sat down beside her husband.

Her eyes held many questions but they rarely reached her lips. She knew better. Carl didn't like being given the third degree about where he'd been or what he did. If he wanted her to know, he'd tell her. Tonight she didn't have to ask, from the strength of the fumes, he had to have been over at the Fisherman's Bar & Grill, drinking with his friends. Only two places Carl could be when he wasn't working: playing pool at the Fisherman's or fishing.

Martha's thin, five-foot frame was deceiving, she was not as fragile as she looked. No one had to tell her she was no glamour girl, but she didn't think of herself as homely either. Her golden, corn-silk hair and pale blue eyes saved her, she thought, from being thought of as too plain.

Helen Dmitri had been her best friend. It was Helen who told her that her eyes were very lovely, sincere and true. A soft sigh escaped before she was able to suppress it. Helen Dmitri's opinion had meant a great deal to her. Helen had been on her mind more than usual lately.

She supposed it was because of the resort and all. Funny how it came to her mind about Helen asking her what was the worst day in her life, and what was the most fantastic. At the time she was embarrassed because she couldn't come up with any definite answers. All she could think of to say was there were so many good days she couldn't think of a really rotten day, and the only truly fantastic day was when she married Carl. Today was different. If Helen were here she could tell her without hesitation that this was her most fantastic day. No exceptions either.

She hoped Mike realized how much his kindness was appreciated. Since he agreed to lend Carl the money, Carl's disposition had improved tremendously.

Carl's spirits were flying so high she could just picture him bumping into clouds. He was behaving like a little boy. And no one could be happier for him than she. If anyone deserved the chance to see his dream come true, it was her husband. According to what he told her, he'd worked hard all his life. And he was still working hard.

Some women made the mistake of thinking they could change their men, but she knew better. She was foolish enough to try once. She offered to help him correct his lazy grammar, his habit of dropping his g's. She never brought it up again. She was satisfied and proud that Carl showed respect for her feelings by being careful with his language in front of Helen, knowing how much Helen's opinion meant to her. He never cussed around Helen. When Helen was around, he'd use words like dang, or futzed up or goshdarnit.

Carl's pretending to be indifferent about what people thought of him didn't fool her. He cared. She could tell he had been genuinely pleased when she repeated what Helen said about him, that he was a very fastidious man. Which he was. During the summer there wasn't a day he didn't shower less than three times a day, and every time he showered he put on clean clothes, including all his underwear

Another sigh almost escaped but she caught it before it did. She didn't want him to think she was discontented about something, or wasn't excited about his dream coming true. She was looking forward to the resort, having people around. Since Helen's passing hardly anyone came around and she missed having company. Carl didn't care much for company. He had some strange ideas about people being nosey, snooping around, finding out his business.

Talent for Deception

She nearly jumped off the swing when Carl flung his arm around her shoulder. "I'm gonna have it all, Marth. It's all gonna come true." He lifted his hand to her hair and started stroking it, something he hadn't done for quite some time. He said he liked walking his fingers through her hair. She liked having him do it.

Hugging her close to him, he kissed her cheek. Marrying her was the smartest move he ever made. She was easy to get along with, good at dealing with people. That was gonna help when the resort was done. He was never good at suckin' up to people. She was. Everyone liked Marth. Most of all, the prince, Mike Dmitri liked her.

Marth was no chatterbox around the house. She liked to chew the fat with all the windbags in town, but that was okay, as long as she did it in town and he didn't have to listen to it. He knew full well that all the years he worked for Dmitri, none of it counted as much as Marth. She was the real reason Mike agreed to lend him the money. And all because Marth was Helen's best friend, and took good care of Helen when things got bad.

He had no quarrel with that. What he wouldn't have liked was if Marth started acting like Helen. When women got to thinking they were smarter than men, they got bossy and were nothing but trouble. He was no Mike Dmitri; he wore the pants in his house.

He squeezed her shoulder "Almost there, Marth. Before you know it, dream's gonna be a reality."

"I'm so happy for you, hon. I know it's going to take hard work on both our parts, but we'll make it a success."

"Hard work never bothered us. Neither one of us is afraid of that." He patted the pocket that had the check in it. It didn't make any difference why Mike handed him the check, he had it and that's what counted.

"Gonna be a gold mine, Marth. There'll be people coming from Wisconsin, Iowa, Illinois, Minnesota, probably even Canada, to stay at Anderson's Resort."

"Hon? Don't you think maybe it might be a good idea to have Mike over for dinner or maybe we should take him out for dinner over at the Norseman's…"

He shot up off the swing. "What the hell for? Show Mike our gratitude? This is business. Get it through your head that Mike did not give me the damn money. I borrowed it. I'm gonna pay him back, with int'rest. Hell, the bastard's gonna make money off the money I'm paying him to use. Where do you think the lumber is coming from? He's giving with his right hand and taking it back twice with his left. I swear, woman, you got some real lamebrain notions." She was about to say something else but he cut her off.

"Don't be giving me any sob stories about the poor Dmitris and how tough they had it. Mike Dmitri never had bill collectors pounding on his door. Makes me laugh when people talk about being poor. They don't know what poor is. People lookin' at you like you was a piece of dirt, like you had bugs all over you. I've had it tough all my life. Started workin' when I was twelve. Not any kid jobs, either. And how about us, you and me haven't been on easy street, or maybe you haven't been payin' attention. I ain't been working all that much this year."

"I know that, I just thought…"

"Thought what? Don't think. I'm not int'rested in what you think about what we should do. And don't be cryin' on my shoulder about poor Mike. You think so much of him, pack up and move in with him."

"Carl!"

"Oh, forget it. No use talking sense to you." She looked like she was going to start crying. He sat down on the swing. As nice as he knew how, he said, "I've been planning on telling you, starting next Sunday, I'm going to start going to church with you. How do you like that? Tomorrow after I put the check in the bank, we're drivin' to the Cities to get some decent clothes. I need some suits and ties and shoes and you could use some nice dresses."

Talent for Deception

She didn't know what to say. She didn't want him to see her cry so she laid her head on his chest and squeezed his hand, wishing there were a way to stop this day from ending.

"Know what else? I'm gonna start joining some of the clubs. Eagles maybe. And the Moose." The American Legion was out, so was the VFW. "Places where I can rub elbows with other businessmen in the area. Make contacts. I'll be bringin' money into this town and that means I'll have influence. Be important."

The smell of her shampoo and the touch of her chamois skin made him grow hard and tense. "Let's forget about the damn Dmitris and hit the sack, have a roll in the hay." He pulled her off the swing and nuzzled her neck.

Tonight, lovemaking was the last thing Martha wanted to do. She was tired, sticky and hurt. But no wife had any right to deny her husband.

Long ago, when she was young, she'd had her fantasies about what it would be like to be married and have a family. The day after their wedding, she learned how silly her fantasies were, and promised herself not to waste time thinking about such foolishness again. It wasn't until they moved to Hid'n Oaks and she saw how Mike and Helen were together, and how they were with their children, Paul and Dina, that Martha knew her fantasy was possible. The Dmitris were living it, proof that people were kind and loving and weren't afraid to show it. And they were kind and friendly, and giving to strangers. No one could tell her that her fantasies weren't possible, she just had to come to terms with the fact that they weren't possible for her, they were only going to happen to special people. Today she became one of those special people.

CHAPTER THREE

WHAT MOST PEOPLE SAW WHEN THEY FIRST MET KAREN DMITRI WAS AN extremely beautiful, blonde girl with a lovely smile and deep sapphire eyes. The bonus was discovering how sweet and uncomplicated she was.

Until the age of fourteen, Karen believed what her mother told her, that if she kissed a boy she would get pregnant. After she compared notes with her friends she understood her mother told her the story to discourage her from getting too cozy with the opposite sex. The truth did nothing to encourage her to go on a kissing spree, because there was only one person of the opposite sex she wanted to kiss, and that was Paul Dmitri. When he did finally kiss her, it was not as memorable as she imagined it would be, it was more sweet than passionate. She didn't mind because what he said meant more, he told her she was his angel with a Christmas tree smile, stardust in her eyes and moonlight in her heart.

Today, at seventeen, there was no Christmas tree smile, no stardust in her eyes, or any moonlight in her heart. They were overshadowed by a festering resentment and a hatred she had never experienced before Carl.

Standing before the Cheval mirror, her sapphire eyes were unconcerned that her honey blonde hair was a tangled mess and that her nose resembled a giant cranberry. What her eyes were concerned with was the unmistakable roundness of her belly. Distressed and getting closer to panic by the minute because she knew Paul's shirts wouldn't hide it much longer, she had to decide what to do. If she walked out of this house without saying a word to anyone, where would she go? Not to her parents. She'd die before telling her friends. The one person she felt she could trust was Dina, who was also the one person she didn't want to confide in. Next to Paul, Dina's respect meant a great deal to her. She was in a…quandary. That was the word for it. A strange sounding word with such a terrible meaning.

She felt she was in this *quandary* partly because of her mother. Her mother was the one who told her not to worry about her irregular periods, so she didn't bother keeping a record. And because she didn't, now she had no idea of how pregnant she was. The other part of the reason was because she had been so successful in erasing that night from her memory. Little help it did, because now she was forced into trying to remember so she could figure it out. As if that weren't enough, she had to put up with her mother's constant bragging ringing in her ears, hearing her mother telling her what a blessing it was that she had her mother's body structure and probably wouldn't show she was pregnant until the last few months like her mother did. And that she too would probably be blessed with not having to put up with morning sickness. She put Paul's shirt back on and looked at her belly.

This was blessed? Having her life turned into an ugly nightmare was a blessing? Dealing with the strain of having to lie and pretend all the time was a blessing? Being on constant guard every day, every hour, afraid something would slip, or someone would notice how big her belly was getting was no blessing. Last night she could have died when Mike commented at dinner that she looked better with a few pounds on her. And Dina! Four times this past week she asked her if she was okay. She used to write Paul every day, now he was lucky if she wrote twice a month. She was afraid if she wrote more often he would read between the lines. He might be able to tell how much she held back from him.

It was so unfair! What would be fair, was if Carl had some kind of mark or telltale sign on his body so people could tell what he'd done to her. Every time she spotted him, it made her angrier than the last time, seeing him walking around with a big smile and talking friendly to everyone. The only reason she didn't pray for him to die was because she was afraid it would put a hex on her prayers for Paul.

As always, thinking of him filled her with a need to see him. Looking through their wedding albums usually helped make her feel better. She took them out of the drawer and sat by the window and started to page through the albums. If she were to ask herself why she needed to see the pictures, she couldn't say if it was a way to find solace, punish herself by remembering what was, or finding yet another way to stall. She didn't know or care. What she knew was that it helped her to freeze so many memories of that day in her mind. When she turned to the page with her favorite picture of Paul, she traced the contour of his face with her finger. He was looking directly into the camera, staring back at her with what she called his bedroom eyes. She couldn't let herself think of them that way today.

Their first year anniversary was almost here. Thanksgiving Day. Sometimes it seemed like decades ago, sometimes like yesterday. Three years ago the world stood still. She was just fourteen and she and her friends had gone to see *Gone with the Wind*. There was a long line at the Grand Theater that day. Paul and Dina were in line four people ahead of them. She was looking toward the front of the line when Paul happened to turn around. Maybe he was looking to see how long the line was, or for someone he knew, but when he got to her, his eyes stopped. Before he turned away, he smiled and winked. It was the first time she had seen him up that close. His eyes were very dark, like melted chocolate, and his lashes were so thick that when he closed them they locked together like zippers. She knew from that moment they were destined to be together. Meant for each other.

For half an hour they all stood in that line waiting. Long enough for her friends to notice her staring at Paul. Naturally, they teased her about having a crush on him, and let her know that he was at least six years older than she, and a college man at that. No college man, they said, was going to bother with a child, a high school freshman. He'd be accused of robbing the cradle. She told them they were too immature to understand. It wasn't a crush. And she asked what did five or six years difference make? Everyone knew that girls matured faster than boys. And didn't they know that Paul's father was fourteen or sixteen years older than his wife, Helen? And, besides that, her own father was eight years older than her mother. If nothing else, it stopped them from teasing her.

When they all got inside the theater and the usher showed them to their seats, she wanted to tip him. She ended up sitting directly behind Paul. For her girlfriends' sake, she pretended to be engrossed in the movie, but her eyes rarely left the back of Paul's head. Every now and then he turned to look or say something to Dina and she saw his profile. She had to fight to restrain herself from leaning forward and touching his beautiful black hair. If it weren't for his curly hair and the bump on his nose that got broken in some stupid hockey game, people would mistake him for Tyrone Power. She knew her friends thought so too, but he was her dreamboat, not theirs.

While Rhett was telling Scarlett that what she needed was a man, Karen pretended Paul was sitting next to her saying the very same words to her.

It took him two years to ask her for a date. She could still see how impressed her parents were when he arrived at their door, by appointment yet, and asked them for permission to take their daughter sailing. Her parents hadn't been able to say yes fast enough. Thinking back on it, Karen couldn't think of any parent who wouldn't allow their daughter to date Paul Dmitri. For weeks her father went around like some gossip columnist, reminding her what an honor it was to have a young man from a family with an impeccable reputation interested in her, and how Mike Dmitri was what they used to call a gentlemen of the old school and could anyone tell him of any other young man who would make an appointment with a young lady's parents to ask for their permission to date their daughter? Her mother was more impressed by the Dmitri Place and money. But they both agreed the family had class. "Breeding" her father called it. To this day, Karen suspected her father had a crush of his own–on Helen Dmitri.

The money was something Karen didn't care much about. She knew she would have married Paul if he was dirt poor. What she cared about was the way he treated her. Like a princess. Not with gifts and things, but by being attentive, and kind and respectful.

She smiled wistfully, thinking that on that day, Hid'n Oaks became her Hollywood, and she and Paul were like two movie stars. A handsome couple with the world in their lap. The newlyweds who were surrounded by people who cared about them and loved them and wished them nothing but the best. She sighed. Living in the beauty and comfort of the Dmitri Place was wonderful. Yet, as corny as it sounded, she would have been satisfied with a small house and a small picket fence.

Unexpectedly, the movie, *Leave Her to Heaven* edged its way into her mind. She had gone to see it at the Grand months ago, and had given some serious consideration to doing what Gene Tierney had done in the movie. To lose the baby she didn't want, she purposely tripped over the carpet and fell down the stairs. She didn't have to go looking for the stairs and carpet, they were forty feet from her bedroom door. But every time she thought she was close to actually doing it, she couldn't. Why was it easy to be brave thinking things, but actually doing them wasn't so easy? In this case, she reasoned, it wouldn't make any sense to risk a bad fall that might leave her paralyzed, because all it would accomplish was having people find out she was pregnant sooner. She wiped the tears off the album and slammed it shut.

It was time to quit stalling and face the inevitable. Her plan was to leave before Mike or anyone else found out—before Mike threw her out. But she wanted someone to hear her side, which she found was grotesquely funny in a way. After all the time she spent being so afraid someone would find out, she was going to confide in someone, and she was afraid Dina wouldn't believe her.

* * *

Karen put on a robe to walk across the hall to Dina's bedroom. No one left their bedroom in a nightgown or pajamas in the Dmitri house without putting on a robe first.

As she stood outside in front of Dina's bedroom door, her eyes so swollen they hurt, her nose plugged and red, Karen concentrated on rallying the courage to say the words as eloquently as they were in her head. Her feet hurt something awful and her ankles were so swollen they were practically bulging over her slippers. She didn't know whether to laugh or to cry. Before the tears had a chance to start, she tapped on the door. It seemed to take Dina forever to respond, but Karen knew only seconds had passed when she heard Dina's voice call out to her.

"C'mon in."

For a split second Karen thought about running back to her own room. Instead, she took a deep breath, opened the door, and stepped inside Dina's bedroom.

CHAPTER FOUR

DINA WAS SITTING AT THE OAK ROLLTOP DESK PAUL HAD MADE FOR HER, TO match her bedroom set and the built-in bookcase. All had been stained with what Karen called pecan pie brown. As usual, Dina's coppery black hair was pulled back away from her face and she had a law book in front of her.

"Hi. I'm not disturbing you am I? If I am, I can come back later."

"No, make yourself comfortable. Just give me a few minutes to finish this chapter."

"Sure." Karen's first choice to be comfortable was the window seat, but it would mean having to circle around Dina and distracting her again. Her second choice was the bed. It was close to the door, the fastest way out in case Dina asked her to leave. Her heart was thumping like a bass fiddle and her head ached.

After a minute or two went by she was sorry she didn't have a movie magazine to look through. To pass the time and keep her mind on something else, she settled for a visual tour of Dina's room, making sure she didn't linger too long in any one spot, or leapfrog around the room. She didn't want Dina to think she was being nosy, or impatient.

She didn't much care for the pale aqua walls or the caramel carpet, but there was something about the room that was soothing, and the thick carpet felt good to her feet. Karen was thinking of how many times she'd been in this room and she estimated no more than five. The Dmitris treated their bedrooms like private sanctuaries. She used to think it was strange, but when Paul was home it was wonderful. No one disturbed them.

She looked over at the wall opposite her, at a portrait of Mike and Helen. It was an anniversary portrait. Their eyes looked alive and accusing. She shifted her attention away from the wall and over to Dina. Her head was still in her book.

Dina's head was buried in a book the first time she saw her at the library. Dina was probably fourteen then, and was already five-eight. It was a good thing she hadn't grown much taller, the only boys in town taller than her then were Paul and Jake.

If she ever told anyone she used to feel sorry for Dina, they'd say she was cuckoo. Dina was considered the richest and the most beautiful girl in town. Karen always thought she was, too. With her apple-green eyes and thick coppery-black hair, she looked a lot like Ava Gardner, without the dimple. Her hair was wavy, not curly like Paul's. From what she could gather, boys were attracted to Dina, but she intimidated them with that no nonsense air she had about her. That was the reason Karen felt sorry for Dina, for that, and Dina must have born with an old mind. She was only a little more than two years older, but sometimes she acted like she was twenty years older. From what Karen was able to observe, the only boy—*man*—she corrected herself, who was not intimidated by Dina, besides Paul, was Jake Tanner. Which was fortunate, because he was probably going to marry her.

The portrait on the wall drew her attention back to it. Anyone who looked at Mike and Paul knew instantly they were father and son. And there could never be any doubt that Dina was Mike's daughter. Both of them had Mike's dark Mediterranean-like looks; they always looked tan, which made her feel a little envious. Mike was a very handsome man. People were always saying that Paul was the spitting image of his father.

She gasped. What if the thing inside her came out looking like Carl?

30

"Oohh, God, Dina. *Please, please* help me. I'm in very bad trouble."

The anguished despair in Karen's voice alarmed Dina so much that she was sitting beside her and had Karen cradled in her arms within seconds.

"Karen, what is it? What's wrong?"

In an effort to keep her face hidden from Dina, she buried it down deep into Dina's shoulder, afraid to see the disgust on Dina's face as the sickening, shameful words spilled from her mouth.

After Karen pulled out all the buried memories she could recall, she continued to cling to Dina, unable to look at Dina or have Dina see her face. For a long time Dina sat and held her and stroked her head without speaking. Finally, she lifted Karen's head and held it inches from her own. When she did speak, her normally soft voice was sharp and sounded mean. "Karen, look at me."

Dina sounded as though she were angry at her. Karen pulled away and slowly raised her head. She was encouraged by the smile on Dina's face, relieved not to see disgust. It took a few seconds for her to realize that although Dina was smiling, her eyes were like stone. And her face was very dark and rigid. It made her ask herself if Dina thought she was lying?

"Honest to God, Dina, I didn't flirt or egg him on."

"Karen, the damn troglodyte raped you! You have a right to feel many things, but not shame. The shame is his. Not yours. Don't let that worm rape your mind by making you feel ashamed. My God, Karen, you didn't have an affair. That wasn't some rendezvous you had with him. He raped you."

"But I…I didn't tell you the worst part. I'm pregnant!"

It was Dina's turn to gasp. "How long?"

"I. . . I don't know! I can't remember! I wanted to forget it ever happened. I never wanted to think about it ever. Oh, God! I just want it to be over and done with…" Her tears were hot and burned her cheeks.

Talent for Deception

"Shhh. It's okay, Karen. Just try, try to give me an idea."

"I'm not sure. Four months, maybe five?" She paused as if she expected Dina to provide the exact number of months.

Dina covered up any telltale signs of her own anxiety as best she could. It wasn't going to help and it would make matters worse, if possible. To distract Karen while she recovered her own composure, she took Karen's hands in hers and squeezed them, then released them and hugged Karen close. It wasn't a good time to ask questions that couldn't be answered. It only made Karen feel worse.

"It's okay. Let's not worry about it now." It was hard to believe Karen could be four months pregnant, much less five. She then realized Karen hadn't been to see a doctor. She leaned back to look at Karen.

"How do you feel? Do you feel sick, or are you in any sort of physical discomfort?"

"Physical discomfort? Oh, you mean pain? No, I'm okay that way." Karen saw Dina's right eyebrow was arched, like an open stepladder. It was something she did when she was deep in thought.

Dina's mind searched for a path through the scrambled mass of thoughts, but she couldn't get beyond the irony that Thanksgiving was three days away: Karen and Paul's first wedding anniversary. Of all the things in the world Karen needed, it wasn't the anniversary celebration Mike had been planning. How was she going to convince him that a party was not a good idea? How in the world was she going to tell him period? It would devastate him to learn that the daughter-in-law entrusted to his care was raped by the man to whom he had loaned $100,000. No. She couldn't allow that to happen. Mike could never know. So deep in thought, Dina wasn't aware that Karen was talking, until she heard her name repeated.

"Dina. Dina? Are you listening?"

"Sorry. I guess I was wool gathering, lost in thought for a second."

"I know this isn't easy for you, finding out…"

"Karen, please, stop talking as if you and Carl were engaged in some secret rendezvous and you have to apologize for it. Rape is not pleasant to experience or hear about, but you have to put it this in its proper perspective."

A lot of times Karen didn't understand what Dina was talking about, but she did know that she felt better for having confided in Dina. Someone shared her trouble.

"I just wanted to say thank you. Considering the short time Paul and I had together, we had many wonderful times. I'll remember them forever. They kept me going, and will keep me going for a long time. I don't think I'll ever get married again."

"What? What are you talking about?"

"I know Paul. What keeps going 'round in my head is the night he told me how much it meant to him that both of us were virgins. It was after he asked me to marry him. I knew he wasn't a liar, but I took it for granted that he…you know what they say about boys sowing their wild oats before they settle down. I guess he could tell I didn't believe him, not completely. That must have been why he told me about the promise he made to your father and mother, about never doing anything to bring shame on them by stealing a girl's most precious gift to her husband. All I had to do was watch his face while he was telling me. He had the same expression I've seen on the faces of boys, and even grown men, when they're watching a John Wayne movie. I guess it's adoration. Paul loved your mother, but he idolizes Mike. And Paul is so much like Mike. Don't be mad, but it seems to me they both sort of see everything in black or white. Their margin for gray isn't any wider than a sliver. I'm sorry, I don't mean to be critical, but it's hard to think of them as forgiving."

"Karen, what you have to get straight in your mind is that you have done nothing to be forgiven for. As for Paul, well, let's not talk about it now. We'll sleep on it and talk tomorrow. You're exhausted; what you need is some sleep. Do you want to sleep in here tonight?"

"Can I? I mean, I'd really like to, if you're sure you don't mind?"

"Of course I don't mind." While she pulled back the covers she was thinking to herself that it was better if Karen were not alone tonight. She was also handing herself messages of guilt for having passed off Karen's moodiness these past few months as lonely bride blues, or some sort of growing pains she herself somehow had eluded.

"I can't tell you how relieved I am that you didn't tell me to leave. You don't know how scared I've been. So sick with worry I haven't been able to sleep at night."

"No more talk tonight, try to get some rest." She covered Karen with the blanket, then sat on the bed holding her hand until she was sure she was asleep. She gently removed her hand and walked over to the window seat and sat down.

She stared through the window. Her green, razor-like eyes cut across the lake and stopped at the resort. Her mind was racing in circles. There wasn't much she could see except that the office lights were still on. Carl built the office first so he could work out of it while he built the resort. The resort was finished and open for business. The restaurant was a shell at this point, but it wouldn't take long for Carl to finish it. He'd accomplished quite a bit by himself. Quite a bit.

The thought sent a chill through her, yet she was damp with perspiration. She wanted a cigarette and a strong cup of coffee. She had to forego the coffee. Mike was a light sleeper and he'd be up before she poured the coffee into the pot. She wasn't up to talking to him tonight. The cigarette was no problem, she kept a carton in her desk drawer for the nights she stayed up late to study or work on invoices. One of these days she was going to quit the filthy habit, but it definitely wasn't going to be tonight. She opened the drawer, took a pack out and tore off the cellophane. She picked up an ashtray and carried it with her to the window.

Karen's soft snores were snuffed out by the memory of Dina's vacation in Sarasota four years ago, before her mother was diagnosed with her brain tumor. Flashbacks flickered in the window pane. She, her friend Carol, and Carol's brother, Tim, were swimming in the ocean. None of them saw the dorsal fin approach. It was suddenly just there, circling them with a lazy grace. Its black button eye didn't seem to notice them until it darted at Tim. It took Tim's leg in its mouth and yanked him up out of the water, shaking him as though he were a rag doll. After it ripped Tim's leg open, it seemed to have lost all interest and let Tim go and swam off.

It was the first time in her life Dina experienced terror. It took Carol's screams to bring her back to her senses. Somehow, they got Tim to shore and he was taken to the hospital. It appalled her that any creature would attack for no apparent reason. It wasn't in danger, or angry, and it couldn't have been hungry; it left Tim's leg. It had simply gone after something that was in its path. Vulnerable, easy prey.

To this day, she still couldn't appreciate Tim's twisted sense of humor whenever she remembered how he sat up in his hospital bed saying he didn't hold any grudges against the shark; after all, the ocean was the shark's chomping grounds. His window ledge was covered with books about sharks and he was only too happy to share the tidbits he thought everyone else would find as fascinating as he did. She didn't. One tidbit that had stuck in her mind was that sharks could smell a drop of blood up to one hundred yards away. It was all she needed to remind her never to swim in the ocean when she had her period.

After what Karen had told her tonight, she knew that from now on that's how she would think of Carl—as that shark, waiting for easy prey to enter his domain. The difference was that she had no fear of Carl.

Talent for Deception

She didn't know if Karen could feel any forgiveness in her heart for Carl, but she herself fully agreed with the women, and men, who said rapists should be castrated. If it didn't solve the problem, at least it gave women who were raped some small reason to celebrate.

Carl had forced her sister-in-law to experience something no woman, no girl, no child should ever have to know: the difference between rape and being made love to. She lit another cigarette and rested her head against the wall. The lights went out in the resort office.

Her mind had entered an arena of debate. When a thought came up, it was questioned about how feasible it would be. Several were possible, some were absolutely not. It was four in the morning when it was down to the one idea that demanded serious consideration.

At this point, accusing Carl was out of the question, not only was it too long after the fact, a trial was out of the question. It would be far too horrendous of an ordeal for all of them. Especially Karen, and Mike most of all—he would blame himself and that was something he could never live with. He might go as far as killing Carl. She couldn't take a chance on that. She'd fought too long and hard to get Mike to care about life again, she was not going to see him spend any of it in prison, especially not for a piece of scum like Carl Anderson.

At the moment, for the first time in her life she was thinking she was glad her mother was not alive to have to live through this, although she had to admit her mother would probably take it better than Mike. In retrospect, she understood it had been very short-sighted of her and Paul to have recognized Mike's strengths and not their mother's. Regrettably, for her, it took seeing her mother battle the cancer that ravaged her once strong, active body for Dina to realize how much she had overlooked. The iron will entwined inside the deep blue eyes. The more frail and weak her mother's body became, the more visible the determination became in her eyes, as she worked

36

to get around the abyss that was pulling her body and mind away from them, the abyss that had swallowed her ability to communicate verbally. Her communication came from her eyes and silent lips, and with those, *she* consoled *them*.

Before that, all those years she had credited Mike for being the one who taught her and Paul independence, to be self-reliant and respect themselves enough to stand up for what they believed in, and credited her mother with having taught her and Paul how to brush their teeth, comb their hair, sing and dance, share, forgive and be kind. She didn't want to believe she could have been so obtuse, but facts were facts. Her mother taught them far more than what her small list read, and in the end, she also showed them how to die with dignity.

And here she was, as bizarre as it seemed, devising a plan that she thought unthinkable yesterday. She, who abhorred liars, was sitting here planning how to deceive her father and as many people as necessary. Deception had never been part of the guidelines for growing up, but neither was how to deal with rapists. If it took some sort of talent to deceive people, she was going to have to develop it. Whatever it took, she had to do it—if Karen agreed. The final word had to be Karen's.

As she was mashing out the cigarette, something that had been stirring around on the bottom of her thoughts had worked its way up and become the center of attention: Was Karen the first? Were there others?

The night Mike told her he had loaned Carl $100,000 she was not tactful about how she felt. Yet, when Mike asked her to give him a specific reason why she disapproved of Carl so much, the only answer she had to offer sounded obscure even to her. There was just something about the man. Tonight, she had an answer for Mike, but wouldn't be able to tell him, or anyone else what it was. She no longer disliked "something" about Carl, she despised him. It sickened her to think of the way he had paraded around town these past months, slapping backs and shaking hands, assuming the role of the successful businessman of the year. People in town talked about the amazing changes that had come over Carl. How he had traded in his overalls and tee shirts for white shirts and dress pants. Gave up drinking on Sunday mornings at the Fisherman's to attend church with Martha, even wore a suit and tie!

Did he think it was going to bring him absolution? Did he think he deserved to be thought of as an upstanding citizen? Carl Anderson deserved to be castrated. What she had in mind was something he would feel was far worse. It would cost him dearly, a price painful and difficult for him to pay.

She walked back over to the desk, sat down, and tore off yesterday's page from the calendar. It was now November 18. Thanksgiving was four days away. Her eyes widened when November hit her hard enough to jog her memory. Karen said Carl raped her on a night she went for a swim, and that she never went for a swim at night after that. Dina distinctly remembered it was in May because she asked Karen why she didn't go for evening swims any more. Karen had said she didn't care to swim alone at night, that she'd wait until Paul got home. That was practically six months ago! Karen wasn't four or five months pregnant, she had to be in her *sixth month!*

CHAPTER FIVE

THE SUN HAD RECLAIMED MOST OF THE TERRITORY IT HAD SURRENDERED last night by the time Dina came up with the only practical solution. A solution she wished wasn't necessary. She had committed herself to the deception and she didn't want to worry about principles right now. What she needed was to have Karen hear her out and understand that if she agreed they both would have to live with the consequences, and it wasn't going to be easy. If Karen agreed, and they went through with it, it also meant Carl would not have to face going to prison. But it was going to cost him more than he could imagine.

She checked her watch. It was five before nine. Her neck was stiff, she rocked her head from side to side, then forward and back, trying not to think about how inviting the bed was. There was too much to do. It was a good thing it was Sunday, she couldn't work today.

Karen sensed she was being willed awake and she opened her eyes, not sure where she was for a few seconds. Then it all came rushing back. She didn't see Dina right away. She heard a sound over at the window. Somewhat sheepishly she sat up and said, "Morning."

"Good morning. How are you feeling?" Karen looked rested, less tense. Something Dina wished she was.

"Oh, better. Didn't you sleep at all?" Her voice was tangled in a mixture of relief, guilt and embarrassment.

"I don't need more than a few hours. Karen, I want you to listen very carefully to what I have to say, and then I want you to think it over. Okay?"

"Sure, okay."

"First of all, you have to understand, it isn't going to be easy. Both of us will have to live with it for the rest of our lives. Maybe in time it will be easier, I don't know. But you have to decide if you want to do it. After you hear me out, think it over, sleep on it, then we'll talk about it, when you decide whether or not you want to do it. I don't want you to make any instantaneous, rash decisions."

Karen listened without interruption. When Dina finished, she knew it was what she wanted to do. She didn't want to think it over, didn't need to sleep on it, or discuss it any more. She was sick of waking up in the middle of the night trying to think of a way out. She was tired of feeling ashamed and guilty. She had used all her guilt up, she didn't have any more left.

"I agree to everything."

"Karen, I can't give you any guarantees. As I said in the beginning, it isn't going to be easy for either of us. Once committed, there will be no turning back."

"I don't care. I want to do it. Anything is better than..."

"Don't be too quick to agree. I want you to seriously think this over."

"No! Let's do it. I can't bear to be miserable any more. I'm sick of being scared, afraid of your father finding out. I'd die if Paul ever found out." She didn't want to admit it to Dina, but she was positive Paul would divorce her if he found out. "Dina, I'm so sorry I had to drag you into this, but honest to God, I didn't know what to do. I've been so scared. I swear I'll be forever grateful to you."

"You don't have to be grateful for anything, Karen. We're family. And family comes first, above all else. Remember?"

"Yes, I remember. But I still want to thank you just the same."

"You're welcome. How about some breakfast?"

"I am kind of hungry."

"Good. Why don't you get the coffee started and I'll be down in about twenty minutes. I have a few calls to make."

Karen's spirits and confidence were blossoming, she felt good about all of it. Paul had told her he would trust Dina with his life. She was trusting Dina with hers.

As soon as Karen left, Dina dialed her friend Carol's number in Sarasota. Carol answered on the fourth ring.

"Carol? It's Dina. Are you and Tim still going to tour Europe this winter?"

"You bet. We've been trying to decide what not to take, seems we're taking all the clothes in both our closets."

"Carol, how long are you going to be gone?"

"Oh, probably until May, maybe June. We're not sure, why?"

"I was thinking of taking a few months' vacation with my sister-in-law."

"Sister-in-law? Brother, don't that beat all. I'm going to Europe with my brother and you're taking a vacation with your sister-in-law. How's Jake Tanner doing?"

"Far as I know, fine. Carol, I was wondering if you'd be interested in renting out your place while you're away?"

"Hey, are you kidding? You don't have to pay me; I'd pay you if you needed the money." She chuckled. "It'd set my mind at ease having someone I trust house-sit. How soon are you coming?"

"A week or so."

"Oh, that's too bad. We're going to miss each other, Tim and I are leaving the day after Thanksgiving. You know where we keep the key…it's still there."

"Great. Oh, and Carol? What's the name of the doctor Tim had? The one who went into private practice?"

41

TALENT FOR DECEPTION

"Can't remember off the top of my head, and Tim's outside somewhere. I'll find it and write his name and number on a notepad. I'll leave it on the kitchen table. Good enough?"

"Good enough. Thanks, Carol. You and Tim have a great tour, and send me a postcard or two. Love to both you guys."

"You too, from us. Hope you have a good time here—you and your sister-in-law. Make yourselves at home. Maybe we'll see you in June or July, if we get up your way. Gotta go…Bye."

Anyone else would have asked for some explanation or have thrown out some nosy questions, but not Carol. Carol accepted things at face value. It was one of the reasons she liked her so much.

CHAPTER SIX

THE TEAKETTLE WHISTLED, ANNOYINGLY IMPATIENT IN ITS DEMAND FOR attention. Martha removed it from the burner and poured the scalding water into the two cups, first filling Dina's cup, then her own. It was so nice having company. But it was also making her a little nervous having Dina over. If Carl walked in and found Dina Dmitri sitting in his kitchen he'd have a terrible conniption.

The kitchen had a faint smell of Lysol and the floor had been freshly waxed. Other than the teacups and saucers, there wasn't a dish in sight, the counters were clean and polished.

"It's so nice having you here. You know, your mother and I, we used to get together and have lunch at least once a week. Sometimes she'd come over here, pick me up and we'd go into town to the Norseman's Retreat, or we'd drive to the Cities and have lunch, or have it over at your place. Oh, how I enjoyed those lunches. I loved your mother very much."

Dina hadn't thought much about loneliness, but now, seeing the expression on Martha's face, it occurred to her how lonely Martha must be without her mother's companionship. Carl's supposed magical turnaround hadn't injected him with a magnetic personality. They were so totally opposite. Martha was bright and cheery. Kind and always thoughtful. She was the town's unofficial makeshift nurse and welcoming committee. She tended bee stings and scraped elbows, and handed out Band-Aids. To Dina's knowledge, Carl had never brightened anyone's day—including hers.

Talent for Deception

Tiny, soft-spoken Martha had surprised a lot of people by revealing a hidden talent of her own. The woman had a knack for business. She was the one who took care of the resort office and supervised the restaurant they were adding. Dina thought of the many words of praise Phil Tanner had for Martha, that she was the sweetest, nicest, and calmest person he'd ever known and he admired her very much. Whether he knew it or not, Phil was more than a little infatuated with Martha.

"I remember those lunches, and how hard the two of you laughed when you were together. My mother loved you too, Martha, and felt very close to you."

"Isn't a day goes by I don't think of her. I miss her so. Sorry. I know all of you do, too." She rolled her spoon in her napkin, then unrolled it. She was aware she was fidgeting but she couldn't help herself. Keeping her hands busy kept her mind off the clock. She did not want to give Dina the impression she wasn't welcome. Carl did not keep a regular schedule.

Her intuition was telling her that Dina had stopped by for more than a small chat. The girl was preoccupied and though she would never come right out and ask, she tried to think of a way to get Dina to say what was really on her mind.

"Did you know your father used to drive to the Cities every Thursday, to some dance studio so he could surprise your mother on their fifth wedding anniversary and take her dancing? They were quite a pair."

"Yes, they were." Mike had said over and over that he wouldn't dance again until he danced at Dina's wedding.

"Have you seen the resort office yet—or the restaurant?"

"No, I haven't had the time. We've been very busy."

"Carl's so proud. Did all the interior work himself, you know. Cabinets and everything. Dina, I can't tell you how grateful we are to your father, lending us the $100,000, and then that extra $75,000 to add on the restaurant. Made a real difference in our business. Folks

44

like to have things convenient, like to have food close to where they're staying. Carl's already working on some extra cabins, should have them finished by Christmas. He wants to have eight total by spring." Martha knew she was rambling but couldn't stop herself.

Unable to offer any response, Dina was relieved that Martha was doing all the talking. Hearing about the extra $75,000 left her temporarily speechless although she was confident she had masked her surprise fairly well. It was her anger she was having trouble with.

To conceal her own nervousness, Martha placed her hand over Dina's and saw something strange in Dina's eyes. "I'm glad you came by. You know that you, Mike and Paul mean a great deal to me."

Without saying a word, Dina removed the tea bag, placed it on the saucer, and took a long sip of her tea. Then she smiled, looked straight into her mother's loyal and trusted friend's eyes, and asked, "Martha, how would you like to adopt a baby?"

* * *

Long after Dina left, Martha's head was still spinning so fast she was afraid to stand up, afraid that if she did, everything she had heard would turn into another of her foolish fantasies. Torn between excitement and guilt, her heart was bursting with enough happiness to almost shut out the guilt. Was it wrong? Should she feel guilty for being so happy about what was really Dina's troubles? The girl was pregnant and unmarried. It was going to break Mike Dmitri's heart. But how could she not be happy, having her prayers answered? Thinking of all the years she prayed to have a child of her own, how heartbroken she was for so long, how could her heart not be dancing? Better than that, she was going to have her best friend's grandchild. How could it possibly be wrong to be glad about that? She was doing it for Dina as much as herself.

She loved Dina like an older sister and was very defensive about her. Wasn't more than six years ago she had told the town busybodies, Cassie and Edith, they were full of horse manure when they predicted that while all the other girls in town were out buying dresses for the prom, Dina "tomboy" Dmitri was going to be sitting on the dentist's chair getting fitted for dentures because of the way she was always playing baseball and basketball with the boys.

Tickled her so much she was embarrassed by it when it happened, the magical transformation that turned the tomboy into a beautiful young lady made Cassie and Edith's mouths hang to the ground. And overnight their sons, who had played baseball and basketball with Dina, became all awkward and red whenever they were around her. They could barely say "hi."

The hypocrites changed their tune in a hurry when the tomboy turned into a graceful young lady. Now the mean old biddies were dying to have Dina for a daughter-in-law.

It pleased her no end when Jake and Dina took a liking to each other and ruined Cassie and Edith's plots. Neither of their sons stood a chance.

Up until now, she hadn't thought about Jake. It was for sure he wasn't the father. She shouldn't even be speculating about the father. It was none of her business, period. It was just that she couldn't imagine Dina with anyone but Jake. It would break his heart if he ever found out. Whoever it was, she hoped it wasn't one of the old biddies' sons. If it were one of them, she didn't want to know.

While she was rinsing out the cups, something made her forget all about speculations. Something that was far more important to think about—what she was going to say to Carl. How was she going to tell him that she had already told Dina they would take the baby? Never before had she made a decision without first asking him. Even with his good mood these days, it wasn't going to be easy to convince him to adopt a baby. He didn't care much for small children, but Dina's baby?

Martha made up her mind. Why shouldn't she have her dream come true too?

46

CHAPTER SEVEN

THEY STOOD ON TOP OF A HILL ACROSS THE LAKE FROM THE DMITRI PLACE. While Dina watched patchy streams of clouds float past a pale blue sky, Carl leaned against a tree trying not to show on the outside how worried he was on the inside. His breath was coming out in puffs, creating thin, miniature clouds.

Uppermost in Carl's mind was how hard he had worked for what was down the hill and across the way from him. He'd finished up two cabins yesterday, and they were booked for the whole summer and fall seasons next year. But this winter wasn't looking too good. Reservations for the hunting season were falling way short of what he'd planned on. And if the damn lake didn't freeze over soon, there wouldn't be any ice fishing. And if the damn snow didn't get here, there wouldn't be any skiers, either. As if that wasn't enough to worry about, now he was hit with this, thanks to the meddling bitch going behind his back, putting the screws to him.

His gut was killing him. She was going to give him an ulcer—if she hadn't already. He could see out of the corner of his eye that she was looking the other way, so he turned just enough so he could see the expression on her face. It was the same look she had on her puss on the day he quit, like she couldn't stand to be in the same office with him. He hated her puss, the way it made him feel. Worst of all, he hated that she knew how she made him feel. Damn giant thistle was what she was, churning around in the middle of his stomach. If there was a way to get rid of her now, without being seen, he'd do it in a flash.

Talent for Deception

While Carl was trying to think of a way to get rid of her, Dina was asking herself if it was lack of wisdom that enabled her to chew up any doubts about this whole plan not working out the way she constructed it in her mind, or was she being over-confident?

She wondered if someday she would become one of those people who suspect others of having ulterior motives because she attributed her own motives to them. What did Mike say? Liars and deceivers see themselves in others. Is that why she understood Carl's priorities so well? Because she was like him? She found her own question repulsive. Her priorities had to do with family, not buildings. She sensed rather than heard Carl circling her.

A gust of wind snapped her coat against her legs and bit at her face. She stiffened slightly to hold back a shiver, refusing to give him the impression that it was fear rather than the cold that prompted the shiver. She turned just enough to make him stop circling her and she moved toward him. Obviously feeling threatened, he moved back, away from her. It brought a smile to her face, he saw it and looked away.

"There isn't much else to say. The baby is clearly your responsibility. This way, Martha need never know the baby is, in fact, yours."

He moved back toward her, so angry he almost lost his balance.

"Shut up! Don't you threaten me about telling my wife…"

"It's not a threat. If you think you have an alternative, go ahead, try it. But bear in mind that you're the one with everything to lose, and I promise you, it will be everything." She looked down the hill, directly at the resort.

His attempt at a derisive laugh caught in his throat and he nearly choked. "How about Mike? What does he think 'bout your…what did you tell Marth…your 'indiscretion'?"

When she responded, there was no inflection in her voice, nor any sign in her face that gave away the loathing she felt for him. Carl stood quietly waiting for some sign that he'd hit a nerve, something to give him some satisfaction. When it didn't come, he looked away from her.

"It's best that you don't ever misinterpret my motives for telling Martha that I'm going to have the baby. It would be stupid to think that it gives you any leverage. Your protection depends on Mike knowing, believing, what Martha believes. Your silence is not in Mike's best interests, nor Karen's, nor mine. It's in yours. I know how much the resort means to you. If you don't want to lose it, you won't try anything that will jeopardize your keeping it. If you do try anything at all, I promise you'll lose everything."

"Oh, yeah? What're you gonna do? Haul me to court? Think 'bout this, can your ole man handle a scandal?" In spite of the cold, he was sweaty, even the hair underneath his cap was damp. Last thing he wanted was to have some sheriff pokin' around in his past. A smile spread over his face. "What do you think people would say, her waitin' all this time to pin it on me?"

"You seem to have difficulty grasping what your position is. What do you think your chances are of being believed? Do you want to test how credible your word is compared to the word of the Dmitri family? Are you that much of a gambler? Ask yourself if you could handle a scandal? Are you able to repay your loan today? What would Martha do?"

She watched Carl's face twitch, and it may have been because of the wind that his eyes were tearing but, from the pained expression on his face, she was certain he was visualizing everything he cared about disappearing from the spot he was staring at.

"Frankly, I don't care one way or the other. Make your choice, adoption or face a rape charge, which means Anderson's Resort will probably become just another part of Dmitri Enterprises."

The words put a horrible taste in his mouth and he wanted to throw up. His stomach was acting up worse than it ever had before, because he knew it was true. His feet were nearly frozen. He took a deep breath and looked over at her. She was smiling, the witch liked the idea of him losing his resort. The witch could see right through him. Knew exactly how bad it would hurt and how afraid he was of losing everything, and she was standing here and enjoying it. Poisonous blister on his ass. Some day he'd pay her back. Maybe even pay to have someone bump her off. The thought made him feel a little bit better.

Nothing was going to spoil things, force him to lose his resort. He'd planned too long, worked too long and too hard. He drew up the plans. Only thing he was going to need help with was the restaurant, but it damn well was going to be according to his specifications. Summertime next year he planned on making enough dough to double up on the loan payments. But for now, he didn't have a dime to spare. No one was gonna take it away from him, especially not her.

"Okay. OKAY!"

"As I told Martha, all medical expenses will be paid. What you and Martha have to do is start talking about your plans to adopt a baby, starting tomorrow. I'll contact Martha when it's time and tell her when and where you and Martha can claim your baby."

"Yeah, yeah, yeah. Martha already told me 'bout your generous offer," he said sarcastically. He wanted to tell her to stick her money, but he was in no position to take on any more expenses.

"Generosity has nothing to do with it. And unless you want to turn your resort into a foster home, I suggest you behave in a civilized manner, because if you try this again, I'll see to it personally that it does become a foster home."

"Don't you threaten me. Scram! Beat it. I don't want Marth seein' me here with you." He had an urge to grab her and choke her to death. She was going to see to it personally! Who in hell did she think she was scaring? "You got anything else to say? If you do, tell it to

Martha. I'm not int'rested in anything you got to say." He turned and trudged down the hill, measuring his pace, making sure it wasn't too fast. He didn't want her to think he was running away like some scared animal with its tail between its legs.

When he got to the bottom of the hill, Dina turned and headed for her car, regretting that there wasn't a way to lock him away for the rest of his life. A way that wouldn't require Karen having to go to court, without Mike or Paul finding out, or risking Mike's health. If there were a way, she'd do it in a second—if it were her choice to make.

The smell of leaves burning gave her a feeling of melancholia. She didn't like it when nature's brilliant fall production was reduced to ashes. Even though the leaves were brown and lifeless now, it was still depressing. Or maybe it was her frame of mind. The lake she loved so much didn't make her feel any better. It had a silvery sheen and curling rows of whitecaps were sending a message that winter was going to be very harsh this year.

It started to snow and flakes collected on her nose and hair, the kind of big fluffy flakes she liked seeing on Christmas Eve. Christmas in Florida was going to be a new experience. It was hard to imagine a green and balmy holiday. Yuletide without snow was going to be a first for her, as well as for Karen.

She got into her car and drove home at the slowest speed possible without stopping. She wasn't looking forward to getting there and facing Mike. This was the difficult part and she was afraid she wasn't going to be able to do it. She was almost ashamed of the fact it had been so easy to deceive Martha. Mike was entirely different. His respect meant as much to her as her own. But she couldn't think about it, those thoughts had to be put aside. Mike had done a good job of instilling in her and Paul that no problem was insurmountable for them.

TALENT FOR DECEPTION

She had committed to this deception and that's the way it was. Karen needed her support and understanding and that's the way it had to be. Karen had gone through the worst part, but what was still ahead was going to be far from easy.

CHAPTER EIGHT

MIKHAIL DMITRIANDROVICH WAS FIFTEEN THE DAY HE ARRIVED AT ELLIS Island in 1917. He looked closer to thirty. A clump of blue-black hair hung just above cliffs of eyebrows. Plush eyelashes flicked over licorice eyes studying an old piece of cardboard with a photograph of Grand Uncle Vladimir that he was trying to memorize. It was the only photograph he had of any family member. His grand uncle—a stranger he had never met—was his only blood relative still alive. From the stories his father and grandfather told, Vladimir left Russia when he was seventeen to see the American Wild West and never came back.

Mikhail had a firm grip on the cloth bag in his right hand. Other than the clothes he had on, his worldly possessions were crammed into the bag: two changes each of pants and shirts, six pairs of socks, a sweater, an extra pair of shoes and his mother's samovar. The rubies, emeralds and black pearls from her necklaces were sewn inside his jacket. Necklaces that would have been passed on to his sisters Nadya and Irina, had they lived.

He didn't like thinking about it, because when he did, all his pent-up anger at his father took over and it took him hours to calm down. What good did it do? There was nothing he could do to change the facts. It was true, his father did try to convince his mother to take him and his two sisters out of Russia. His father made arrangements for them to go to Grand Uncle Vladimir in Minnesota, America.

His father's mistake was saying that he would join them later. That was all his mother had to hear. Her response was, "Above all else, we are family, and we will all leave together or we will all stay here together."

His father responded with words Mikhail had heard so often he could recite them along with his father, "My dear, I am a colonel in the Russian army and have pledged my loyalty to my czar and will not break an oath." Mikhail did not understand why the family did not come first, above all, to his father. For years Mikhail's mind tormented him, questioning whether his father had time to regret not being more forceful about making his family leave before extremists shot his wife, raped his two daughters, then killed his own parents before the savages mercifully killed him.

Mikhail wanted to know if his father spent those last few minutes thinking about the story he liked telling his son and daughters. About how he paid for their mother's hand with six magnificent white horses from the czar's own stables. And how their future mother was so impressed she ran away from him—three times. Mikhail wanted to know if his father, in the last few minutes of his life, considered those six *magnificent* white horses worth his mother's love and loyalty, because his father's loyalty to the czar cost her and his daughters their lives. How had his father felt watching them die? What was he thinking when his daughters were raped? And his own parents murdered?

Mikhail only knew how he felt. It was he who had to live with the guilt and shame of watching it happen from the safety of the woods with friends of his fathers holding him down and stuffing his mouth with a glove. He knew that seeing them all die would be with him forever, and his sisters' screams as they were being raped would haunt him the rest of his life. And he would remember making his father's friends swear never to repeat what happened to his sisters because he needed to know his sisters wouldn't be violated again by having it retold.

The old man who met him at Ellis Island didn't look anything like the photograph he held in his hand, yet he did introduce himself, in very poor Russian, as his Uncle Vladimir Dmitriandrovich. He was old. Healthy, but *so old*. He took the photograph from Mikhail, looked at it and gave it back.

"You speak English?"

"Yes, Grand Uncle. My mother hired a tutor so we would be able to speak it when we…came here."

"That photograph is old. Not as old as me, but old. I mailed it over fifty years ago. I'm seventy now, maybe a year or two older. Don't look at me like I'm going to fall over dead. If I do, you won't have to worry, you'll be taken care of."

"No disrespect, Grand Uncle, but I came here because my father arranged it, not to be taken care of. You're all I have left. We're the last of the Dmitriandroviches."

"Yes, yes, I know. From now on, remember, your name is Mike Dmitri. Dmitri is what they stamped on my papers when I came here and I requested yours be the same. And call me Uncle Walter. Grand Uncle is not necessary, too formal. America is your country now. Things are much simpler here. How old are you now?"

"I'll be sixteen, Uncle Walter."

"You look older, strong. Did you work in the fields?"

"Yes, in the fields, and I helped build houses in summer."

"Houses, eh? Good. You can help me start a construction company. You'll have to run it, I'm not so young as I used to be."

"Me? Grand Uncle, I don't know anything about running a…"

"So, you'll learn. Don't make too many mistakes though, or the boss will fire you. Then maybe you'll stop calling me Grand Uncle. It makes me sound too old." He laughed. He had an easy, hearty laugh, like that of a much younger man. Mikhail liked him very much.

During the trip to Minnesota, Walter told him that he came to America to see the Wild West when he was only a year or two older than Mikhail was now.

Talent for Deception

"Didn't get there. Worked as a lumberjack and a walker, somehow I ended up in Canada, mined for gold in the Yukon, got lucky. Came back to Minnesota. Started a mill, made railroad ties, gunstocks for the army. The weather reminds me of Mother Russia."

"Does it get so cold that when you open your mouth to breathe your throat feels like ice?"

"Wait and you'll see. Misha?"

"Yes, Uncle Walter."

"I'm sorry about your mother and sisters. And your father too, of course."

Neither of them said what they were both thinking, that his father's loyalty should have been for the family, not Czar Nicholas. If it had been, if he'd taken them all out of Russia when he had the chance, they would all be alive today. Standing right here beside him and Uncle Walter.

Walter lived another ten years. A week after the funeral, Mike sat in the lawyer's office, prepared for the formalities of changing the mill and yard over into his name. The construction company was already in his name. He was stunned to learn that he also owned four oil wells, AT&T stock, plus a few stocks in something called Tabulating and Recording Company, which changed its name in 1924 to International Business Machines. He sold the oil wells and kept the stock. The events of 1929 made him question his business judgment, but he held on to the stock, asking himself how long could a depression last?

* * *

On this November twenty first, Mike was feeling closer to eighty than fifty, his ever-firm jaw was slightly slackened and his eyelids had three tiers instead of one, but neither did anything to diminish his presence, nor his handsomeness.

On the desk in front of him was a list of what he wanted Dina to pick up at the store. He was disappointed when Dina put the kibosh on his party plans for Karen, but Dina was right, it wouldn't have done much to lift Karen's spirits without Paul. He reached over and spun the radio dial to find the station that played two hours of big band music, most of the vocals sung by Sinatra. He rolled the dial one way, then another, his frustration building while he promised to write the numbers of the station down so he wouldn't have to go through this every week. It took one more roll before he caught Frank singing a couple notes of "Polka Dots and Moonbeams." It was reassuring, hearing familiar lyrics.

He had too much on his mind and was having difficulty concentrating on the things at hand. His mind had been doing a lot of drifting lately and he knew it didn't slide by Dina. The girl noticed every little thing. From the time she was a tyke sitting here on his lap, it was far from easy keeping anything from Dina. He was annoyed with himself for checking his watch for what might have been the third or the thirtieth time. It was quarter after three.

Dina usually didn't get home before six, but he heard her leave at four-thirty this morning so he expected her to get home earlier tonight. When she did, he was going to suggest she start making plans to go back to college. Maybe take a week or two of vacation first. There was no reason for her not to. He was getting around good without his walker and putting in four, sometimes five days a week down at the yard. He was feeling fine and had most of his strength back. He and Phil could alternate Saturdays.

Frank was singing "Where or When." It was one of his all time favorites. He settled back in his chair and closed his eyes, willing Frank's voice to transport him back to Miller's General Store, on that cold and dreary October day in 1929. Helen was wearing a pale blue dress on the day fate brought him into town for supplies. She was with her parents.

Helen was sixteen. As captivatingly beautiful as a butterfly on its errands. Her hair was the color of burnished gold and hung down past her shoulders. He had never seen such warm blue eyes. When she stopped dashing about and smiled up at him, he felt as though he'd been drenched with sunshine. Having previously met her parents, Mike immediately asked Axel and Ingrid Larsen if they would please introduce him to their daughter. Axel, perhaps duly concerned with their ten-year age difference, frowned but he complied with Mike's request.

When introduced, Helen laughed and it was like a rainbow had suddenly broken through the clouds and burned away all the dark shadows in his mind, and in those few moments he knew he could not live without her. She had opened something deep inside of him that he didn't want to close. She was warmth and joy, feelings he had been without for so long he was afraid he'd forgotten how to accept them. He felt if he lost it he would never feel anything like it again. He was encouraged by the fact Helen did nothing to hide her obvious attraction to him. She had the carefree spirit only the young seem entitled to. But he never thought of her as a child.

And then he did lose it. He never thought of himself as a weak man. But when Helen died, she left him with an ache that made it hard for him to breathe. Whenever he thought about her, it was like losing her all over again. He missed her laugh and her playfulness. And their talks late into the night. He even missed her stubborn independence. But more than anything, right now, he missed the touch of her lips on his and having her body lying next to him.

Not the body he held those last few weeks she was alive. He did not want to see the frustration in her eyes as she fought to decipher the notes her ears were scribbling to her brain. He watched helplessly as despair turned into terror, as she ran down passages in her mind, trying to find the misplaced keys to the door to the room where the dictionary was kept.

The doctors were wrong when they said she wouldn't be aware

of much. She was aware of what was going on right up to the end. And he swore she was aware the day his prayers ceased to ask for her recovery and became requests for her quick and peaceful passing.

Since he was prepared to lose her, he didn't expect the blow to hit as hard as it did. For days after she was gone, his heart felt like it had been pulled through barbed wire. He still wasn't sure if he had fallen or jumped into that pit of depression that he wasn't able to climb out of, nor was he able to understand why he didn't want to try. He relied on memories to get him through the lonely nights and days, until the trips to yesterdays became more pleasant than facing life and Dina put an end to his "wallowing in self-pity" as she called it. She was right.

The clock's ticking broke into his thoughts. It was almost five. Dina had to be coming home before much longer. He didn't want her to see him moping, she would start to worry that he'd fallen into the pit she'd worked so hard to help him climb out of. Her and that male nurse. He could smile about it now, but not then. They were unrelentingly merciless in making demands on his body to get it to respond to therapy. There were times he wanted to strangle both of them, but he couldn't deny he would have done the same thing. If it hadn't been for them, he'd probably be in a wheelchair today. The only thing he missed from his recuperating days was having someone shave him. That was very relaxing.

His hands reached over and picked up Helen's picture. In it, she looked so alive, so healthy. He let out a sigh of resignation. Twenty years were not long enough, but he had the twenty and they were the best. He kissed her lips and put her picture back on the desk.

He glanced over at the clock: it was almost five-thirty. He was close to breaking his own rule and calling the yard to see if she was still there. He set the rule for himself when Dina took charge of the yard. He'd only call if it was an emergency. He didn't want Dina being needled about her over-protective father checking up on his little girl.

He signed the check Martha had dropped off earlier, vowing to make an effort to go over and have a look at Carl's resort. He had stayed away all this time intentionally. He didn't want Carl to think he was leaning on him or breathing down his neck. He knew Carl would pay off the loan before the ten years were up.

From what he could see from this side of the lake, the exterior of the place looked charmingly rustic. He knew the interior had to be a showcase. Carl had enormous pride in his work and well he should. He was a quality carpenter; with that meticulous eye he had for detail no one would ever find any sags or humps on his floors or cabinets, or any rough edges on his doors or shelves. He always had everything lined up perfectly.

He heard the front door close, followed by familiar footsteps coming down the hall toward his den. Dina had an unmistakable walk, determined, full of purpose, yet she was very light on her feet. It was the dancer in her. She got that from her mother.

She walked in and sat in the chair across the desk from him. "Mike, I have something to tell you that I know is going to upset you, but I have to tell you anyway."

Dina saw the confusion register in Mike's face, then came acknowledgment and finally anger. She felt how immensely painful it was for him to accept, just as difficult and painful as it was for her to sit and see her father turn into an ashen-faced, disappointed old man before her eyes. She was about to ask him if he was all right, but he spoke before she had the chance.

"Do you remember the talk we had on your twelfth birthday?"

"Yes."

"I told you not to let anyone treat you with less respect than your mother and I had for you and your own."

"Yes, I remember."

His hand smashed down on the desk with a forcefulness she hadn't seen since before he had his stroke.

"Then how could you do this?! 'Indiscretion' you call it? Call it what it is, a cheap favor. What else can it be, since you apparently didn't think enough of him to bring him to the house and introduce him to me?" For a very long minute he sat staring at his daughter and saw his sisters, while their screams echoed inside his head. He recalled his sisters' maidenly innocence taken from them, and when he looked at Dina he saw someone who had willingly given it away, as if it were something cheap. His rage erupted and for the first time in his life he struck a woman.

The slap was quick and took both of them by surprise, yet Dina never flinched. There was a shadow of remorse in Mike's eyes but he immediately blinked it away. He noticed the tears start to form in her eyes just before she suppressed them. "You've dishonored yourself, your mother, and my sisters. Get out of my sight, I can't look at you."

Dina thought it was an odd for him to bring his sisters into it, but brushed it from her mind. She started to leave, then turned to see if he had normal color back in his face. He did. "Are you going to be all right? Karen and I will be gone for about five months."

He glanced up at her and saw the red mark his hand had left on her face, and for a brief moment his remorse was visible. He answered quickly, "Phil and I handled things for twenty-five years, we can still do it. Go on, get out. Leave me alone."

She turned around and walked out of the den, down the hall and out the front door, got in her car and headed in the direction of the lumberyard, not with pride in her newfound talent for deception but with regretful relief.

Mike's first impulse when he heard her car drive away was to burn Helen's wedding dress that Helen had stored in the attic. She had hoped Dina would wear it on her own wedding day. Instead, he slammed his desk with his fist. And then he cried.

By the time Dina pulled into the yard parking lot, her cheek was no longer smarting and Mike's handprint was hidden behind the flush the cold wind had provided.

She found Phil Tanner in the huge pole barn with Mike's collection of antique cars. He was wiping the Duesenberg with a cotton diaper. He had already done the 1935 Auburn and the Rolls. There was a 1925 Packard convertible in the corner, covered with mosquito netting.

He barely looked up when Dina walked in. "Well, look who's here. You know it wouldn't surprise me if you brought a cot down here so you could spend the whole twenty-four hours a day here."

"Mike said the same thing the other day. What about you? You're here! I think these cars mean more to you than they do to Mike."

He smiled and when he did she could see why Karen said he had the impish smile of a leprechaun, like the actor who played Kris Kringle in *Miracle on 34th Street*. Phil was short and burly like Edmund Gwenn, too. Dina wondered if there was one person in Hid'n Oaks that Karen hadn't compared to some movie star or other.

"You might be right. I do sort of think of them as my girls." His voice had about as much mischief as his smile.

"Do you know the reason I'm attracted to Jake? Because he reminds me of you. He's just as mischievous and as caring as you. Perhaps not as handsome, but close."

"I'm daffy about you, too. Say, meant to ask you, have you heard from Jake?" He saw her smile fade. It was replaced with something close to uncertainty.

"No, I haven't. Phil, I have some paperwork to do. When you can tear yourself away from your girls, stop up at the office—I want to talk over a few things with you."

Phil didn't poke his head into the office until two hours later. Dina was just finishing the billings and payroll, getting ready to file everything and lock things up.

"Sorry, Dina, I lost track of time."

"That's okay, gave me time to do what I had to. Phil, Karen and I are going on an extended vacation, leaving either tomorrow or Monday. Now that Mike is putting in full days…"

"Tomorrow? On Thanksgiving?" The look on Dina's face made him change his tone. She wasn't herself today. And he noticed she was getting thin. Too thin. "Well…hey, that's great! About time you took some time out for yourself. You deserve a vacation. Don't worry about things here. Any real problems we'll save them for you, the rest Mike and me can handle. Be good to get you out of our hair for a while." He winked as though she wouldn't know he was kidding if he didn't. He wanted to tell her about the letter he got from Jake saying he was expecting to be home for Christmas, but Jake had specifically asked him not to, he wanted to surprise her. "How long you going to be gone?"

"Don't know. We're going to play it by ear, travel here and there. Karen hasn't seen much of this country, and you know Paul, once he gets back home he'll plant himself here. He doesn't care much for traveling. Now seems as good a time as any, before I go back to law school." She was rambling. It was the lying. Today she'd told more lies than she had in her entire life.

He could tell she was either nervous or tense. "Don't have to tell me, I know how Paul feels. I couldn't wait to get back home. I love this place too. When you're thousands of miles away, all you think about is home, what you're going to do when you get there, who you're going to see. Travel is the furthest thing from your mind. Do both you and Karen good to get away."

He thought he saw something in her face that wasn't quite right, something different. Something peculiar. "Dina, are you okay? You seem kinda out of sorts."

"Must be the excitement over the vacation. Lot of last minute things to do, to get in order."

63

"Where you headed on the first leg of your journey?"

"I'm not sure. We don't actually have a definite plan or destination. We're just going to head down south, maybe Florida for a while, then who knows? We'll see. I'll call from time to time. See how things are going."

He didn't know why she was being evasive, but she was. He and Dina were tight, she knew she could talk to him about anything. He didn't feel offended. She was like Mike, kept her own counsel. "Well you two have a great time. Don't feel you have to hurry back."

She walked over to him and gave him a hug so tight it hurt. "Hey! Give a guy some air."

"I love you, Phil. Been crazy about you forever it seems. You and that nephew of yours."

"Well, that's good. Makes it nice for all of us. One big happy family. Say, it's late, you get on home. Go on, take off. I'll lock everything up."

"Thanks. Take care of yourself—and Mike. Wherever we are, I'll call twice a week, just to touch base."

"Not to worry. Have a nice time and a safe trip."

"Good night."

"'Night, Dina."

He watched her get in her car and drive off, thinking of the day she had first come in to take charge of things. She had walked across the lumberyard on long, coltish legs, her copper-black hair flying all over the place. He had watched with as much amusement as pride at the way she stood on the platform, introducing herself to the men gathered around her, their new boss.

Other than Carl, most of the men didn't have much trouble accepting her as a temporary boss. A few of the newer ones did a little grumbling at first, they didn't much like having to take orders from a girl, the boss' kid at that. But resentment was minimal, and the resistance soon faded when it was pretty clear Dina wasn't some spoiled brat who had come to play boss. She knew her stuff and she pitched in, working as hard, if not harder, than most of them.

They tested her to see if she knew the differences between hard woods and soft and their best use. She did. She also understood foundation, framing and structure, knew all the names of every nail, screw and bolt and every one of the tools and how to use them. And she often did.

She listened to their beefs objectively and always made the right calls. Even the men who didn't like the calls had to admit the calls were fair.

There were a few times he was tempted to ask her if she knew that the men called her the spike in lamb's clothing, but he didn't have to, they handed her a bronze spike wrapped in lambswool on her birthday.

Like most people, Phil took it for granted that his goddaughter and Jake would end up getting married to each other. It made him smile thinking about it. They were going to make some pair.

They'd make mistakes. Everyone does, but they had advantages. The word made him stop to consider why the word came to his mind. It was a strange word to use, but he couldn't think of any other word to describe it. Both Dina and Jake had been through some rough times and they weathered them very well. They knew no one was going to hand them any merit badges getting through tough times, and that life had a way of eating up crybabies and quitters. They'd make it okay. They were durable.

Things might have turned out differently if he had said no when his brother, Will, called from Hawaii to ask him to take care of Jake for a few extra days so Will and his wife, Sue, could spend two more days in Hawaii. If he'd said no, they would have left on the fifth of December, instead of changing it to the eighth. They would have been home before Pearl was bombed. But he'd said yes, and that was that.

Talent for Deception

He hadn't done such a bad job of raising Jake, all things considered. A lot of the credit had to go to Mike and Helen, they helped raise Jake, too. Will would have been proud of all of them, including Jake.

When he noticed the time he told himself he shouldn't be surprised it was after nine. Working late had been ingrained into him, something he shared with Mike, before Mike had his stroke. Dina was just as bad. And before long, Mike would be back to his old bad habits, too, if they didn't watch him and make sure he didn't overdo it by pushing himself too hard. He had to admit he *did* look forward to just the two of them working as a team again. They worked hard, and loved every minute of it. He turned out the lights, set the alarms, locked up and went home.

The following afternoon, Dina and Karen left for Tampa.

CHAPTER NINE

GREEN CHRISTMASES ARE NOT TOO POPULAR WITH THE MAJORITY OF Midwesterners, especially kids and businessmen in resort areas. When the forecast is "no snow" the standard adult response is: "It's not going to seem like Christmas." With kids it's: "What are we going to do? Without snow, vacation is boring." In resort areas, when the lakes don't freeze, ice fishing and skating are out. And if the hills and slopes are green, sledding and skiing are out, too.

Anderson's Resort had a profitable first summer, but so far, winter hadn't been very good to Carl and Martha. The reservations book was filled with the dates, lines, and empty spaces that were there when they bought the book. Carl went to church every Sunday with Martha, and insisted they both pray real hard for snow from the first of January through March.

Mike heard that Carl was talking about converting to Catholicism so he could stop in church anytime he wanted to pray. Looking over at the resort, Mike's black eyes surveyed the grounds, then counted the empty parking spaces. For Martha's sake, as well as Carl's, he hoped business picked up for them so they wouldn't be in the red.

"Hey, Mike, you want to take your pies out of the oven so I can put my turkey in?" Phil stood in the dining room doorway to the kitchen, holding a roaster with a twelve-pound stuffed turkey.

"Be right there. They should be done by now." He walked

through the dining room and into the kitchen, grabbed two hot pads and pulled out his apple and pumpkin pies.

Phil shoved the turkey in and Mike started to grind his Christmas specialty: cranberries mixed with oranges. Phil peeked over to see how much sugar Mike put in, just out of curiosity. After putting up with the cantankerous mood Mike had been in for the past few weeks, feeling like he was buck-naked in a roomful of por-cupines, Phil wouldn't say a word if Mike put four cups of sugar in; it was fine by him.

Four hours later, Phil transferred the turkey to a platter using the same care he would use in transferring six dozen raw eggs in their shells. He set it on the table and stood back to admire his culinary skills. "Mike, we've got to take a picture of this bird. Brown to per-fection. Even looks succulent. Bet you it'd win first prize in a con-test." He reached for his camera and snapped a few shots.

"You going to carve it or elope with it?"

"Uh-uh. Your house, you're the host, you carve it. I'll make the gravy and mash the potatoes."

"If you promise you're not going to break down and cry when I carve it up…"

Phil emptied the water out of the kettle and dumped the potatoes into a big bowl, threw in a stick of butter and poured a cup of milk on top. "Ran into Martha yesterday over at the store. Boy, is she excit-ed about that baby she and Carl are adopting."

"She'll make a good mother." The tone in Mike's voice was sharp, an indication he didn't care to talk any more about the subject. He didn't offer any phony explanation or apologize. He was plainly in no mood to discuss a grandchild that wasn't here yet, or talk about it as if it wasn't his grandchild. However, Phil didn't pick up on the message.

Mike started carving the turkey. "You want white or dark meat?"

"Little of both. Yeah, I think Martha will make a good mother. The woman's a jewel. I can't understand why she married Carl. I can't see him being a father. Hope the kid's not a girl."

Mike's head shot up and he nearly cut his hand. "What makes you say that?"

"Tell you the truth, I can't say exactly. It's complicated."

"Carl's a complicated man."

"Maybe. Have you ever noticed how he sort of sneaks looks at young, pretty girls? Not that I don't like looking at pretty girls. Handsome women are nice to see, and admire. When I look at young girls, it warms my heart and I wish them fun and carefree days. They're kids, for cryin' out loud. The way Carl looks at them seems strange, that's all I'm saying."

"Carl's shy when it comes to women. I think he has some kind of an inferiority complex. Makes him feel out of place. Or used to. I don't think he feels that way now. Having the resort helped give him self-confidence. Seems that way to me anyway."

Phil stopped to consider this. "I don't know. Maybe it has, maybe it hasn't. Hasn't Dina ever mentioned to you that she didn't care much for him? I always said my goddaughter had good judgment, especially when I agree with her." He waited for Mike to respond, and when he didn't, Phil stopped mashing the potatoes and looked up. Mike was way out in space and he was wearing a troubled, clouded look. "Hey, Mike! You having a good time on your trip?"

"Sorry. I was thinking about a phone call I have to make. Mind holding off on dinner for a few minutes?"

"No, go ahead. I'll have a beer and set the table."

From the phone in his den, Mike called Sam Olsen at home. Helen's uncle was more than a trusted friend and lawyer, he was family.

Talent for Deception

Sam picked up before the fourth ring. "Hello and Merry Christmas to you, whoever you are."

"Same to you and the family, Sam. It's Mike. I hate to bother you on a holiday, but I need you to check on something for me when you get back to your office again."

"Will do, if it can wait until we get back from Denmark. Lois and I are taking the kids to see their cousins. I haven't seen my brothers and their families since they moved back to Copenhagen."

"When d'you plan on coming back?"

"We're leaving tomorrow, won't be back for six, maybe seven weeks. If it's urgent, I can have someone else check for you."

"No. Don't bother. It's nothing urgent. It'll wait till you get back."

"All right. Say, I hear you and Phil are batching it until Dina and Karen get back. When you talk to Dina, tell her as soon as she gets her law degree, she has a place in my office. I should be entitled to be her first consideration since it was here in my office that her interest in law was born, in a matter of speaking."

"Phil's staying here with me while he has some work done on his place. Dina's checking some colleges out east. When she gets back, you can tell her about your offer. Well, I won't keep you, tell everyone there and in Denmark we all wish them a Merry Christmas and a healthy, happy New Year. And, Sam? Put me down on your calendar the earliest date you have open. Goodbye."

"Will do, Mike. And we wish you all the same. Goodbye, Mike."

Reflecting on his earlier phone conversation with Dina gave him a feeling of discontent. Nothing had been accomplished. Neither of them were able to talk, say the things that were on their minds. It was a short, stilted conversation. There were things he wanted to ask, to say, but wasn't able to in front of Phil, and he would never ask Phil to leave the room. He wanted to ask when his grandchild was due to be born? How much longer would she and Karen be away? And, yes, he conceded, he wanted to apologize for slapping her. He thought about writing her a letter, but changed his mind. There were things he wanted to tell her face to face.

Carl's baby insisted on an early appearance, and on the fifteenth of January Dina spent most of the afternoon pacing the waiting room floor with six expectant fathers. She had the feeling they felt as comfortable here as they would shopping in the lingerie department at J.C. Penney's on a sale day.

The mounds of magazines were all male related: *Sports, Popular Mechanics, Esquire* and a few comic books. Dina paged through the most recent *Popular Mechanics.* One of the men was passing out cigars, two to each of the other five men, in honor of his newborn twins. When he got to Dina he stuck two in her hand, too. He left before she had a chance to give them back.

While she dozed in the chair, the two remaining men took their minds off their nerves by trying to figure out if the dusky brown woman in the room with them was American or East Indian. Their guessing game was interrupted by a nurse who gently touched Dina's shoulder.

"Karen Dmitri? Your sister-in-law had a baby boy. For a preemie, he's doing just fine. And Dina's doing just fine too. It'll be a while before you can see her. Why don't you go into her room and get some shut-eye. I'll call you as soon as she's awake, before they bring her out of recovery."

Dina stood and handed a cigar to each of the remaining men and left the waiting room.

* * *

Karen walked out of the hospital carrying her suitcase, the baby's formula and his clothes. Dina carried Peter Dmitri.

From the beach house, Dina phoned Martha to tell her that their son was doing well and that she named him Peter, the name Martha said she wanted if it was a boy. While she was talking to Martha,

71

Talent for Deception

Karen was taking her daily swim in the pool. The day they got back to the beach house, Karen had begun a grueling regimen of diet and exercise. As soon as she got up she started with a walk, then a half-hour swim in the pool, followed by half an hour of calisthenics, and, if Dina wasn't watching, a swim in the ocean, otherwise she did more laps in the pool.

It didn't take long for her body to tap into its memory and coax the muscles into responding to familiar routines. By the end of January, she was pleased with the results. She had her definition back, slim hips and narrow waist, topped off with a deep golden tan that made her teeth gleam, white as tiny snowballs. Her honey blonde hair was streaked with platinum. She looked and felt freer, more relaxed. Her time in hell was over.

While Karen exercised, Dina looked after Peter. She was the one who bathed, dressed and fed him. Changed his diapers and rocked him to sleep on the rare occasions he cried.

Karen refused to look at him, much less hold him. It was one of the happiest days of her life when the final arrangements for the adoption had been made and he was out of her life.

The more joy Martha exhibited over Peter's arrival, the more sullen Carl became. Her jabbering was going to drive him nuts for sure. Jabbering away about Peter this and Peter that. He was already sick to death of people calling him Daddy.

CHAPTER TEN

INSIDE THE TANNER CABIN, THE SOUNDS COMING OUT OF THE RADIO WERE bouncing off the walls. "…There's sunshine in the Cities folks, but don't let it fool you, we're in for a pip of a storm. Present temp is twenty degrees but that wind…" Jake fumbled for the knob and twisted it to off. He didn't think it was that loud last night. He could not remember much of anything after twelve last night, except the usual dreams about Dina.

He gently placed his fingers on his temples. He was fairly sure there weren't any thorns there. Encouraged by the discovery, he vigorously brushed his fingers through his wiry chestnut hair. Those scotch and sodas went down good last night, but he'd pay for it today.

He swung his legs out of bed, groaned and groped his way into the bathroom. Shivering, he grabbed a towel and wrapped it around his lean frame.

Assessing the damages in the mirror, he could barely make out the tiny blue patches that peered back at him through red cobwebs. He was afraid to blink for fear there was glass mixed in all those cobwebs. He took a chance and blinked. His eyelids weren't shredded which made him feel better, except for a raw throat that some clown had raked over.

Generally he preferred to shave before showering. Today it seemed saner, wiser and safer to shower first.

It took the shower and three cups of very black coffee to make the red cobwebs disappear and for his tongue to lose the cigarette taste in his mouth.

A vague recollection was coming back to him of someone driving him home from the Norseman's Retreat while he was trying to talk whoever it was into stopping at Dmitri's. Good thing they didn't listen. Not a smart thing to do, drop in on your future father-in-law marinated in Scotch. He also recalled someone telling him that Dina and Karen weren't back from Florida yet, and his Uncle Phil was staying over at the Dmitri Place.

He poured out another cup of coffee and went over to the window facing the channel. He looked over at Carl's resort. There was not much to see as it was camouflaged with snow. He crossed over to the opposite window that faced the Dmitri Place. He started rubbing a circle into the frosted glass, and jumped back immediately when the sun's brilliant rays attacked his eyes.

He gave them a few minutes to recuperate, then made another try. Last night's snowfall had covered everything with a puffy white blanket. He didn't expect to see anyone walking around over at the Dmitri Place, nonetheless he felt disappointed when no one was.

He drained the rest of his cup and gave his teeth and tongue a second brushing. When he finished, he picked up the phone to call Phil over at the yard. The line was dead. That took care of calling Dmitri's, too.

The sun had disappeared behind a massively gray sky and it was starting to snow. Again. And it was coming down heavier by the minute. He knew if he was going to walk over to the Dmitris he had better get a move on before it got worse.

He put on a pair of dark blue cords and the maroon sweater Helen had knitted for him four years ago. He hunted for a pair of Phil's boots and put them on, grabbed his pea coat and started out across the lake, into what was promising to be another bad snowstorm.

74

The first hundred feet was refreshing. Then the wind picked up and the snow got heavier. Walking through last night's three feet of snow wasn't too bad, but the six- and eight-foot-high drifts were turning the walk into a survival march. He was caked with snow.

It didn't make much sense to turn back now; he was almost halfway and he could see where he was going better than he could see where he had come from. Behind him a whiteout had already begun building its wall. He told himself a saner man would have been satisfied with sticking his head out the door, breathing deeply and going back inside, instead of playing dumbbell in a snowstorm.

Trudging blindly in a snowstorm was a good place to rehearse his speech. Mike had always been a tough audience. And he didn't think Mike would be any different today than he was the first time Jake declared his feelings for Dina, telling Mike he was going to marry his daughter. Mike never said a word, he just smiled. Jake still wasn't sure if the smile was because Mike was pleased, amused or being extremely polite. That was ten years ago, when he was thirteen. He was a man now and when he walked into Mike's house today he was going to find out what Mike's smile represented: amusement, manners, or acceptance.

He stopped for a few seconds to see if he was still headed in the right direction. He couldn't see the top of the hill, but he could make out some of the oak trees. He estimated it was going to take him another fifteen minutes.

Watching the Dmitri Place was more than idle curiosity for Carl. Keeping tabs on Mike, watching for any sign that might cause trouble was a vital part of his routine. He had seen Phil take off in his truck with the plow attached over an hour ago, probably to plow the yard out. That had to take him a few hours. Time to give him and Grandpa a chance to talk. From the way it was snowing, the talk had to be short and sweet.

Talent for Deception

Grandpa Mike was gonna have to kick in something for his grandson. Now that he was saddled with the kid, it only seemed right that Grandpa pay his share. Kids cost a lotta dough. Marth was driving him nuts, talking about college and insurance. Christ! The kid wasn't more than a few months old and she was harping about college! It was the meddling bitch's fault.

Dina thought she was so damn clever. Did she think he wasn't smart? Too stupid not to see some advantages in having Mike believe the kid was hers and *his own* grandson?

Life was a vicious circle, or cycle, whatever the hell they called it. Every time he paid one thing off and turned around there was something else he had to shell out for. Boats and motors just cost him over twenty grand. At this rate he'd never get the damn loan paid off.

When he got to the front door, he decided not to use the bell. The way the wind was howling, Mike wouldn't hear it anyway. And he stood a better chance of catching Mike off guard. He gave the door two soft raps and walked in.

Standing in the foyer he could see into the living room. Mike was sitting in a chair in front of his fancy marble fireplace. He took off his snowshoes and set them in the corner, walked across the living room and stood behind Mike's chair.

The fire was blazing. A log shifted, crackled, then spit sparks at the screen. The crack caused Carl to jump back. He gave the log a sneer before sitting down in a chair next to Mike, who didn't look too happy about having company. "I knocked, but you didn't hear."

* * *

Old habits did die hard, especially the ones you wanted to keep. Jake stepped out of Phil's boots, shook out his jacket and hung it on a hook on the outside porch. He walked into the kitchen without knocking; if Mike was napping he didn't want to disturb him.

Aromas of breads, pies and a thousand cookies greeted him as if they were in the oven right now. He sat down in his usual chair, the

76

chair he jumped up from to kiss Dina for the first time, for which she promptly thanked him by giving him a black eye.

When he stretched out his legs, he noticed his socks were as wet as his hair. As soon as he got the chill out of his bones, he'd find Mike and ask if it was okay if he borrowed a pair of Paul's pants. From the way it looked outside, he wasn't going anywhere for at least three or four hours.

The storm was turning into a whiteout. Visibility had to be down to ten, fifteen feet. He was lucky he'd left the house when he did or he'd be wandering around in circles in the middle of the lake.

He was tempted to make some hot chocolate, and then he realized why: he smelled apples and cinnamon. When he heard and saw the red light click on the oven panel he knew it wasn't imagination. He opened the oven door. Two apple pies. He was rescuing them just in time. They were close to burning.

He took them out and put them on the trivets sitting on the counter. If they weren't so hot, he would have cut himself a huge slice. He could hang on for half an hour.

This kitchen with its aromas of a thousand breads and cookies had followed him to Korea and kept him awake many nights. He'd invested a lot of hours in this kitchen just to be with Dina. And, he had to admit, he liked being with Helen, too. This was where Helen had washed all of their bruises and scraped knees, and made soup and sandwiches for the ailing Musketeers while they recovered from mumps, measles and countless colds.

Icy snow began to pelt the windows. The wind was getting more serious. He opened a cabinet door, retrieved an ashtray and was about to light up when someone shouting from the living room or Mike's den distracted him.

Curious, as well as surprised, he went over to the door leading to the dining room. He was about to make his presence known when Carl Anderson's voice stopped him cold, and his palms froze inches away from the door.

"…gonna cost me a bundle to raise that grandson of yours. Hell, I'm the one doing you a favor, took the bastard off your daughter's hands. Gave him my name. Seems to me, I'm the one making all the sacrifices so that snooty daughter of yours can walk around with her head up in the air, like nothing ever happened."

Carl's words chiseled through Jake's temples like jackhammers. He tried to move but his feet felt as if they were glued to the floor. He lifted his hands slowly and placed them on the door and rested his head against them.

Mike's fists were balled at his sides, his eyes strained their sockets, the vessels in his neck swelled.

"You're in my house, Carl. And my daughter is not open for discussion, not by you, or anyone else. What makes you think I'd hold still for extortion?"

"Extortion! You want to talk about extortion? That slut daughter of yours went behind my back, running to Martha so's I—"

Mike shot up out of his chair. "You're in my house, and out of line. Watch your mouth…" There was a click in the back of his mind, then it clicked again. And he knew what had been bothering him: he saw a thin, pale Dina, and a fuller-faced Karen. Quietly he repeated , "Dina went behind your back? *Why?* Why would she do that?" The guilty look on Carl's face was all the confirmation Mike needed. Mike's face twisted with a knowing rage. "You miserable scum!"

Carl didn't expect Mike to be able to move so fast and it threw him off guard, but Carl lurched forward when he saw the look in Mike's eyes. Mike wanted to have a go at him about as much as he wanted Mike. All he cared about now was finally getting the chance to knock Mike Dmitri on his ass. He was only sorry there wasn't someone here to see it.

They were an arm's length away from each other when the kitchen door smashed into the wall behind them. They both turned to see what caused it.

Carl's anger disappeared when he saw the look in Jake's eyes. A split-second evaluation told him Jake was in better shape. Knowing making a run for the door was smart, he ate up the distance in time a running back would envy. Jake was about to take him when he heard a crash behind him and spun around. Mike was sprawled on the floor. Jake slammed the front door and ran to Mike.

His face was distorted and ashy blue. Jake quickly loosened his belt and unbuttoned his shirt. "Take it easy, Mike. Don't move, I'll call an ambulance." He went to the phone, but the lines were still down. Knowing it was impossible to drive anywhere in the whiteout, he walked back over to Mike and held him.

"I'm sorry Mike, the line's dead. I don't think anyone could get here if it was working. It's bad out there."

Mike grabbed Jake's sweater with a desperation that sent a chill down Jake's spine. "Tell Dina, tell her…I'm sorry…"

"I will. I will. Mike? Mike!" Jake watched life leave Mike's eyes, leaving a lonely, vacant stare behind. A stare he'd seen too many times before.

"Ahh, Mike." He started to cry. "Goddamn it! Mike, can you hear me? God, don't let this happen…"

Three hours later, Jake heard the scraping sounds of the snow-plow making its way down the driveway, and he knew it had to be Phil.

* * *

Martha added hot water to a huge mug half-filled with brandy and handed it to Carl, bundled in a heavy blanket, his feet in a tub of hot water. He cupped the mug in both hands.

"Honest to goodness, Carl. It was crazy for you to be wandering around out there in this storm. I don't know how you ever found your way home in this…"

Peter stared to cry.

"There's your answer. That's how I found my way, I heard the kid bawling. Pour me another brandy, then go take care of the kid. See if you can shut him up."

Martha poured out a triple shot of brandy.

"Peter. The kid's name is *Peter.*" She went into the bedroom and the crying stopped.

CHAPTER ELEVEN

THE DECOR IN THE NORSEMAN'S RETREAT WASN'T SPECTACULAR OR EVEN special. The walls were painted with a variety of swan- and drag-on-necked longboats, the inevitable Viking helmet hung above the back bar, and the carpet, tablecloths and chairs were burgundy. It wasn't the decor that drew the locals or why the tourists kept coming back once they found it. Hardly anyone would argue that the food wasn't the best within fifty or sixty miles. Some people said it was the ambiance. The word that had passed for decades was that the Norseman's Retreat was the kind of place where anyone who walked in a stranger, left as one only if they wanted to. Casual dress, shorts, tee shirts and sandals were acceptable in the lounge. Bare feet, profanity and fights were exit visas. Shorts and tee shirts were not acceptable in the dining room. Tourists took their cues from the locals, dressing up for dinner. No one was allowed to drive home drunk; Gus and Gertie made certain of that.

A Wurlitzer jukebox, loaded with songs from the thirties and forties, sat in a corner of the lounge. To accommodate wedding and anniversary parties there was a huge dance floor and a bandstand in the opposite corner. A large stone fireplace was shared by the lounge and dining room.

No one was dancing tonight. The few customers there were locals who had heard about Mike. They sat at the bar quietly sipping their drinks.

Talent for Deception

Phil and Jake walked to the end of the bar and sat down. Gus had their beers drawn and set on coasters, waiting for them.

Gus's gray hair was thinning, and to compensate he had grown a beard. Normally a gregarious man who always had a smile and a funny story, tonight he was somber, like most everyone else who had heard about Mike. He leaned over the bar in front of Phil. "I can't believe Mike's gone. Sheriff stopped in...said it was a coronary occlusion?"

Without looking up from his beer Phil said, "That's what the doc says." He took a long swallow of beer.

Gus shook his head. "Dina know?"

Phil looked up at him. "She knows. Called her before we left the house. She and Karen are flying home tomorrow."

Gus wiped an imaginary water spot with a bar rag. "I can't believe it. I know he wasn't in the best of health, but he was doing so good. Gonna miss him."

Jake picked up two quarters and walked over to the jukebox, wishing it were still last night and he was still pie-eyed. And Mike Dmitri wasn't dead.

Phil sat staring at the shelves on the back bar. "Heck of it is, Paul called the yard from California. He tried calling the house but the lines have been down there most of the day. He left a message with one of the office girls that he and an army buddy were on their way to Omaha. He wanted to stop and meet his buddy's folks before coming home. Said that once he got home, he wasn't leaving Minnesota, or Hid'n Oaks again. No way we can reach him now, the office gal didn't catch his buddy's name. So, we'll have to wait and tell him when he gets home. Hell of a thing to have to do."

Jake had punched in his selections and returned to his stool. He lifted his mug and drank until it was empty. Then nodded to Gus to pour him and Phil another.

After the Mills Brothers finished singing "You Always Hurt the One You Love" Dooley Wilson started "As Time Goes By."

Jake made no attempt to join in on the conversation between Phil and Gus. Passed on a refill. He didn't want to drink or talk. He wanted to find Carl and punch his lights out. Make him apologize for calling Dina a slut.

Perry Como finished "Girl of My Dreams" and Harry James, with Betty Grable doing the vocal, played "You'll Never Know."

Jake wanted to be alone. Go someplace where he could think. He waited another ten minutes before reminding Phil he had to drive to the Cities tomorrow.

Before leaving, they all drank a toast to Mike, then before they left, Phil said loud enough for everyone in the lounge to hear, "If anyone wants to get hold of us, call the Dmitri Place. We'll be there until Dina and Karen get home. 'Night everybody."

When they walked back outside, they both shuddered at the drastic temperature change as it pinched at their faces. Shivering, Jake swore under his breath. They ran to the truck.

Phil's fingers were so cold when he turned the ignition it took four tries before he got it to connect. "Got to be fifteen below."

They sat blowing on their hands to get them warm while they waited for the defrosters to clear the windshield.

"Phil, has Dina been seeing anyone? I mean dating anyone special?"

"You kidding? She hasn't had time for a date. All she's been doing is working. While she was home, anyway. Relax, if she met someone down in Florida, she would've said something to me or Mike. What's the matter, you getting nervous?"

It seemed pretty obvious to him that she had time for more than work. "Just curious. So, has she been going out with anyone on an irregular basis?"

"Jeez, Jake, I told you, no. Stop stewing about it. Let's get over to

Dmitri's and get some rest." He backed up the truck and turned around.

It was noon before Jake hopped into the shower. He heard Phil leave around nine and intended to sleep for fifteen minutes longer and zonked out for another two hours.

Half an hour later, he was on the highway heading for Minneapolis. The highway was like a black inchworm stretching around piles of snow, then it became humped to climb over the hills. The plows had done their best, but the wind won out, shaping bladed drifts across the highway. Every now and then he had to slow down to swing around them.

The car hit an icy patch and skidded sideways nearly hitting a bank. Jake dropped his speed to thirty. At least the slow ride would give him time to think.

He pulled into the parking lot half an hour before the plane was due in. The extra time to think sorted out nothing. Everything was all jumbled up.

He stopped to buy a pack of cigarettes out of a machine and walked down the concourse to the gate, trying to sidestep the deplaned human cannonballs hurrying toward him either to the baggage claim or the bar.

He found an isolated spot in front of the door to the men's room. Seemed no one else wanted it. From there he could see the passengers as they filed out of the concourse into the airport lobby. He pulled out a cigarette and stuck it in his mouth but didn't light it.

A voice battling static announced the flight from Chicago had landed and was headed for the gate. He put the cigarette back in the pack and popped two mints in his mouth.

Suddenly the moment he'd been dreaming of had happened all too soon. He wasn't prepared, but there she was, forty feet away, walking straight at him. She didn't seem to recognize him, giving him the few seconds he needed to slow his breathing and heartbeat.

She looked about the same as when he last saw her, skin the color of dark mahogany, hair pulled back. Only her eyes were different, they were puffy and red.

His corpuscles were doing a dance and he felt his stomach take a dive down a long elevator shaft. He hesitated, then stepped in front of her, and took her arm with a possessiveness that surprised her as much as it did him.

"Hi, stranger." He led her to the side, out of the line of traffic and took her in his arms and whispered into her ear. "Sorry about Mike. I loved him too, you know." He smiled over her shoulder at Karen and winked.

"Some homecoming, for both of us. Welcome home. I'm glad you're back safe and sound." She kissed his cheek and moved back, away from him.

There was something in her voice, in her eyes, that made him feel vulnerable, and he didn't like it.

After giving Karen a hug and kiss on the cheek, he took both their arms. "C'mon ladies, let's go get your luggage."

The ride home was quiet, each one of them relieved by not having to work at making up small talk. They were all closed in with their own thoughts.

It didn't take Karen long to doze off. Dina sat with her hands folded in her lap, staring into the road ahead, barely aware of the distance the car was putting behind them. Jake occasionally glanced over in her direction. He thought about taking hold of her hand but didn't want to risk having her pull it away.

Before long, she too dozed off.

Jake pulled the car as close as possible to the house, waking Dina first, then Karen.

"We're home, ladies. Let me warn you, it's cold as the arctic out here. I can manage the luggage, you two get in the house."

By the time he brought in all the luggage, Dina had just finished a note Phil had left on the dining room table. She handed it to Karen.

"Paul is arriving tomorrow in Minneapolis!" Karen's face was flushed. She wanted to jump and shout, instead she put her joy on hold. Under the circumstances, it didn't seem right to do anything else.

Jake pulled her up in a hug. "That's great. Want me to drive you?"

"No, thanks, Jake. Dina and I will pick him up."

Dina smiled. "Karen, it's okay to be happy." She turned to Jake. Trying not to sound insincere, but dreading a positive response she asked politely, "Would you like a cup of coffee?"

"Yes. I could use something warm. Must be thirty below out there. I don't want you to go through any trouble making a pot of coffee, a little brandy will take the chill out of my bones."

Karen passed on the coffee, thinking they wanted to be alone. "All I want, and need, is sleep. Good night you two."

Jake put his arm around her. "Before you go, since I missed the wedding, you owe me a kiss." He leaned over and gave her a brotherly kiss. "Bet you were a beautiful bride."

Dina moved closer to Karen and put her hand on her shoulder. Somehow the gesture seemed almost protective to Jake, but he felt he was reading too much into it.

"Yes, she was a beautiful bride. Paul's a lucky guy." Karen blushed and ran up the stairs.

They said good night to Karen, then stood looking at the empty stairway as if they were two strangers waiting for a bus. Dina was the first to move away.

"I'll make the coffee, brandy's in the same place."

Jake followed her into the kitchen, took off his coat and laid it over a chair, without saying anything.

He hadn't made up his mind whether to stay and get it all out, stall for time, or just walk out and come back tomorrow.

It wasn't easy to ignore the crazy thoughts knocking away his plans, telling him he was going to end up falling in some crack, a hopeless bystander watching the life he counted on slip away from him. He got the brandy out of the cupboard and poured two shots in his cup. His eyebrows became fuzzy furrowed question marks while he waited for Dina to look his way. She saw the question and held up an index finger. He poured out a single shot for her, a double for himself.

"I half expect your mother to come in and tell us what we need is hot cocoa, not brandy."

"Jake? Tell me about what happened here yesterday."

For a full thirty seconds he didn't respond, he looked down inside his cup, thinking about how the last two days had taken him on one hell of a roller coaster ride, and asking himself how he could have gone from sitting on top of the world, to surviving the worst hangover in, if not the world, at least Hid'n Oaks, recovering from that, only to wind up being gutted. Now she wanted him to talk about it. He didn't want to talk. He wanted to hold her in his arms, kiss her until they didn't have a breath left. Tell her he loved her, and he wanted to marry her. He didn't want to look into those penetrating green eyes that always saw through him. He slowly lifted his eyes out of the cup, looked into those beautiful green eyes he'd been dreaming about for four years, and gave her a brief, doctored version of what had happened.

She listened without asking questions, poured the freshly brewed coffee over their brandies, then sat across from him, quietly sipping her coffee, thinking there was something besides Mike that was bothering him. She knew Jake Tanner too well. He was holding something back.

"Jake, we grew up together, you've been part of this family ever since I can remember. We're part of each other's history. Neither of us has ever lied to the other. Omission is lying, Jake. We both know that. You've left something out. I have to know what it is—it's very important."

Something inside him exploded and blew away control, caution and fear. An ugly compulsion was coiled inside him and he had to let it out.

"You want to know everything? Okay, no holds barred. You're going to hear it exactly like I did." He proceeded to tell her, word for word, what he heard, and what happened, tracking her reaction. He wanted to see pain. If not that, guilt would do. He wanted her to tell him he was mistaken, it wasn't true. Tell him he was nuts. He told her everything.

What he saw in her face clogged his throat with lumps of desperation and his heart took another drop down deep within him. He had never regretted anything he said or did in his life, until now. For some stupid, mean, little-boy satisfaction he had just risked everything he cared about most in the world and he desperately wanted to take it all back.

"Christ, Dina! I've loved you since the first day your dad brought me here. There's never been anyone else for me."

"Jake, please, don't say any more."

"Why not? A few minutes ago you wanted to hear everything. Why not hear how I feel? What's the problem? Bad timing? I'm sick of waiting for the right time. Pardon me to hell for coming home at such an *inconvenient* time. This is my life we're talking about here. Our life. I apologize for my lousy timing, for being rude and a complete ass. I screwed up. For crying out loud, you seem to feel I should keep on shoving my life on hold, keep what's important to me on some back burner. For how long? A year? It's been on a back burner for four years. The plans I had for us were what kept me going…"

"Plans *you* made. Plans you never consulted with me about. You take too much for granted, Jake." The truth was no longer possible.

If Jake knew, Paul would know. She could picture one of them killing Carl and winding up in prison. Telling Jake she loved him would only complicate things more. Right now, she wasn't sure how she felt.

"Take you for granted? That's a laugh. You love me, or you did, I know you did. Know how I feel? Like one big horse's ass. What I want to know, what I think I deserve to know, is why? Why didn't you marry this guy?"

"Oh Jake, it doesn't matter. The reasons are none of your concern."

And there it was. The words and her attitude said it all, *none of his concern.* He gulped down the rest of his coffee, grabbed his jacket, punched his arms into the sleeves. On impulse, he took Dina in his arms and kissed her long and hard.

"Thanks for the welcome home kiss. If you need anything, call, you know the number." Before he walked out he remembered what Mike said. "I almost forgot, Mike said to tell you he was sorry. He didn't say why, he didn't have a chance."

"Thank you, Jake. Good night."

Upstairs, lying in her bed, Karen moved her hand up and down across her flat, hard stomach thinking no one could tell she'd had a baby. Her stomach growled, letting her know she hadn't eaten anything since breakfast.

She heard Jake's car start up and jumped out of bed to look out the window. It was too late to see if there were two people in the car, it was too far away. She put on her robe and shoved her feet into her slippers and hurried downstairs.

The kitchen light was off, but the light in Mike's room was on. She peeked in. Mike's navy blue suit, a white shirt and a multi-blue striped tie were in a neat pile on the bed. Dina was inside Mike's closet looking for something. Karen lost her appetite and retreated back upstairs where she jumped into bed and scrunched way down under

89

the blankets. When you cremated people, why on earth did you dress them up?

All that was missing was a tie pin. Knowing Mike's habit of tossing pins and cufflinks in the desk drawer in his den, Dina went in to find one.

She flicked on the light switch and the bayberry aftershave and cherry pipe tobacco were so strong she expected to see Mike sitting in his chair.

She opened the top drawer on the right hand side of the desk and picked up a letter that was addressed to her in Florida. There was a stamp on it but it was unsealed. Either he didn't have time to mail it, or was considering not mailing it. She pulled the letter out.

It was dated the eighteenth of December. It began very formally, briefly informing her that he had Sam Olsen draw up a will and a few other documents. She scanned the next few sentences until the words, *I've extended Carl's loan* got her attention. She lifted the letter closer and read the entire paragraph. Anger made her stop and she dropped it on the desk. She waited to calm down before picking it up again.

The entire mood of the letter changed in the next few paragraphs.

> *I don't like this estrangement between us any more than*
> *you do. I don't look into crystal balls but I cannot shake*
> *the feeling that Paul isn't going to make it back, that you*
> *will be the last of the Dmitris. You and I know all too well*
> *death doesn't make reservations to let you know, it just*
> *sneaks up and snaps loved ones away.*
> *I'm not proud of the valuable time I wasted feeling sorry*
> *for myself when she died. I know it was hard for you, and*
> *that other Cossack, that male nurse you hired to make me*
> *care about life again. How ironic it is that death comes when*
> *life means the most. Funny how when we're healthy we don't*
> *resent people helping us, but when we're limited in what*

we can do, we do resent it.

Your mother's death was difficult for all of us, but you handled it far better than your brother and I. There is a nagging urgency going on inside me insisting that I get my house in order, and that includes telling you that when you came in here that day to tell me about your indiscretion, it was like having someone rip my heart open. You destroyed something very precious to both of us; my faith in your judgment.

Perhaps as a father, as a man, I always thought of Paul as an extension of myself. But you, Dina, were more a part of the woman I cherished. Mothers and daughters share a special, unique mystery that husbands and fathers can only stand in awe of, and appreciate. Fathers and husbands, and brothers, want their wives, sisters and daughters to be safe. Want them to be respected. To be respected, you have to be respectable. Your mother was my world. My rainbow. She gave me love and joy, you and Paul. She brought grace and beauty back into my life. And tenderness. You were an extension of her, of your grandmother, and my sisters. It cut deep into my soul to think all that didn't seem important to you.

Life is full of choices, as well as chances, but we have to be careful of the shortcuts and detours. They can cause terrible problems, can turn into dead-ends and often take us so far away from our goals, it's hard to find our way back. We all make mistakes, I've made them too. We have to forgive and forget. Go on with life. I will never speak to you about this and I ask you never to bring it up to me. Take care of yourself and Karen. Love, Mike.

Dina refolded the letter, placed it back in the envelope and carried it into the living room, opened the fireplace screen and threw the envelope on top of the logs, lit it and watched the letter turn into flimsy ashes. A letter never mailed, never read. As far as she was concerned, there would be no breaks for Carl, not while she was alive.

CHAPTER TWELVE

DINA RAPPED ONCE ON KAREN'S DOOR AND ENTERED WITHOUT WAITING for an invitation. "Karen, are you asleep?"

Karen sat up, groggily blinking her eyes into focus. "What? What time is it?"

"I know it's late and I'm sorry, but this can't wait." Dina sat on the edge of the bed, thinking the last thing she wanted to do was send Karen into a panic, but the risk was unavoidable.

Karen's first reaction was what Dina expected it to be: fear. She thought of her leaving as desertion. "Why? Why do you have to go to New York? Why so far away…why not some college near here?"

Dina took the accusatory tone as a good sign. It was better for Karen to be angry than scared. "Karen, listen to me. I'm going to explain and I want you to stay calm and listen to every word."

Karen sat back against the headboard with folded arms, doing her best to show she was not going to be intimidated by Dina or agree to something she didn't like. "I'm listening."

"I have to tell Paul about Peter." She held up her hand to cut off Karen's protests. "We discussed it, I told you that night we talked that it was likely I'd have to tell Paul something. I'll tell him what I told Martha and Mike." She took a short breath. "And what Jake overheard."

"Jake overheard what? What did you tell him? I can't believe this! I trusted you."

"Karen, getting hysterical isn't going to help. Listen! When Jake got here, Carl was here with Mike. Apparently they were having an argument and Jake overheard some of what they said, most importantly, that I had a baby. Don't you see? I have to tell Paul."

"Soon everyone is going to know!"

"Stop it. Karen, it has to be this way. We can't take the chance; Paul has to hear it from me."

"*Chance?* What chance? Do you think Jake told you everything? What if he tells—"

"Karen, you know better than that. Jake will not repeat what he heard. He only told me because I insisted, he knew I could tell he was holding something back. I forced him to tell me."

"Oh my God, do you think *he'd* tell someone? *He* wouldn't dare, would he?"

"Carl is not going to breathe a word. He isn't going to risk saying anything to anyone. Trust me."

She said it with such conviction that Karen felt herself relax and let her mind occupy itself with things easier to deal with.

"I wish you didn't have to go all the way to New York; you could go to college some place closer, live here and—"

"My being here would only make things more difficult. Try to imagine the strain. You'd always be wondering if something slipped, if I mentioned anything, or if Jake and I discussed Carl, if we were overheard. You want to live in a house filled with suspicions and whispers? It would be like a prison. With me gone, what risk is there of any discussions? Who is Jake going to talk to? And you?"

"I know you would never tell anyone, or Jake."

"No? A few minutes ago you weren't so sure."

Karen started twisting her hair, a nervous habit she broke when Paul said it was unattractive.

"Karen, this is your home, yours and Paul's. You'll be living here for the rest of your lives. I want you to promise me that no matter what Paul says, you will not try to defend me. If you do, you might say something more than you intend to say, so don't risk it."

It was terrible having such mixed feelings. She was sorry Dina was leaving, but she felt relieved too. With Dina gone, she wouldn't feel like someone was around to judge how good or bad she was at pretending. Things didn't seem to be good between Dina and Jake. She felt bad about that. And if Dina left and never came back, she'd feel awful.

"Oh, Dina! I'm so damn sorry. This is all my fault..."

"Don't say it, or think it. Carl's to blame. Don't let your conscience hang you up on his guilt. I need to leave because, for the first time in my life, I know what it is to loathe someone, and frankly, the prospect of seeing him dead doesn't bother me."

"I know what you mean," she sighed. "I just hope I can pull it off."

"You can and will. Trust in yourself, you've done a marvelous job so far."

"I've relied on you too much, but you're right, I can do it. Paul means everything to me. Dina, I can't lose him, or his respect. If I did, I'd die. I keep telling myself I had an operation to get rid of something evil. It's over. I refuse to think about it."

Karen's view of Peter being something evil to get rid of bothered Dina, but who was she to tell her what she needed to do to go on with her life. Her plan hadn't proven to be so hot either.

"Concentrate on your happiness, yours and Paul's. Just be happy."

"We will. It's been so terrible, so unfair. I wish you didn't have to go away. Maybe if..."

"Oh Karen, wishes, ifs and maybes are words for people who refuse to accept what is." She knew Karen could see she was losing patience and tried to distract her by imitating Mike. "You know girls, life's neither fair nor unfair, it simply is. Up to you to make it what you want it to be."

Karen laughed. "He was such a serious man. Oh, he was wonderful, but..."

"I know. But he was right. Don't count on wishes and maybes, count on you."

"I will. From now on, I have to. Thank you Dina, for everything."

"Karen, for the last time, you don't have to thank me, we're family, and family always comes first, above all else, remember? Get some sleep. You have a long drive tomorrow and I have a lot to do. See you in the morning, or I should say later this morning."

"Good night, see you around ten."

Once she was in the shower it didn't take long for the fiery needles to stab away the control she had been able to maintain since she arrived back home. Tears started to flow, mixing with the water. But they soon stopped when Carl's image invaded her privacy, igniting an anger so fierce the water washed away the tears. She felt herself losing control of something she had relied on most of her life: reason. Carl was not going to get away with it. He'd raped Karen, and brought on Mike's death. Whatever she had to do, she'd do with no regrets. No apologies.

CHAPTER THIRTEEN

THE SKY WAS A FROSTY BLUE, THE AIR BRISK AND FILLED WITH THE FRESH scent of pine. It felt strange, sitting in her car in the deserted parking lot. Deserted except for Phil's truck.

The meeting with Sam Olsen had taken half an hour, the same amount of time it took to drive from his office to the yard.

She stayed in her car for fifteen minutes, then got out. As soon as the car door closed, a rabbit scooted out from behind the office building and almost collided with a squirrel. They both looked stunned for a second, then ran in separate directions.

When she looked over at the office, she spotted Phil standing by the window. She waved and so did he. He continued to watch her walk across the parking lot on the same long, coltish legs that brought her into the yard the day she became his protégé. Now she wasn't anyone's protégé, or the temporary boss, she was the acting head of Dmitri Enterprises. She was his boss and he was her assistant.

He grabbed his jacket and hat and went out to meet her.

"What are you doing here? Go on home, Dina."

"It's beautiful out here. Smell the pines?"

"You come out to smell the pines?"

"I stopped by to let you know I'm leaving after the services. Going to New York to finish law school."

"What's the big rush? Can't it wait a few weeks? Why New York?"

"Can't wait any longer. Phil, I want you to run things. Paul's going to need someone he can trust, count on, to bring him along. You know how he's always hated paperwork, the financial end of the business. All he wanted to do was to work with wood...create what he called his masterpieces."

"Yeah, he said paperwork was a contagious disease to be avoided whenever possible."

"Karen knows how to process bills of lading, do billings. It'll be good for her and Paul to work together with you."

"Be nice if all of us would be working together again. Paul, Jake, you and me."

"Maybe some day. Later. For now, if you agree, I'd like you to manage things. Everyone knows and respects you—you've been here forever it seems."

"Sure. I can take care of things. For how long?"

"I...I don't know. We'll have to see. I came down to type up a notice and post it on the board so there won't be any questions or misunderstandings. I'll call you as soon as I get settled, give you my number."

"Dina, do you mind if your godfather asks what the hell is going on? Jake's back home, you just got back, Paul's on his way home and you seem to be in an all-fired hurry to leave."

"Nothing. No questions right now. It's time I finished college, got my degree. Corporate law has been my goal, and that's what I'm going to do." It sounded rather curt, but it was just as well. She did not want to encourage a discussion about it.

"Sure. Don't get sore. I wasn't asking you to explain...well, I was in a way, I guess. Just took me by surprise is all. But you're right, you have put everything on hold long enough."

She kissed his cheek. "I knew I could depend on you. Oh, did Mike tell you he was going to offer Jake a job designing model homes for Dmitri Construction?"

"He mentioned it, nothing was definite. Mike liked to talk details directly with the person concerned."

"I know. Well, it's definite now, there was a...notation in Mike's desk drawer. So, godfather, as acting head of the Dmitri companies it's up to you to offer him the job."

"Me? Shouldn't you be the one to ask him?"

"Nope. You're in charge now. Your first official act as the chief."

"Okay, if you say so." Tears began to gather and he was having trouble swallowing. "Woulda tickled Mike to see Jake and Paul working together again. Last time they worked together, they were in high school. I wish Mike could have been around to know Paul made it home..."

She cupped his cheeks in her hands. "He knows. Now don't you cry on me." She kissed his wet cheek. "You need a shave. Do you know what whiskers can do in this weather?"

"What do you mean, do I know? You think I haven't given my share of whisker burns?"

Dina rubbed his shoulder. "Oh, I'm sure you have."

"Go on, type up your notice, I'll lock things up." He reached in his pocket and pulled out his keys and dropped a set of car keys. "I almost forgot. Here, these keys are yours. Mike ordered your birthday present, it was delivered a week ago. It's a Packard Caribbean, in the pole shed. It's a honey. Test drove it myself."

"Keep it here for me, take it for an airing now and then like you do the others."

"Aren't you even going to look at it?"

"Not right now, have to type up the notice, then I have one more stop to make. See you tomorrow, at the services."

It was the first time she had been anywhere near the resort. The setting did have a kind of Currier & Ives look to it. The lake was all covered with snow, except for the patches shoveled out for skaters.

Talent for Deception

There were ten cabins to the right of the Swiss chalet lodge, the restaurant was on the left. Every cabin door, as well as the restaurant and lodge, had large circular plaques with *Wilkommen* stenciled on them.

She knew Martha was at some social doings at church and it was Carl's night to work in the office. Jim Olsen's wife, Kaye, was taking care of the restaurant.

She walked into the lodge, and decided immediately a prairie house style would have been a better choice. The lodge inside had old west, country furnishings: oak-planked floors, a pot-bellied stove surrounded by oak captain's chairs. The walls shared Carl's trophies with different pieces of western memorabilia.

Heads of deer, elk, bear and wolf hung on the wall, staring down at her. Just as she was thinking that one head was missing, the door behind her opened.

She didn't have to turn to see who it was, she could feel his eyes crawling over her.

For a few seconds, Carl stood without saying a word, debating whether to walk back out.

"What do you want? I thought I told you to stay away..."

Dina turned to face him and caught him trying to avert his eyes, trying to hide the fear. He didn't look much like a shark now...he reminded her of a cornered animal. She didn't say anything, just stared.

His efforts to avoid looking at her failed. He couldn't help himself. The hate she felt for him was like a magnet, drawing his attention to her. With a sick fascination, he become absorbed in the hatred in her eyes and mouth.

When she spoke, there was nothing soft or remotely polite in her voice. The look she gave him was a warning and he was prepared not to jump when she did speak.

"I don't care what you said. I have something to tell you. Something I want you to know."

"Yeah? Well, say it and scram. I'm a busy man."

"You don't have to tell me that. I know how busy you've been." She watched his mouth open, then close. "Stay away from the Dmitri Place, the yard, the quarry, and the construction offices. If you need any building materials, call Phil Tanner directly. He will handle whatever you need to purchase and have it delivered."

"Just who do you think you're talking to, like I was some damn kid. Like—"

"I had a meeting with Sam Olsen this morning."

"So? You had to run over here to tell me that?" He started to reach under the counter for his roll of Tums, then slowly withdrew his empty hand. He was dying for one but he didn't want her to think she was the reason for his insides burning like he swallowed razors. After she was out of here, he was going to chew the whole damn roll.

"I went over your loan agreement with Sam. It appears you've defaulted on your loan."

"What the hell you talking about? Me and Mike had a—an understanding. Said we didn't need it on paper, didn't need some formal thing—addendum, that was it! Mike and me had a gentleman's agreement, he said it was okay with him if I didn't make all or any payments for the first year, until things—"

"What do you know about being a gentleman? It doesn't matter. What's relevant is that I, as administrator of Dmitri Enterprises, am not legally bound by some secret understanding between the two of you. I read the contract and that's what I'm holding you to. Or you can go to Sam Olsen's office and sign an adhesion contract."

"I ain't signing nothing. This is my place." He didn't have any idea of what an adhesion contract was, but he wasn't going to ask her.

"Virtually nothing is yours, Carl, except Peter. If you choose to file bankruptcy, that's your choice. I'll have you in court for breach of contract. You'll lose everything. I'll make it a point to search your entire background and lay it bare for everyone to see. I strongly suspect that Karen was not your first rape."

"What? You don't know what in hell you're talkin' 'bout." Beads of perspiration broke out across his forehead. He saw his whole life deteriorating in her hands. And she knew it, he could see it in her wasp eyes, green wasp eyes sticking poison into his gut. He'd give anything to be rid of her, to get her out of his life for good.

"If you don't think I will, try me. I want you to try me. Because I don't care any more. You lost your insurance when Mike died. You either sign, or everything you have will disappear with the crack of a judge's gavel."

His gut was gonna split open, right here on the spot. In front of her. He turned away from her, wishing he had a gun behind the desk so he could shoot her, drag her sorry-ass body out in the woods and bury her.

"Incidentally, I'll be leaving Hid'n Oaks." She could almost hear the relief on his face. "But I'll never be more than a phone call or plane away. I will take a great deal of interest in how our resort is doing, and I'll make it a point to check everything twice."

"You snot-nosed bitch..." The pain in his stomach was killing him. He was afraid to move. Some day, some day he'd make her life miserable, worse than what she had done to his.

"I strongly suggest you sign the contract. That way, neither Martha nor anyone else need ever know that Peter's adoptive father, is, in fact, the bastard that raped his mother."

He pounded the counter, but didn't say a word, trying to calm himself by thinking she was leaving, going to be out of his hair. Something else made him feel better. Partners shared losses.

"Yeah, okay. I'll go and see Sam tomorrow and sign the goddamn paper."

Once she was out the door, he started to laugh. Then the laughter stopped. She lied to her old man. He was willing to bet Mike discussed everything with her, just like he did with Helen. For now, it was smart to play along. He couldn't afford any more trouble. Not that kind. No one's luck lasts forever, sooner or later she'd run out of hers. If she didn't, maybe he'd do something to help it run out for her. Something he should have done to the other one. If he'd been smart, he would have dragged her into the lake and held her underwater until she ran out of air. If he had, his life would have been a whole lot simpler. And he wouldn't have to sit here wracking his brain, trying to think of a way to get her out of his hair for good.

CHAPTER FOURTEEN

ONCE PAUL UNDERSTOOD IT WASN'T A JOKE, ANGER SINGED AWAY ALL THE humor that had covered his face seconds ago. He anchored his hands in his pockets to keep them from striking the sister he'd adored all his life.

"Who is this...*man* who charmed you out of your pants?"

"Who he is doesn't matter. I've told you all I'm going to, all you need to know."

"Who else knows?"

"Karen, Jake, the Andersons, of course, and now you."

"How considerate of you to keep it so exclusive. Must have done wonders for Jake, hearing about his lady. No wonder he acted so funny at the memorial services this morning. And Martha, she acted like her feet were on fire, she couldn't get out of here fast enough when she brought the food over." He walked to the far side of Mike's den and stared at the books on the shelves. "Did you ever stop to think that Karen and I have to live here, that eventually we'll have to raise our children here? You've dishonored the whole family."

"No one is perfect, Paul. Not you, not Mike, and not me."

"What? You're making judgments? Pardon my choice of words, but don't you think your judgment is a tad screwed up?"

"Oh stop it, Paul! Stop behaving as though the words 'created in God's image' were meant specifically for you."

"Don't you dare try putting me on the defensive. I'm not on trial."

"*Neither am I, Paul.* Neither am I. I told you what you need to know. I wanted to make sure you heard it from me."

"Gee, I can't tell you how grateful I am." He started to say more, but held back.

"Paul, I'm not asking for absolution and I won't do penance. As for Mike, he was not happy when I told him, but he came to terms with it."

"How about some good news, like when are you leaving?"

"Early tomorrow. I have a lot of packing to do, so, if you'll excuse me, I'll get started."

His words followed her out of the den. "Excuse you? I'll never forgive you, Dina. *Never.*" They stood and stared at one another for some time, then Dina turned and walked out.

After she closed the door, Paul sat down in Mike's chair and leaned back. Sitting in it, in this room, brought back the sense of security he always had when he was in here with Mike. He closed his eyes and could hear echoes of *Gang Busters* and *Inner Sanctum*. Radio programs and the ball games he and Mike spent hundreds of hours listening to. He could still hear the crack of Joltin' Joe's bat.

Here in this room, he and Mike had discussed what presents to buy for his mother and Dina for their birthdays and holidays. It was their hideaway. They talked about girls and life.

Whenever anyone asked him what he wanted to be when he grew up, without hesitation he said, "Mike. I want to be my dad." With Jake it was different, every day he wanted to be something else. Only one thing was always the same...he ended by saying "and Dina's husband."

He looked over at the bottom shelf of the bookcase. There was a picture of Jake with his parents, himself and Dina. "Who are you going to marry now, ole buddy?"

He slid open the bottom drawer where Mike kept his brandy. There was an unopened bottle of Napoleon Brandy. He twisted off the cap and added two jiggers to the coffee he had sitting on the corner of the desk and lifted the cup in a toast.

"To you, Mike, the one true man among men. Always were, always will be my idol. I promise, somehow I'll make this up to you, I'll erase this mark on the family."

Karen rapped twice, then entered the den and sat down in what used to be Paul's chair, opposite Mike's. She could see he had been crying.

"Why didn't you tell me about Dina when you picked me up at the airport?"

"Dina asked me not to."

"Who is he, do you know?"

"No, I don't."

"Did Mike know?"

"She didn't tell anyone."

"I'll find out. Karen, don't ever withhold anything about the family from me again. Your first loyalty is to me, just as mine is to you."

"I…"

"What? Is there something else you haven't told me?"

"No. I was thinking, maybe someone forced…"

"Don't be ridiculous. Do you seriously think any guy would try to force himself on any Dmitri woman? Especially Dina? She'd have sent his gonads through his ass, or died trying. Excuse me for being so crass, but it's so ridiculous." He realized he hurt her feelings. "I'm sorry, sweetheart. I didn't mean you were ridiculous. I know this must have been difficult for you. Tell you what, I haven't seen the workshop yet, what do you say we take a ride over and take a look at it?"

"Sure, fine."

For Paul, the workshop was a bona fide stamp of approval from Mike. They had argued long and hard about his quitting college after one semester. It wasn't often they disagreed, and when they did, Mike usually won. It took Paul a year to wash out the resentment he felt over Mike's basing his final decision to let him quit college on Carl's say-so. That Carl's praises had carried more weight than his own merits as a craftsman. Having Carl tell Mike that "the kid" had a good eye for detail and had a real gift for working with wood. Paul understood Mike's having respect for Carl's opinion—the man was a master craftsman—but he would have preferred that Mike base his judgment on what he saw personally. Carl's praise was flattering, but Mike's respect meant far more. Besides, he never asked for or needed Carl's recommendations. He didn't care much for Carl and wasn't comfortable being on the receiving end of praise from a man he did not like. But it did get him out of college.

He took a long swallow of his coffee mix, thinking about the funny way things worked out. Korea had got him out of college faster but gave him something harder to live with, some very bad memories.

CHAPTER FIFTEEN

THE SUN HAD PUSHED THE TEMPERATURE UP A GOOD TEN OR FIFTEEN degrees by the time Dina reached the outskirts of town on her cross-country skis. The additional help from the sun took the chill out of her bones. The clock on the bank read seven forty-five, she had left the house at six. By now, Karen had to be up and about, or would be by the time Dina got back home.

She removed her skis, setting them up against the house, and waved when she saw Karen through the window. She brushed herself off and walked into the kitchen.

"Morning. Coffee sure smells good."

"Morning. It's not quite ready. The first pot I made went into Paul's Thermos. He took it with him to the shop. Left about seven."

The red light lit up on the coffeepot. Karen poured out a cup for Dina, then herself.

Dina took a sip and put the cup back down. "Wow. Little too hot for me."

"Guess I'm used to it. Dina, I'm so sorry. I hate to see you leave like this…"

Dina reached over and placed her hand on Karen's arm.

"Don't worry about it. It'll all blow over."

She shook her head. "I don't think so. He told me if a man tried to force himself on you, you'd push his…gonads up through his ass, or you'd be dead. Is dying more acceptable than rape? Is that what all men think?"

"There are women who think the same thing. Not all men think that death is preferable. Death is a dreadfully high price to pay for the person not guilty of any crime. Conclusions drawn from speculations are a fool's pastime anyway. Karen? You have to stop acting as if you're the other woman. You're not. Carl raped you. It is not your fault. Don't let him ruin your life, or Paul's. Can you do that?"

"Yes. I'm...trying to put it behind me."

"Don't try, it's essential that you *do* it."

"I will."

"You know, my mother once told me that we Dmitris don't march to a different drummer, we're our own orchestra. Maybe that's so, but circumstances sometimes call for us to dance to someone else's music. The thing to do is make sure it's a short dance."

"I'll try. Oh, Jake called. Again. He wants to talk to you. Said it's important. Please call him."

"Don't have the time, I have to get going. I'll call him when I get to New York."

It was obvious to Karen, from the tone in Dina's voice and from the way she looked, she wouldn't call.

Karen said, "C'mon, I'll help you load your suitcases."

She waved until the station wagon disappeared, then went back into the house and dialed the shop.

"Hello...Dmitri's Fine Furniture."

"Dina just left. You should have been here, Paul. You should have said goodbye." Before he could answer she hung up.

A minute later, the phone rang at the Dmitri Place.

"I said goodbye yesterday. As far as I'm concerned, she's dead."

"Paul, I don't want you to talk about Dina like—"

"You don't understand, honey!" She could hear him slam his hand on a desk or maybe a chair. "We both grew up with the same set of values. Mom used to worry about her becoming a tomboy, can you imagine? Mike told her not to worry, Dina needed more competition than what other girls had to offer. She was…the best. Better than me, at everything. And I, we all, thought she was something special. We put her on a pedestal…"

"Do me a favor, Paul, don't put me on a pedestal. I'm afraid of heights, and the fall's too far."

"I put you on one long ago."

"Take me off."

"Christ! I don't get it. I go off to some foreign place, put my life on the line…for what? To make their world over there a better place, only to find my world is screw…turned upside down. Is it too much to expect my world to stay the same? Well, is it?"

"Things change, things happen here too."

Karen was staring down at the carpet, not trusting herself to speak.

"Sweetheart, I didn't mean to upset you. Karen, I love you. You're the one constant in my life now. You are my life. My rainbow. I need you more than ever."

She raised her head, repeating, "Take me off," then hung up.

CHAPTER SIXTEEN

By the time Phil remembered to look at the clock, everyone else had been gone for hours. He started to dial Paul's number at the shop, saw that all the lights were out, and replaced the phone. Thinking he might catch Jake and Paul at the Norseman's, he locked up and drove there.

On his way in, he passed a man on his way out. When he walked into the lounge, he realized the man he had passed was the last customer. Other than Gus, there wasn't another soul in the place.

Since it was going to be a short night, he ordered a boilermaker.

"So it's just you and me? Been quiet all night?"

Gus set a beer down and poured out a brandy. Despite the improbability of being overheard, he leaned over the bar. "It's quiet now, but it was fairly busy earlier. Look, Phil, I don't want to be a hard-ass, but can you keep Jake out of here until he learns how to behave himself?"

"What happened?"

"He started a fight with Carl Anderson. I was going to call in the sheriff."

Putting a call in to the sheriff was drastic action for Gus. "How'd it start?"

"Jake got himself tanked up, got to playing all those damn torch songs he's taken such a liking to, then he spots Carl. I might be wrong, but it seemed to me Jake was laying for him. Now, I gotta say, Carl was minding his own business. Jake goes over to him and whispers in his ear. I don't think anyone heard what it was, but whatever it was, it set their fists to flying and they started to clobber away at each other. This is a family place, Phil. It isn't the Fisherman's Bar."

"I know, Gus. Any damages?"

He rapped on the bar. "No, knock on wood, and not to anyone else besides the two of them. Carl's face is in bad shape and let me warn you, Jake don't look pretty neither."

"Sorry for the trouble, Gus. I'll have a talk with him."

"I'd appreciate it. You know, Gert and me, we've always liked Jake. Hell, Phil, we both served overseas, we know how it is. When we got back, we did our share of drinking and hell-raising, happy to be alive and home again. But there's such a thing as going too far. Jake was always a level-headed, easy-going guy. Him and the Dmitri kid. Paul's doing all right. What's eating at Jake?"

"Must be readjustment blues or something. I'll get it straightened out, talk to him when I get home. Don't feel bad about it. Someone doesn't behave in your place, you have every right to make them leave, with a sheriff's help if necessary." He tossed down the brandy and took long swallows of beer.

"I didn't mean to chase you away."

"I only came in for one nightcap. Time for me to go home and hit the sack. So long, Gus."

"Good night, Phil. Take 'er easy."

The stale fumes of beer, nicotine and recycled brandy attacked his nostrils as soon as he opened the door. Jake was sprawled out on the sofa, snoring. By turning his head slightly, a badly swollen cheek and puffy black eye were revealed.

Without bothering to be gentle, he shook Jake until his eyes rolled into a blurry focus. A silly grin inched its way into his face. He tilted his head and pointed to his face. "Arm rasslin' wit' Carl—on'y shot he got."

"Is that so, hotshot?" With one yank he pulled Jake up off the sofa, half dragged, half marched him into the shower, turned on the cold water full blast, and shoved him in.

"Stay in there till your head shrinks back to its normal size. I'll make some coffee."

The shower helped but the coffee smelled like dishwater, and tasted like it. Jake knew better than to offer excuses. His jaw hurt too much to give any.

"Jake, you got to pull yourself together. You're not some swabbie on shore leave, you're home. You can't keep going around getting tanked up, getting into stupid brawls."

He waited for Jake to respond but he was staring at his coffee, like he was considering diving in to escape.

"Listen kid, I know how it is adjusting to civilian life again, but the sooner you do it, the better. Make up your mind what you're going to do with your life. Paul's not going to hold that job open much longer."

"Talked to him today, I took the job. Worked out a few designs this afternoon." He motioned to the sketches he had laid out on the coffee table.

Phil picked them up and flipped through them. "Should have stayed home and worked on them all night. Better yet, maybe you ought to get in your car and drive to New York, have it out with Dina. Settle things. Get on with your life, one way or another."

"Gimme a break. My head feels like ventilated concrete." He held his head in his hands. "Dina knows where I am, knows my number."

"You want to play stubborn, go ahead, but do yourself a favor and lay off the boilermakers. You can't handle 'em."

"I know, I know."

Meanwhile, on the other side of the lake, Carl barely recognized himself in the bathroom mirror. His ears were still ringing with the maniac's threat. "You ever call Nadine Dmitri a slut again, you'll be pissing through your nostrils." Goddamn maniac never did have all his marbles. He should have known better than to go into the place when he saw Jake's truck out in front.

Wasn't a person there could say he was looking for any trouble when he walked in. But he wasn't about to run and hide neither, have the punk think he was scared of him.

Martha handed him an ice pack. "You're lucky you didn't break your neck or get a concussion. You don't feel tired, or woozy?"

"No, I'm okay. Just leave me be."

Trying to talk him into going to see a doctor was useless. First thing tomorrow, she was going to insist that he get additional insurance. He had a son to think about now. It was beyond her how he fell between the sink and the toilet. Men.

CHAPTER SEVENTEEN

IT WASN'T AS THOUGH DINA HAD NEVER BEEN AWAY FROM HOME BEFORE. There were family vacations to California, Wyoming and Texas, and she'd gone down to Florida twice, on her own, to stay with her friend Carol. Those places were nothing like New York. The noise, the concrete buildings—steep stepping stones to the stars, continuous crowds of strangers rushing by with a manic urgency to reach destinations they seemed to fear were going to perish if they didn't get to them yesterday. It wasn't a city, it was an arena.

Apartment hunting wasn't a challenge, it was a perverse way of using the scarce free time she had. It took three weeks to find a suitable place, one that was centrally located, close enough to the university and to the law office that Sam Olsen had referred her to.

The rooms were ample, but not too. Classes, study time and a part-time job weren't going to allow her much time to fuss with anything larger. It did have two bedrooms and the kitchen didn't threaten to close in when she bent over. The living room could easily accommodate three chairs, a sofa, floor lamps and three tables.

Private time was something she had always needed, from the time she was a child. She cherished space, the luxury of stealing uninterrupted hours to sort out mental kinks, or simply sit and reflect. Loneliness was altogether different and three months of it was more than she was willing to endure. She placed an ad for "Female to Share."

Talent for Deception

Two weeks of phone call interviews gave her second thoughts about the merits of loneliness. Some calls were disgusting, some downright ridiculous and some she wasn't sure she understood. She agreed to one last interview before resigning herself to becoming a part-time recluse.

She barely had the door open when a tall, auburn-haired arrow whizzed past her and into the living room, throwing questions over her shoulder as she darted through the rooms, leaving Dina in her wake.

"Two bedrooms? Yes, good. Full bath? Hmm, also good. I like to soak in the tub. What hours do you have? Mine are sort of irregular, I hope you're not one of those cheery early morning risers. I can't stand pot banging symphonies at six a.m. Or flushing toilets. Tell me you don't drink sugar in your coffee. Clinking teaspoons circling 'round and 'round in coffee cups drive me nuts. Do you sing? I'm not fond of arias in the shower either." The arrow stopped to look her over. "Tell me you're not a model, competition is tough enough as it is. You are stunning, I have to say. Yes, *stunning*, does suit you. I doubt very much that I'm the first to tell you. So? Tell me you're anything but a model."

"I'm not a model. I'm attending Columbia University, and I work part-time in a law office."

"You're not one of those pseudo-intellectuals who go around saying, 'I have a law degree' in every pause in every conversation? Magpie cum loudies I call them." She waited a second or two and when there was no response she said, "So, Gabby, this is fine by me, how about it? Do I pass your inspection? God! You're about as green as your eyes. What kind of lawyer do you intend to be when you grow up?"

"Corporate attorney. Have *you* ever thought about law as a career?"

The arrow let out a hearty laugh that sounded almost evil and extended her hand. "Name's Amanda Adams. Believe me, I try to keep law furthest from my mind."

Dina shook Amanda's hand. "Nadine Dmitri. Most everyone calls me Dina."

"Dmitri, is that Greek?"

"Russian."

"You're not a communist, are you?"

"No, are you?"

"No, I'm Jewish—you have a problem with that?"

"Problem? No. Why would I?"

"Oh, kiddo. Where are you from? I'd guess Kansas—or Iowa."

"Neither. Minnesota. Hid'n Oaks, Minnesota."

"Hmm. Sounds ominous. How long have you been in the big, wicked city? I'm surprised your parents let you leave home."

"Small towns aren't all that unwicked. Both my parents are deceased. And I'm too old to be a runaway."

"Sorry, I'm too blunt sometimes. I'm a native, parents live upstate. Well, Gabby, you pass inspection, do I?"

"One thing I want understood. No overnight guests—not men."

"Overnight guests? You mean no shacking up? Tell me, do they still do the minuet in Hidden—whatever?"

"Hid'n Oaks. Why shucks, not hardly ever these days. We've done graduated to the turkey trot."

"Touché. Normally I'm quite open-minded. Fact is, my mother is fond of telling me that I'm so open-minded my brain must be made of hair netting. By the way, I don't smoke and except for an occasional glass or two of wine, I don't drink. Booze is as unkind to the figure as it is to the complexion. I won't be here all that much…I do a lot of, uh, location layouts. Gotta do 'em while I'm still in demand. Before my eyebrows end up on my upper lip, my ass no longer sways, it plops, and I have to buy size 36-vertical bras. So, what do you say?"

"I guess so. Yes."

"I hope by the time you finish law school, you develop a silver tongue. As for the drudgeries: cleaning, cooking, laundry. I hope you cook. I have a thing about eating out. Used to be a waitress myself. Know the old joke about men washing their hands after visiting the little boys' room? Well honey, I've seen plenty of women who act like they touched gold behind those stall doors and refuse to wash it away. Gives a body such a sense of pride in the personal hygiene of the feminine sex. Then they wonder where all those pesky germs come from."

"I enjoy eating out."

"You know it's not going to cost you anything to expand a little, what are you, a conversational mime? So, when will it be convenient for me to move in?"

Dina wasn't sure which of her instincts to follow, was Amanda Adams intelligent, or too knowing? She was likable. The vibrant brown eyes didn't seem all that earnest, or maybe it was the fact that she apparently didn't take life all that seriously.

"How will next weekend work for you?"

"Well, this Friday would work out better, is that okay with you?"

"Uh, sure, I guess it'll be fine."

They shook hands again and Dina told herself it was going to work out all right. It was going to be fine. Fine. She hoped.

In the cab, on the way back to her soon-to-be vacated apartment, Amanda congratulated herself. Dina Dmitri was made to order, right down to her strait-laced manner and somewhat introverted personality. She was looking forward to introducing Dina to her parents. When they saw Gabby, their worries were going to drop off their shoulders with a bang so loud California was going to think they were having an earthquake. Gabby was probably the epitome of the daughter they had hoped Amanda would be. She doubted she

120

and Miss Dmitri were going to be friends, but as long as the arrangement was tolerable she'd hang on, at least until something better came along.

As questionable as it seemed at first, the arrangement did work out. Amanda found, to her surprise, that she got a kick out of being Dina's tour guide to the real New York, was proud of the fact that in less than two weeks time she had shown Dina more of New York than she'd seen in three months on her own.

Amanda introduced her to pizza, Coney Island, and bagels and lox. They toured Manhattan, took a ferry ride where Amanda pointed out Ellis Island, sat in St. Patrick's Cathedral, stood on top of the Empire State Building and saw all the current Broadway shows. Amanda also took her to see the Dodgers, Giants and the Yankees play.

Dina found Amanda to be perversely unpretentious, fortunately possessing a sense of humor that saved her from offending people most of the time. Beneath the tough facade, she was a sucker for panhandlers, dogs and, despite her efforts to seem otherwise, children. She was an extraordinary teacher who knew all sorts of interesting things and places. A loyal, trustworthy friend, the kind of person who would not only give you the blouse off her back, she'd pay you for taking it off her hands, *if* she liked you.

CHAPTER EIGHTEEN

SPRING OF 1954 INFECTED EVERYONE IN HID'N OAKS WITH ITS YEARLY DOSE of lightheadedness. In Paul's case, it was more than spring fever. On the fifteenth of June, he became the proud father of a six-pound, eight-ounce girl.

Leslie Joanne Dmitri was slightly wrinkled, bald and very squirmy. She was perfect—or would be once her belly lost the look of a cereal bowl tipped on its edge.

The expansive mood fatherhood had put him in stopped Paul from objecting to Karen's calling Dina to tell her the good news, that she was an aunt. His mood ended when she tried to hand the phone to him. He responded by walking out of the hospital room.

The morning before Paul was to bring his wife and baby home from the hospital, he felt out of sorts. Lonely. He decided to drive over to Tanner's.

Carl held the binoculars tight against his face as he watched Paul stroll down the hill. He disappeared into the boathouse. Two minutes later, his boat came out and he pointed it in the direction of Tanner's place.

He kept Paul in his sights until he docked at Tanner's pier, satisfied that he knew where he was and what he was doing. Had to check on his buddy's progress, as if he couldn't tell by the racket.

The pounding had started at nine o'clock. Soon after, screeching saws joined it. He counted twenty straw bosses standing around watching five men work on Jake's Folly. Jake's Joke is what it was. Goofy house was sticking up in the air like some dry-docked boat. He heard that Jake said he intended for it to look like that. Like hell.

When the thing was finished, all the people who hung around watching it being built were going to be looking for something else to waste their time on. If they thought they were going to plant their asses on his property while the new cabins were being built, they had another think coming. He didn't want people hanging around, getting in the way.

He never heard Martha come up behind him. When she spoke, he jumped.

"Lake busy?"

"Damn it, woman! You trying to give me a heart attack, sneaking up on me like that?" He swung the binoculars to the other side, across the bay from Tanners, to Dmitris. "Ten, twelve fishing boats. Coupla speedboats pulling skiers. More and more people want to go waterskiing. We have to buy some boats for it, accommodate our guests."

Martha was standing beside him, and looked out at the skiers. "Can't afford to buy boats now, hon." The commotion over at Jake's drew her attention to his place. "He's really coming along with the place. Don't know how he does it, works night and day, that man."

"Hard work never hurt nobody."

"Doesn't leave much time for a social life."

"He gets around."

Martha was going to ask how he would know, but decided not to.

CHAPTER NINETEEN

THE FIRST FIVE YEARS OF LESLIE'S LIFE WERE PURE HEAVEN. SHE WAS THE center of her mommy and daddy's world; she had their undivided attention, and everyone else's who came to visit. She was swaddled in love, and she basked in their praise and perpetual concern for her well being. She was her daddy's little rainbow, his piece of sunshine, and her mother's look-alike angel.

Paul readily agreed with his wife, Leslie was every bit as beautiful as Elizabeth Taylor had been at five. Golden honey hair framed her diamond-shaped, peaches and cream face, and gorgeous little sapphire eyes danced behind a forest of eyelashes. She was a delight, so adorably precocious. A most charming little girl, who, everyone predicted, was going to be a terrible heartbreaker.

For the first four years, Karen thought her look-alike angel's talent for imitating was amusing, and at times she was proud of how perceptive she was for such a youngster. Leslie was a natural mime. Karen even envisioned her being on the stage, an acclaimed actress. But as time went on, every now and then things got out of hand. She didn't know what it was, exactly, but the imitations began to bother her. Sometimes her impersonations seemed almost mean. Karen told herself she was being silly, four-year-olds were not sly, or sarcastic. Not intentionally.

Paul didn't need people to tell him he was the luckiest man on earth. He knew he had all he wanted—a great life, a wonderful, beautiful wife and now he had a little rainbow with the same angel face as his wife.

He didn't think about it getting better. When it did, he declared a holiday and took the mother-to-be and his daughter on a three-day vacation to Wisconsin to see The Dells and the Milwaukee Zoo. While they were at the zoo, they broke the news to Leslie that she was going to have a baby sister or a baby brother to love and play with, someone they could share their love and happiness with.

Neither of them seemed to notice the massive dark cloud that covered their little angel's face. The cloud disappeared when, two months later, Leslie found out she wouldn't have to share after all, because her mother lost her baby brother. Leslie celebrated by giving a tea party for all her stuffed animal friends in her bedroom.

On the other side of the lake, Leslie's half brother was living a very different life. By the age of four, Peter understood that being *chosen* didn't mean by both Martha and Carl. Maybe by Martha, but Carl hadn't chosen him.

By age five, he had logged countless hours sitting on the porch steps watching for a car to drive up with his real mommy and daddy in it, come to rescue him. Hope turned to despair, then anger, when he concluded they weren't going to come get him, they had ditched him.

It took time, but eventually he learned that no matter what he did, he was never going to please Carl. Carl didn't like him tugging at his pant leg or touching his arm to get his attention. All Carl did was shake him off and tell him to scram. Except when Martha was around, then he'd pay attention to him—for a while.

Martha said he had a guardian angel to watch out for him. He knew there had to be someone invisible helping him to stay out of trouble. Like staying out of Carl's way when Martha wasn't around.

He learned how to be careful, pretend he wasn't doing something when he was, like watching Carl when the letters from Martha's friend came. Carl pretended too, he tried to look like he wasn't interested in them, but he was. As soon as Martha was done with them, she'd put them on top of the refrigerator and, soon as her back was turned, Carl snatched them up and studied them like they were treasure maps. Peter found this very puzzling. If Carl hated this bitch so much, why was he so interested in her letters?

Every time one of Dina Dmitri's letters came, he grew more and more curious, but he knew better than to ask. He promised himself he was going to find out what it was about her and her letters that made Carl so crazy mad. He'd find out before he ran away.

CHAPTER TWENTY

JUNE 1959, NEW YORK. IT WAS HOT, STICKY, MISERABLE. THE VERY FIRST thing Amanda did when she got inside the apartment was kick off her shoes, the second was to pull off her blouse, soured and stained with perspiration. Then she checked the refrigerator for a snack, anything to tide her over until dinner. Everything that looked tasty was too fattening. Nothing fell into the sensible snack category. Since dinner was going to be her treat tonight, she wasn't going to spoil her appetite.

Her conscience told her she was kidding herself, it wasn't hunger. It was the damn kvetching pangs of guilt gnawing at her.

Nothing in the meat keeper looked good enough to satisfy a starving roach. Without enthusiasm, she picked out salami and mozzarella, then grabbed the jar of mayo and a head of lettuce and carried it all to the counter.

With an uncaring deftness, she slathered two pieces of bread with mayo, slapped on the salami and cheese, and topped it with a lettuce leaf. She cut the sandwich in half, wrapped one half up in wax paper and along with all the other ingredients, put it in the refrigerator.

She bit into the sandwich half just as the cuckoo emerged from its hidey hole to announce it was six o'clock in its usual aggravating tone. One of these days she was going to catch the little pain in the ass and rip it off its perch before it could get back inside.

The snack lost its appeal so she pushed the plate away, knowing very well it wasn't the food—her conscience had a death grip on her.

Her father was a great believer in getting things off his chest, claiming that it was best to tell the truth up front, for truth was its own reward.

And that's what she fully intended to do once she and Gabby stopped being two women sharing an apartment and became good friends.

For her, past experience with good intentions had never proved rewarding. The last time she acted on a good intention, it cost her five hundred dollars. She had made up her mind on the spot that if she ever had good intentions again, she was going to shove them so far up her ass, her brain would never find them.

If Gabby had only asked, things would have been so much simpler. She would have fessed up and got it over with. Her less judgmental side suggested there was no reason to, Gabby never asked. It wasn't in Gabby to ask personal questions of someone. Why would she? Getting her to open up about anything personal was about as productive as trying to scratch through steel with a toothpick.

Why was she beating herself over the head? Because she had placed Gabby in a very awkward position. There was not a judge in New York, nor any cop, who would believe an intelligent, sharp lawyer with a prestigious law firm was so gullible she didn't know she was sharing her apartment with someone who made a living as a prostitute.

The day she answered the ad and walked into this apartment, all she cared about was having a nice place to stay, sharing it with someone who her parents could meet and be assured that Amanda wasn't living with someone who reeked of aftershave lotion or wore jockey shorts. It was a kick seeing them so intoxicated with relief when they met Dina for the first time.

Now here she was feeling guilty about leading a lamb into a mess. Not that Gabby wasn't able to hold her own with con artists and triple-lipping lawyers with a penchant for superfluous theatrics, but Gabby would always be stuck with the small town affliction: trust.

Right now, it had the so-called merits of sophistication beat all to hell.

The phone rang, putting a temporary end to her self-recriminations. She waited until after the third ring before picking it up. She didn't even get a chance to say hello.

"Congratulations, your crystal ball is working. We won the antitrust case!"

"So? Am I supposed to be surprised? What took so long?"

"Lawyers. I'm on my way home. Where do you want to go for dinner? It's on me. Are you in the mood for Italian, Jewish, Chinese, Russian, what?"

"Dinner is supposed to be on me. Would you mind eating in, picking up some Italian on your way? I have to talk to you about something important."

"You can buy next time. Tonight dinner's on me, okay? Italian it is. See you about seven."

It was ten before seven when Dina charged into the apartment.

"Damn it Amanda! Why isn't the door locked?"

"I left it open purposely because I figured you'd have your hands full…" The disheveled woman standing before her looked nothing like the impeccably dressed woman Amanda saw every day. The one who always looked as if she stepped off the cover of *Vogue.* "Either you were in a fight over a taxi and lost, or you were mugged. Is that tomato sauce on your coat?"

Dina looked down. She was about to answer when a loud knock on the door stopped her.

Amanda motioned to her to open it. "Muggers don't make house calls, as a rule. Unless they want a reward."

Talent for Deception

Dina opened the door a crack and a tall, dark-haired man flashed a badge at her as he practically barreled past her. He was dressed too casually for a policeman.

"Miss Dmitri? Detective Ben Coleman. I happened to be in the neighborhood, saw some perp snatch your purse. I tried to chase him down, but I lost him."

"Since you don't have my purse, how do you know my name?"

"Saw you enter this building and described you to a guy downstairs. He and three other guys said it had to be you. Seems you're a very popular...lady."

Off in the corner, sitting quietly in a chair next to the window, which was turning out to be the best seat in the house, Amanda took in the scene playing out for her and was finding it difficult to hide her amusement. She concentrated on detecting the detective.

Detective Coleman had quite a technique It started out as a cop doing his thing, committing all the little details to memory. But...his big brown eyes toured the room while making intermittent probes of Gabby's body. His orbs were better than tentacles. Amanda was pretty sure he loved playing doctor when he was a boy. Maybe the badge was a fake and he was a voyeur.

While the detective probed away, Gabby was trying hard to be polite and cooperative, but her jaw was beginning to jut. If the detective wasn't careful, she was going to poke a hole in his chest. Either the notebook in his hand was more than a prop, and he was being a conscientious cop, or his brain needed a transfusion because he was missing signals.

It was almost as if he heard Amanda thinking, or finally remembered she was in the room. The look he gave was about as subtle as a knuckle sandwich. She responded with a raised eyebrow and a smirk. He returned his attention to Gabby.

Detective Coleman wasn't a bad looker, in an off-beat sort of way.

There was intelligence in the brown eyes, and his dark brown hair was actually shiny. From the looks of his tush, he was in damn fine physical condition. His mouth was a real problem. So was his ego. Given the narrow confines that held so much ego, it was amazing his head did not explode. The man had as much finesse as a storm trooper.

"You married?"

"I beg your pardon. What does my marital status have to do with my purse being stolen? There seems to be some confusion here. I'm not applying for some government position."

He flipped the notebook closed and shoved it into his shirt pocket. He spent all of ten seconds looking at the portrait on the wall. The woman was fair, with very fine features. The man was dark, and looked very much like the woman standing in front of him.

"Well, that's about all for now, Miz Dmitri." He started to turn toward the door. "Oh, one more thing, where can I reach you during the day? In case anything turns up. You do work *outside* the apartment?"

Dina's head jerked back and her eyes narrowed. "Has anyone ever told you that your attitude is about as palatable as crushed glass?"

He smiled. "Ma'am, I'm just a public servant doing my job. Asking questions goes with it. You don't get my vote for Miss Congeniality either. You keep those eyes in the freezer overnight?" He held up his hands. "Not to worry, I'm well insulated."

"I can see that. What you need, Detective, is a course in diplomacy and help for your inferiority complex."

"Tsk, tsk. Such a smart mouth for a lady. I'm just a diligent pro, like yourself."

"What is your problem, Detective?"

"You still didn't answer my question, is that slow thinking or clever evasion?"

Talent for Deception

"Unlike you, thinking is not a rare occurrence for me." She reached over and picked up a card from the table and handed it to him. "In case you can't find someone to read it to you, it says I'm an attorney with Strauss and O'Brien. Usual hours from 8:00 a.m. until 6:00."

Barely able to contain a mocking grin, Amanda watched it start to register, watched the big bad wolf's eyes jump over to the desk, rest for a few seconds on the law books sitting on top and presto, the big bad wolf turned into a sheep. She waited until he got around to remembering she was still in the room, and when he did, she put more mock into the grin.

He started backing up toward the door.

"Well, uh, Miss Dmitri, if there's anything I can do, if anything turns up I'll call you. For now, I'll get out of your hair." He nodded slightly, gave Amanda a look that told her he knew he wasn't wrong about her, and left the room.

Dina stood in the doorway until he got on the elevator and the doors closed before closing the apartment door and bolting it.

"I hope I don't have to see or hear from him again. And may I ask why you're sitting there gloating?"

"Am I gloating? Take my word, you'll be hearing from him."

"I hope not."

"He may be lacking in the savoir-faire department, but he's quite a hunk, if you go for tall, dark, battering rams."

"I don't."

"No? Hmm. Do you, uh, have any bruises?"

"No, he just grabbed my purse. He didn't lay a hand on me."

"I wasn't referring to the purse snatcher. I meant your detective."

"My detect...he's not my anything. What do you mean 'do I have any bruises'?"

"Never mind. Detective Coleman will be calling you. Trust me, I know people. It's...sort of an occupational necessity, or hazard,

134

depending on how you look at it. Take care, he's definitely the 'me man, you woman, lay down I want to talk to you' type."

"Are you out of your mind?"

"Dina, Dina. He took time to go over every inch of you. This Ben Coleman is going to work his way into your life and he's going to make sure that you have the time for him."

"Don't be absurd. That badge-flashing Neanderthal will stay clear of me if he has half a functioning brain. He's obnoxious. Subtle as chartreuse."

"I think the reason he was so rude is because he's attracted to you. Interested. But he was having a problem with what he thought was your choice of careers."

"What? What possible difference does it make—"

"Dina, do you have any idea of how many models make it to the big bucks bracket? What you Midwesterners so modestly refer to as a comfortable living? Damn few. And I'm not cut out to be a smiling, posing pencil. I have very expensive habits, not the least of which are eating and wearing warm clothes in winter. I like living indoors. Look, what I'm trying to tell you is that the reason I think Detective Coleman was in the neighborhood is he may have been tailing me. He may have me under surveillance—I'm a hooker." There. It was out. "I model to make contacts, and to show Uncle Sam proof of legal employment."

"Amanda, I know."

"What do you mean, you know? For how long?"

"Remember that fantastic fashion layout you told me you had in Paris? Two days after you left, your answering service called—"

"Cassie! That bimbo! I gave her strict instructions never to call me here unless it was a life or death situation. What did she say?"

"She was excited for you, knew you hadn't had any modeling for some time. She assumed I knew about—"

"Did she say what the shoot was for?"

"Beer commercial, I believe."

"Figures. I hate beer. It's so damn bloating. Dina, I want you to know I'm so sorry about all this. I honestly meant to tell you. I—"

"Amanda, don't apologize, you've taken great pains to be discreet. You've never had any of your...clients...here or allowed them to call. If you had, things might have been different, I don't know. You've always respected my privacy; I had no desire to intrude on yours."

"I've placed you in an awkward position. When I moved in here, I didn't think it was any of your business, but once we became friends, things got difficult. I was all set to tell you the other night, but it seemed like a better idea to wait until you won this case. And now you have."

"I didn't win it alone, it was Max's case as much as mine."

"All right, your half of the case. Anyway, I suspected I was being tailed about a week ago, and I was going to tell you, then something happened I thought got me off the hook, so to speak, gave me a way out. That fantastic fashion layout I told you I had in Rome, Paris, Athens...well, he asked me to marry him."

"Amanda! That's wonderful! I'm so happy for you."

"His name, by the way, is Robert Ryan. How's that for a reverse *Abie's Irish Rose?*"

"And you never said a word. When did all this happen?"

"Oh, he's asked me to marry him off and on for a month. I didn't want to leap into a fire without some assurances. Then I asked myself, how much longer can I go on alone? It's not that I don't love him, but with Bob the only worry I'll have about old age is growing old. He's not exactly rolling in change, if you catch my drift."

"Looking at you, I don't have to ask if you're happy. This is great, it really puts the topper on my day."

"Mine, too. Gabby, he's handsome, smart, has a great sense of humor and he loves me. I am really crazy about him."

136

"What does he do?"

"Do? For now, he's in insurance, eventually he's going into real estate."

"Well? When's the day? The wedding, I mean."

"Two weeks, maybe three. Don't worry, I'm not going to skip out on the lease, I'll pay whatever I owe on—"

"Don't be silly."

"Okay, I won't. Dina, I want you to be my witness, can't ask you to be my maid-of-honor, don't want to risk having a synagogue fall on me. It'll be a justice of the peace sort of thing."

"I'd be hurt if you asked anyone else."

"Thanks. Now that I've got everything off my chest, I'd like to put something in my stomach. Not what you're wearing. How about you taking a shower and I'll order a pizza from down the block."

Dina looked down at her spaghetti-sauced dress. "I'm surprised Detective Coleman didn't ask what kind of sauce it was. I'll be ready in about twenty minutes."

Amanda picked up the phone but didn't dial. Through the window she saw Detective Coleman sitting in a car across the street. A scruffy looking guy was handing him a purse through the driver's window. She smiled.

She yelled down the hallway to Dina. "Say, Gabby, how about we go out for pizza?"

"Fine with me." She stepped into the shower.

Amanda divided her attention between the action on the street and dialing the pizzeria.

"Carlo's. Take your order?"

She gave him the order.

"Lady, you sure you want extra salt on the pizza to go?"

"I'm absolutely positive. I'll pay for it when my friend and I get there. We'll be having our pizza there, in the restaurant."

"Okay lady. Twenty minutes?"

"Perfect."

"Twenty bucks! I coulda been killed, and you want me to settle for a lousy twenty bucks? Guy chased me ten blocks yelling 'purse-snatcher.' I swear he woulda caught me, if the traffic wasn't so heavy."

"Twenty bucks is what we agreed on, Ernie, and twenty bucks is what you're getting. We both know where you're going to spend it. I'm not giving you a dime more."

Ben held the twenty out the window. Ernie shrugged, took the twenty and walked away grumbling to himself about cheap cops as he purposely passed the first liquor store and crossed the street. There was a bigger liquor store down the next block, around the corner, where Ben wouldn't be able to see him go in.

Ben pulled a cigarette out of his shirt pocket and pushed the lighter in. As soon as he inhaled, his stomach started complaining. He glanced at the clock on the dashboard, wishing he hadn't skipped lunch.

Before he had a chance to slump down he saw the redhead, Amanda, look right at him, and nod. They walked halfway down the block and went inside the pizza place.

He was tempted to walk in the restaurant, bluff his way through, say he was checking out a few things and decided to grab something to eat. Instead he took out Miss Dmitri's card and fingered it, trying to figure her out.

If she worked for Max Strauss, she couldn't be tied in with anything illegal. Max would bounce her out of his office if she was. *If* he knew.

If she were on the level, what was she doing living with Charmaine Colbert, a.k.a. Amanda Adams, prostitute, and Bob Ryan's sweetie. Ryan could wear five hundred dollar suits, fifty dollar ties and get his fingernails manicured, but his hands were still dirty.

He made up his mind to call Max the first chance he got. If she worked for Max, why didn't one guy from the squad mention seeing Max in court with a looker? Looker like her was hard to miss. They might have intentionally kept it a secret.

A kid came out of the pizzeria carrying a box, heading straight for his car. When he got to the window, Ben rolled it down.

"What's up?"

The kid handed him the pizza. "Compliments of a red-headed dame inside. Said you couldn't get outta your car, 'counta your fallen arches."

Ben started to reach in his pocket but the kid waved him off.

"Keep it, she tipped me. Said ya didn't want anything to drink, cuz it'd give ya too much discomfort."

"I bet she did. Thanks, kid."

Ravenous, he took a large bite of the one of the bigger pieces. He knew right away that she must have asked for extra salt. Three pieces were all he could take. His throat felt like it did the morning after a night of heavy drinking.

They finally came out of the restaurant and went directly to the apartment building. Just before she went in, the redhead paused for just a second and waved.

He started the car and drove to the first diner he came to. He ordered two hamburgers with raw onions and a pitcher of ice water to drink while he was waiting. He poured himself a glassful and carried it over to the phone booth, found Max's home number and dialed it.

"Max Strauss here."

"Hello, Max, it's Ben Coleman."

"Benjamin? How are your mother and father? Haven't seen your father at the synagogue in a few weeks."

"We're all fine. My father was down with the flu, but he's fine now."

Talent for Deception

"Haven't seen you in the halls of justice for some time now. You got things so much in control you don't have to do court time?"

"I wish things were under control. I haven't had to testify in any cases for a while. Max, reason I'm calling is, I need to talk with you. Can you meet with me tomorrow?"

"Tomorrow my day's full. Tomorrow evening is reserved for my wife. Once a month, we have dinner out. Alone. We have two drinks, dinner, dance around the floor once or twice, then come home. Tomorrow it's Sardi's. I made our reservations for eight. If you can get there by seven we can talk before Irene arrives."

"Thanks Max, I appreciate it. I'll be there."

He was pouring the last of the ice water when the waitress brought over his hamburgers. He barely chewed the first one, took his time with the second while reviewing his track record. He had a reputation to protect; the other detectives in the squad swore he was a warlock because of his skill in spotting phonies.

If he was wrong about Miss Dmitri, they were never going to find out about it. The thing that threw him off, what he was having trouble with, was separating his instincts from his desires. He wanted her to be what she said she was. But was she? Was she a legit attorney or a shrewd broad in some hood's pocket learning all the legal loopholes? He tossed a twenty on the counter and stormed out of the diner.

The waitress shrugged and picked up the bill. Who knew what got people upset? Since it wasn't the food or the service, who cared? Dissatisfied customers didn't leave a ten dollar tip.

CHAPTER TWENTY-ONE

Ben was sitting at the bar when Max walked in and stopped to check his hat and coat.

First time he saw Max Strauss was fifteen years ago and the first thing he thought was how short he was. A shrimp. His mother said Max had a sexy saunter, like the actor Robert Mitchum. It made him smile. It was hard to picture a guy five-three with Brillo-pad hair walking like a man six-two or better.

Even back then Max's face looked like the old baseball glove he had when he was a kid. He wondered whatever happened to that glove.

So much for first impressions. Max may have had a weathered face, but he had a pair of mesmerizing, glacier blue eyes that could cut any man down to his size, that and a regal air about him that many men over six feet couldn't acquire if it were sold over the counter. Max Strauss was a bona fide mensch, who wore survival like everything else in his life, including success, with a graceful dignity. The man had survived Hitler…nothing intimidated him. Max made Ben proud to be a Jew.

By the time Max reached him, Ben was standing. They shook hands.

"Hello, Max."

"Evening, Benjamin."

They both ordered a couple of old-fashioneds, ran through the usual amenities, and then Max, who was never one to waste time, especially his own, asked what he could do for him.

"Max, does a Nadine Dmitri work for you?"

"Nadine? Yes, she does. And is, in my opinion, our most promising attorney. Took her under my wing personally. Are you asking about her for professional reasons or personal?"

"Professional. She had her purse snatched; I was in the area, saw it happen. Guy took off like smoke, so I went to interview her. I just want some verification, some background on a few things."

"Was she hurt?"

"No, a little shaken, but other than that she's fine. Where is she from? She's not a New Yorker."

"Small town in Minnesota. Hid'n Oaks."

"How long's she been working for you?"

"Four years, or maybe five; she did paralegal while she was attending college."

"Do you know the kinds of people she socializes with? I mean does she, you know…"

Max leaned slightly toward Ben and the look of amusement fell away as he did. "If this is a personal inquiry, call and ask her. Professionally, Dina Dmitri is a woman of integrity, fine character and high morals. Understand? I trust her, have complete faith in her. May I offer a word of advice—free. She doesn't like games."

Ben held up both his hands. "Max, I wasn't implying she wasn't…any of those things you said."

"No? Then you'd better work on your tone, there's a definite lack of respect."

"I apologize if I sounded disrespectful. I'm not, believe me. Has she ever been married, or is she engaged?"

"Not personal, eh? Not to my knowledge."

Ben's mouth curved upward. "Thanks, Max. I appreciate your making time for me; I won't take up any more of it. Regards to Anna."

His eyebrows grew into hills. "Is that all? Is there anything else you want *verified?*"

"No. That's it. Shalom, Max."

Two days after Amanda moved out of the apartment, Ben knocked on the door. Dina's smile vanished as soon as she saw who it was.

"Detective Coleman. I thought it might be...someone else."

He handed her the purse. "Take a look, see if anything is missing."

She opened it, glanced inside and closed it. "Not even a hairpin. Thanks."

"Thieves aren't much interested in hairpins. Mind if I step in? I don't want to discuss this in the hall."

It didn't take a detective to realize there was a definite lack of warmth in the air. To annoy her further, he gave her his warmest smile as he stepped inside.

The place was less cluttered now, which he found strange, since there wasn't all that much furniture missing. It was quality stuff, nothing boxy or busy. The records that remained in the cabinets had to belong to her. At least they shared one thing in common, an appreciation for great musical talent: Sinatra, Ella, Margaret Whiting, Mel Torme, Nat King Cole and surprise, surprise, Jo Stafford. Some show tunes and some classical. A woman after his own heart.

"Detective, was there something you overlooked on your last visit?"

"Saw your roomie leave. You wouldn't be in the market for a new one to share expenses and the comforts of home?"

"Detective Coleman..."

"Call me Ben."

"Detective Coleman, how tall are you?"

"Six-two in socks."

"How much do you weigh?"

"One ninety, ninety-five. Depends."

"Amazing. How do you cram your ego into such a small space?"

"Must be magic." He smiled. "What do you eat for breakfast—thorns?"

"Detective, I don't like you. I find you insufferable. You seem to think you're being cute and charming. You're not. Thank you for returning my purse."

"You're welcome. I was beginning to think it was against your principles to be polite. Can we find some neutral ground here? I got off on the wrong floor, I'm sorry. How about dinner, a few drinks, maybe a dance or two." He nodded toward the cabinet. "It seems we enjoy the same type of music."

"Frankly, it's difficult for me to believe we have anything in common. Good night."

"Might have been—a good night, that is."

She opened the door, wide. "Will be, after you leave."

"I take it that's a rain check on the dinner. All right, I'm going. I'll call you in a few days, give you a chance to change your mind. I'm really a nice, fun guy once you get to know me."

"I'll deprive myself of the pleasure." She closed the door after him.

He smiled when he heard the bolt slide into place.

* * *

Dina was finding Detective Coleman about as easy to discourage as lint. He sent flowers. Called every other night, sent engraved invitations to Broadway shows to the apartment. When that didn't bring any response, he sent them to the office.

The joy in Ben's voice when at last she agreed to have dinner with him gave her a tiny bubble of guilt. The bubble wasn't easy to dismiss, considering her motive. She was going to make it a night neither of them would want repeated.

When he came to call for her, his foot never got past the threshold. She rushed him out of the building and followed him to his car, got in before he had a chance to hold the door for her and didn't throw out one lifeline to the conversation during the ride to the restaurant.

Jimmy's was one of Ben's favorite restaurants. The food was excellent, all the waiters and bartenders knew him, and he had gone to school with the owner.

Inwardly he could feel his blood pressure overheating, which only made him put out extra effort to appear as nonchalant as he knew how. Miss Dmitri shot down every one of his suggestions, forcing him to relinquish his role as king of his turf.

He didn't mind when she passed on the Caesar salad he suggested and ordered tossed. He did mind when he suggested the house special, prime rib, and she ordered New York strip. He smiled pleasantly when he suggested Burgundy and she nixed that for a Chablis. He assumed it wasn't ignorance, it was some deep character flaw in her nature. By the time they ordered dessert, he understood she was not only being intentionally insulting, she was practically drawing diagrams to let him know it. He ignored her efforts to irritate him, and turned up the charm.

Max was right, she didn't like playing games. He liked that. She was no phony. She didn't pull out a mirror to check whatever it was that women supposedly checked for. He suspected that was a ploy to get noticed. And she didn't do that whip your head thing to draw attention to her hair, or do the finger comb. She didn't have to do anything to get noticed, except exist.

He liked that she didn't attach much importance to being on the receiving end of all the admiring stares she was getting from men and women. She had to know she was the most attractive woman in the place. Not that he was a slouch, some of the those admiring looks were directed at him, from the women.

The first time he saw her walking into the apartment building, it was her legs he noticed first. They were nice, long and well-propor-

145

tioned. His educated guess was five-eight, one twenty-five. Her driver's license proved him wrong by two pounds, she was one twenty-seven.

Her voice was soft and low. Not timid, just soft, one of those pleasant voices you don't mind hearing early in the morning or late at night.

Having a good time was never hard for him, but he was hard-pressed to think of anyone he enjoyed being with as much as he did her. Having her sit across the table from him or walking beside him made him feel good. Content.

What he wanted was to have her like him. He wanted to make her laugh, hear her laugh. He wanted to get down on his knees right now and ask her to—Jesus! Marry him? The words made him so nervous he spilled his wine.

She laughed. Her laugh was one of those infectious ones that got everyone going. And it did. It seemed like the entire restaurant was with her. He did his best to soak up the wine while smiling at the crowd to let them know he thought it was funny too.

"Glad I wore a dark blue suit."

Mid-way through her dinner, Dina changed her mind, she didn't want to make Ben's evening miserable. True, he had enough pride to give him a hernia, but there was *something* about him that sort of appealed to her. She liked the fact that he didn't take himself too seriously. He could laugh at himself. She was half certain the self-deprecating humor wasn't strictly for her benefit, that the glimpses she was getting were genuine, not part of some game plan to make a good impression. In some ways he reminded her of Jake. Only Jake was…it was getting harder to remember *what* Jake was like.

"Why did you become a policeman?"

"Simple, my mother wanted me to become cultured, my dad wanted me to be a lawyer. I compromised. For my mother, I took up stickball, hockey, bought stacks of Spike Jones records and spent Saturday afternoons at the movies watching the Three Stooges. For my dad, I graduated from high school, hung out at college for two years, and took some courses in law to help me understand the system so I could, hopefully, make lieutenant some day." For a second his smile flickered and he became very sober. "And I will."

"I believe you will. With all your charm, how could you not?"

"Charm has nothing to do with it, Miss Dmitri. Charm is a lawyer's stock in trade. Sorry. Let's forget serious. There's a little club not far from here called Harry's where there's a guy, Ray Miller, plays the piano better than Eddy Duchin and he lets me sing. We can have our after-dinner drinks there and dance to Berlin, Porter and Kern. Any music you want."

He didn't bother mentioning that the dance floor was the size of a beach blanket and was usually crowded, when he was lucky.

There were only four couples on the dance floor, but once he and Dina started dancing, the other couples moved off to the side to watch.

His instincts about her had been right, she was a feather on her feet. She anticipated all his fancy maneuvers as if they had been dancing partners for years.

They breezed through a foxtrot, the lindy, a tango and two rumbas. He wanted to dance the night away, holding her so close he could feel her heartbeat. Never in his life had he been so attracted to a woman, been so reluctant to end an evening.

During the drive back to her apartment, she seemed to be as comfortable as he with the empty spaces in their conversation. He liked not having to suffer through the effort of trying to fill the spaces with small talk.

Outside her apartment door, Ben kissed her cheek, as softly as possible, keeping a non-threatening distance.

"Thanks, Ben. I had a lovely time."

"So did I, Miss Dmitri. I'd like one cup of coffee and a little conversation, after which, I promise to go on my unmerry way. Scout's honor."

"It's late…"

"Dina, the name's Ben, not Lenny the Lecher. I'm not going to force myself on you."

"That doesn't change the time."

He held up his index finger. "One small cup."

By the time she brought a tray with a coffee pot and two cups into the living room, he was sitting on the far end of the sofa. His jacket was off and his tie was loosened. He had Sinatra singing "I've Got You Under My Skin" on the hi-fi.

"I've spent most of the evening talking about me, now I'd like to hear about you. I'm sure you had a life too."

"Not much to talk about really. My mother died of a brain tumor, my father a coronary. My brother Paul, his wife Karen, and their daughter Leslie live in the house we grew up in."

"What does your brother do?"

"Has a wood shop, makes furniture."

"How long has it been since you've been back there?"

"Quite a while."

"You sound…wistful. You miss it a lot?"

"I do, but not as much as I used to. It's a wonderful place to live, grow up. It has everything. Nice people, most of them. Spring-fed lake, skiing, winter and summer. Golf courses within twenty miles. It's a nice place to be."

As he listened to her, he tried to overlook the pluses to find the minuses. He was glad there wasn't a mirror in the room, thinking if there were and he looked into it, he'd see a dopey, love-struck kid smiling back at him. The crazy thing was, he didn't care. He'd bedded his share of women, none of whom made him think seriously of marriage. Guys in the squad dubbed him the Home Run King. A rep he didn't deserve nor deny. Who wanted to admit they had more slumps than home runs?

Making love to her was something he wanted to do very much. But he wanted more. He wanted to know her, get inside her head.

"Did you always call your father 'Mike'?"

"Habit. My brother Paul and I spent so much time around the yard, before either of us worked there, we didn't want to go around saying 'daddy' all the time. After a while it just came natural."

"I've always called my dad Pop, up until I was eighteen or twenty, then it was Sam. Before leaving for Korea, I was back to calling him Pop. He was a cop too. I hope to be half as good a man—and cop—as he was. My mother's folks had a farm in the Catskills and turned it into a boardinghouse, like many did, to make a go of it."

When he talked about his parents there was a touching softness in his eyes, which she found very appealing.

He looked at his watch. "It's late. I'd better be going. I asked for one cup of coffee and conversation…thank you. How about tomorrow? You doing anything?

"Can't. I have a wedding to go to. Amanda's getting married."

"So Bobby-boy really thinks he can make a housewife out of her. Happy for her, good news for me. One less hooker in circulation." The minute it was out, he knew it was a bad mistake.

"Your enthusiasm warms my heart. This *hooker* happens to be a friend, my best friend."

"Bad choice, shows a lack of discrimination."

"Thanks for dinner. It was a nice evening." She was heading straight for the door.

"Hold on a minute. Don't get your nose out of joint. Look, Dina, this is my city. I'm a realistic optimist, okay? Experience has given me a good dose of cynicism. You're from some isolated small town in the Midwest where a horse is a beautiful four-legged animal, a joint is a juncture, and where bones in the body can bend. Where VD is whispered about after the kids are out of earshot. And coke is—"

"I know what horse is, and I know that coke is more than a soft drink."

"Let's get this settled, here and now. I'm a cop. A *good* cop. An honest cop. Pimps, pushers, prostitutes, the mob and sleaze-ball politicians are personal affronts to me." He took a deep breath. He knew he was risking his chances but this had to be said. He had to know if she understood his perspective. "Prostitutes and addicts keep the scums in business by allowing themselves to be used and abused. Hookers refuse to file charges, like wives with husbands who smack them around. They convince themselves over and over that it'll get better. It'll stop. Who knows what goes on in their heads? I've seen too many sweet, bright, fresh-faced kids turn into drooly-mouthed, runny-nosed, vacant-eyed blobs with all the coordination of dry, rotted string."

"Amanda doesn't have anything to do with any of that."

"No? She's an innocent bystander? What? Would you have preferred me to call her a party girl? Hostess? Or maybe courtesan sounds better? Wise up, she knows people you wouldn't want to meet, much less talk to. Knows them well, if you know what I mean. Vicious people. These guys aren't amusing, tough but dumb mischief-makers out of some Damon Runyon story. I'm talking about buckets of slime who latch onto young girls. Sweet Sallys and Sues who should be going to high school dances with Joe College or Stan Schmuck, not hustling for some bastard. Maybe I can't clean it all up, but I intend doing what I can. I care, about them and my city."

"I know you do. It's just that, at times, you come across so judgmental. Amanda is my friend."

"Judgmental? Wise up, baby. You and Max deal with a different class of people than I do. I see the seamier side of the world. A world you don't know or understand. You and Max deal with ladies and gentlemen, some of whom cheat, lie and steal, but rarely kill for what they want. They play a different game. Your best friend's husband-to-be has had people killed, did you know that? If you're hot under the collar because of the way I feel, tough." Before she had a chance to utter a word, he held up his hand.

"You ever stood beside a mother, holding her hand when she identified her baby in the city morgue? By baby, I mean any kid from one to fifty. They're still their momma's babies. Maybe you'd be judgmental too if you stood beside a cop's widow and his kids, at his funeral, trying to give them strength to get through *Amazing Grace*. You know, there are a lot of people who don't like cops. I guess I can add you to the list. Thanks for the lovely evening, the coffee, and the somewhat limited conversation. Good night."

Sleep refused all invitations and pleas, making the night endless. When the alarm finally did go off, she was tempted to try for half an hour of real sleep, but was afraid she'd fall into a deep sleep and be late for the wedding. She tossed the covers back and pushed herself out of bed.

The cold shower helped wash away the grogginess but left annoying images of Ben Coleman. Intuition told her he was not going away easily.

Amanda's civil ceremony was small, simple and brief. The bride wore a simple, short-sleeved turquoise dress, the groom wore gray. Dina had on a tailored pale green dress. The other witness, introduced as Bob's brother Al, wore a midnight blue suit that was borrowed, outgrown, or some cleaner had simply shrunk it. Amanda called him King Kong in a tutu, which he didn't seem to mind. He was not a smiley-face person, but pleasant enough. Dina thought he seemed almost shy, despite his size.

Talent for Deception

After the ceremony, everyone kissed everyone, except Al. He stood back and offered a handshake, then vanished. Then the bride and groom's car vanished and she found herself standing alone on the steps of the courthouse waving at the back of a car she could barely see. When she turned, Ben was inches away.

"Hi. Green is definitely your color."

"I traded in all my small town calico for it."

"What do you say we call a truce? I'm here to give you a second chance, see?" He did a slow spin. "Got dressed in my Saturday best: cocoa brown suit and brown shoes, polished, I might add. Note the sparkly white shirt and the dark brown silk tie. Can't afford to spill anything today."

"How nice. Color coordinated."

"I thought I'd take you to dinner and if you play your cards right, I'll let you order. I know how much you like to order."

"I don't think so."

"C'mon, don't you feel just a little let down, all dressed up and no place to go? Way it goes with these civil ceremonies. Leaves you with the feeling that the party is being held in some secret place and no one told you where."

She smiled, yet at the same time resented his ability to see through her. She did feel let down for some stupid reason. And she was hungry.

He could see she was wavering. "How about it? Dinner, a few dances at a nice, quiet place. We get tired of dancing, we can talk."

"Okay, but let's go Dutch."

"Uh-uh. I ask a lady out, she compliments me by dining with me, I reciprocate by picking up the tab. No one owes anything, okay?"

"Okay."

"Best of all, I won't try to order for you."

"I have to apologize. I was being miserably obnoxious. You order, if it isn't what I like, you can eat it."

152

"Deal. My car's around the corner." They started walking and he suddenly stopped. He turned her around to face him. "Look, Dina, I'm sorry for hurting your feelings. A long time ago, Pop told me not to leave unsaid what I'll wind up wishing I'd said a thousand times. He also told me not to say or do anything I'd regret by midnight, because regrets are hard to sleep with, and it's worse having to eat crow the next morning. Bad for the digestion."

"I know."

He smiled. "Let's get something to wash down the taste of crow."

Halfway through their Chateaubriand, Dina began to see how much of Ben's tough-guy abrasiveness was a façade, that he was more sensitive and caring than he allowed people to see until he trusted them. The more convinced she became, the less she wanted the evening to end. His cynicism was practically endearing, once she understood it stemmed more from his disappointment than anger or apathy. He poured out another glass of wine for each of them.

"When I was growing up, it's all I wanted to be was a cop. I love catching the bad guys, getting them off the streets."

"You ever catch someone who turned out to be a good guy?"

"Yes, Miss Dmitri, I have. Hey, I'm not a vigilante. I've given people breaks. The ones who made minor mistakes. Kids mostly. They deserve a second chance, maybe a third, to live up to their potential." He shook his head. "I can't deny that I've made some errors in judgment. Not many, but one or two. Makes me very unhappy when the ones I do give a break don't follow through, keep their word."

"This 'potential,' is that their potential, or your view of what their potential should be?"

He shrugged his shoulders. "All I want is for everybody to be the best they can be. Behave, you know? Follow the rules. You think that's wrong?"

"No. We have to have rules. Sometimes some of us find them hard to follow."

"Oh? And what rules have you broken?"

"I'm a lawyer, I know better than to incriminate myself."

His smiled, ignoring the small shadow of suspicion that was squatting in the corner of his mind. He picked up the tab. On the way out of the restaurant he asked if she'd like to stop and have a drink and a dance at Harry's.

This time, neither one of them seemed to be willing to end the evening. Ben's friend Ray played all their requests from Rodgers and Hart, Gershwin, and Berlin. They danced to almost every song. They didn't notice the time until Ray played what Ben and other regulars recognized as his personal favorite and his last tune for the evening, Hoagy Carmichael's "Stardust." While they were leaving, Ray played a few bars of "What'll I Do?"

During the drive back to her apartment, Ben mentioned an older brother who didn't come back from Korea, then quickly changed the subject and talked about his rookie years on the force.

"Before I joined the force, I was pretty good at sizing people up. Things like whether someone looked directly at you, or if they had shifty eyes, like they felt guilty or were nervous about something. Once I got on the job I learned to pay more attention to the way people dressed. Did they wear expensive clothes? Was it to impress someone in particular, or everyone? Did they wear a cross or a crucifix? Or a star of David? Did they wear clothes that clashed because they were color blind, or did they think they looked chic? You learn to look at the total person, fingers for wedding or engagement rings, or high school and college rings. Frat pins, watches. Your eyes have to take everything in. Everything means something. And sometimes it's nothing more than to intentionally throw cops off."

He was getting the feeling that at the rate things were going he was going to be an old man before he found out if he and Dina were at all compatible. He had tossed the ball at her fifty times or more, asking her about her own background, about her goals. A few of the questions she let fly by like a batter who chooses not to swing, the others she answered with a brevity he didn't think any lawyer was capable of.

He was almost glad when he pulled over to the curb, in front of her apartment building. He decided to take a chance on a way to speed things up. He turned off the engine, and made no move to let her out.

"Dina, I have a few days off coming up. How about the two of us get away from the city? My folks still have a place in the Catskills. We used to go there every summer, my brother, me, and my mom and dad. We loved it. I know I did. Fresh, clean air. Fresh fruit and vegetables. Probably the same kind of environment you had while you were growing up. Lakes, boats, swimming. These days, Mom and Dad don't like to drive anywhere, if they can't get there on foot, it's out. I go there a couple of times a year to check things out, make sure the place is still standing. It's beautiful up there. They have great food, and the entertainment is tops. What do you think?"

"You don't want to know what I think."

"Don't jump to conclusions. I warn you, I'll resist to the death even the subtlest of advances."

"Thanks, but no thanks. I don't have the time or the inclination."

"Dina, I'm not Jack the Ripper. You think I'd try to seduce you? Honey, it wasn't my brain that was circumcised. I don't want to make you…well, that's not true. I did and I do, but I won't. I want more than that. I want to get to know you. I know you make a fair pot of coffee, although it's a little weak for my taste and you don't give out second cups, not to me anyway."

"You want a cup of coffee? I'll make some. And it'll be strong.

The last time, you didn't deserve a cup, weak or strong." She opened her car door and got out. He slid out after her and they walked into the building.

As soon as they walked in to the apartment, Dina hung up her coat. She laid Ben's on the arm of the chair nearest the door.

"Dina, I'm serious about the Catskills. I want us to get to know each other. I'd really like to know if you're grumpy in the morning. Do you jabber away, or are you mildly cheerful, like me? Can you cook? Bake? Can you get to the point where you feel comfortable with me? Trust me with who you are inside. Other than me, what are your pet peeves? I want to know what you like and don't like. If you're a good sport."

"Not that good."

"I don't mean that kind of sport and you know it. You seem pretty well balanced. That's good. I need balance in my life, I get kind of moody sometimes. I'm impulsive and I know I can be brash at times. You're self-assured like I am. That's good, I like that. I'm not asking you to bare your soul, or anything else you're not comfortable with." He started to walk in circles.

"Damn it!" he said suddenly. "I'm losing control here. Everything is moving too slow or too fast, I don't know any more. What I do know is that I have this feeling that it's imperative for us to get to know one another—fast. Because if we don't, I'm afraid some hotshot attorney is going to beat me to it and sweep you off your feet and I'll be left humming "I'm Walking Behind You" at your wedding. He stopped pacing to take a long look at her. "No, I take that back, I don't think anyone can sweep you off your feet. Dina Dmitri, I think I'm in love with you. I feel like my life, my happiness depends on you."

"Ben, be serious. You don't know me."

"Be *serious*? You think this isn't serious? I have never been more serious in my life. I'm so damn serious, it scares the hell out of me.

Saying I thought I was in love with you was an understatement, I know I'm in love with you. And I want to marry you. But hey, don't let me put any pressure on you. It's not my style. I'll give you a month. Under this cocky exterior lies a tender, romantic, irresistible heart. I love kids, I'm kind to animals, and as you can see, I'm very patient and reserved."

"Ben, this *is* going too fast. I am attracted to you. I like you more than I thought possible, believe me..."

"Dina, I'll bet you never did anything on impulse in your life. Be impulsive for once in your life. I promise you, you won't regret it. Give me the chance to show you another side of me. I promise I'll be a gentleman, for as long as you want me to be. I'm thirty years old, kiddo, and I'm aging mighty damn fast."

"I have to say no for now. I'm just not comfortable with the idea."

He looked into her eyes for a long time, trying to think of a way, short of coercion, to get her to agree. Slowly he leaned forward to kiss her cheek, then brushed her lips with a soft kiss.

"I understand. Good night. I had a wonderful time tonight. I'll call you tomorrow. And tomorrow, and tomorrow, until you say yes."

Without planning it, Ben chose the same cocoa brown suit, same brown tie and shoes, even the same shirt and socks that he had on the day of Amanda's wedding. Once he realized they were the clothes he wore that day, he took it as a good omen. He needed all the help he could get, and number seven was his lucky number. Dina had turned him down six times in six months. This was his last proposal.

When he went to pick her up at her office, his spirits climbed higher. She was wearing the same green dress she wore for Amanda's wedding.

At Harry's, Dina stopped in the ladies room and Ben went over to the piano and arranged to have Ray play "All of Me" six times consecutively, then if and when he gave him a nod, to play it once more.

TALENT FOR DECEPTION

Then he walked over to the ladies room and waited for Dina to come out. When she did, he signaled Ray and led Dina to the dance floor.

Dina lost track of how many times Ray had played "All of Me" but knew it was more than three. Concerned, she turned and whispered in Ben's ear. "How many refreshment breaks has Ray had?"

Ben angled his head so his lips were touching her ear. "He's fine. I asked him to play it six times in a row, one for every time you've turned me down. I'm asking once more: Dina, will you take all of me? I love you more than the Three Stooges and Spike Jones. Will you marry me?"

She laughed. "How can I refuse a proposal like that?"

"What?"

"Yes, I will marry you."

"You're serious, you're not kidding?"

"Serious, but probably not sane."

"Okay with me. Serious is good enough."

CHAPTER TWENTY-TWO

Jake's Folly was built into a foundation of brick and stucco, and jutted out over the embankment of the bay's entrance. He had accomplished what he intended, it did resemble the aft of an old frigate and did appear to be moored, like some pirate ship waiting for the crew to come aboard and set sail.

The bumped-out quarter gallery and after decks served as the master bedroom and shower; below was the galley and under that, the below decks was the boathouse. Midships consisted of a narrow mountain of Montana stone with a fireplace in its center, dividing the living room from the dining room. Phil's bedroom and a guest room were in the stern. The foyer was the landing, complete with planked floors and pilings in four separate groupings along the walls. Barrels and kegs served as chairs and tables. The ground floor of the attached lighthouse was Phil's putter shop, the tower, Jake's studio.

Gus and Gertie were so impressed with Jake's Folly that they begged Jake to give the Norseman a facelift. They knew he wasn't keen to do it, but they were fairly confident he wouldn't trust any one else to do it.

Three, four times a week he drove into the Twin Cities, visiting restaurants and bars. He interviewed decorators until he found the one he was looking for, someone who knew more about Vikings than he or all the others he interviewed. Someone who understood that the Norseman was synonymous with Hid'n Oaks and wanted to retain that. Jake was determined not to turn it into one of the pretentious, ritzy city places he'd seen too often.

Ann Taylor understood exactly what Jake wanted, that the Norseman keep its small town ambiance, a place where tourists and vacationers fit in with the natives, not the other way around. In her opinion, Jake wanted the place slightly sandpapered, not too polished.

Ann was an attractive brunette, tall, with an athlete's body, brown tiger eyes and a hearty laugh that wasn't forced. She was also, Jake thought, fond of small towns and shared his love of the outdoors.

The first two weeks were spent planning on how to mesh Ann's suggestions and ideas with Jake's determination to keep everything the same, only slightly different. Halfway into their second week of working together, things became more social than professional. It took Jake a month to realize that Ann was strictly a big city girl, one who didn't mind spending a weekend or so in the sticks, but she didn't want to live in Hid'n Oaks, and once she realized Jake was as good as buried in his hometown, she began finding other things to do with her evenings, became unavailable.

After the Norseman had its facelift, they drifted apart, agreeing that it was better to be friends, knowing that if they saw each other again, it would be more by chance than design.

Jake began to give some thought to taking some time off to sail around the world, visit islands, do some fishing, play golf in exotic places. But Phil was adamant, he had been to more places than he wanted to see during the war, and he was content to stay right where he was, planted on earth, not going on some ocean voyage and getting tossed around like three men in a tub. Jake didn't bring the subject up again, telling himself he didn't want to be an ocean away if something happened to Phil. But he knew that was only part of it; he didn't want to be an ocean away when and if Dina came back.

Winter had never been Paul's favorite season. Morning came too late, evening too early and stayed on too long. It was still dark at 7:00 a.m., then dark again before 5:00 p.m. Yet here he was sitting in a six-by-eight-foot ice shack in ten below weather with fingers as supple as Popsicle sticks, trying to put a damn minnow on a hook. Why? Because Jake wanted to go ice fishing.

If they'd waited a few months to do something together, they could go golfing.

Every time he looked over at Jake, saw him contentedly puffing away on his pipe, checking his bobber, sipping his brandy, he had an urge to cram him down the ice hole.

Feeling Paul's lack of enthusiasm, Jake cocked his head, smiled and held out the bottle of brandy. "You look a mite chilled. Here, have a brandy."

Paul took the bottle and poured out a double. "Chilled? I think I turned to marble. You love this, don't you? Ice cracking under your frozen toes, smoking your pipe, waiting for some dumb fish to unlock its frozen mouth wide enough to take the bait."

"Fresh air's good for you. I love being out in it, lets me unwind a little. Something you can use."

"Why can't we unwind in the Fisherman's over a couple games of pool? Where we wouldn't have to see our breath, or hear this damn wind howling."

"Winter weather is part of winter, goes with the territory."

Paul handed the brandy bottle back and sighed.

"Dina called Karen the other day; she's getting married. Asked Karen to be a bridesmaid and Leslie to be flower girl. Wanted me to give her away. Can you imagine that?"

Jake gulped the rest of the brandy he had been nursing for half an hour. There was a constriction in his chest and for a few moments he found it hard to breathe. "When's she getting married?"

"Couple months."

"Who is he?"

"A cop. Detective Ben Coleman. Karen insists on going, and of course, Leslie's all excited about getting a fancy dress, being part of the wedding."

"How about you?"

"What? Going, you mean? Not on your life."

"Why not? Don't you think it's time to stop treating Dina as if she were some sort of outcast? You keep building that wall, and it's going to be harder and harder to get over it. Dina's the only sister you have, buddy. Time you got beyond the bullshit."

"Bullshit? It's not bullshit to me. And it shouldn't be to Dina. She grew up with the same principles and should have shown more respect for who she was and how she was raised."

Jake stood up. "Spare me the sanctimonious crap. I'll give you a tip, Paul. Stop trying to be like Mike. Be your own man, and you will be like Mike."

Paul stood up too, and when he did his pole slid down into the hole in the ice. He made no attempt to catch it before it disappeared. "Drop it, Jake. Get off my back."

"How about you?" he continued, defensively. "Isn't it time you move on with your life, get married and have kids of your own?"

"What am I, on some kind of time schedule?"

For a few minutes Paul stared at the hole that swallowed his fishing pole. "Jake? Do you think the Anderson kid looks like her, like Dina?"

"No, I don't. My guess would be he looks like the father."

"You think so? So help me, if he lives around here, if I find him I'll make him wish he never touched her."

"Why? What's it going to accomplish? Let it go, Paul."

162

"I can't. I honestly wish I could, but I can't." He couldn't explain it if Jake didn't understand him by now. And he wasn't able to tell Jake he was right about the walls. He'd already waited too long.

"Paul, do you remember when we were fourteen, and you said that when you're an old man you want memories that will put a smile on your face and rainbows in your heart? Do you remember telling me that?"

"Vaguely."

"Vaguely, huh? Well, buddy, miserable memories don't put rainbows in your heart."

"It wasn't me that created the misery. And who are you to talk? Have you ever called Dina?" They stared at one another for a few seconds. "Are *you* going to the wedding?"

"Haven't been asked. If I am, I'll probably pass."

"Then mind your own goddamn business." He grabbed his tackle box. "I'm freezing. I don't know about you, but I want to go where I can get feeling back in the lower part of my body. Want to shoot some pool or keep sitting here, become part of the ice and have to wait till spring to get to shore?"

"Ten bucks a game?"

"You're on, I can use a new fishing pole."

Jake looked down at the hole. "What's wrong with the old one? Hole's big enough, little dip might improve your disposition."

"It'll improve when I get out of this ice cave and get someplace where I can thaw out. Winning a new pole will make me ecstatic."

"I got a better idea. How about if you win, I buy you a new pole, if I win, you go to Dina's wedding?"

"Go to hell."

* * *

Up until they boarded the plane and taxied down the runway, Karen held on to the hope Paul would change his mind and come along.

For most of the flight, Leslie kept her mother's mind off her disappointment with a barrage of questions: Why didn't Aunt Dina ever come to visit? What did flower girls have to do? How did the plane stay up in the air? How high were they? How soon would they get there?

Karen was exhausted when Leslie finally fell asleep and soon dozed off herself.

It seemed like only minutes later when the pilot's voice called them both back from their naps by announcing they would be landing at La Guardia in fifteen minutes.

Leslie sensed a holiday spirit was swirling all around them and decided it was very nice having an aunt and uncle. They were something new and different and they were crazy about her, thought she was adorable and so preciously precocious. Leslie reveled in the compliments Aunt Dina and Uncle Ben showered on her.

Karen caught Dina looking back toward the gate and when they returned to her, she slowly moved her head from side to side.

Ben saw the exchange, and the shadow that passed over Dina's face. He put his arm around her and gave her a squeeze, then picked Leslie up.

"How about you and me go to Central Park, let your mom and Aunt Dina do their shopping? We'll give the ladies a chance to get reacquainted and we'll meet someplace for dinner. What do you say, Mom?"

Dina thought she saw a tinge of apprehension on Karen's face while she was bending down to consult with her daughter but it seemed only natural for a mother to be somewhat apprehensive about leaving her child alone with a stranger.

Karen accepted instantly after seeing the "Don't you spoil my fun" look on Leslie's face. She wasn't up to having to deal with one of Leslie's week-long sulks and she did want to have some time with Dina alone. Maybe they could have lunch at one of the places she'd read so much about in the St. Paul papers—the Russian Tea Room, or Sardi's, or the Stork Club. Or Luchow's. Maybe they'd shop at Macy's or Tiffany's.

They did shop at Macy's and Tiffany's, and decided to have lunch in the Russian Tea Room. Karen spent the first five minutes searching for a familiar famous face. If there were any stars there having lunch, she didn't recognize them. No Greta Garbo, Marlon or Audrey today.

After they finished their salads, tired from the strain of rubbernecking, Karen gave up trying to spot famous faces, and concentrated on answering Dina questions about home.

"How are the Tanners doing?"

"Oh, you know Phil. He's the same leprechaun, sweet and adorable. I wrote and told you about what a tremendous success Paul's furniture shop has been. And construction is booming. Jake's been designing some beautiful spec homes. And of course, they're all being furnished with the furniture Paul makes. And I, my dear sister-in-law, have a degree in Interior Decorating."

"Karen, that's wonderful!"

"Yes, it is, thank you very much. I don't know if I'll ever use it, but I have it. Something to show that I can accomplish something on my own."

"Good for you. How's Jake Tanner doing?"

"Oh, he's so unbelievably busy, we hardly get to see him these days. I don't think he has time for himself. Hard to say if he's more in demand professionally or socially. He designed four very expensive homes, mansions I'd say, in the Cities. He spends a lot time there since he started dating Ann Taylor. She's an interior decorator, a really nice gal. They worked together on the Norseman; Gus and Gert wanted to give it a facelift. They started seeing each other on a regular basis after working hours."

"I'm happy for him. Jake's a very special man. Can't think of anyone who deserves success and happiness more."

"Paul and I said the same thing. Oh, Dina! There's something I have to tell you that's better than the degree in decorating. Now, don't be hurt that I didn't tell you before, we've been sort of nervous, superstitious I guess, after losing the last one. I'm six months pregnant." She patted her stomach. "Although it won't be a secret much longer."

"Karen, how wonderful! It'll be so nice for Leslie to have a sister or brother. She seems highly inquisitive and observant." It was just as hard to believe now as it was the first time Karen was pregnant.

"Yes, she is quite an exceptional child, very clever for her age."

Dina thought she detected something rather odd in the way Karen said the words, but dismissed it, thinking it had been a hectic day and her ears were as tired as the rest of her.

"Who's…giving you away?"

"Max Strauss."

"Oh, I'm glad it's someone you know."

"Yes, Max is about the best stand-in I could have. I'm sorry, that was nasty. Time for a change in subjects…Leslie has to be the apple of Paul's eye, she looks so much like you and, as I recall, Paul didn't let a day pass without saying how beautiful you were, inside and out." Dina expected a smile, instead, Karen looked more pensive than pleased.

"Yes, she does, doesn't she? But her temperament is very different. Oh, never mind. I'm so happy for you and Ben. Ben seems so nice. And so handsome."

"You think so? When I first met him, I didn't think he was either. But I've changed my mind. He is nice. And handsome."

"Dina, I've never seen you so glowing and happy. I can't tell you how glad I am that you found someone. You're going to make an absolutely beautiful bride. I just wish..."

Dina placed her hand over Karen's. "Don't. Someday, we'll all get together and remember all the good times. That's what I remember. What's important is we're all happy. Life does go on, Karen. It has for me. And look at you, you're going to have another Dmitri."

"I do hope it's a boy." Very different from Leslie, she almost said, but caught herself and pushed all unpleasant thoughts out of her mind. Today she wanted to think about only happy thoughts. Today she felt as though she'd been exonerated. Dina had someone to share her life with now, she wasn't alone. And Karen didn't have to feel guilty anymore.

Peter's name was never mentioned, although Karen knew Dina kept in touch with Martha to show she had some interest in how *her* son was doing.

Whenever possible, Leslie ignored her mother's silly movie star observations. She didn't care if Amanda was just like Eve Arden or Rosalind Russell or that Uncle Ben looked like John Garfield. Her mother was a silly person and she wished she would just go away. Far, far, away.

Karen tried to look as if she was interested and knowing about the various ongoing conversations and discussions Dina and Ben's friends were having about politics, jet airplanes, civil rights, Alaska becoming the forty-ninth state. They talked about some satellite going into orbit, about careers, Univac and IBM. She didn't like feeling out of her depth. She knew she wasn't particularly bright or talented and the only career she cared about was being Mrs. Paul Dmitri and Leslie's mother. And the mother of the baby she was carrying.

The best of Leslie's times came to an end the day of the wedding. The adventures she'd enjoyed, and all the attention, came to an abrupt halt. It made her angry that Dina was spoiling everything. When Leslie overheard some of Dina's friends talking about Madame Butterfly, she immediately thought that was who Aunt Dina was, Madame Zero.

Uncle Ben had paid attention to Leslie all week, but now he did not seem to know or care that she was there. He was so busy looking cow-eyed at Madame Zero and he hung onto her like she was going to run away. He danced almost every dance with her. Everyone wanted to dance with *her*. Kiss her. Her lips were going to wear out. Weddings stank. Aunt Dina stank. She was nothing. Zero. A big fat zero. Uncle Ben stank too. And so did Mommy.

She scouted around until she found the perfect spot, a corner where she was able to see everything that went on, *if* she felt like looking. Anyone who glanced in her direction got a scowl. But no one seemed to care that she wasn't having a good time.

The band started to play "I Only Have Eyes for You" and Ben took Dina's arm and led her onto the dance floor.

"Have to dance to this one, my song, you know."

"What about 'All of Me.'"

"Uh-huh. I knew you'd come around. Now you have to wait. Later, my dear."

Karen motioned for Leslie to come over to her. Leslie stubbornly held her ground, she wasn't giving up her corner. Karen had to walk over to her and take her by the hand.

"Come on and say goodbye to Auntie Dina and Uncle Ben, they're going to be leaving after this dance."

She planted a bright smile across her face, skipped over to them and allowed them to kiss her. With a wide, innocent smile still in place she looked up at her aunt. "Bye, Auntie Dina. I'm so happy to have met you. Thank you for inviting me. You're very pretty...I don't know why my daddy hates you so much."

Too mortified to speak, too embarrassed to look at Dina, Karen's initial thought was to escape to the ladies room. Instead, she turned to Amanda with a pleading expression on her face. What she saw in Amanda's knowing eyes distressed her more. Out of the corner of her eye, she saw Dina kneeling and holding Leslie's face in her hands.

"Sweetie, your daddy doesn't hate me. Sometimes, when people are angry or upset they say things they don't really mean."

Amanda took Ben's arm and steered him out of earshot.

"What a little charmer. The sweet little girl next door, if you're a Borgia."

"She's a kid. They say anything that pops into their heads."

"Even as a kid, I knew you can't say *everything* that pops into your head."

"You were older and wiser than most."

"Mmmm. Times don't change much. Innocent, harmless kids still get away with saying the darndest little things. All I have to say is, if the big bad wolf plans on eating her, he'd better make sure he has all his shots."

"Some grandma you're going to make."

"Relax. Motherhood's not in the cards for me."

"Oops. Sorry. And I mean it."

Amanda lifted her shoulders. "Don't be. It's probably just as well. I think I'd be like Karen is today, as tense as an overwound guitar string. Only she has patience."

"Kids are kids."

"Uh-huh. Sure. By the way, Bob and I both want to congratulate you, *Lieutenant* Coleman."

"Thanks." He leaned closer. "You can fess up to me, did Bob really have an important previous commitment or has matrimony made him shy?"

"He didn't want to embarrass you or Dina. Looks to me like it

169

was a sensible decision. There are enough cops here to have the Policeman's Ball."

"There are, at that. Tell Bob I'm touched by his consideration."

"Don't be such a smartass. It is your wedding day, and pretty difficult to have sex when you're all asshole. As it is, I hope you can do better than give Dina the best two seconds of her life."

"Ouch. I think I'll prove I'm a little better than that."

"I'm sure you'll have fun trying." Frown lines formed across her forehead. "Ben, you and me are veterans of the streets, too well acquainted with the darker side of human nature. And it tends to make us less extravagant with our trust and feelings. Dina has chutzpah, but she's not like us. I'd trust Dina with my life. She's the best friend I have and her friendship means a lot to me, so you don't have to worry about my coming around much, putting her in any more awkward situations."

"Your friendship means a lot to her too. Don't be a stranger on my account. And whether you believe this or not, I sincerely hope Bob's successful with his insurance business—isn't that what you said it was?"

She ignored the insinuating smile on his face and before he had a chance to add the words to go along with the smile, she cut him off. "Thanks. It's a stepping stone. Eventually, he wants to go into real estate and I'm going to be the broker's little helper. You know going the straight and narrow route isn't easy. Narrow's too narrow, straight's too straight."

"Works out okay for most people. What the hell, late is better than never."

"It's harder for late starters." She rested her hand on his arm. "Take care of her, Ben. Since you came into her life, she smiles and laughs a lot more. And you know what they say about life without humor? It's like sex without a climax."

"You would make that comparison."

"One tends to think in terms one understands." They watched Karen walk Leslie to the ladies' room. "Looks like Mrs. Coleman is free now; you'd best get back to her before she suspects something is going on between the two of us."

"Ha ha." The hug and kiss were as much of a surprise to him as they were to Amanda. Without thinking, she returned the kiss, and when she wiped the lipstick from his cheek, she saw he was blushing.

"What a tough guy. Take care, Lieutenant. Of yourself and the missus."

"Will do. You, too."

He turned and walked over to his wife's side, slipped his arms around her and whispered into her ear. "I love ya more den bagels. What say we blow dis joint, hit da road to da cabin in da Catskills?"

"That's the worst Bogart I ever heard."

"Bogart! You kiddin' me? My dear Mrs. Coleman, that was Cagney."

"Cagney who?"

"Time to go now. Smile nice and wave to the people."

* * *

The place Ben kept referring to as a farmhouse was actually a two-and-a-half-story Victorian: half timbers, bay windows, turret, huge chimney, with open upper and lower porches. Inside, the floors and trim were stained a medium oak. There were four bedrooms and a bath upstairs, and the master bedroom with its own bathroom was downstairs and shared a fireplace with the living room. The living room and dining room were divided by pocket doors; the ceilings in these two rooms were coved.

Ben piled a few logs into the fireplace while Dina walked around inspecting and asking questions, making suggestions on what to do about the squeaks in the floor, saying it was the carpenter's fault for not crowning the natural humps in the wood.

"How do you know so much about construction? Tensile…compression…crowning humps?"

"My father owned a lumber and construction business. I spent a lot of time at the yard. Worked there for a while. My brother runs it now."

"I thought you said your brother had a furniture shop."

"He does. Construction is a…sideline."

"Sideline? He has a construction company as a sideline? Why is it you didn't mention this before?"

"What for? I'm an attorney. I'm no longer a part of the business."

"Exactly what are we talking about here? I mean what did you come from? Financially, I mean."

"Dmitri Enterprises is probably worth about five, maybe six million dollars. I'm not sure anymore. I'm no longer minding the store so to speak."

"*What?* Let me get this straight. Are you telling me I married an heiress?"

"No. I'm telling you I'm out of it. It all belongs to my brother and his family now."

"That's not what I meant. What kind of lifestyle are you accustomed to?"

"My parents were not indulgent people. We, my brother and I, were not brought up with any exaggerated emphasis on what monetary advantages we had. We were aware of them, of course, but we were taught that our true value was who we were as individuals, not by how much money we had."

There was nothing in her voice or attitude to indicate she was trying to impress him or making excuses. From the tone of her voice, she could have been telling him her date of birth or her social security number. Maybe that was why it didn't knock him off his feet, or make him feel she'd been less than up front with him from the start. But then, there were a few things he hadn't told her either. Like what his first impression of her had been. Someday he would, when he was sure she'd find it tearfully hilarious that he thought she was a hooker.

He took her in his arms. "Today, I became the richest man in the world, because I have you, Mrs. Coleman. And we don't need any more than us."

The chilled champagne was left unopened.

CHAPTER TWENTY-THREE

On July 4, 1960, Karen and Paul's many prayers were answered: Andrew Mikhail Dmitri arrived with all his fingers and toes in place.

Leslie's excitement over seeing the bulge in mommy's tummy ended when she found out Andy's visit was not on a trial basis. He was here to stay and that was that, whether she liked it or not.

They had tricked her into believing it was all going to be so wonderful to have a baby brother. Andy stank, was too noisy, was too much trouble, and he was far too visible. Everybody made such big fusses over him with all their oohing and aahing and going on and on about his black curly hair, Mommy mushing over his big milk chocolate eyes and forest of eyelashes that were just like Daddy's and Grandpa Mike's. Leslie demanded to know how Mike could be a grandpa when he was dead.

They promised things would get better but they didn't. They lied. It got worse when Andy started to walk. He was into everything, he slobbered all over his toys and her toys, and, worse than that, he broke some of her toys.

They didn't care that she was unhappy. And it didn't matter how long she pouted, stomped or cried. None of it did any good.

They had played one dirty rotten trick on her and they were going to *pay*. She sensed that the best way to deal with them was to go underground.

Outwardly, she was helpful and eager to please everyone. She controlled her temper. The rare times she complained, she did it with a sweet voice and a smile. She volunteered to be Mommy's little helper when it was Mommy's turn to have the girls over for bridge, and she was Daddy's helper when he had his cribbage tournaments. She passed out platters of little sandwiches and cheese and crackers. She placed bowls of pretzels and chips around the tables. While she did, she studied facial expressions, individual patterns of behavior, memorized conversations. She noticed the smirks, heard all the "between you and me" and the "don't breathe a word about what I told you" confidential conversations and put it all in her memory bank. People were puzzles to be solved. Some were more challenging than others, some were very simple. She was the little mouse that no one seemed to notice had the ears of an elephant and a brain as thirsty as a Turkish towel, and they were force-feeding her volumes of valuable, often secret information. Leslie forgot nothing.

Her bedroom became her private rehearsal hall, a place to sift through the gathered bits of information, practice mannerisms, expressions and voices of her teachers: Mommy and Daddy, Jake and Phil Tanner, neighbors, employees, and Andy.

When her mother got the call from Madame Zero to tell her that Leslie had a cousin, Benjamin Michael Coleman, her only comment was that she hoped they didn't plan on bringing him to her house, she had enough trouble with Andy, now that he was walking.

The value of friends was something she understood very well by the time she started second grade. Friends were not only physical proof of one's popularity, they were available to perform certain unpleasant tasks. They were most helpful to her as studies in the differences of personalities. It amused her that adults weren't all that different from kids. They were all full of false pride, hated to admit they were wrong, and found it humiliating to apologize. Which was not very smart. Apologies threw people off the track, made them think you were actually sorry, or a dumb good sport.

CHAPTER TWENTY-FOUR

THE WIDE BAND OF SKY HAD A GAUZY LOOK TO IT. THERE WERE A FEW clouds that reminded Peter of the pompadour hairdos women wore in the forties that he saw in some of Martha's old magazines. The breeze was too weak to offer any relief, the air so humid it felt like he had a soggy towel hanging over him. Had to be near a hundred.

He had intentionally anchored his boat two hundred feet off to the right of the Dmitri pier. Paul Dmitri didn't own the lake. It wasn't as deep as it was over at Tanners, but the bottom was rocky, a good place for walleyes. Martha loved walleyes. He had three of them and a largemouth bass hanging on a chain alongside the boat.

Peter leaned over, checking them to make sure they were still alive. While he did that, he casually glanced over at the Dmitri shoreline to see how much progress Jake and Paul Dmitri were making on the dance platform they were setting up. Wasn't a person in town who wasn't buzzing about the two parties the Dmitris were having. An afternoon deal for Queen Leslie and an evening one for adults.

Even if Peter had been invited to Leslie's afternoon party, he wouldn't go anyway. Not that they would've invited him, he wasn't a pedigree. He had a hunch it was more than that. Whatever bug he'd put up Mr. Dmitri's ass he had no idea, but he did know Mr. Dmitri had no use for him.

Maybe he was all wet, but it was more than a father afraid of having a mongrel coming too close to his precious daughter. He guessed Paul Dmitri didn't trust any teenaged boys around his spoiled brat.

Talent for Deception

Mr. Dmitri didn't have to worry about him, this mongrel didn't have the slightest interest in her. She wasn't his type.

All things considered, Peter respected Mr. Dmitri for being protective of his daughter. It made sense that Mr. Dmitri looked upon him and all sixteen-year-old boys as possible threats. Leslie was a beautiful thirteen-year-old girl who looked and acted as if she were eighteen. She was spooky.

Sometimes he wondered if his own mother had been fifteen or sixteen when she was pregnant with him and that was why she had to give him away. If that had been the case, his grandfather, whoever the hell he was, should have been more concerned, so his real mother wouldn't have ended up with a kid she didn't want. So what if that meant he wouldn't have been born? It was better than spending all those years being lonesome for people he didn't know.

It wasn't that he blamed Paul Dmitri for anything, he just wanted to know and understand what it was that Paul had against him. He had to admit, Paul was civil to him at least. Mrs. Dmitri was something else. She made it very clear she didn't like him, the night he bumped into her at the Grand Theater and almost knocked her off her feet. When he tried to apologize it all came out mumbled because of the way she reacted when she saw it was him. Her usual smile she had for everyone vanished and her eyes made a beeline for cover. She acted as if she saw something too ugly to look at. The look should have been enough to tell him to shut the hell up, but no, stupe that he was he had to go on about having a common interest, old movies. The look she gave him made him want to bite his tongue off.

Like him, she'd always come alone those Wednesday nights. Far as he knew, that was the last time she came. She never showed up the two times he went after that. He wondered if she'd be happy that he stopped going too, because he felt bad for taking away a special pleasure for her.

Laughter snared his attention and pulled it back to the shore.

178

Jake and Paul laughed a lot when they were together, it was easy to see they had a good time together. Like he imagined brothers would. People always laughed when they were around Jake. He was a pretty cool guy.

Peter was beginning to feel stupid, trying to act like he wasn't interested in what Paul and Jake were doing. What was Mr. Dmitri going to do if he caught him looking at his property—shoot him? It was a free country.

He threw a long, defiant cast toward the Dmitri shoreline and watched them openly. For two older guys, they weren't in bad shape. Jake was leaner, Mr. Dmitri had the start of a paunch. If he didn't do more than weekend swims, he was going to get flabby. If Paul Dmitri weren't such a pisshead, he'd ask him to run a few miles with him in the mornings.

Paul's back was covered with perspiration. Salty streams ran down his temples, stinging his eyes. In an attempt to divert the flow away from his eyes, he wiped a path down his jawline. It did no more than give him an opportunity to check on what the Anderson kid was doing. There still wasn't any sign of similarity to Dina that Paul could see. Maybe it was true, what the wise, mysterious *they* said, about adopted kids getting to look like their adoptive parents.

From everything he'd heard and seen, Peter was a good kid, except for the one incident with Joe Grady's kid, Ryan. He was known to be polite, respectful. Smart. He knew the kid was a hard worker. Watched him mowing, picking up litter off the resort grounds, scraping old paint off the rental boats, then painting them. Far too lanky for his size. He turned to Jake.

"Think the kid knows he's starting to get a bad burn?"

Jake flicked away a tiny river of sweat that flooded the crease in his forehead and waved over at Pete.

"He knows. Doesn't like looking pale, so he's willing to live with the pain." He kicked off his moccasins and gave Paul's shoulder a shove.

"C'mon old man, let's cool off, last one in's a rotten egg." He ran down the pier and dove in. Paul was just diving in as Jake broke the surface.

Cooling off turned into a diving contest. They took turns doing tucks, jackknives and backflips, and ended up with cannonballs.

Paul pulled himself up onto the pier and grabbed two towels, tossing one to Jake. He noticed the Anderson kid was gone.

Jake sat down beside him and lit up a cigarette, made a face and put it out. "Too hot to smoke. What time does Leslie's shindig start?"

"Four. I told her the music stops at 7:00 P.M. I have to be, as the kids say, out of my gourd—I hired a rock and roll band."

"Count me out, too old to rock."

"Me too. Remember when we ran up and down this hill twenty, thirty times a day without getting winded? Now I wheeze halfway up the first time." Paul took a second look around the lake but there was no sign of Peter. "Uh, you and the Anderson boy seem pretty thick."

"Pete's a good kid. Whenever we can, me and Phil take him along with us fishing. Once in a while I take him golfing, give him a few tips."

"When did the two of you get so chummy?"

"Can't tell you when. One day he showed up at my place and asked if he could use my diving board to practice for some competitions that were coming up. I said okay. He's got terrific form, makes it look effortless. But there's a lot of discipline there. Quite a runner too."

"I know. Seen him out running near the yard early in the morning, two, three times a week. Seems to alternate, walk a mile, run a mile…" He waited for Jake to make a comment, but he didn't. "You

180

know what went on between him and Joe Grady's kid, Ryan?"

"Ryan's a little shithead. Likes to taunt. Kept asking Pete, 'Hey, Peter, how's your peter? Find it yet?' One day, Pete decided he'd had enough. Told him no, but he knew where a knuckle sandwich was, and served it to him. Dropped him with one punch. It was too bad, but, as fortune would have it, Pete broke Ryan's nose. Way I heard it, tightass Carl didn't say a word about having to pay the hospital bill. Fact is, he gloated for a week."

"If the kid's thinking about boxing as a career, he'd better start putting on some weight. I hope Carl pays him a decent salary."

"Carl pays him. Pete saves practically all of it. Has his heart set on going to college. No boxing career in his future. He was not happy with himself for breaking Ryan's nose because it made Carl proud. He swore he'd never lose his cool again."

"Going to college, huh? Good for him. Way Carl feels about higher education, that must warm the cockles of his heart."

"That's my guess."

"He tell you what he wants to do with his life? What his major will be, what college he plans on going to?"

"Doesn't say much about long-range plans. Carl's been teaching him carpentry. Pete says he hates it, but he's kidding himself. He's good with his hands. I'll say this for Carl, he is a damn good carpenter. Whatever Pete decides to do with his life, I'm sure he'll do fine. What's the sudden interest in him?"

"I just wondered is all. Hope that college he goes to is out of state."

The conversation ended there. Each man sat thinking his own thoughts. Jake thinking it was better not to mention that Pete was leaning toward law as a career. Paul wished Peter well. Hoped he learned all he could from Carl and used it to his advantage. Jake was right, Carl was a wizard when it came to carpentry. Other than that, he was an asshole.

TALENT FOR DECEPTION

After a few minutes, Jake got up, said he'd see him later and left Paul sitting on the pier by himself.

Paul stayed on the pier for quite a while, gazing out at the lake. He reached over and picked up the binoculars Karen kept on the bench for watching the kids when they waterskied.

He slowly panned the lake, starting down at the far end, worked his way back, and stopped when he got to the resort. The beach was covered with sunbathers and kids building sandcastles, or knocking them down. There were a couple of kids having a water fight in shallow water. Speedboats were whizzing by, slapping waves.

The Anderson kid was on the beach too, picking up litter. Some summer vacations he had. The laird probably docked the kid when he took off to go fishing or play golf with Jake.

He swung the binoculars up toward the office, and almost dropped them when he saw another pair of binoculars trained on him. Carl. Something told him Carl had been watching him for a long time. He was tempted to give him a finger salute but didn't want some woman or kid seeing it. Instead, he laid the binoculars back down on the bench and walked off the pier and up toward the house.

Carl watched him until he disappeared beneath the cover of the oak trees. He smiled to himself.

"That's right you snooty son of a bitch, I'm keeping tabs on you. Pays to keep an eye on the enemy."

Just like it paid to keep in touch with old friends, like good ole Charlie up in Toronto.

They had raised their share of hell together during the time they worked for Charlie's uncle, doing their apprenticeship. Drank a lot of whisky, chewed a lot of fat, told some lies and shared a few dreams.

Nineteen thirty-two was a tough year in Toronto, they were lucky to get work in the Catskills. Things might've turned out a lot different if he hadn't gone there. Might have taken him a lot longer to get the idea in his head of having a resort if he hadn't worked there.

What counted was, he had it now. And Charlie had his place on Lake Simcoe. It was no palace, but it was good enough for Charlie. And it served his purposes too. Charlie's place was ideal as a base for his scouting missions. From there he could go check up on her and get back to Charlie's without him ever knowing how long he was gone or when he came back. Cost a fair-sized bundle to keep Charlie boozed up so he didn't know what time of day it was for a solid week, but it was worth every dime. Canadian whisky was cheap on that side of the border, long as you drank it there.

For eight years now, he'd been keeping track of her. Not that it took a genius to find her husband's place, she did everything but draw a map in her letters to Marth. What a dumb fox she was, telling when they were going on vacation and how long they were staying.

Mrs. Coleman would wet her ritzy pants if she knew how much he knew about her and her husband, and the brat. How they liked to take long walks, ride their bikes, go for boat rides and swim. They liked to go to Grossinger's to see the entertainers they had there. Smack in the middle of his old stomping grounds. He'd been wise not telling anyone about those years in the Catskills.

The idea of her trying to make trouble for him made him smile. He had the upper hand now and he was going to make sure she never took it away from him.

* * *

Sundays were Peter's favorite day of the week. After church, Carl drove them over to the Fisherman's and got out of the car, and then he and Martha rode home and she fixed pancakes and sausages. They ate in peace; they didn't have to worry about saying or doing the wrong thing that would set Carl off into one of his pissfits. Sundays were Carl's day out, but it was a holiday for Peter. Carl did not get home until late in the afternoon. When he came through the front door, he went straight to bed to sleep off his *plasma* as he liked calling it.

TALENT FOR DECEPTION

Peter wouldn't have cared if they just had toast and jam, it would have been okay with him. It was the peace and quiet he enjoyed. Like today, sitting across from Martha, reading *The Count of Monte Cristo,* every now and then glancing over at her. Made him feel good to see the pleasure in her face while she read Dina's letters. He liked watching the smiles roll across her face.

An unexpected memory of two years ago filtered in and he flushed with embarrassment. He had almost written a letter to Dina, to let her know how much her letters meant to Martha and how nice it was for her to have someone close to her own age to communicate with. It would have been one of the uncoolest things he had ever done. At the time, he didn't realize how women felt about their ages, and Martha was probably ten or twelve years older than Dina. She would have been insulted.

For a long time it was confusing. Martha constantly referring to Mrs. Coleman as "Dina Dmitri" until one day it hit him and he understood. Martha thought of her as Dina Dmitri because that's how she remembered her, the girl who grew up across the lake, the girl she sewed outfits for. Dina Dmitri was the person she knew, not Mrs. Coleman, the same as it was for him, and he'd never seen her, much less met her.

He didn't have to see her. He got to see Carl's reactions when her letters came and whenever her name was mentioned. It gave him joy to see Carl's face turn a fantastic purplish, blotchy red. Then he'd get all twitchy and so upset he couldn't talk sometimes. For that reason alone, Dina Dmitri became his secret ally, his tool to irritate Carl. He was probably about ten when he understood it, and made up his mind on the spot, that when he went to college, he was going to study law. Scare the living hell out of Carl.

Carl was everything he was determined not to be. He was mean, and he was a slob. Even if he wore a tux like Jake had on the other night, he'd still be a slob. Freshly laundered clothes and suits back from the cleaners didn't hide the fact he was a pig. Belching all the time with his mouth open, cleaning his fingernails with his jackknife at the table.

More than anything else, he hated it when Carl started making dirty, nasty remarks about women, especially girls. Sneaky pig, he always made sure Martha wasn't around when he talked dirty. As if that made him respectful or more of a gentleman.

There were times, like now, when he wanted to tell Martha she was still young and healthy, still attractive enough to find someone else. That she deserved someone better than Carl. He couldn't understand why she stayed with Carl. Was it because of him? He couldn't count the times he wanted to tell her to leave Carl. In a little over two years, he'd be eighteen. Responsible for himself. Considered an adult. He could take care of himself now.

Martha slid the letter back into the envelope. Her smile was gone now, she seemed far away and her eyes were sort of moist.

"Everything okay with Dina and her family?"

"Yes, things are okay. They're getting ready to go to the Catskills on vacation, like they do every year. Ben Jr. is doing well in school. Ben Sr. is chief of detectives now." Her forehead wrinkled and she sighed. "Dina must be bored staying home. That girl was never one to sit around…she had to be active, especially her mind. I think she misses practicing law. I should have taught her how to sew." Helen had claimed she didn't know how to sew, but Martha always knew in her heart that the reason Helen asked her to sew outfits for Dina and sometimes herself was because she knew they needed the extra money.

Peter waited, expecting Martha to continue. When she didn't he decided to say something about what was on his mind. "Last week when I was over at Jake's, Sam Olsen dropped in. He and Phil got to talking about the old days, like they do, and Sam was telling Phil about the time he tried to talk Dina into hanging her shingle up at his office. She turned him down, said she liked the challenges in New York. Seems unfair, ungrateful of her. Sam was the one who taught her how to pick through details, weed out what was pertinent and all that. Don't you think it was ungrateful?"

Martha was half-listening…her thoughts were on a time some-time back, to the day Dina sat exactly where the handsome young man was sitting now and asked if she wanted to adopt a baby.

She stared at Peter's hair, thinking how summer sun always streaked his dark brown hair with gold. His jaw was firm, it wasn't a sharp, bony jaw like the Dmitris had. His temper got the best of him sometimes, and he tried pretending he was tough, but he wasn't. It was his eyes that gave him away. He had such a sweet softness in those eyes. Of all the things that came to her mind when she thought of Dina, sweetness wasn't one of them. Kind and thoughtful, yes. Even gentle, but not sweet. Dina did not have a soft nature.

His foot scraped the floor under his chair, bringing her back, and she caught him trying to find the secrets she kept locked behind her eyes. She quickly dropped them down to her hands which were busy rolling her knife in a napkin.

He cleared his throat. "Mom? What do you think? Doesn't it seem kind of ungrateful to you that Dina didn't come back here? Sam is family, he's her great uncle or something. You told me the Dmitris believed strongly that family comes first, above everything else."

She shook her head. "They still do. I'm sure Sam doesn't feel that Dina owes him. She became a lawyer after she got her degree in New York. Sam didn't hire her and show her the ropes so she could be his assistant, or to take his place. Sam knows folks have to do what's best for themselves. Live where they're comfortable."

Now he stared out at a faraway place, a place he was lonesome for, only he had no idea where it was. "That's a fact."

186

When their eyes met again, each had a slight mistiness in their eyes.

She got up from the table and left the room. Some twenty minutes passed before she returned and laid a picture on the table.

"Forgot I had this. Woman on my right is my friend Helen, the girl standing in front of us is Dina, she was about your age when it was taken."

She watched him trying to appear less interested than he was, and she thought it might have been unwise sharing Dina's letters with him. It wasn't as though she broke her promise to Dina. A child had a right to know what the woman who bore him was like, what she looked like, even if he didn't actually know who she was. No one alive knew Dina like she did. And the talks kept them from discussing Carl behind his back, something she always tried to discourage.

Seeing what she looked like spoiled everything. He didn't care that she was tall and skinny. It was the resemblance to Paul Dmitri he didn't like. He passed the picture back to Martha as if it were a smelly fish.

"Nice." He got up and began clearing dishes. "You go relax, watch the roller derby that you like on TV, I'll do dishes." It made him smile to think Martha, who didn't like to argue or hurt a person's feelings, loved to watch women bat and shove each other around.

"Sometimes pictures don't do a person justice, especially old ones." The words weren't meant as an apology, but she could see Peter was bothered by the picture and she didn't know why.

"I know, Mom. A picture's just a picture."

CHAPTER TWENTY-FIVE

WEARING A LIGHT BLUE SUNDRESS, HER HAIR PULLED BACK IN A LOOSE ponytail, Karen looked much younger than thirty-three. She was at the kitchen counter preparing canapes. Leslie was unhappily assisting, feeling she was being forced to do someone else's job.

"I don't see why we don't have someone come in to prepare all this junk. It isn't like we can't afford it."

"It's not going to kill you to learn how to do these things. I enjoy cooking and baking. Your father appreciates it and so does Andy. That makes it worthwhile to me."

"My, what high standards you set for yourself. The best little cook and baker in Hid'n Oaks. So who all's coming to the old folks' party?"

"The usual…the Olsens, Jake and Phil, people from the yard and office, about thirty people altogether."

"Hmm. You know, sometimes I have to wonder about Jake. He never brings chicks to these parties. Think he's queer?"

Karen refused to respond. She'd made up her mind that today Leslie wasn't going to get under her skin. And the best way to avoid an argument was to ignore Leslie's remarks. Sometimes Leslie would drop the subject.

"Hello, Ma, are you there?"

"You know very well that Uncle Jake dates women."

"*Dating* is not marrying. Isn't he getting a little long in the tooth?"

"Hasn't found the right woman."

"Which is a polite way of saying he's queer."

"Oh, Leslie, stop. Don't cast aspersions—"

"Oh, wowee! Ma, you've been reading again. One of these days, if you're not careful, you're going to choke on that dictionary you swallowed."

"Stop it, Les. I want this to be a pleasant day for all of us."

"Oh, c'mon, Ma. I was just joking. It's just that if Jake is a homo, it'd be a shame, all that bread he makes. Any woman who marries him would have it made. By the way, my birthday's coming up. I'm putting in my order for a new bedroom suite."

"I know when your birthday is. And there's nothing wrong with the one you have. Your father made all the furniture in that room for Dina…You can't have everything you want."

"Ma, you said the D word! It's okay, I won't tell Dad. Anyway, I don't want *everything*, just the best. I'm not Dina, or you. You're satisfied having these Salvation Army rejects around here, like that stupid triangular guitar and the goofy teapot. Why are you hanging onto them anyway? It'd be better if you hid…stored them someplace instead of having them on display. They're nothing but eyesores."

"Those eyesores, as you put it, are the only possessions your grandfather had left of his family. That and his mother's jewelry."

"For shame, Ma. You forget the greatest possession of all, the family name."

"Don't be snide. Why not tell your father how you feel about the eyesores?"

Leslie grinned. "You know why. If he knew how I felt about a lot of things around here, he'd be devastated."

"Go find Andy and tell him to come in and have something to eat. I want you to make sure Andy is in bed by nine. He has a busy day tomorrow. I don't want him too tired to enjoy his camp-out with the Olsens. And you, I want you in bed by eleven, at the latest."

190

"Okay." She kissed her mother's cheek. "Thanks for the reprieve. I'll go find Andy."

Karen's felt her festive mood dropping and her irritation growing. She was too tired to deal with Leslie and her nasty little games.

The mothers in her bridge club constantly complimented her on having a daughter who was a mother's dream. There were times she wished they were right. Yes, Leslie was a straight A student. She was polite, pleasant and even kind—when she wanted to be. She wasn't neat, she was a clean freak. There was never so much as a dirty sock on her bedroom floor, her room as well as her bathroom were pristine. All the clothes in her closet were arranged by outfits, and they were all color coordinated.

And she did have a voracious appetite for knowledge and was inquisitive about people, wanted to know all about them. It wasn't out of concern, however. She had motives.

Twice, perhaps three times, Karen had suggested to Leslie she might seriously consider becoming a psychologist or psychiatrist. Leslie only laughed and said she wasn't about to baby-sit a bunch of loonies, she had enough to put up with around her own house.

One of the women dubbed Leslie a montage of the all-American girl after looking through an album containing hundreds of pictures of Leslie swimming, playing tennis and volleyball, waterskiing, and swinging a golf club. All the women agreed. Leslie was blonde and beautiful, blessed with flawless skin, brilliant blue eyes and snow white teeth.

What would they say if they knew what went on behind that montage? If they had held a sobbing Andy when he told her about the night Leslie woke him, took him by the hand, and led him down the hall to place his ear up against Mommy and Daddy's bedroom door to listen to how bad Daddy treated Mommy, so bad that he heard Mommy cry out to God for help, and how he wished Leslie hadn't yanked him away when he was going to try to rescue her.

TALENT FOR DECEPTION

Andy said Leslie pushed him down the hallway, back to his bedroom and made him promise never to tell a soul. If he did, people would know how mean Daddy was and there would be a divorce and he would be put in an orphanage. She read him *Oliver Twist* to prove there were such awful places. To save them all, Leslie had a plan...what she had to do was keep Daddy happy, and he had to keep Mommy out of Daddy's way as much as possible.

How would those women feel if they knew her Leslie was as wholesome as pyorrhea? God forgive her for having such horrible thoughts. She made the sign of the cross.

Andy came bursting into the kitchen and the disruption saved her from unpleasant musings. He took one look at her long face, came to an abrupt halt and cupped his hand over hers.

"Hi, Mom. You okay?" His black curly hair was still wet, and his brown eyes were bloodshot.

"I am now. You've been swimming underwater over in the Olsens' pool. Your eyes look like they were soaking in tomato juice." She tousled his hair. He was the color of maple syrup. "You'd better get out of those trunks, shower and get dressed for dinner. I want you in bed by nine if you want to go camping tomorrow. Leslie will be home too, if you need anything."

"Boy, Mom, you look nice."

He had a quarter-moon smile on his face and Karen wanted to pick him up and hug him. Instead, she returned his smile.

"Thank you, kind sir."

"What are we having to eat anyway? I'm so hungry I could eat cow chips."

"Andrew! Where on earth did you pick that up?"

"Leslie says 'horseshit' all the time."

She pointed to the ceiling. "Scoot upstairs and take your shower. I'll have a roast beef sandwich and milk ready for you when you get back down."

"Okay, alley-gator, see ya later." He raced out of the kitchen and stomped up the stairs, leaving his mother to contemplate how to go about impressing on Leslie to be more careful what she said around her brother.

Phil Tanner's retirement and love for the bubbly malt had caught up with him. His Buddha-shaped body made his waist visible only from behind.

"C'mon, Jake, snap it up. Time we get to the Dmitris', everyone will be home in bed. You need order in your life. A wife."

Jake smiled. "That's why I have you, dear, to give me orders."

"Very funny. I'm not going to be around forever, *dear*. High time you had kids of your own, 'stead of playing second father to other people's. You should be going to the party with a lady friend."

"How could I enjoy myself? I'd have to keep my eye on you, make sure you didn't muscle in."

"Don't talk crazy." He stopped and lifted his chin in the direction of the Dmitri Place. "Forget her, Jake, she's married."

"Phil, I know you mean well, but drop it, okay? Stop worrying about me. Look at you, you're what, sixty? You're not doing too bad."

"I'm sixty-two. Never mind about me. You do that all the time, change things around. We're discussing you, not me. I don't want you ending up alone. Lonely."

"Thanks for the concern. If I promise you'll be the second to know if I find *the* woman, will you get off my case?" There were two women he'd come close to proposing to, but didn't. Couldn't. It would've been like asking a lady to dance, then spending the entire evening wishing she were someone else. No woman should have to accept being second-best.

"Okay, okay. So let's go."

Phil tossed the keys to the Chris Craft to Jake. "You drive over, I'll drive back."

Talent for Deception

The polka music from the Dmitris surrounded them as soon as they stepped outside.

Karen was already on the pier, anxiously waiting for Jake to get out of the boat. As soon as his feet hit the pier, she shouted a greeting to Phil and grabbed Jake by the arm and steered him toward the dance floor.

"I've been waiting for you, mister—had the band play ten polkas in a row. We're down to five and I'm nabbing you before anyone else has the chance or they start playing foxtrots."

Paul watched from the bar. These days the foxtrot was as exuberant as he wanted to get. He counted six women clumped together, waiting for their chance to dance with Jake, and laughed to himself. Jake was not just the best polka dancer, he was the best dancer in town period.

A piece of long ago dropped in and for a moment, Paul caught a glimpse of Jake and Dina dancing at the prom. He held it for a few seconds, then blinked it away.

As a favor, the band played two extra polkas. After that, they threatened, they were switching to foxtrots. After the first extra polka Jake begged off, saying he had to have something tall and cool to drink before he was completely dehydrated.

On his way over to the bar, he stopped at a few tables to say hello, but didn't linger. He wasn't about to get embroiled in any long-winded debates. Dialectic bull. Parties weren't the place for them. Too many solutions were soaked in alcohol.

Twenty feet from the bar he passed Leslie and they nodded to one another. He considered himself lucky to be out of breath, it kept him from laughing out loud. She was dressed up like a cat burglar: black slacks, black blouse, black shoes, and her hair was piled under some sort of goofy black scarf. From the corner of his mouth he whispered, "Nice outfit."

She glared up at him but didn't say a word. The chinos-and-loafers man making fun of her outfit. He had about as much chic as Norton on *The Honeymooners.*

Circling the guests, being careful to avoid being seen by her parents, she scouted for each vantage point that would enable her to see and hear while she remained unseen. Her temper had almost cooled down. If she missed anything important because Andy took so long to fall asleep she was going to fix him good tomorrow.

Over at Phil Tanner's table, they were talking about space and astronauts. She was about to move on when she heard Fred Cole mention Mike's car collection. It was difficult to restrain herself. She wanted to inform him that Mike Dmitri was deceased…the cars belonged to her dad now, and would eventually belong to her. But she didn't want to let anyone know she was there, so she kept her mouth shut and listened.

"Boy, I tell you, I'd love to have the Duesey and the Auburn. The Cord or Bentley would be okay too."

"Packard Caribbean can't have more than five thousand miles on it."

"Not vintage yet, too new. Mike bought it for Paul's sister. From what I understand, she never drove it. Karen takes it for an airing once in a while. Phil here takes the others out for a monthly spin."

"How about that Indian motorcycle—Paul doesn't drive that much either, that baby's in prime shape."

Leslie was taking in every word. It was Fred Cole who grabbed her complete attention.

"I know a guy owns a dealership up in Canada, goes to all these antique car shows. Goes to Harrah's out in Reno once, twice a year. Flies to Europe, Asia, all over. He deals in Rolls Royces, Bentleys, Mercedes, all these luxury cars. Buys only the cream of the crop. There's a big market for them overseas. I know he's making money hand over foot. Lives in Canada in summer, spends part of the winter in Jamaica or Bermuda, and he has a place in Switzerland. I won't vouch that he's on the up and up, but I could overlook a little larceny if it paid well."

The conversation soon drifted to fishing, and Leslie moved on, passing a table of ladies discussing vegetarian diets. She recognized Maggie Cole's voice, who claimed to be a vegetarian, moaning about pesticides and ranchers pumping up cattle to fatten them for market. Maggie was no more a vegetarian than she was. Earlier, from her bedroom window, she saw Maggie packing away a pretty hefty roast beef and three ham sandwiches.

She was so busy paying attention to the tables, she didn't duck soon enough. She saw her father coming straight for her, wearing his no-mood-to-bargain face. She saved herself the trouble of making up a reason for being lakeside, and from being ordered up to the house, by walking directly to the path that led up to the house.

Paul stood and watched, making sure she went all the way up. When she opened the door to the kitchen, he turned back to his guests.

He was going to sit down with Jake and Jim Olsen until he heard the topic of their conversation, his least favorite: computers. He grabbed a beer out of one of the tubs and went over to Phil Tanner's table and sat down. He was more comfortable with his father's contemporaries than his own. He supposed it was because he felt he had more in common with them: similar values such as respect, similar rules of conduct. It was better if those were the reasons, instead of thinking of himself as middle-aged. But who was kidding whom? The Dmitris, as he reminded himself too often, didn't have much of a longevity record.

Karen was always after him to go for checkups, yet she balked at going for pap smears and those breast exams. But she did go.

He realized the band had all their instruments packed up. Three of the musicians had already left, the two still remaining were having drinks over at Jim and Elaine Olsen's table. Jake was still there too. That left only Jake and Phil who weren't from this side of the lake. He put a few quieter LPs on the hi-fi: The Three Suns, *Moonlight and Roses,* and four of Mantovani's albums. Strings were a good way to wind things down.

Laughter was sporadic and conversation had stopped flowing; only tired words stumbled into the night air. The ice in the tubs had become wading pools for the mixes and bottles of beer.

Halfway through the first record, Jim and Elaine Olsen left Jake at the table alone, said good night to everyone and took off, leaving Jake to decide if he wanted to have the proverbial one for the road at Phil's table, or be sensible and have coffee.

Phil wasn't going to leave, not with a captive audience. So coffee it was.

The urn on the serving table was empty. Thinking there had to be some up in the kitchen, he started climbing up the brick path to the house. The hill was by no means steep, it was just uphill. A breeze when you're twelve or fourteen, an effort when you're more mature.

Before his foot touched the top step he caught a slight movement on the patio, just outside the spill of light from the kitchen window.

"Hello there, Mr. Tanner. Searching for the absentee hostess?" Karen was comfortably stretched out on a chaise lounge, holding a martini in her left hand. She patted the chair next to her, then poured out a martini from the Thermos and held it out to him.

Against his better judgment he took it. "I came up here for a cup of coffee."

"Oh, no you don't. No coffee. This is a party." She poured out another for herself.

"Last time I had one of these mind-mushers, I made a pig out of myself and had six. Things were fine until I stood up. My feet were on a rolling pin and my head was on Mars. I was deaf too, as I recall."

"You're a nut, Tanner. Humor me, I've had one hell of a day." Karen raised her glass to his. "Here's looking at you, pal."

"*Casablanca*, right?"

"No, that was 'kid.'" She sighed wistfully. "We're not kids anymore, are we, Jake?"

"Hope not. Be terrible to come all this way and find out we're still kids. By the way, Andy like his rod and reel?"

"Loved it! Can't wait to go fishing with you, just the two of you." It sounded like she meant, without having to say, without Peter. "Like all the kids around here, he's *crazy* about you. And, as you well know, so are all the women. You're a very nice man, my friend. I mean that sincerely."

"Thank you, I'm crazy about you too. And all the kids, and all the women, too."

"Tell me something, Jake. Do you ever miss the nifty fifties?"

"You mean beatniks and Mister Peepers?"

"Ah, yes, I forgot about Mister Peepers, and the funny Mrs. Gurney. I used to listen to Arthur Godfrey with my mom when he was on radio. Remember *Life with Luigi?* And Fibber McGee and Molly with their closet full of stuff?"

"It was *Gang Busters* for me. And I liked Charlie McCarthy and Mortimer. Edgar Bergen got away with a lot of racy zingers using those dummies."

She laughed. "He did, didn't he." She let out a sigh. It had a lot of gin in it.

"Young people are so angry now, if they're not doped up. We didn't have any damn generation gap back when we were growing up. Not that I remember anyway."

"Synchronized disharmony's what it is." He took a small sip of his martini.

"Not funny, Jake. I hate it. Makes me feel out of touch. Old."

"Seasoned, not old. You can't complain, age hasn't held any

grudges against you. If it's possible, you're more beautiful now than you were at sixteen."

"Flatterer. Parenthood's not easy these days."

"I don't think parenting's ever easy. If it is, people are doing it wrong."

"Jaakke! I'm serious. Our kids have always been my career. Things are so upside-down today. I feel like I missed the boat, or the train, or whatever it was that took women to where they are today. I even feel like I'm the child and Leslie is…in charge."

"You didn't miss any boat, Karen. You're not a crack-the-whip type person. You're sweet and gentle. We all love you the way you are. Want to feel bad for someone, how about me? I wait for you to grow up and what did you do? Married Paul as soon as my back was turned."

"That's bull, Jake. And you know it. You never looked at any other girl than Dina."

"Guilty."

She poured herself another martini, picked up Jake's glass, dumped it out, and poured him a fresh one. "Nothing worse than a warm martini."

"Yes there is, being passed out on cold martinis. I don't think I can handle this one."

Karen tried looking at Jake through objective eyes and found it impossible, as always. Except for Paul, he was the most handsome man around. And a real sweetheart to boot. He'd make a wonderful father. His kids would be beautiful, or handsome.

"Anyone ever tell you, you look like Robert Wagner?"

"I'm getting younger? You used to tell me I looked like William Holden."

"I changed my mind. Woman's prerogative, you know."

Spurts of what sounded like slap-happy laughter floated up from the table down by the lake, and for a time they just sat and listened, trying to identify whose voice was saying what. Then they lost interest.

"Say, Tanner, isn't it about time you, 'took a wife' as they say?"

"I'll let you in on a secret. I have taken a wife."

She punched his arm. "Why you stinker. Why didn't you bring her to the party?"

"No, can do. If her husband found out, there'd be hell to pay. She's with him but ever an echo in my soul." He patted his chest.

"Sorry, Jake. I guess I misunderstood...I didn't mean to pry. Is there any chance she'll get a divorce?"

"Not going to happen. She's happy. Although she wouldn't be, she'd be peeved if she knew I can have her anytime I want. I can see her now, giving me of one of those rigor mortis looks of hers. She sure could drill you with those eyes." It was out before he was aware he'd actually said it.

"My...God! You're talking about Dina! You're still in love with her? Oh, *Jake*. I'm so terribly, terribly sorry." She wanted to cry, but was afraid if she did, she wouldn't be able to stop.

"Why be sorry? No one gets through life without a heart scar or two. If they do, they haven't been using it. She's happy, that's what counts." He leaned forward, closer to her. "She *is* happy, isn't she?"

"Yes, she is. Oh, damn it Jake, Peter isn't Dina's...Carl raped me." She was aware of the tears rolling down her cheeks, but didn't try to stop, knowing if she did, she'd start bawling and attract unwanted attention. "I've never told anyone except Dina. If it hadn't been for her, I don't know what I would have done."

Without saying a word, he took her hands in his and held them, trying not to guess how things might have been if Dina had trusted him enough to confide in him. Guesses were useless. Water under the bridge. He pulled out his hankie and wiped her cheeks.

"Must have been difficult for you, keeping it inside all these years."

"It was another life ago. Hard to believe it was mine. Dina's the one's had it difficult."

There was a rustling coming from the bushes behind them and Karen spun around.

"Did you hear something moving around over there?"

"Relax, it's probably just a raccoon or a cat."

She waited a few minutes, listening. After a few minutes she felt it was safe to go on.

"Dina left a letter here for Martha, asked me to mail it. I read it. I know I shouldn't have, but I read it. In it she said if Martha needed help, anything at all, she should let her know and she would take care of it. She'd let her know her address when she was settled. You know, to this day she keeps in touch with Martha, asks about him. I think it's because she knows Martha would think it was strange if she didn't; she would think she was uncaring. I waited until I knew Carl wasn't going to be around and I stuck it in the mailbox. After Dina and Ben got married, I used to worry about how she was going to explain it to Ben, *if* Martha ever asked her for help." This time she distinctly heard something moving around in the bushes behind them.

"Did you hear that?"

"Not to worry. I'll protect you if a big bear comes crashing out at us. If I can stand."

A cat meowed.

Relieved, Karen laughed. "I guess I'm jumpy. Shouldn't be with all the liquid tranquilizers I've had tonight. Tell the truth, I am a little woozy. Should go down and say good night to who's left."

"You handle those mind-warpers pretty good, but they're very sneaky. Go on in to bed, I'll say good night for you. I think Phil and Paul are the only ones left." He stood up and wasn't surprised that he too was wobbly. It sounded funny, but it was better than bombed.

"Ask Paul to drive you and Phil home, he never drinks more than a couple beers…"

"Nah, we'll be fine. Phil's okay, he talks more than he drinks. I gotta lot to do tomorrow."

"Jake? You won't say anything to anyone about Peter?"

"About what? Generation gaps? Not me." He leaned over to kiss her forehead, and almost missed. He held her tight, more for his support than hers. "Good night, angel face."

"Good night."

She stayed long enough to make sure he made it down and was about to go into the house when she was sure she heard someone running along the side of the house, toward the front.

Panic exploded and she tried to follow, but lost her balance and fell. She got up and hurried around to the front porch. No one was there. She opened the front door and stepped inside and immediately went upstairs, praying Leslie was fast asleep.

Standing at the foot of Leslie's bed, she knew it was impossible to tell if Leslie had been running because her own heart was pounding so hard she was afraid it would burst out of her rib cage. She did hear her snoring lightly.

"Les? Are you awake?"

Leslie continued to snore.

Karen tiptoed back to the door and breathed a sigh of relief. She took care to close the door quietly. When Leslie heard the door click, her eyelids flipped open.

Putrid Peter Anderson was Dina's bastard! If Andy had fallen asleep faster, she might have heard who the father was.

Now she understood why her father always referred to Dina as *your* aunt, and *your* sister-in-law to her mother. He never referred to Dina as *his* sister.

While mulling over this information, Fred Cole popped into her mind. The grab-a-free-feel man. Be interesting to see how Maggie would react if she knew he was cheating on her. Probably drop him like a ham sandwich at a vegetarian meeting.

At the same time Karen was pulling her nightgown over her head, her daughter's intricate receiving mechanism was busily screening and interpreting the information that her suction cup ears and microscopic eyes had amassed. She sorted it and embedded it .
into her personal archives. When she was finished, she promptly fell asleep.

CHAPTER TWENTY-SIX

THE NEXT MORNING, A MALICIOUSLY UNSYMPATHETIC SUN THREW GAUDY rays of green, purple and orange through the bedroom window. She tried taking refuge behind a pillow, but it didn't help. Paul's snoring vibrated right through it.

Her last hope was the shower. As the cold water pounded out the stupor, she swore she was never going to drink another martini as long as she lived.

Bits of last night's conversation with Jake skipped in and out. None of it seemed to matter much, until the noise in the bushes and the sound of someone running flashed in. She was cold sober when she stepped out of the shower. She dressed in a hurry and rushed downstairs.

The clock on the kitchen wall read twelve noon. She smelled bacon frying. Andy was buttering toast. Across from him, Leslie was slicing tomatoes.

Leslie smiled. "Good morning, Ma. I thought I'd make the least offensive lunch I could think of, BLTs."

"Good morning. And thank you. I didn't realize it was so late."

Leslie knew her mother was looking for verification for her suspicions, afraid she'd find it. She went over to the stove and removed the bacon strips from the frying pan, grinned, and held out the pan to her mother.

"Hey Ma, where do you want me to pour all this globby bacon grease?"

She got the reaction she hoped for. Her mother ran for the bathroom. She shrugged her shoulders at Andy.

"You're mean."

"Oh, be quiet and eat your sandwich."

After they finished eating, Leslie went into her father's den, took three family albums off the shelf and started paging through the frozen images of younger, living Dmitris.

They never held much interest for her before, but now she was curious. Her grandparents did make a nice looking pair. The older he was getting, the more Peter Pan looked like her grandfather. She flipped past a few pages until she came to Dina's graduation picture.

She hated to admit it, but she had to agree with her mother. Madame Zero did sort of resemble Ava Gardner in that movie she was forever watching on TV. *Mogambo.* That was it. Only Dina's skin was dark, like her father and grandfather. There was no hiding the fact they were from the same family. There was something different about Madame Zero, but it wasn't just the green eyes. Exactly what it was, she couldn't put her finger on. It was no big deal anyway. She had info that was more important. She continued to stare at the photograph for a few more minutes nonetheless.

So she was pretty, so what? So were millions of other women, including herself. She didn't recall there was anything special about Dina when she saw her in person. Anyway, why was she wasting her time looking at pictures of someone she probably would never see again?

She tossed the albums back on the shelf and ran up to her bedroom, went directly into her bathroom, and removed the toilet tissue from the roller. The key to her secret box was still securely taped inside. She pulled it out and walked over to her dresser, opened her secret compartment that Peter Pan had made special for her and lifted out the secret box. It was supposed to be for special mementoes. It was.

Dina's old bedroom had undergone extensive changes. It had been a painful process for Paul. By his daughter's request, he had pulled out the built-in bookcase he made for Dina and put in floor-to-ceiling mirrors. He gave the bed, dresser, armoire and desk that he made for Dina to Jake and stood numbly by as the movers brought in the junky French Provincial suite Leslie had ordered from some store in Minneapolis.

The aqua walls were now dove gray, the furniture white, the carpet and drapery bordeaux. Lying on the pale rose bedspread, she fingered the stacks of one hundred dollar bills, one hundred in each stack. She was going to have to talk to her dad about getting her own safety deposit box at the bank. It was comforting to have the $80,000 close by, but it was risky. Pollyanna might come in her room and snoop around.

These hundred dollar bills had been accumulating for nearly four years, since the day she decided to take a peek inside one of the envelopes her father gave her to drop off at the post office on her way to school. After she found three crisp hundred dollar bills in the first envelope, she opened the other two. And they too contained crisp new hundred bills. One had five!

Two were addressed to churches, the other to some charity foundation in the Twin Cities. There was no note inside any of them to explain who the money was from. She held on to them, and went to school. It was the longest day she spent. She couldn't wait to get home to ask about the envelopes.

When she did get home, she had to wait for him to finish his end-of-the-day relaxers, two dry Manhattans.

As he explained, it took all the willpower she had to suppress the anger it ignited inside her.

The envelopes, he said, were a tradition that his father started long ago, the money placed inside them was a small payback for the good life they enjoyed. Like his father, he did not claim it on his taxes, or tell anyone else outside the family about it. If he did, it would spoil the whole purpose.

At first, she was too stunned to speak, but somewhere in the middle of his spiel, she wanted to tell him he was full of shit, preaching about the family first, getting on her about saving for college. From that day on, Paul became Peter Pan in her mind and her mother, Pollyanna.

To avoid suspicion, she didn't break her routine. She walked into the post office and mailed two of the envelopes, the other remained in her schoolbag and stayed there until she got home from school. The bills were then removed and stacked in the bottom drawer of her dresser.

On subsequent delivery days, she alternated. One day she robbed one church to pay Leslie, the next it was some other church to pay Leslie. Another day it was the charity organization that paid Leslie. The bills in the envelopes were not always the same—sometimes they were less, other times more. She assumed it depended on how much profit her father made each month.

After a month, Leslie didn't bother mailing anything, she walked into the post office to buy stamps or envelopes then left. The envelopes her father had written out were either shoved deep down into garbage bags, or if there was a fire going in the fireplace and no one was around, she tore them in tiny pieces and tossed them in.

She was ten at the time. By fourteen, her savings amounted to a little under $80,000.

Peter Anderson was in the principal's office trying to convince himself his ears weren't playing some cruel joke, that he had actually won a $35,000 scholarship to the law school of his choice. At the same time, Leslie was in study hall composing a résumé to submit to her father, listing the reasons why she should learn the family business, starting with working in the office, and explaining why she did not want to be given an allowance, she wanted to earn a salary.

At the time, she wasn't aware that she didn't have to work so hard on her résumé. Paul had his mind made up already, because he was banking on her taking over the family business after she finished college.

Paul didn't need a written résumé. He knew firsthand the hours she sat at his side watching him at his craft, learning lumber grades and the differences in hickory, oak, pine, cherry, fir, birch and burl. Knew which were best for cabinetry, doors, windows and foundations. She was a straight A student, a whiz in math, and he was willing to bet, if she wanted, she could be a college professor. He knew the countless hours she sat in the office during the slow times learning the filing and billing systems; she knew how to fill out bills of lading when she was ten. His daughter was a genius. She also happened to be the most beautiful and captivating girl in the state. In any state. And she had his heart wrapped in her little finger. She was also sharper than Dina was at her age, or damn close.

The only thing Paul had a hard time with was the idea of her missing out on the few years she had left to have fun, carefree summers.

Sitting across from her in Mike's den, he in Mike's old chair and she in his old chair, he looked at Leslie's résumé on the desk in front of him. Paul had trouble speaking without choking on the pride that welled in his throat, yet he did have some reservations.

"Sunshine, are you sure you want to do this? You're not quite fifteen yet. I see no problem with working weekends, or a few days after school, but do you really want to work all week during the summer? You only have two summers left to enjoy doing the things you and your friends like to do."

"To do what? Hang around in town, see movies? Go for a swim or waterski? Movies are a bore. When and if I want, I can always find time to take a dip after work. Or have Mom pull me across the lake on skis. Most of my friends have to work to earn spending money or save for college. I want to get a head start. I don't want to work for spending money, I want to learn everything there is about the business, how things work, how to run it. I will eventually anyway."

He smiled, catching himself before telling her how much he wanted her to do exactly that. He didn't want to put any more pressure on her than she had already put on herself.

"Okay, Rainbow. It's your call. But if your grades start to suffer, then we have to sit down and talk this over again, to decide if you should cut back, work just weekends."

"I promise you, my grades won't change. Tell you what, let's make a deal. If my grades fall, I'll quit. If I keep a straight A, when I'm sixteen, I get a Corvette. Red. Deal?"

He laughed and threw back his head. "Thanks for the year's warning. I know who's going to be driving around in a red car in a year."

"Not 'car,' Dad, a 'vette. Come to think of it, maybe it's a good idea if I get a head start on that too. You know, start learning to drive this year?"

"Uh-uh. No dice on that. You get the Corvette when you're sixteen. It's only a year away. Oh, and seventy-five percent of what you make goes into the bank, toward your college education. I know you've saved quite a bit from your allowance, odd jobs and money you got as gifts over the years and I'm proud of you, but a really good education doesn't come cheap."

"Deal." While they shook hands on it, she wondered what her father would say if he knew how much she had upstairs in her dresser drawer. "Oh Dad, I keep meaning to ask, I want to have my own safety deposit box, to keep my jewelry and stuff."

"Sure, sunshine, we can go tomorrow and get it set up."

The following day, as he promised, they went to the bank and she got her safety deposit box. Over the next three weeks, she slowly moved the money hidden in her dresser into the bank. It had become a morning ritual: she checked to make sure the key to her safety deposit box was still taped to the toilet tissue holder. It was always intact.

She wasn't keen on giving the money up and knew she'd miss the security of having the money readily accessible. But the risk of keeping it near was too great. If Andy or her mother discovered it, she'd have difficulty explaining having all that money. She didn't think her mother would find it, but Andy was unpredictable at times. A nosy fink.

Before Leslie received her first paycheck, praises from her co-workers poured into Paul's ears, telling him what a difference his daughter made in the office, how everything was so much more organized, and files that had been missing were magically where they were supposed to be. "She's a real hard worker," "Sharp as a tack, and so efficient," and, "So like her mother, refreshing and pleasant as a spring day." Paul agreed. He could tell the difference in his own office since Leslie started. She had taken it upon herself to straighten things up and there wasn't an invoice or bill of lading that was further than where his fingertips could reach.

Paul was so proud of her, he ordered a red Corvette, to be delivered June 15 of next year.

CHAPTER TWENTY-SEVEN

For the past two years the seasons seemed to swish by so fast he barely recognized the remnants of the special days of family celebrations: Birthdays, anniversaries and holidays. Mike had told him and Dina often enough to take the years one day at a time, not cram their lives into empty spaces. Jake was right, he was a sanctimonious ass.

He looked out the window, up at the hill where he, Dina and Jake used to slide down on their sleds. He walked over to the door and stuck his head out.

"Les? I don't want to be disturbed for a while…any calls come in, take a message. I'll call back."

He picked up the phone in his office and dialed the familiar number. His hands were clammy and his mouth hadn't been this dry since Korea. Unlike previous times, this time he let it ring until she answered.

"Hello."

"Hi, Dina. I'm early for Russian Easter, so Happy Passover. It's Paul."

"I still recognize your voice. I hope everything's okay there."

He caught the concern in her voice. "Oh, hey, nothing's wrong. Everything's fine. I'm a little—no, I take that back—I'm a lot nervous. I wasn't sure you'd speak to me."

"You're my brother, Paul, so of course I'd speak to you. I love you, nothing will ever change that."

Talent for Deception

The sigh of relief was embarrassingly pronounced and he laughed to cover it up.

On the other side of his office door, Leslie was busy going over inventory lists, musing how nice it was being Russian Orthodox. All the employees left at noon using the pretext that they were going to church. That was a laugh. While they were probably sitting at home or shopping for Easter, she was getting time-and-a-half for working Good Friday.

Finished with the inventory lists, she started scanning some cost sheets, amazed to see how expensive construction machinery was. She become so absorbed in making mental notes totaling values of each piece that she never noticed Carl Anderson coming into the office until he was there in front of her.

The first time she saw him she thought he was the oddest duck she ever laid eyes on. He had two colors: in winter and early spring he looked like he walked off the set of *Dracula*, trying to find a blood donor. In summer and fall he was coronary crimson. Today he was sort of in-between until he opened his mouth, then he flushed.

"Your father in?" She gave him the willies, the way she looked like her mother. He could swear he was looking at Karen. Like time really had stood still.

"Hello, Mr. Anderson. My father is in, but he's tied up with an important call. If you wait just a sec, I'll check to see if he's free. Have a seat."

She knocked on her father's office door then walked in without waiting to be asked.

"Dad? Mr. Anderson is here."

The look on her father's face made it clear he didn't appreciate being interrupted. He held up his hand.

"Dina, I have to go. I'll call again. Take care. Love you."

214

Leslie's mouth dropped. Dina? Love you? She went back out to the front office.

"He'll be right with you, Mr. Anderson."

The words were no sooner said before Paul came out, gave Carl a nod and held the door for him, then followed Carl back into his office and closed the door.

Leslie didn't have to pretend she wasn't eavesdropping, there wasn't anyone around to pretend for. Her father's voice could have iced the walls, there was not even a feeble attempt to be polite.

"What do you want? I have a lot of work piled up, I don't have much time."

"One thing about your old man, he was a good businessman. He took the time to hear a man out." Paul Dmitri was still a snotty little punk.

"Well?"

"I'm adding on more cabins, need some work done. Thing is, I'm kinda strapped right now, just shelled out a bundle for plumbing repairs, couple boats and motors. I can't put out the cash right now. I thought you could have one of your crews get the cabins up and I'll pay you soon as some of the deposits come in for next summer."

"Can't do it."

"Can't, or won't?"

"Can't. All the crews are committed to jobs until fall. I don't have anyone available."

"Not available to me, right?"

"Let's just say I'm not going to strain myself to try to accommodate you."

"Some day, wise guy, you're going to need a favor from me. Summers are my busiest times. I need the kid working for me, but since you hired him to work construction for you, I had to hire people to do his work."

Paul smiled. Any remaining doubts he had left about hiring Peter

215

were all dispelled in this moment. "I hear you had to hire three to do the work Peter did. Why complain? Peter still helps you out when he can. And you won't have to pay a dime to send him to college."

"Oh yeah, the scholarship…"

Paul saw the idea formulating in Carl's eyes. He wanted to blow it to bits. "From what I understand, there's no way in hell you can touch that money. Not legally. If you tried, it would be very embarrassing. Now get the hell out before I throw you out."

Carl slammed the door and stomped out. Leslie's smile was wide enough to push dimples into her cheeks. She let out a low 'hmm.'

Her eyes followed him back to his truck, shaking her head and admonishing herself for being so dense. He was right here, all the time. Had friends who drove semis. Drove? They probably owned them.

She had found her partner. He wasn't going to be easy to approach, she'd have to dispel any suspicions he might have first. He didn't appear to be particularly bright. His eyes had about as much warmth as a glacier, and his eyebrows could use a dab or two of Nair, but dating him wasn't what she had in mind.

Paul came out of his office while she was contemplating the best way to approach Carl. He was surprised to find her still in the office.

"Hey, sunshine, about time you punched out. You go on home, tell your mother I'm going to be late for dinner, and all of you should go ahead and eat. I'll grab a bite at the Norseman on the way home." Before she had a chance to ask how she was going to get home, he pulled out a set of keys out of his pocket.

He didn't have to say anything, his smile gave it away. "Guess now is as good a time as any; these belong to you. Car's in the shed, and yes, it's a Corvette, and it is red."

She jumped up, grabbed the keys and threw her arms around his neck.

216

"Oh, Daddy! Thank you, thank you."

"Don't forget to thank your mother, she's the one who taught you how to drive. And be careful."

She ran to the shed and opened the door, slid in behind the wheel, turned on the ignition and carefully eased the car out of the shed. She drove out of the parking lot slow and easy, as though the car were made of glass. Once she swung onto the highway, she floored the accelerator.

* * *

She drove straight home, ran up to her bedroom, and went directly into the bathroom. She removed the toilet tissue holder and looked inside. The key to her safety deposit box was intact. She put the roller back and walked across the room to the window and sat down. She peered out over the lake, at the resort.

The view was bleak. Leafless trees and bark skeletons, with fussy wind twirling ground leaves in circles. Hid'n Oaks was one huge, debilitating pit of boredom. If it weren't for confidence, her talent, and an ability to focus, she'd be out of her mind. She didn't know if she could hold out through two more tortuous years until she was eighteen and free to get out. 'Course now, she didn't have to spend her own money on a Corvette.

She didn't belong in this town, or in this family. The town was full of crippled souls who wanted dreams to happen, like by accident good things were going to come their way. They sat around waiting for luck to come their way. Not her. She wasn't going to wait around for anything. Years ago she had set her goals and worked to make them reality.

College was one goal she gave serious consideration. From the information she had been able to glean, it was one of the best places to deal drugs. The financial prospects were tempting for a while. But after weighing the pros and cons she didn't like the risks. It meant having to deal with the unpredictability of elastic-headed creeps, the

217

junkies and acidheads she'd have to do business with, or worse, socialize with, mingling with oatmeal brains. That had about as much appeal as swimming in a septic tank. How long would it take one of the zeros to turn her in for a fix or a dime bag? Dealing was out. She wanted no part of prison. She had something far safer in mind.

The sound of her mother's car pulling up next to the back door interrupted her train of thought and she suddenly remembered it was market day. Pollyanna's car would be loaded down with corn, fresh eggs, tomatoes and anything else she could stuff in it. And she'd have her gladiolas. Pollyanna was a kook when it came to flowers. The house smelled like a funeral parlor already. But helping her unload it all was a perfect time for a little chat. She took the backstairs down to the kitchen.

Since Leslie didn't appear bored, Karen assumed she had some ulterior motive in mind for helping her put away the groceries.

Leslie loved poking around inside her victims' heads. The less forthcoming they were, the more she enjoyed the challenge. The girl had a wicked knack for setting people up, creating certain moods, then zap!

Up until a year or two ago, Karen suffered tremendous pangs of guilt for thinking such thoughts. Now she only smiled at her own reflection in the window above the sink.

Her reflection wasn't what it used to be and she had to ask herself why? The Christmas tree glow was gone, and what had become of the girl with moonlight in her heart?

What happened, she told herself, was the sandpapered realities of life had rubbed away the glow and the moonlight and it left her with a suspicious and cynical mind. She had to admit it was a swap she had been gladly willing to make. It enabled her to look at Carl and see him as just a man who owned the resort across the lake. A man who meant absolutely nothing to her. Less than his son did.

She saw Leslie waving at her and turned her back to the window.

"Ma, what planet are you on? I said Dad told me to tell you we should go ahead and have dinner without him. He's working on something and he'll catch a bite at the Norseman."

"Sorry, I didn't hear you, I had my mind elsewhere. How do you like your car?"

"Oh, it's terrific, thanks. Would you believe it? Dad called Madame...I heard him talking to Dina."

"I know, he called earlier, said he was going to. What's with this 'madam'?"

"Nothing. Just being silly. Oh! Guess who stopped by the office today?"

"I'm not good at guessing...I haven't a clue."

"Oh, Ma, don't be so modest. Carl Anderson."

"What did he want?"

"I don't know. Dad hustled him into his office and shut the door. Carl sure is an odd old boy. Has about as much animation as a rock, hair's about as lustrous as pumpernickel rye bread. In some ways, he reminds me of that skinny actor, the one that acts so bashful. Gary Cooper, that's who he acts like."

"*Gary Cooper!* Never. You stay away from him...I mean out of his way. He's a very unpleasant man."

"Not really. Say, Ma? What do you think? You think the bastard looks like his mother, or his da-da?"

The room closed in on her as her worst fear crept over her and she felt her sanity start to slip away. Something snapped and she quickly snatched it back.

"What did you say?! Tell me what you mean!" Her voice was so shrill it made the hair on her arms stand up. She grabbed Leslie's arm. "It was you out there that night!"

219

"Ma, let go of my arm—you're hurting me! You flipped out or something?" Her mother was totally freaked.

She dug her fingers into Leslie's arm. "Tell me what you heard."

"Ouch! I heard you tell Jake that Peter was Dina's kid. That she keeps in touch with Martha...*Ma!* Let go of me."

She released her. "What else?"

"Nothing. I took off."

"You pretended to be asleep when I came into your room—why? Kept quiet all this time."

"Because I knew I'd heard something I wasn't supposed to. What's the big deal anyway? Who cares if Dina had a kid out of wed-lock? Isn't that how your generation so delicately puts it?"

"Have you ever said anything about any of this to your father?"

"You kidding? Why would I do that? I knew he was super p.o.'d at her. He never said her name for eons. She's been on his shitlist from the time I can remember, and I thought she always would be. Until this afternoon."

"I want you to promise me you won't ever bring this up to him."

"Oh Ma, you must have fallen out of some *Mother Goose* book. You'll never outgrow your fantasies. You're the perennial Pollyanna. This isn't the '40s or '50s—who cares if Dina screwed around? It's no big deal."

"It's a big deal to a lot of people. It may be that people your age might not see it that way, but my generation does. Parents—"

"Parents! You're all alike when it comes down to the nitty-gritty. Kids are your ego trips, puppets to fulfill your dreams. You want us to turn out well so you can take bows for your accomplishments, reward yourselves for your many sacrifices. Tell me Ma, what sacrifices have you made? What aspirations have you had? To be Paul Dmitri's wife? To be the best cook and housekeeper in town? Congratulations! You made it. All you'll ever be is the great Mike Dmitri's daughter-in-law. A shadow. Just like Dad will always be

Mike Dmitri's shadow. And Andy, he'll always be Mike Dmitri's grandson. One isn't born into this family, they're inducted. Well, not me. I'm nobody's shadow. Paul Dmitri is *my* father, Mike was *my* grandfather. This whole 'family first above all' bullshit is a joke. Like some slogan for an insurance company."

Stunned, Karen could only stand and stare. Finally she found her voice. It had an eeriness to it, as though it was working its way out of a heavy fog. "Does your conscience ever whisper in your ear?"

"Get real, I can't be bothered with pests or shadows."

"Shadows, huh? Les, your conscience would vanish in the shadow of a flea. Do you realize what you could do with your insight, that you could be a great help to people? Instead of digging around in their private souls to exploit people, you might do something to—"

"Don't start on the looney thing again. If I do go to college, I'm not going to waste my time on shrink courses. I don't need them. I understand people just great, and I didn't get it out of books…"

Karen stood silently watching Leslie, her eyes forcing her to recognize the actress giving a performance as her entire manner changed and she became the personification of contrition.

"Mom, I'm sorry I got carried away. Things are just different today than they were for you and Dad, and people of your generation. Today people think differently, have expanded views and values. Things are…different."

"Regardless of what you think of your father and me and our generation, you will respect what's important to us. I don't want you to say anything to your father about any of this. I don't want anything to ruin your father and Aunt Dina patching things up."

"I promise, I won't say a word to him. You know Ma, you may not think so, but I do care about this family. I'd never do anything to hurt any of us. Don't sell me short, I might be more than you think I am. You could give me a little more credit."

"I hope and pray that's so, for all of our sakes."

"I'm sorry if I upset you. Oh, I wanted to ask you—"

"Later. I can't talk to you right now."

"Sure, later Ma...Mom. It can wait till a better time."

"And Leslie, values are not passing fancies."

She gave her mother a respectful nod and walked away.

After making sure her safety deposit key was intact, she flopped down on her bed trying to imagine what secrets these walls held. What whispered promises and curses? Was Madame Zero a dreamer too?

While she deliberated over these things, another thought came in. Her mother had gone absolutely freaky frantic. Why?

Pollyanna went berserk when she asked if she thought Peter looked like his mother or his da-da. He definitely didn't look like Dina...and she had mentioned Carl earlier. Carl! She shot up straight, giving her complete concentration to the clicking of the piece falling into place.

* * *

The $35,000 scholarship was a curse wrapped inside a blessing as far as Peter was concerned. Things were simpler when he didn't have it. Work, pay Carl back every penny he'd had to shell out for him from the day he set foot in his goddamn house. According to his estimates, he owed Carl $75,000. Long ago he had made a promise to himself that everything was secondary to his paying Carl off and that included college. The exception was Vietnam. If the war was still going on, that changed things. He was assured that if he did have to go, the scholarship would be there for him when he got back from Vietnam. If he did.

He wanted all of it off his mind. If it weren't for his big mouth, he wouldn't have to worry about it. He was fairly certain it was his high school counselor, Irene Olsen, Connie's mother, who'd arranged to have his name put up as a candidate for the scholarship. As soon he told her he wanted to become a lawyer, if he could work things out, he saw the lights go off in those eyes of hers. Like New Year's Eve in Times Square.

It wasn't like he was pressed for time. He had three months to make up his mind. Time enough to decide what was the right thing to do. If the war was still going on, the choices were easy. Enlist, hand over the $40,000 he hoped to save by then to the shithead, and tell Carl he'd get the rest to him when he got back. Deferment was not totally out, but he didn't like doing it. He wished he could trade the scholarship money in and get it done, just hand it to Carl.

Unfortunately, that was one of the two stipulations—no cash. The other was not a problem to live with, the donors' insistence that their names remain anonymous. Thirty-five thousand dollars. With what he had already saved, he could live where he wanted, would not have to worry about clothes, and he could afford to take Connie out on some real dates.

He didn't mind working construction, it was the best paying job around. And Paul Dmitri wasn't such a bad guy to work for. Addressed him by name now, and he went out of his way to talk to him, ask how he was doing. Couple of times he told him he really appreciated how hard he worked and what a good job he did. It did not mean he was going to invite him over for dinner, but he was more pleasant than Peter expected.

He knew without asking that Paul had hired him on Jake's say-so. Which was okay. Paul had to realize by now that he was worthy of Jake's good words.

Life was pretty good these days. He was finally at a point in his life where he didn't play the depressing scenarios over and over anymore. He no longer cared if his parents were two young lovers who got carried away and weren't allowed to get married, or if they were in some fatal accident, or some asshole just couldn't keep his penis zipped in his pants, or his mother was nothing but a slut. Whatever it was, the conclusion was the same, he wasn't wanted. An inconvenience. Well, someday he, the bastard, was going to be the best damned attorney in the state.

The one thing he tried hard not to do was fall in love. It was not on his agenda. But love ignored plans. It happened, he fell in love and blamed it on fate. Connie Olsen was a kid, one of the sopho-mores he sometimes saw in the hallways on his way in or out of one of his classes at school.

The very first day he reported for work, Paul Dmitri formally introduced him to his daughter Leslie, and her cousin, Connie. As soon as he looked at her in her blue jeans and a pink blouse that made her blue eyes brighter and her skin creamier, he knew he was in trouble. He always thought that love at first sight was just soap opera baloney. It took him less than a minute, for which he was dis-appointed in himself. He gave himself credit for being more sensible than that.

It didn't take long for the disappointment to turn into gratitude. Since he had Connie in his life, things were better. He was better, hap-pier than he'd ever been in his life.

Connie Olsen was tops. Special. He liked her right off because she wasn't anything like her cousin Leslie, the charmer. He never understood why people were so impressed by charm, it wasn't a character trait, it was a ploy to gain something. And the boss's daughter was a perfect example of how to do it.

Sundays were still his favorite days. He and Martha still had breakfast together, but evenings he had a standing date over at the Olsens for dinner and afterwards he played cribbage with Connie's dad and her great Uncle Sam. Whenever they could, Jake and Phil dropped over. When they could make it, it was tournament time.

The games soon became more of a distraction, it was the bull ses-sions that went on that Pete enjoyed. He could tell Jake liked hearing Phil and Sam talk about their king of the hill days as much as he did. And Jake had to have heard their stories often enough to be able to finish them. Lots of times, he and Jake exchanged conspiratorial smiles as they sat listening to the two men discuss law and the lumber business.

Invariably, the stories got around to Mike Dmitri. It was obvious to Peter that Mike must have been quite a man to have all three of these men admire and love him so much. Even though the stories were fascinating, they also made him feel lonely and disconnected. The stories gave the three men a common bond. Family. Something missing in his life, a family heritage. He envied them for having that kind of validity.

When he got to feeling down, he could always count on Jake noticing and getting him out of the dumps. He'd either tell some stupid funny story or ask him to play golf or go for a swim, or play some basketball or pool.

With Jake around, he didn't need a father. Jake was what he imagined an older brother would be like. Or an uncle. Jake was aces. Cool. It meant a lot that Jake liked him too. He loved and respected Jake more than any man he knew.

CHAPTER TWENTY-EIGHT

MONDAY THROUGH FRIDAY, LESLIE WORKED AFTER SCHOOL; ON SATURDAYS, she worked all day. Special sale days were her favorite work days. She hadn't done anything foolish or creative her first year, but mentally she'd worked out in her head how stock could be moved around and how she could bump up her income by overcharging the customers she knew never asked for receipts.

She complimented herself on having made the extra effort to spend time on construction sites to learn all she could about flaws, problems in flooring and cabinets: squeaks, humps and sags. Learned how to read blueprints, differences in roof styles and pitches, and the basics of house structure and foundations.

All this acquired knowledge enabled her to deal shrewdly with the novices who came in to buy lumber. Pathetic handymen and women who didn't know the difference between real wood and veneer and were too proud to admit it. Or too dumb. A portion of overcharges and the differences for substitutes ended up in her safety deposit box, as well as money redirected from customers who were too rushed to bother with receipts.

By her senior year, she had everything down to a science, and in her head planned how to acquire her own private stock of the high demand, higher priced wood. She devised a way to redirect quality, first grade lumber and merchandise to damaged storage areas. Time was the real element of concern. Once she'd amassed her private stock she had to make arrangements to move it out. Then there was all the expensive construction equipment. She was going to have to talk with Fred Cole about unloading it. She didn't doubt for a minute that he'd contact his friend in Canada. Especially now that she knew for certain he was fooling around on Maggie, and Maggie was the one who had the money.

It was amazing what some of those old, klutzy cars were worth. Two, three times more than what her Corvette cost.

Her goody-goody routine was a pain at times, but it was working better than she'd planned. For now she couldn't afford to make any questionable moves, but when the time was right, she'd approach Carl Anderson. If Peter Pan and Pollyanna would make up their minds about when they were going to visit Madame Zero, she could plan to make her move then.

Unloading her private stock wasn't a problem, she hadn't spent years listening to cocktail conversations as she played waitress all these years for nothing. She had a list of people who had no qualms about accepting merchandise that was obtained through questionable means. She had to organize a schedule. Carl was an essential risk. She knew she could get him interested, but convincing him she was serious was going to be harder. Once she got him hooked, then she'd work out a schedule. She had to have a definite schedule to work with, know when she could start redirecting the quality merchandise into the damaged goods areas. Timing was essential. It was everything. She wished she could do something today. Right now there was a sizable backlog of damaged merchandise. There were furniture pieces that wouldn't be hunted for if they were lost. She had to calculate what each piece weighed, how much space it would take up and what the capacity of a moving van was. How many would they need? They couldn't go back and forth five or six times. It was too much activity and it would draw someone's attention.

A broad grin buried her cheeks into dimples. Necessity may have been the father of invention, but boredom was the instigator of brilliant improvisation.

Her parents talked about going to New York in June, sometime after her birthday. Convincing them to go by themselves shouldn't take too much effort. She would insist they needed time alone. They could have a second honeymoon and leave her home with Andy. They'd agree—if they knew Jake would baby-sit her and Andy. That was perfect; Andy would provide the ideal distraction for Jake.

CHAPTER TWENTY-NINE

PAUL AND KAREN HAD BOTH BEEN TRYING TO COAX LESLIE INTO COMING TO New York with them to see Dina and her family since last summer. They gave up trying to convince her when she took them by complete surprise by suggesting that the two of them go to New York alone and have a second honeymoon. Leslie challenged Paul by asking him to trust her enough to take care of the business and Andy—with Uncle Jake's help, of course. Paul had little doubt that Leslie could handle things, but he was still not too keen on the idea, until Jake took him aside and assured him everything would be fine. He and Phil would watch over them without crowding Leslie. But the true deciding factor was Karen. She was extremely touched by Leslie's offer and positively thrilled at the idea of the two of them getting away together. They made arrangements to leave on June 10, promising that when they got back, they would all celebrate Leslie's birthday. Andy didn't mind waiting to meet his aunt and uncle, and cousin Ben. He was happy about staying home and spending time with Uncle Jake. He knew Leslie didn't like Jake very much, but he always had a good time with Jake and his Uncle Phil.

* * *

Having to listen to her parents carry on about the big reunion with Madame Zero was becoming intolerable for Leslie. She was barely able to suppress her annoyance, refraining from letting them know how ridiculous they were behaving. Concentrating on her own objectives is what saved her. It was then she realized how completely and utterly distracted they were. How could the timing be more perfect? Playing the part of little Miss Straight and Narrow must completely have dulled her senses. She laughed out loud over that preposterous idea. A wide grin cracked her somber face and she got into her 'vette and turned it toward the Anderson Resort.

She parked her car at the end of the lot. Carl was not a challenge to pick out in a crowd. It was too early for suntanned tourists, and this time of year he was practically fuchsia.

He was down at the lake, working on some outboard motor and didn't seem happy. He never did.

She stood beside her car for a few minutes to make sure he was alone. She thought about how men who were poverty stricken in the smarts department oftentimes were reasonably handy with their hands.

Carl had the feeling someone was staring at him. He looked up and his heart stopped. He quickly dropped his head back down to the motor, but not before he realized it wasn't her, it was her kid. For a split second he was going to walk away, then changed his mind. This was *his* place, why should he run off? He felt his stomach knot and forced himself to concentrate on the motor. Why was it that every damn one of the Dmitris had the same effect on him? Why didn't they all move east, go live with the bitch?

"Hi, Mr. Anderson. Peter around?"

He refused to look up at her, hoping she'd take the hint and scram. What was she coming around for anyway? She knew damn well Pete was working on some construction site.

He grunted but didn't look up. "You see him around?"

His discomfort amused her. She was used to boys being dopey and awkward around her, and dirty old men who were thinking things they shouldn't, but cranky old Carl? "Oh, that's right. I forgot he was working today. Say, you and Martha must be very proud of him, getting that scholarship and all. He'll be going to college in September, won't he?"

Carl continued to work on the motor without answering, hoping she'd get disgusted and disappear.

"Mr. Anderson? I was hoping you could spare me a few minutes of your valuable time, to listen to something really important to both of us."

He brought unfriendly eyes up slowly, and in an instant he knew he'd never mistake the daughter for the mother again. He saw something in her eyes that the mother didn't have. Something mean and sly.

"Say what you have to say and get it over with, I don't have time to waste."

"Believe me, my time is valuable too. But if you don't hear me out, we'll both regret it."

Something in her tone kept him from turning away. He shrugged. "Say it and make it short."

She glanced over both shoulders. There wasn't a soul within two hundred feet of them.

"Okay, I'll be frank. I know you could use some cash and I know how you can get about sixty thousand dollars. Easy."

"I think you better take yourself back up that hill, get back in your fancy red bucket of bolts and ride the hell outta here."

The lack of congeniality didn't discourage her, because not only did she spot a glimmer of curiosity, she saw greed popping his brown eyes. There was skepticism too. He was easier to read than Andy.

"I'm not kidding around. I've thought this all out...been planning for years. I have a plan that will work, I've got the merchandise, got all the bases covered. I have contacts up in Canada, people who will receive the merchandise. What I need is someone who can supply the means of transporting it. That, and some muscle. I can't do it alone, I need your help. But if you can't use *sixty thousand dollars*, then there's no sense my wasting my time either." She smiled, turned toward her car and slowly walked away, counting off the seconds it would take for greed to eat away any skepticism coiled around his brain. She counted off five.

"Don't cost anything to listen."

While she proposed her scheme, she monitored his reactions by his eyes and mannerisms. She saw his suspicions wavering, watched his greed push his misgivings out of the way and she saw the noose around his thick neck. He was hooked.

He tried to see some sign in that too-pretty face that said it was all a con job. "Let's see if I understand what you're saying. You want me to help you steal from your old man?"

"Not steal, Mr. Anderson. Early possession. It'll all be mine someday anyhow, but I'm not a very patient person. I figure, why wait until my father retires or checks out. By that time there may not be anything left to inherit. Too much feast or famine in the lumber/construction business for me."

Being honest with himself, he readily admitted to himself that he was a selfish man. Still, he was shocked by her cold, barefaced greed. "What business isn't feast or famine these days?" He lost interest in the motor, she had his complete attention. "What about the guard dogs, the Dobermans?"

God, the man was slow! She swore his words fell asleep on his tongue—when his brain got them that far. If he *had* half a brain, he'd be stupid. "The Dobies are no problem. Who do you think feeds them? I have duplicate keys for everything. The back-up alarm system's no problem either, I know where they are and how to shut them off. I'm telling you, it'll be a breeze."

"Nothing in this world's a breeze, girl. You get older, you'll find that out soon enough. Don't you think for a minute that getting that stuff out is gonna be a *breeze*." He almost spit the words out. Another smart-ass Dmitri.

"I've done some preliminary experiments, and believe me it can be done." Now that Jim Olsen was over working with the construction crews and out of her hair, and Connie was no threat, she spent most of her time in the office, filing or filling out bills of lading, or keeping an eye out for Peter Anderson.

"Don't worry about my father, he won't suspect anything. Thinking gives him scabs. Must have a million pounds of scar tissue already, if you get my drift."

"Yeah, yeah. I get it." He grinned. "You don't think much of your old man do you?" This Dmitri he could like.

"You know the saying 'you can't choose your relatives.' Well? You in or out?" She was going to ask him what he thought and decided not to. What was the point?

He wasn't totally convinced this wasn't some kind of trick, but $60,000 sounded interesting all the same.

"Just when you planning on getting all that stuff out of there?"

"My parents are going out east to visit my aunt and uncle in June sometime. When I know the exact date, I'll let you know. In the meantime, you can set up the semis. We'll need three, two will work but it means having to make two trips and that's risky."

"Boy, ain't you something!" There was admiration in his voice and he was practically smiling. "You've been one mighty busy little girl." Seeing her up close like this made him reconsider. She wasn't a little girl, in her head or her body.

She smiled at him. "I don't believe in idle hands or idle minds. I have buyers for the precision tools and most of the construction equipment. As I was about to say, we'll need two, maybe three flatbed trailers and two of those car trailers, the kind car dealers use to haul—"

"Cars? What cars?"

"The cars my grandfather collected, the ones in the storage garage at the yard."

"Oh, no. You hold on right there. You *nuts?* Everyone knows whose cars those are, they'll be traced so fast your head will spin. Too damn risky."

Talent for Deception

She had him! Why else would he be concerned about traceable goods if he wasn't planning on going for it? "Mr. Anderson, just so you have a better idea of who you're working with, I know of at least three people who are very interested in the cars and they aren't worried in the least about having them traced. Those cars are as good as history. We'll need some tarps to cover them. We'll need four drivers. You can drive one of the semis, how much do you think we have to pay the other drivers?" She wondered if he had the vaguest idea of what those cars were worth. From the feelers she'd put out she figured she could get close to $200,000 for the cars alone. They were worth more but she couldn't sell them through normal channels, Carl was right about risk there. Whatever it was going to cost for the drivers she wanted to know up front. The fewer surprises the better.

"Now it's understood that you'll get $60,000. Not bad for one night's work, and the driver's will get $5,000 each van. Think they'll go along with that?"

"Might have to make it $10,000 for each." He'd offer $5,000, might have to go as high as $7,000. The rest he could pocket. George would take whatever a dozen cases of booze cost, but he didn't want to gum things up by them arguing about it.

"You sure that's the cheapest? Try to get them to agree to five; if they won't, don't quibble."

"I know they won't take less than ten."

"Okay. If it has to be, it has to. Soon as you know what they'll settle for, call me at the yard, disguise your voice and when I get on the line, say you're looking for a tall-case American clock. If they'll take nothing less than ten, say you want a clock ten feet high. If they'll take five, say the clock is for a child's room. I'll listen politely, then tell you that we don't make clocks. As soon as I know, definitely, when my parents are leaving for New York, I'll call the resort and ask for reservations for Ava Garfield, and I'll give you a date—that'll be the day they leave. It's best to move on a Saturday. No one works at

236

the yard Sundays. That should give us more than enough time to clear everything out and be long gone by Monday, when Jake Tanner and everyone will notice what's happened. Remember the name, Ava Garfield." Her mother would appreciate that. "You tell me you don't have any openings for that day and we'll have to call it off. And that, Mr. Anderson, would be a shame."

He didn't say a word. He didn't have to. Between his beady eyes and a grin that wasn't quite sinister but was far from innocent, he exuded a confidence she didn't like. Like maybe he had some plan of his own. Some kind of edge. It was important that Carl know she had the edge, not him. "My dad mentioned my Aunt Dina and her family will be coming here this fall. Been a long time since you two saw each other."

"Not near long enough."

"Oh? You sound less than anxious to see her. I thought you'd be glad." She ran her fingers through her hair and smiled. "I have to hand it to the two of you, that was some snow job you gave Martha, getting to take in your bundle of joy."

"What the hell you talking—"

"Mr. Anderson. I don't think I have to spell it out for you, or do I? *I know.* Have known for some time. I want to put your mind at ease, I know how to keep my mouth shut. I don't care if you and my aunt had a thing for each other." She could tell from the look on his face that he was going to lay some bullshit on her and decided to cut him off before he had a chance. "Don't bother denying it. If I may pat myself on the back, I pieced it all together through the years. Apparently my father has no clue about you. My mother was almost catatonic when I hinted you were Peter's father."

A smile began to curl his lips, thinking of the advice he heard long ago. You never go mountain climbing alone with someone who owes you money, and you don't lay all your cards on the table to anyone. Ever. Miss Wisenheimer didn't need to know he was the one with the ace up his sleeve. Not now, maybe not ever, if she played her hand straight. Feeling comfortable with that, he smiled back at her.

"Gotta hand it to you, you're one sharp, hard cookie."

"You can bank on it. And you know I'll keep my mouth shut. Seal it tight as a drum. It's an attribute that's more beneficial to you than me."

"Cut the high-class mumbo jumbo. You sound just like that aunt of yours. *And* your grandmother. Since we're going to be partners, we ought to start off on the right foot. For your information, I wasn't the only one Peter's mother futzed around with, but I'm the one took him in. As a favor to your granddaddy. Don't think you know the whole story. But 'nuff said. We're partners, and gotta trust each other."

"I agree. If my father knew, I'd be out in the cold on my ass. So don't worry about me. I need the money worse than you do—I want out of this burg."

"Just don't try anything cute. If I get caught, *we're* caught—get it?

"I've got it."

"That old man of yours ain't any different than that grandfather of yours. Neither of them take kindly to disloyalty among family."

"Tell me about it. Cut from the same cloth and all that bullshit. Family first, above all."

"Yeah, yeah. I heard the story. Now you better get out of here before someone wonders what we got to talk about for so long."

"Why, Mr. Anderson. Peter is what we're talking about—if anyone asks."

He watched her march back to her car, thinking she sashayed more than walked.

She wasn't back inside her car a second and had the radio turned up so loud he was sure they could hear it across the lake. If that wasn't enough to draw attention to herself, she peeled out of the parking lot like she was at some drag strip.

Girl was dippy, but she had gumption, he had to give her that.

238

That didn't mean he trusted her further than he could spit with his mouth closed. It was too bad Mike Dmitri wasn't around to see her. Hear his granddaughter talk about her scheme to stick it to his son, and steal his precious cars.

Punk had the world by the ass, and it wasn't enough. She wanted more. For the first time in ages, his stomach felt good. Things were on the upswing. A *definite* upswing.

Out on the highway, Leslie started singing along with a group claiming not to give a damn about greenback dollars, wanted to spend it fast. She knew how they felt. Everything was going to work just peachy dandy. Carl had a brain like a spider and the ethics of a snake. A man after her own heart.

She was almost home before she thought to check the gas gauge, moaned when she saw it was nearly empty. She swore, then made a U-turn and headed for town.

It was a pleasant surprise to see the new Sinclair station was open for business earlier than expected, which meant she didn't have to drive all the way into town. Traffic was getting worse every year with all the tourists and summer residents. The little burg was being inundated with progress. Whenever Peter Pan and Pollyanna got into their nostalgia thing they talked about how Main Street consisted of three blocks in their day, and how people had to step out into the street to pass each other because the sidewalks (made of bricks) were so narrow. How, back in their day, there was only a drugstore, small grocery/dry goods store, post office, a gas station and two restaurants. Which were still there.

Big time progress had struck and now there were four service stations, two hardware stores, two supermarkets, an A&W, and the drugstore was expanded to include a gift shop, without giving up the soda fountain and Rock-o-la jukebox. The Twin Cities didn't have to hold its breath worrying about any competition from Hid'n Oaks, that was for sure.

Talent for Deception

As soon as she pulled up to the pump, a dinky little guy wearing a badge that said "Dick Williams, Manager" came out of the office and introduced himself. She nodded politely, asked him to fill it up and got out of the car to take a closer look at the mechanic working on a car in the first stall. There was an Irish Setter lying in the shade, disinterested in anything that wasn't in his direct line of vision. When she stepped into it, the dog didn't lift its head, just shifted his eyes.

She looked inside the garage at the mechanic. The dog still didn't move, but it wagged its tail. She wanted to ask if the dog's name was Peppy or Tiger, but didn't.

"Tony" was embroidered on the pocket flap of his shirt. Six feet she guessed, and with a waist most girls would envy. Most of the girls she knew. His shoulders and arms were having a battle with the seams of his shirt. From the stress in his pants, things were a mite confining there too. His hair was thick and dark, and when he looked up, she noticed he had gray eyes.

To refresh her memory, she strolled back over to her car to look at the manager's shirt again. Williams.

"Mr. Williams? Can you fit me in for a tune-up?"

"You bet, we'll get you set in no time." He yelled over to the body beautiful. "Tony! That's my son over there."

He walked halfway to the stall and the two of them exchanged a few words. The body looked over at her and smiled. His teeth were gorgeous too.

"Tony will take care of you soon's he finishes with the oil change on the Ford."

Tony assured her he didn't mind her looking over his shoulder or asking what he was doing. He thought it was good for girls, women, to learn something about the cars they drove.

In half an hour, she learned more than she wanted to. The

Williams family consisted of five—mom and pop, Tony and two sisters who were married and still lived in some hick town in Indiana that Tony and his parents had left behind. Tony enlisted right after he graduated from high school, served two years in Vietnam and was presently taking night courses in electronics and computer programming.

He was twenty-three years old, and had a voice that must have been born in a cellar.

She noticed he was checking her over every bit as much as she was looking him over. With a slight blush, she bragged about what a wonderful family she had—a cute-as-a-button brother whom she loved like crazy, a mother who was so young looking, so young at heart, they were like sisters, and looked it too. Her father was a master craftsman whom she adored with all her heart. Then she confided she had just recently turned eighteen.

If it hadn't been for Tony's father, Dick, she would have liked to stick around for a while after he finished with her car. But Dickie boy's incessant comedic interruptions were too much. She came close to telling him that he reminded her of those washed-up comics leftover from vaudeville who were forever popping up on TV shows.

She didn't need any more time, she had accomplished everything she wanted already. He had her phone number, and he promised to call.

Tony didn't know it, but he was going to be seeing her exclusively. And he was destined to be her first lover. He was perfect. Not some stumbly-fumbly boy. A man.

There were certain things in life that one had to contend with. Playing the boring, goody-two-shoes role during the getting to know the family routine was one of them. To some it was a relatively small price to pay, but the older she got the lower her tolerance level was.

The only real fly in the proverbial ointment was her parents. If she could stall until they left for New York, Tony wouldn't find out she was not quite seventeen, not eighteen. By the time they came back, he wouldn't care how old she was. She was going to be seventeen in less than a week anyway.

CHAPTER THIRTY

TWO MIDDLE-AGED COUPLES WERE SIGNING IN AT THE DESK AND CARL WAS just about to hand them their cabin keys when Peter walked in.

"Guess we're lucky you had an opening, being a Saturday. Late afternoon at that."

"You got the last two cabins available for the weekend." Carl came around to their side of the desk. "Kid here will get you a bucket of minnows and the trolling motor." He turned to Peter. "Go down to the shed, get the bait, put everything in boat six."

"Uh, thanks sonny. Soon as we get settled in we'll be coming down to the lake. Boat six you said?"

"That's what I said." Carl waited until they were all out the door before pulling the office keys out of his pocket and handing them over to Peter.

"About time you got your ass down here. Marth should be down at ten. Tell her to lock things up at twelve. Did you pack all my fishing gear in the truck?"

"Everything's in the back, including your plasma."

Carl's eyes narrowed. "Don't be a wisenheimer. I'm not drinking it while I'm driving, so shut your mouth."

"Alcohol's bad for you."

"Is that so, wise guy? Like your mouth is for you?" He yelled back over his shoulder as he walked away, "Anyone asks, I'm up in Canada fishing around Lake of the Woods and won't be back for three, four days."

Peter waited for him to pull out of the lot before he went down to the shed for the bait, trying to remember a time when Carl *asked* him to do something, or thanked him afterwards. Carl got his kicks ordering him around, but never in front of Martha.

In his opinion Carl was, plain and simple, an asshole and he wished Carl would stay up in Canada. If Carl drowned up there, that would be fine with him.

He and Martha would get by all right without Carl. In fact, he personally would do a lot better without Carl around. It was getting so bad that at times he felt like a time bomb jammed with all kinds of confusing pressures, ready to explode whenever Carl got on his case and laid his threats on him.

One threat was totally unnecessary—the one about if he ever knocked up a girl, Carl would wring his bastard neck, or knock his goddamn block off.

The next time Carl threatened him about getting a girl pregnant, he was going to tell Carl off. Let Carl know that he would never get any girl in trouble because he wouldn't risk putting another bastard on this earth to wind up living with a son of a bitch like him.

And Carl could take his advice about running off to Canada to avoid the draft and shove it. To hell with Carl. If the war was still on, he was going. Or he might think about taking a deferment. Maybe. What he was going to do for sure was change his last name.

The phone rang. It was Martha, to tell him she'd be down to relieve him at nine-thirty.

"No, don't. Why don't you stay in tonight. I'm not doing anything but going for a run later. I'll lock up."

"You sure? You don't have something you want to do?"

"I don't. You take it easy tonight, Mom. Gonna be a busy one tomorrow. Sundays always are."

"I am kind of pooped tonight. Thank you. Gosh, I wonder if Paul and Karen made it to New York okay."

"I'm sure they did."

"Hope so. There's a snack for you in the refrigerator. Good night, sweetie."

"Thanks. I might be hungry when I get back from my run. Good night, Mom."

He preferred running at night; he slept better. Running was his remedy for getting anger and frustration out of his system. Tonight he was going to take his alternate route; it would be a good twelve-mile run from the resort to the lumberyard and back.

* * *

It was twelve-thirty by the time Peter locked the front door of the resort office.

The night air was sweet and dry. It'd been hot and sunny all day, most of which he had spent working on one of Jake's model home sites. A good run would help get his circulation flowing after sitting drawing and reading law books.

He took the back road, starting off at a lazy pace, then lengthened his strides into an easy but faster gait.

When he got to the turnoff to the lumberyard, there were construction horses blocking the road. Funny, he didn't see them earlier when he left the yard after work. He jogged over to the shoulder of the road. When he realized he was running alongside the yard fence, he veered slightly to the left of it as a precaution.

He was getting closer to the gate, thinking it was unusual for the Dobies not to be somewhere in sight by now. Nonetheless, he kept his distance from the fence. They had lured him into a false sense of security before. He swore they got their jollies by laying for him, waiting for him to relax, then coming out of nowhere to charge the fence and scare the hell out of him. They'd get kind of a smug look, like they were laughing inside.

Talent for Deception

A loud, heavy thud drew his attention over to the loading platform and he stopped to look. Darkness absorbed the halos of lights, giving things a purplish, hazy look.

Someone was on a forklift, loading some heavy equipment onto a truck. There were three trucks. He thought it was odd for them to be loading all this stuff so late at night.

Peter started to turn away to head back to the resort when the horses in the road came to mind. There wasn't any road construction going on. He turned back just as the man on the forklift moved inside the circle of light. It couldn't be anyone else—there was no mistaking it was Carl. A few seconds later, Leslie Dmitri joined him on the platform.

This he found very curious. He walked up to the fence, getting so close his nose was touching the steel. He was fairly sure caution was not necessary. If Carl and the other men were in there moving around so freely, the Dobies had to be locked up.

He watched for a few minutes and then looked for a spot where he could get a better view. He moved along the fence then tripped on something. It was a girl's bike.

Someone was running toward him. Had they heard him? There was barely time to do anything but duck behind the bushes.

Leslie stopped when she got to the gates and swung them open. Carl hopped up into one of the trucks, backed it away from the platform, swung it around and started it toward the gate. There was another truck close behind him, driven by Carl's drinking buddy. There was another truck or trailer with a huge canvas cover over it. He didn't recognize the driver.

He knew what was under the canvas cover, however. *Mike Dmitri's car collection.*

The trucks passed through the gates and headed north. Leslie ran back to the office and let the dogs out and headed back toward him. He watched the dogs wobble around and then lie down on the ground. They acted as if they were *drunk*.

246

Leslie pulled out a hose and washed the road down all the way to the gate. When she finished, she came up to the gate with a large wire cutter. Even with the gloves on, it only took her a minute or two to cut through the chain.

"Could have done it quicker without the gloves."

Her sharp intake of breath made him jump.

"What the hell are you doing skulking around? Scared me half to death."

"I'm out for a run. Important question is, what are you doing out here this time in the morning?"

She gave him what he supposed was meant to be an imperious look. "What does it look like I'm doing, airhead? I'm locking up Dmitri property. This *is* Dmitri property, so buzz off."

"Lock up? Funny way to lock up—by cutting the chain. Why lock up anyway? It's too late—the horses, as they say, are out of the barn. You've already ripped your father off, haven't you?"

"Listen, you simpleton, this is my property. I work here, so what's your problem?"

"I've been here a while. Where are they taking all that construction equipment and the cars?"

"Not that it's any of your business, they're on their way to an auction. My dad's going to buy new stuff."

"Is that right? What about your grandfather's cars?"

"Fire sale, you ditz. Guy called, wanted delivery on it all tonight. Carl, *your dad,* was kind enough to do us a favor—"

"Favor? Why isn't Phil or Jake taking care of it? Jake know about this?"

"What are you, a junior James Bond? Forget it, we don't need Eliot Ness out here either. It's family business."

"Knock it off, Leslie. Carl isn't kind enough to do anyone a favor. How about if we call Jake, or your parents in New York—"

"What for? You stupid, stupid jerk! How much weight do think your words carry? My father refuses to acknowledge that you exist, you pathetic knob, you're an *embarrassment*."

"Let's go to your place—Jake Tanner is baby-sitting you and Andy, isn't he?"

"You're so dense. Christ! Don't you get it? You're my Aunt Dina's big bad boo-boo. My Aunt Dina *is your mother*. What do you care if someone rips off the brother of the mother who pawned you off?"

"*What? You…you're lying!* You're full of shit."

"Am I? So don't believe me, it's no skin off my nose. You want to call my father? Go ahead. Make a fool out of yourself. Do yourself a favor, forget what you think you saw. Forget you were even out here. Your father won't like it if you make waves." She almost felt sorry for the big goof, standing there, looking like someone kicked him in the stomach. Her lack of patience saved her from being a sap, she shrugged her shoulders, brushed past him to retrieve her bike and swung her leg over the seat.

"Carl is not my father."

"Oh, that's right. He's your adoptive father. Well, been nice bumping into you, but I have to get cutting, see you around, *cuz*." She gave the bike a push and began pedaling away, stopped and over her shoulder yelled back at him, "Hey, cuz, when your da-da gets home, why don't you sit down and have a chat with him?"

"Go to hell."

"I'm going there. It's called the Dmitri Place. See ya 'round, cuz." She was sorry she didn't drive over in her car, but she'd reasoned the bike was quieter, and Sherlock Tanner would have heard her 'vette.

Leslie disappeared into the night while Peter stood on same spot, dazed. He began walking, not sure where he was headed. His mind was becoming a battleground he couldn't escape. He thought about all the years he couldn't figure out why Paul Dmitri was so aloof or why Mrs. Dmitri was so uptight around him. Now he understood. Suppressed animosity. That's what it was. Like it was his fault for being born. A rush of past conversations came at him. Martha and the letters from *her*. And him sitting beside her listening to Martha while she read bits and pieces of them to him. He felt betrayed. Martha had to have known all along who his mother was and kept the truth from him. Never said a word. She had no right to do that. How could she have done that to him all these years? His heart was trying to tell him that Martha did it out of love. His head denied it.

He walked along the shoulder of the road kicking at any stone in his path, thinking what a goddamn fool he'd been all these years, moping for his mother, waiting for her to come rescue him. Trying to imagine what it would be like being held and kissed by her. *Loved by her*. For once in his rotten life, Carl had it right, *she* was a bitch. And he was one dumb sucker.

What he'd like to do is get on a plane and go to the Catskills, and in front of everybody say, "Hi, Mom. Take a look at me, I did all right without you. To hell with you."

By the time he got to the house his head felt as though it had been rolling down a bowling alley. He was too tired to retrieve the anger that propelled him back to the resort in record time to confront Martha.

The first thing he heard when he got inside the house was Martha's snoring. It was then he felt like crying. He'd been so involved with how he felt, he hadn't given much thought about Martha's feelings. Did she really know? He truly didn't want to believe she did. He gulped down two aspirins and sat down at the kitchen table. Martha's snoring made him long to lie down, let his head rest on a soft pillow.

He laid down but his eyelids refused to close. The air the breeze brought in through the window was heavy and damp, clingy. Frogs were croaking away, then some crickets started their own symphony. He was tired. Tired of being told what to do and when. He didn't want to think about all the times Martha told him how nice Dina

Dmitri Coleman was. How beautiful she was, inside and out. Did Dina ever in her goddamn selfish life think about him?

Or was that the real reason she wrote to Martha—to keep tabs on him? Did she care? He didn't! The hell with her! And Martha too.

The ticking of the clock on his nightstand grew further and further away as his mind drifted off into space, then fell into a black pool of images.

When he awoke, he couldn't believe it was two o'clock in the afternoon. He'd slept for ten hours! The house was quiet. Martha had to be down in the office. He jumped out of bed and rushed into the bathroom to take a shower.

There was a note from Martha stuck to the door of the refrigerator, saying she was down at the office, and there were cinnamon rolls on the counter and the coffee was all set to brew.

He didn't think he was hungry, but the rolls smelled and looked good. He switched on the coffee and grabbed the smallest roll. By the time the coffee was done, he decided to have another roll.

Carl pulled up alongside the house just as he was pouring himself another cup of coffee.

All he did was take one look at him, check his watch and mumble something about lazy and sleeping late. When Peter seemed to be ignoring him, Carl came right out and asked, "You just getting up?"

"I thought you were going to be gone for a few days, fishing." Peter smiled to himself, knowing Carl didn't know if Martha was home or not. If Carl knew she wasn't around he would have asked if he just hauled his lazy ass out of bed. Carl was a careful man when Martha was around.

"Did a little. Fish weren't biting so I came home. What're you giving me the third degree for?" He never planned to drive a truckload of stolen anything across no foreign border. Eddie could double back and pick up the truck Carl parked at the wayside and drive it over into Canada. Eddie was getting paid enough to take chances.

Eddie didn't have a business at risk if something went wrong. He looked around and when he saw the note Martha left on the refrigerator, he knew they were alone. "I asked you a question, knothead. Did you just get your ass out of bed?"

"Yeah."

Carl's eyes narrowed. There were times he wasn't sure if the punk was being a wise guy or not. Right now, he didn't care. He was beat, dead on his feet. The kid and Marth would have to handle things today.

"Don't you think it's about time you move your ass down to the office, take care of business. I'm going to bed, soon as I have a beer to relax."

He took a bottle of beer out of the refrigerator then motioned to Peter. "Hand me the bottle of brandy." Might as well make it boilermakers, they'd help him relax faster. Driving trucks was hard work, and he had to admit he wasn't no kid anymore.

He poured out a triple shot of brandy, threw it down and took a long swig of the beer. "Christ, I'm beat."

Peter sat watching him, despising him more and more. Sober, Carl didn't have much to say, but when he was drinking, he liked having someone around to listen to him. Without interruptions or any kind of feedback.

Carl poured himself another brandy, cutting it down to a double. "Hand me another beer. Jee-zus, I'm beat. Been fishing all night." The kid would tell Marth and then he wouldn't have to go through any big spiels about where he was. She was getting to be a pain in the ass in her old age with all her questions. Wasn't like that when she was younger. He yawned, thinking things had gone smoother than he hoped. Made the trip in less than ten hours, not bad.

Peter got up from the table. "Where are the fish, I'll clean them."

Was the kid being a wise guy? He had a tone in his voice Carl

251

didn't like. "Ain't any. Told you, the bastards weren't biting. Is there something on your mind, punk?"

"I was out for an early morning run, ended up out at the lumberyard."

Carl was just emptying his second beer. He pulled the bottle back so fast he almost spilled the remaining drop.

"I saw you out there, you and Leslie and those friends of yours." Before Peter had any idea it was coming, it arrived. Carl smacked him with an open hand, pinned him against the wall, then grabbed hold of his shirt collar and twisted it tight around his throat.

"Now you *tell* me, just what you *think* you saw."

Peter tried shoving Carl away. He couldn't breathe. Carl relaxed his hold slightly.

"Let...go...and I'll...tell..." Carl released him.

Peter gasped for air and rubbed his throat, playing for time. Trying to decide if this was the time to see if he could take Carl, if he had the guts, or was he really chicken after all?

"I'm waiting. I ain't got all day." Carl could feel the beads of sweat forming on his forehead and neck.

"I saw you...all of you, loading up the trucks. Talked to Leslie..."

Carl smacked him alongside the head. He was about to hit him again but caught himself. It wasn't smart to leave marks; Marth would raise holy hell. "Talked to Leslie, huh? I'm telling you boy, just so you know where you stand, or should be standing. *I'm your ole man*. Get it? Understand what I'm telling you? Me and you are blood."

Peter's body raged with denial, he went wild and charged at Carl. *"You're a liar!"*

Carl waited for him to get close enough, let him step into it. He hit him in the stomach, stopped him dead, then stepped away to let him slump to the floor. Carl bent over, grabbed him by the shoulders and lifted him up.

"Don't you ever call me a liar. You don't like it, huh? Well, it's the truth. I'm your father."

"You? You can't be. Leslie told me her aunt is my mother. *She* wouldn't have anything to do with you!"

Carl's stomach felt like a pincushion, pitted with needles. He cupped it with his hands, afraid to rub it, cradling it.

So she could keep her goddamn mouth shut! Said she was good at keeping secrets. He should have known better than to trust her. They were all out to ruin him. All the damn Dmitris. He needed time to think. Marth could come walking through the door any minute.

"You think she wouldn't have anything to do with me? You believe all that hogwash Marth's been filling your head with? Well Marth don't know nothing. That *mother* of yours fooled a lot of people. She was a slut. I wasn't the only one had a go at her, only with me it was just the one time. Came onto me when I was drunk."

"Shut up! Just shut the hell up!"

"Tell me, who took care of you all these years? She ever been around to see you? She ever send you a birthday card, or a Christmas present?" Christ! He had to think. No, act.

What the hell was he gonna tell the punk? He had to come up with something and it had to be quick. Something that would shut the kid's mouth. He pushed the brandy bottle away. He felt cornered, just like he did when he was around the Dmitris. Trying desperately to keep panic out of his voice he spoke as quietly as he knew how.

"Well, Mr. Lawyer-man, look at the facts. Old Mike Dmitri paid me to take you off their hands. Why do you think she left town and never looked back?"

"She keeps in touch with…Martha." He resented Carl's judging Dina and was angry with himself for coming to her defense. Why, he asked himself, am I making excuses for her?

"Sure she writes to Marth, the only one, by the way, who was a mother to you. It'd kill Marth if she knew anything about any of this.

TALENT FOR DECEPTION

Listen, son, I took you in, risked having Marth find out. I know I been rough on you at times, but it was for your own good. I didn't want to spoil you, have you get the idea life was some picnic. You gotta be tough to survive, think how tough it's been on me. How do you think I felt all these years not being able to tell you. Fact is, I'm glad that you know. I planned on telling you when you were older. Haven't me and Marth been good to you? Marth's the only real mother you ever had. You think *she*, the bitch, cares anything about you?"

Peter was having difficulty standing, much less clearing his head enough to answer his own question: What was really happening here? Was Carl, who'd made his life miserable ever since he could remember, expecting him to feel some kind of *loyalty* toward him? To feel sorry for *him?* Peter had spent most of his life despising this man. He wasn't about to form any kind of alliance with him. Father? The thought turned his stomach. Deep in his gut he knew it was true. Standing inches away from Carl he thought about spitting in his face.

Instead, he started to laugh. At Carl, and at himself. At all the fantasies he made up about his parents. He stopped laughing when he saw the ugliness in Carl's face. He was well acquainted with what was in it. Hate and fear. With Carl, fear was more dangerous.

Carl stood watching him, sweat pouring out of him, like a man in a corner watching his whole life going down the drain.

They stood staring at one another, neither moving, nor uttering a sound.

Carl wanted to flatten the punk. Put some fear back into his smartass face. Instead, he had to stand like he did that time with Dina Dmitri, acting nice and polite. It was bullshit. He knew what he had to do.

But for now, he had to try to convince the kid he had obligations. He had to give him that much, the kid always met his obligations. He hiked up his pants, walked over to the refrigerator and took out another bottle of cold beer.

254

Peter's eyes never left him. "You slimy creep! You *raped* her! *Didn't* you?"

"What? Know what you are? Ungrateful. Disrespectful and ungrateful. Making these crazy accusations. And you wanting to be a lawyer. I ought to break your face—"

"I know *you.* You think it went over my head all these years? The filthy way you talk about women, the way you act when you think no one's watching or Martha isn't around?"

"Don't talk like a fool. Grow up. Men who don't look and talk about women ain't healthy. Use your head, you think that I'd be dumb enough to try anything like that? Ole man Dmitri would've had me hung—if I'd been rotten enough to try something like that. It cuts me to the quick having my own son say something like that. And here, all the time, I've been putting away some dough for you. Wanted to surprise you when you went off to college. Now that you know you're my kid, it's only right that you know you can count on me. You forget about these wild accusations and everything will be all right—"

Before Peter could tell him to keep the money, use it as payback, Martha walked in with an armload of fish. "Oh, Carl. You're back. I hope you didn't catch many fish, man in cabin three gave me these, he caught more than he and his wife can eat. Peter, clean these for me will you please? We'll have them for dinner."

"Nice looking walleyes, eh Pete?" Carl poked Peter's arm.

Peter took the fish and mumbled "Yes," and went out back of the house to clean them. With the scaling board just outside the kitchen window, he couldn't help but hear them talk. He knew it and he knew Carl knew it.

"Me and the boy were having a nice talk. Told him I was going to help him out with his expenses at college. I've been setting money aside for a few years now. Even you didn't know that, did you?"

Tears formed in Martha's eyes and she clasped her hands. "Oh,

Talent for Deception

Carl. That's *wonderful*. I had no idea." She went to her husband and put her arms around him and whispered into his neck. "You're doing a good thing, Carl. Peter is such a good boy. He deserves his chance to go after what he wants. I know he's been fretting over that scholarship…"

He patted her head. "Kid's worked hard, he's got it coming."

She picked up the empty beer bottles and put them in the case on the floor. "I'm so glad you're going to do this. You catch many fish? You weren't gone very long."

"Didn't get a nibble. But I'm thinking of going up to Lake of the Woods. Yeah, I'm going to call Red and George see if they want to go up to Lake of the Woods and try our luck up there. Things are slow around here…you and Pete can handle things for a few days, can't you?"

"Sure, honey. Do you good to get away for a few days. You go ahead and go on up to Canada, relax and enjoy yourself. How long you plan on staying?"

"Week, maybe." He had to make sure that as far as Marth was concerned, he wasn't going anywhere near Canada. "And we'll be setting up camp and fishing stateside. We won't be going any further than Minnesota." He tried to look like it wasn't important for her to know that. "Say, I got an idea. Why don't you go and get changed and I'll take you over to the Norseman's for supper. Pete can take care of things here. Gonna be a short day for me anyhow." He looked over at the window and waited for Peter to look up. "You don't mind taking care of things around here, do you *son?*"

Martha couldn't believe her ears. It was the first time ever she'd heard Carl call Peter 'son.' There were tears in her eyes as she looked from one to the other.

"Sure, *Dad*, go ahead." He handed the fish to Carl through the window, gave him a little salute then went down to the office.

While Carl waited for Martha to wash up and change clothes, he sat at the table trying to put together a plan. There wasn't much time. The big reunion in the Catskills wasn't going to last more than a week. According to the last letter he read, Dina and her husband were talking about selling the place in the Catskills. He didn't even think of it before—that could mean that they planned on spending their summers here, or worse, moving here. If he could get rid of all of them at the same time, he'd be free. Who knows when he'd get another chance like this? Could he make it look like an accident? Accidents happen all the time. But it wouldn't have to be an accident. Papers always had something in them about New York and crime. Cops getting killed...*and their families*. If the place was blown to smithereens, everyone would think the cop was the target. Yeah. How unfortunate that the family happened to be there.

* * *

A young couple walked into the resort office, signed the register and took the key Peter laid on the desk. After they left, Peter looked out at the sky, thinking there wasn't much daylight left. The sun was already just above the horizon, its receding orange rays blinking off the brightwork of the cruisers and speedboats, like flashes of minuscule fireworks.

He went back to trying to figure out what he was going to do about Carl, trying to sort out his feelings toward Dina Dmitri Coleman. He didn't know if he hated her, or what he felt for her. Or for Martha. Right now he didn't care much for any of them. The three conspirators. The three of them had pretty much determined his life. The only one who cared was Martha. Or was she the only one?

CHAPTER THIRTY-ONE

MOST PEOPLE GRUMBLED WHEN MONDAY MORNING ROLLED IN. NOT PHIL Tanner. He looked forward to Mondays. He'd stop at the bakery at six and slip in the back door to pick up rolls and coffee for the gang at the yard. Everyone sat around gabbing and munching on the rolls before they started work.

This Monday morning, as soon as he got to the gate he knew something was wrong. First he noticed the dogs acting funny, like they were sick. They didn't come to greet him at the gate. Then he saw the chain and lock had been cut and were hanging on the ground. He swung the gate open and drove inside the yard. It took a while before he connected all the empty spaces to machinery that wasn't where it was supposed to be.

He left the rolls and coffee in his truck and ran into the office, then the stockroom. When he got to the pole barn, his stomach fell. He grabbed the phone hanging on the wall.

"Jake, get down to the yard, pronto."

The tightness in Phil's voice told Jake that something was very wrong and he didn't bother asking any questions. All he said was, "Be there as fast as I can."

"Don't make any stops on the way."

Standing with Phil on the loading dock, Jake shook his head. "Did you call the sheriff?"

"No, I wanted you here when I did. I didn't call Paul yet either."

Jake shook his head again. "Don't. What can he do? They'll be home in four days. We can handle things until then. Let's keep this as quiet as possible. You call the sheriff, I want to look around." He picked up two pairs of work gloves, tossed a pair to Phil and pulled on the other pair. "Before you do anything else, put the gloves on. What have you touched?"

"The gate and a couple of doorknobs. Oh, and the phone."

"Try not to move anything."

As Jake walked around the yard, he saw that someone had gone through the trouble of hosing away all the tire tracks.

* * *

Deep in the Canadian woods near Lake Simcoe, Carl and his friend Charlie sat around the campfire. Carl opened the bottle of Canadian Club and passed it to Charlie. Charlie didn't bother passing it back, which is what Carl planned. He started talking to Charlie about the good old days and soon they were laughing about those days, when they were young and tough. When they were punk kids with more guts than brains. When they started drinking at noon and didn't stop until dawn, when they laughed in the face of the grim reaper, and had more than their share of nooky every night.

It took the whole quart of Canadian Club to get Charlie drunk enough to be stupid, but sober enough to answer some casual questions, saving the important one for last.

"Charlie, you still got any of those sticks of dynamite you had around?"

"Yeah. Couple, three boxes, stored in the shed." Then he promptly passed out.

After he was sure Charlie was out, Carl checked the shed. Charlie was almost as good a carpenter as he was. The shed was well constructed and dry as a bone. Carl opened the satchel he'd brought along. He counted out five sticks and then, as an afterthought, counted out five more. Better too much than too little, he thought.

It was after ten by the time he had everything organized. Charlie was snoring loudly enough to wake everyone within ten miles of Lake Simcoe. To be safe, Carl waited half an hour extra to make sure Charlie was really as drunk as he seemed before he loaded up Charlie's car. Carl was tired and wanted to sleep for an hour himself. If he had one drink, he'd be giving Charlie competition in the snoring department. As he packed up the car he mumbled about how much it had cost him tonight. He liked to think it was worth it—especially the three hundred bucks he shelled out to charter a plane in International Falls. He had to make sure that anyone nosy enough to check up would think he was up in Lake of the Woods, not Lake Simcoe. Guy who flew him in needed the dough and he'd keep his mouth shut.

He crossed over into the States, stopped long enough to take a quick pee and splash water on his face, and then drove as far as he could. He pulled down a side road just outside Binghamton and settled in for the night.

CHAPTER THIRTY-TWO

PAUL TOOK THE BEER BEN OFFERED AND TOOK A LONG SWALLOW AS HE FOL-
lowed Ben out on the porch. They went outside and sat down on the
steps.

The difference in their ages was only a year, yet Ben couldn't help
but think of Paul as being six or eight years older. He had been prepared not to like his reclusive brother-in-law, but he did like Paul,
very much in fact. Physically, there was a strong resemblance
between Paul and Dina, and they shared some similar personality
traits, but Ben appreciated their differences. If Dina could read his
thoughts, she'd say he had a lot of nerve thinking Paul was too rigid
in his views on certain issues. Paul was more reserved than Dina,
played things closer to the vest than she did, if that were possible.
What Ben liked very much about Paul was he didn't hide how he felt
about Dina. He loved her very much and was obviously as glad as
she was that they had finally patched things up. Ben took a long
swallow of his beer wondering if they were as happy as he was about
it. The buried hatchet had put one heck of a radiant smile on Dina's
face. And he wanted it to stay there.

Paul took another swig of his beer. "It's nice here."

"Yeah. Times change. I'm glad we sold the place. I've loved it
here ever since I was about eight, nine years old. Originally these
were all farmlands. To make a go of it, many of the farmers ran
boardinghouses, some of which eventually became hotels. Years
back, they had strolling violinists, and tummelers went around enter-

taining guests, making them feel welcome, getting them involved."

"Like social directors."

"In a way, but more than that. Hard to explain. We had our share of a lot of different types of people mixing. Movie stars, theater people. Frank Sinatra was here. Danny Kaye, Red Buttons. I think Eddie Fisher got married up here and Rocky Marciano trained up here. Had our share of gangsters, too, but while they were here, they behaved themselves. They spread their dough around pretty freely." He could feel Paul staring at him. When he looked up at him, Paul was smiling.

"Thanks, Ben."

"For the little history?"

"Well, that too, but mostly for being so good for my sister. And your hospitality."

"Don't thank me for being good for Dina, the pleasure has been all mine, believe me. You know, the day we got married, I wanted to fly to Hid'n Oaks, bust your chops, then drag you back with me so you could be here for our wedding. I have to say, I didn't like you much."

"I can understand that."

"That's all in the past. I'm glad you and Dina squared away your differences. I don't mind admitting that I'd hate to have either of you pissed off at me."

"Well, I can't speak for my sister, but as for me, I take it hard when someone beats me at pool. You can ask my buddy, Jake, about that."

As he was saying it, a younger version of Ben joined them on the porch. "Did I hear someone mention pool?" Ben Jr. was already showing signs that he was going to be taller than his father. Like his father, Ben Jr. was outgoing but had a serious side Paul liked seeing in a young man. He was never too serious, however, to pass up a chance to have fun.

Ben felt it was only fair to warn his brother-in-law, "Paul, my advice is don't play with him unless you're as good as Masconi. My son is a born hustler. A pool shark."

"I may be a little rusty, but I'm sure I can beat a man a fourth my age."

"You're on, Uncle Paul."

Ben saw tears begin to form in Paul's eyes and looked away, not sure if Paul was moved by Ben Jr.'s easily given affection and acceptance of him, or if was it hearing himself being called "uncle" for the first time. Ben gave Paul a few seconds to recover, gave him a soft punch on his arm, followed by a shrug, and said, "Remember, I warned you." He put his arm around his brother-in-law's shoulder and walked him over to the doorway and stuck his head in.

"Would you ladies care to join us? We're going to run into town and have a big pool play-off."

Dina was shaking popcorn kernels into a pot and Karen was melting butter.

"No, you menfolk go on, we women are going to stuff ourselves with popcorn and watch *Casablanca.*"

Ben smiled. Making sure the women heard, he turned to Paul and asked, "Brother Paul, I ask you, are we not the luckiest menfolk on earth?"

"That we are. And we thank God for undeserved riches."

"Hey, speak for yourself." Paul gave his brother-in-law a nudge.

Ben Jr. pushed his way in between them. "Hey, if you two keep this brown-nosing up, they'll never let you go." He pulled his father and uncle out of the doorway and marched them down to the car.

Dina smiled, and Karen grinned back at her. "Nice that they get along so well. I'm so happy that we're here."

"Me, too. It's been wonderful. Good weather, good company, good food and wine. I haven't had such peace in a long, long time.

Next time you have to bring Les and Andy with you. We can take a trip to Jamaica or the Bahamas."

"Yes, that would be nice. Andy would have come but when Leslie offered to take care of him and the business we couldn't resist. Paul and I haven't had much time to ourselves lately. And why wait until next year—how about you and Ben bringing Ben Jr. out our way? Say sometime in late summer or fall?"

"Yes, I'd like that very much. I'll talk with Ben about it. If we're still awake when the guys get back, we'll figure out the best time."

"Good for us anytime…hey, the movie's starting."

Sometime in the early hours, Dina woke up with a pounding heart and a slight headache, covered with perspiration. She could still feel the shark circling her, the flat, black button eyes staring, pretending not to be interested. She sat up, then got out of bed very carefully, trying not to disturb Ben. He rolled over on his side and began snoring lightly.

She put on her robe and went downstairs to look for Paul's cigarettes. She had quit smoking when she found out she was pregnant. But she wanted a cup of coffee and needed a cigarette. The dream had unnerved her enough so that it didn't surprise her when she noticed her hand was trembling.

She picked up Paul's pack of cigarettes, pulled one out and grabbed his lighter. She poured out a cold cup of coffee that was left over from dinner. Then she remembered Ben's remark about Ben Jr. being a pool shark. That was probably why she had the dream after all these years! It must have lodged in the back of her mind. Suddenly she felt better.

Her mother had been right when she told her so many years ago that you can't lock liars or bad dreams out of your house.

Armed with cigarette and coffee, she went outside and sat on the

266

porch swing. She half hoped she'd have a coughing fit with her first drag to discourage her, but she didn't.

The moon wasn't full, and the sky wasn't without clouds, but there were a few thousand stars blinking. She was about to sit down on the top step when she noticed a car some twenty feet or so beyond the end of the driveway. It was either parked in the ditch or ended up there. Thinking that perhaps someone went off the road or had car trouble she decided to walk down and check it out.

She was thirty feet from the house when things exploded behind her and she flew through the air, along with all kinds of debris. Somewhere in her subconscious state she was aware of the car driving off, and then everything went black.

CHAPTER THIRTY-THREE

Since they'd begun dating, most of Tony's spare time belonged to Leslie. She was the most impossible chick he'd ever met. One minute she was seductive, the next she was flirting with someone else to make him jealous. Then she'd turn around and get all cool and detached. Aloof. She made him think of a book he'd read years ago. The main character called his girl a vixen. That was Leslie all right.

She was the most beautiful, demanding, fascinating girl he'd ever met. Sweet and childlike one minute, then a sharp-tongued witch the next. She tantalized him, then shunned him. Ticked him off, drove him up a wall. And he loved it, for the most part.

When they finally did make love, and he found out she was a virgin, he wasn't sure how he felt. First he felt guilty, then cocky, knowing he was her first. She was far from his first, but she was his first virgin.

Then the other shoe fell. He found out she wasn't eighteen like she'd said. Tony was convinced his life was over, or would be as soon as Paul Dmitri got back home and found out.

Paul's finding out wasn't the only thing that worried him. What judge was going to believe he didn't know how old she was? A spear of terror struck him in the middle of his skull, and he saw his dreams of having his own body shop turn into Technicolor shit with stereophonic sound provided by the explosion from Paul Dmitri's shotgun.

He tried several times to break off with Leslie, but it was useless. She was sexy and exciting. Gorgeous. He was nuts about her and knew there wasn't a guy in town who didn't want to be in his shorts. Breaking it off with her was impossible, so he made sure he always had three or four condoms with him at all times. He made Leslie swear she'd get birth control pills.

When it happened he wasn't sure, but one day it was in his head and he was thinking marriage wasn't really a bad idea. Life with Leslie wouldn't be dull. The thoughts turned to a plan of action. Tony had his mind made up. Soon as Paul and Karen Dmitri came back from New York, he was going to be up front, honest with them. Tell them how he felt. Ask for her hand in marriage. Parents liked being asked for their permission. They might like it well enough not to charge him with statutory rape.

Marriage wasn't a hasty decision. Not something easy to do. His parents had recently celebrated their twenty-seventh anniversary. They'd been through some financially tough times, but they'd hung on. They were happy. So were the Dmitris. His mom and pop seemed to like Leslie well enough. His mother always said the apple didn't fall far from the tree. If she was right, Leslie couldn't do better than be like her mother. Karen Dmitri was an all-around doll. What Leslie needed was maturity, to grow up a little more.

Leslie tossed the dirty towels down the laundry chute, placed fresh towels on the rack, checked the tissue holder to make sure the key was in place, and sat down on the window seat.

She was getting sick of having the warden around, but his decision not to notify her parents about the robbery until they got back home tomorrow worked out perfectly. She was glad now that she hadn't split when all hell broke loose after the big cheese's discovery. It would have led everyone to the same conclusion, that she had something to do with the robbery. But, so what? What if Peter Pan did find out about her part in it? What could he do, send her to prison? Not likely.

What did concern her was Jake's mentioning something about the possibility of having the feds in. She didn't much care for that at all. Didn't want to think about it. That was a decision for her father to make.

For one of the few times in her life, she didn't know what she wanted to do. Tony had to work all day so they weren't going out until he finished, after he took a shower and got all that filthy grease off of him.

Tony was somewhat of a disappointment. His aspirations were on a much lower level than her own. She had hoped he'd be more ambitious. Not that she didn't have enough for both of them, but that was a no-deal proposition. She wasn't going to knock herself out for someone whose highest goal in life was to be a grease monkey.

He was a hick at heart and always would be. Still, he was a handsome son of a bitch. True, matching wits with him was less taxing than daydreaming or playing Scrabble with Andy, but there was no denying he was the best thing around, and, since she had to stick around for at least another year or until she was eighteen, it would be fun to use her powers of persuasion to try to convince him to reconsider his career choices.

It would just blow his mind if he knew she was in a position to set him up in something far more lucrative than a damn two-bit garage shop. Maybe she would tell him, just to see the expression on his face. She knew Tony had never seen $200,000 at one time.

The shrill buzz of a speedboat drew her attention to the lake. Jake Tanner was pulling Andy on water skis and they were heading in toward the pier.

She rushed downstairs to make dinner for Andy and the warden. Phil was at some old men's thing, so he was out of the way. She wanted it to be special, something the scoutmaster liked. Men talked more freely with a stomach full of the food they liked. Jake could fill her in on how much he knew about the robbery investigation while digesting roast beef and mashed potatoes with gravy and green beans. The man could pile away food. As long as the TV was on, Andy would not interrupt them.

She didn't know if she should be relieved or not when Jake said no one knew much of anything yet. Was it a fact, or were they keeping something back? She insisted on making popcorn for everyone to eat while they watched TV.

Andy didn't last long. He was fast asleep before the first commercial break.

It took effort, but Jake watched her attempts at being provocative without laughing out loud. She pranced and swiveled, adjusted the color on the TV because it looked too orangey or it was too blurry. Every move was well-choreographed to aim her hot little buns in his direction. Then there were the subtle but strategic stretches so her sweater would ride up high enough to expose her rib cage.

Before it got to the point where he had to laugh, he decided to put an end to it.

"Knock it off, kiddo."

"Knock what off?"

"Your amateurish attempts to be seductive. You ought to be more careful about how you come across."

"Hah! Do you think I'm trying to seduce *you* of all people? Only thing macho about you is your aftershave."

"There you go again. You're such a flowery flatterer. You know, in my day we used to call girls who acted like you 'fast.'"

"In your day, snails were jets."

"Uh-huh. Look kiddo, tease entrapment games can get you into situations you can't control or walk away from. Takes a lot more than a training bra and big feet to fill Mommy's shoes."

She had to force herself not to look down at her feet. "My feet are *not* big, they're just right for my height. And it takes more than a jock-strap to be a man." She stood there giving him the full impact of her haughtiest look for a few seconds, then went over to shake Andy awake.

"C'mon, Andy. Time for bed."

Andy looked at Jake with a silent plea for intervention in his eyes. When it didn't come, he mumbled a good night and headed for the stairway.

Leslie paused to cast what she meant to be her best look of contempt at Jake, then slowly followed Andy up the stairs.

Jake kept the smirk inside, but shuddered when she looked down at him from the top of the stairs. "Good night, kids."

CHAPTER THIRTY-FOUR

THE RINGING OF THE PHONE STARTLED HIM AWAKE. ONCE HE WAS AWAKE, he wasn't sure it was the phone until it rang again. It was while he was picking up the phone that he realized he'd fallen asleep on the couch. He checked his watch: 4:00 a.m. Once it came into focus, he was wide awake. Who would be calling at 4:00 a.m.?

"Hello."

"Is this Philip Tanner?"

"No, this is Jake Tanner, Phil's nephew. Who is this?"

"This is Amanda Ryan, a friend of Dina Coleman's. Sorry to be calling you at this hour but it took a while to track down the phone number. Are Leslie and Andrew Dmitri there with you?"

"Yes. What is this about?"

"I'm afraid I have some bad news. There's been an explosion and at this time, the cause is undetermined. Four people were killed. Paul and Karen Dmitri were among the four."

"Who...else?" There was an awful feeling of fear building in his chest and he fought to keep his concentration centered so he would be able to comprehend what his mind was not going to want to hear.

The person on the other end took a long time to answer. When she did, she sounded like she was having trouble keeping her concentration as much as he was.

"Dina was the only survivor. As of now, she's in critical condition."

"The boy, Ben Jr..."

"Dead. And his father, too."

"Jesus."

For a long time, Jake sat in the living room staring at nothing, tears streaming down his face, thinking thoughts he didn't want inside his head. Sad thoughts, happy thoughts and ugly thoughts. Amanda Ryan told him she was calling from the hospital and would call if there were any changes in Dina's condition. She sounded like the type of person who wasn't intimidated by doctors, she'd make sure she got answers.

What he needed to do was pack a bag and get a flight to New York...Christ! What was he going to tell Leslie and Andy?

He punched in the numbers of his home phone.

"Phil? Can you get over to the Dmitri Place right away?"

"What's up?"

"Something bad. Real bad. Talk to you when you get here. Come in the back way, I'll be in the kitchen."

"Be right there."

For one of the few times in her life, Leslie felt numb, unsure of how she felt or how she should react. She never had to reflect on what was honestly in her heart. Remorse was something completely foreign to her, imagined or real. She thought what she was feeling was either shock, or some strange sense of loss. Why would someone want to kill four people? She wasn't sure if she should cry, or be brave for Andy, who was carrying on enough for both of them.

She had loved Pollyanna and Peter Pan in her own way. She only half understood what Phil and Jake were talking about. Jake was flying to New York, to make some arrangements and to see Dina.

* * *

On his way back home, Carl made it a point not to rehearse how he was going to act when he heard the terrible news about Dina and her family. He didn't buy or read a newspaper or listen to the radio.

He wanted to be natural, convincing. Unprepared.

When he stepped onto his porch, he heard Marth and the kid going round about something. It surprised him. Marth never argued with the kid. And the kid *never* gave her any lip. He decided to stay where he was and listen a while before letting them know he was back.

"I can't forbid you to go to New York to see Dina. But be reasonable, Peter. Stop and think. You can't just go barging into that hospital. She might be home by now. They might have protection around the house. You'll never get in. It wouldn't be right, it would be too much for her to deal with. Too painful."

"I don't want to cause her pain. I just want *to see her*. I want to know she's all right. I want to *be with her*. Let her know…"

Carl's stomach lurched, then fell into his shoes. Was she *alive*? The bitch! The goddamn lucky bitch!

He booted the door open and stepped inside. "What's going on here?" He had his tackle box in one hand and a case of beer in the other. He dropped his tackle box and put the beer on the table.

"We were talking about Dina."

"So? What about her?" His mouth was dry as hay.

"Oh, Carl! You haven't heard?"

"Heard a lot of things, what're you talking about?"

"Something awful's happened. Paul, Karen, Dina and her husband and son were bombed or something. Terrible. First the robbery, now this."

"Robbery, what robbery?" He half-expected the kid to horn in and when he didn't, Carl looked over at him. It took him by surprise—he'd never noticed before, the kid was tall, had to be close to six foot now.

Martha put her hand to her head, trying to think back. "I don't even know now, I'm so upset. The robbery happened while you were gone the last time. I can't remember now, was it four, five nights ago? Then this bomb thing just the other night."

"What happened with the bomb?"

"Someone set a bomb under their house or something, I'm not sure of all the details. It killed everyone except Dina. Jake called, said she's critical, but holding her own. He's catching a plane, leaving tomorrow morning."

The razor blades were chopping away in his gut again. What went wrong? He did everything right, sat and watched them through his binoculars. Retracing his steps, watching Paul, her husband and the kid go out, leaving the two of them watching some movie. Carl waited until the others got back and went to bed. Purposely waited nearly two hours after the lights went off before he crawled under the house and set up the dynamite and timer.

There was no way around it, the bitch had a four-leaf clover up her ass.

He began rubbing his stomach then stopped...the motion made the razor chopping worse. It was then he became aware that Peter was staring at him with a wise guy look on his face. Carl took his keys out of his pocket and tossed them over to him.

"Go get the stuff out of the trunk. I bought a couple things up in Canada for you two, pair of leather slippers for you and one of those quilts for you, Marth. And there's a cooler full of Canadian fish I caught up there. Stick 'em in the freezer." Cost him plenty, too, but it was worth it. Proof that he was in Canada—there were tags on the gifts.

He motioned with his chin after Peter went out. "What's with him?"

"He's upset, mixed-up. He knows about Dina. He won't tell me how, but he knows. He's hurting and he's angry about being lied to, and, somewhere in all that, he's worried about his *mother*."

Something about the way she said it didn't set right, made Carl think she had suspicions. But about what? Something. He'd have to ask her later. Right now, he had other problems on his mind.

278

Goddamn it to hell! What else could go wrong? The question made him nervous, made him feel like someone was sitting on his shoulder, listening to his thoughts, waiting to dump something else on him. Zing him again for good measure.

"So, what does he want to do, go see her?"

"Yes."

Nothing ever came easy for him in his whole goddamn life. And it sure as hell wasn't getting any better.

"So send him."

Peter came in, his arms loaded down with fish and the gifts Carl had brought home. Without saying a word he put the fish in the freezer, placed the gifts on the table, then waited for Carl to look him in the eye before he said, "I changed my mind about going to New York. I'm staying put."

Carl watched him. The smartass look on Peter's face told him there was something else on the kid's mind. But he didn't say anything. He was keeping his trap shut. For how long? The kid was going to cause him more grief—he could see it. He could feel it in his gut.

Martha looked from one to the other. She saw the hostility in Peter's eyes, and felt the strange tension in Carl.

"I think that's wisest. It's best you wait until things calm down a bit." She tried to keep her nervousness out of her voice, but when they both turned to look at her she knew she hadn't.

Suddenly, Peter's face softened. "Yeah, I think so too. I'm going for a run. I'll be back to cover the office."

Martha looked at Carl, then turned away. He finished his beer and went to bed.

Out of habit, Peter started out in the direction of the yard, then veered off toward town, trying to outrun the tears streaming down his cheeks. If Dina Dmitri was his mother, that meant Connie Olsen was his cousin. Damn *her,* and damn Carl for screwing up his life. He wished she would die. No, he didn't. He wanted her to live long enough for him to tell her what he thought of her. To thank her for his wonderful life.

CHAPTER THIRTY-FIVE

ACTING OUT REHEARSED EMOTIONS, MANIPULATING SOMEONE ELSE'S emotions, had never been difficult for Leslie. She could spill tears, pout, or gush over something stupid with ease...she could sympathize, flatter and deceive, but now, for the first time in her life, she was faced with something that wasn't part of a game. Honest, genuine emotion. She didn't know if what she was feeling was loss, pain or anger. It was difficult to sort out the mixed-up feelings that were thrashing about inside her.

She never knew anyone who was killed on purpose. People died from accidents, like Johnny Jackson in a car accident a year ago. And Tina Meyer who had dived into the stone quarry, hit a big rock and broke her neck.

Things weren't going the way she'd planned. *They* weren't supposed to leave her, she was the one who was supposed to leave them, leave this tiny dot-on-the-map town. She had lost the two people who loved her the way she was. The two people she could count on no matter what. Pollyanna and Peter Pan were tiresome at times, and they did dumb things, but she never thought they would die on her.

If they hadn't gone to see Madame Zero, they would still be alive. It was her fault.

There were too many thoughts coming at her from so many different places. She was on her own. No, she was going to be responsible for Andy, and not just for a week or a month. She was going to be stuck with Andy for who knew how long? Forever? Now she had responsibilities that she couldn't pick and choose. She wasn't anyone's little girl anymore.

Her tears started to dry as she began to realize that in eleven months she was going to be eighteen! The yard, the construction company. She was going to own everything. She was Dmitri Enterprises!

The recovery process had begun.

* * *

Gabby hadn't moved a muscle, much less opened an eye. On her worst day no one would have called her Chipmunk Cheeks, until today. Her face was one big puffball.

This was as good a time as any to slip out and make a few phone calls. There was a cop in the hallway. Amanda tiptoed past him, took the elevator down to the lobby and chose the phone furthest away from the ones being used.

She poked in numbers she knew better than her own home phone number.

The phone was picked up on the second ring.

"'Lo."

"Al, it's me. Anything?"

Al Ryan looked around his living room, checking it over to make sure things were tidy. "A few leads, nothing definite. I'm on my way out now to check on them."

"That's encouraging. Simmons is ready to lend a hand when you need it. You have his number. I won't keep you. Let us know how things work out. Good luck. Your brother Bob sends his love along with his best wishes too."

"Yeah. Call you when there's something to call about."

After he hung up, he finished packing, carefully wrapping the magnum and silencer before placing them in the bottom of his suitcase. He double-checked all the appliances; they were all off. He locked up the house and got into his car.

He preferred working alone, but Simmons was what he wasn't: a people person. Regular good neighbor Ned. He fit in easily. He was…what was it brother Bob called him? Oh yeah, Simmons was folksy.

The next call Amanda made was to her home.

"How's she doing?"

"About the same. Talked to your congenial brother, Al. Says he's following up on a couple of leads."

"Cops are turning the state upside down. Checking Ben's busts, going back ten years. Plus everything he's been working on now. I'm having some people look into her cases."

"Her cases? She hasn't worked in—"

"Gotta cover all the bases, sweetheart. She did handle a few touchy cases that ruffled more than a few feathers, cost some important people a lot of dough. So far nothing fits. This was no random thing. Someone went through a lot of trouble to do this. Dina ever tell you that the Dmitris are worth mucho pesos?"

"You trying to be funny? She's a Midwesterner, they don't brag or discuss money—theirs or anyone else's. Doesn't surprise me, though. I had a feeling she came from what they so charmingly refer to as *comfortable* means. But she's been away a long time and hasn't been on the best of terms with her brother for years, until just recently." She ran her fingers up and down the cord, thinking how happy Gabby sounded when she called to tell her that her brother and sister-in-law were coming out for a few days. "I'm glad that things pulled together on that front, before this happened. Bob? I think checking her out will be a dead-end. Futile."

"Nothing's futile. If she was the target, whoever it is knows by now that they failed, that she's alive. By the way, there's someone in place to see nothing does happen to her while she's in the hospital. I know there's a cop posted, but it doesn't hurt to have back-up."

"Bob, I appreciate all you're doing. I know it puts you on the spot, calling in favors from old acquaintances. It's just that I owe her, and Ben."

"You didn't ask, I volunteered. Besides, what you owe, I owe. I want to nail this s.o.b. I'm doing it for us, as well as her family. Ben and I were never friends, but he was a fair guy. And I want to see the maniac who kills kids go down."

"Hell of a world we live in, isn't it? Seems like it's come down to three categories: victims, protectors and killers. Least you and I get some choices."

He glanced out the window, watched a peregrine falcon circle, then glide off. "Do we?"

"I like to think so, gives me a false sense of security."

"Have to go. See you at dinner."

Amanda had a moment of panic when she saw the empty chair outside Gabby's room. She pushed the door open and terror gripped her when she saw a tall, dark-haired man standing beside the bed. He looked up for a second, then back down. She wanted him to be the *someone in place* her husband Bob had referred to. But he was being too familiar, he had Gabby's hand in his. Was he pretending to be a concerned relative to throw her off?

Amanda rushed in. "Who the hell are you? How did you get clearance?"

He put his finger to his lips and whispered. "I'm Jake Tanner, an old friend of Dina's, uh, Mrs. Coleman's."

"Sorry. I talked to you on the phone last night. I'm Amanda Ryan."

He reached over and shook her hand. He was bronze. His hand was firm and calloused, yet there was a gentleness about it. In his eyes, too.

If she didn't know better, she'd swear he just stepped off the

Busted Flush, that she was seeing John D. MacDonald's Travis McGee in the flesh. Only his eyes weren't gray, they were ocean blue, and his hair wasn't blond, it was dark brown.

"I flew in to make arrangements to have the...family returned to Hid'n Oaks. I had to see Dina for myself, so I can tell everyone at home she's doing okay. Doc was in a bit ago, he said she's off the critical list. She's stable."

"Whatever that means. Has she been awake since you got here?"

"No. And I'm afraid I have to leave. There are a lot of things that need to be taken care of back home. When she wakes up, tell her I stopped in and not to worry about her niece and nephew. Leslie and Andy are staying with us, me and my Uncle Phil, for as long as they need to."

She watched him lean over and give Dina's cheek a feathery kiss. There was a fondness in his touch and his face that prompted her to wonder if they were ever lovers. He walked around the bed with the lazy agility of a cat.

He handed her a card. "If you need me, something comes up, call me anytime. Day or night."

"I will."

As he was walking out, he turned. "Ben and the boy?..."

"Mr. and Mrs. Coleman have made arrangements."

"Please let me know when she's ready to take calls. Nice meeting you, Amanda."

"Same here. I'll keep you posted on her progress."

"Appreciate it. Bye."

CHAPTER THIRTY-SIX

AMANDA WAS WORKING ON HER SECOND PECAN CARAMEL ROLL. DINA WAS staring out the window. The roll on her plate was untouched, her coffee had to be cold.

"Gabby, help me out here, this is about as domestic as I get. Baked the rolls myself. Want me to get discouraged? Forgive me for boasting, but they're not bad."

It was beginning to frighten her. Gabby either wasn't listening or hearing. She was staring into the middle of nowhere with a lost, wounded look. It wasn't like her.

"How about it? One roll?"

"No, thanks."

The cynical smile Dina had embedded in her too-thin face was troubling as well. It wasn't good. From everything that Amanda had seen, everyone was pussyfooting around Dina and it wasn't helping her. She was falling deeper into her hole.

"Dina, I know you're going through a difficult period. Losing loved ones is tough. It's tough being a survivor. God—"

"I didn't survive, I was left behind. God had nothing to do with what happened. This was planned by some person or persons unknown as they say."

"I know. But God—"

"Don't say it. Don't say He *spared* me. I never have understood people who claim to have been spared from some disaster, as if they were worthy of being saved and the others were not. Do they, do you, honestly believe God sits on His throne and decides who gets the thumb up, who gets the thumb down, as though we were all in some goddamn arena in long ago Rome? Arrogant idiots!"

Aha! Anger. Anger was good. "Well, however it happened, you were given a second chance. You did survive."

"I was left behind."

"Oh, knock it off, Gabby. Whether you were spared or left behind, what difference does it make? You're alive. What the hell is wrong with you? And do me one favor—lose that cynic's smirk, it doesn't become you. Don't feed ghosts, Gabby, they'll hang around forever."

"Do you think I don't want them to?"

"I'm not talking about memories, I'm talking about guilt. Ghosts thrive on it. They'll drive you away from yourself. Memories are gold, but life is silver. You have to use it or it loses its luster."

"Spare me the homilies."

"If your face wasn't so puffy, I'd smack you."

"They're releasing me tomorrow." There was a heavy note of regret in her voice. Amanda ignored it.

"I know. It's all arranged, you're staying with Bob and me until you're on your feet. You have a niece and nephew who need you."

"I'm well aware of that. I don't know how I can help them, when I can't seem to help myself. I miss my family. Miss their company. Miss holding them and being held by Ben. I want to talk to them, see them. I want to tell them I love them one more time."

"They knew, Gabby. You told them a million times, in a million ways. What you need is time away from here, away from all this medicine smell. All this white. It gives me the creeps, it's so...virginal."

288

CHAPTER THIRTY-SEVEN

From the day Sammy Breen discovered he had it, he loved impressing people with his photographic memory. It gave him a sense of importance, got him dates, and brought all kinds of financial rewards.

That changed the night beefy Al, no-last-name Al, came nosing around his bait shop. The instant he laid eyes on Al, he knew the guy was someone he didn't want to see, much less talk to. He was a walking mausoleum. Kind of guy hard to forget, but your survival instinct told you it was better if you had a memory lapse if anyone asked about him. The guy wouldn't have stood out in a buffalo herd, but anywhere else he'd be the main attraction. His smile wasn't nice, but it was his eyes that threatened destruction. He was connected. No two ways about it. It had to be how Al found him. These people could find breath.

He didn't bother trying to bullshit his way out of getting involved, Beefy Al saw through him like he was made of gauze.

He gladly gave Al a description, the best description of the car he could, and of the guy who was driving it. He knew it was vital to his well being. He'd have given Al his mother, if he asked.

Wrong place at the wrong time, that's what it was. It was dumb rolling around in the Catskills with Betty. If his wife ever found out, he was a dead man. He'd lose her, the kids and his bait shop. He and Betty were lucky they weren't closer when things exploded like a crazy Fourth of July. They would have been flying through the air just like the dame who came at them like a missile. He should have just picked Betty up and walked away. No, he had to play Good Samaritan, send Betty for help and sit there with the dame until help came.

What else could he do? Leave her there, with that big chunk of wood in her neck? She'd've bled to death. Damn thing was like an arrow.

Least he had the presence of mind to disappear before any cop came around. Didn't give his name to nobody. But Beefy Al found him anyway. And if anyone asked him about Beefy Al, all he was going to say was "Al who?"

CHAPTER THIRTY-EIGHT

THE RESTAURANT AND LOUNGE IN LA GUARDIA WAS RATHER QUIET, EXCEPT for the planes landing and taking off.

Amanda watched her waitress skillfully avoid the maze of outstretched legs and jutting elbows in her path. Did all these people thoughtlessly move tables and chairs around to complicate the poor woman's life, or was it the plan of management—maximum seating, minimum maneuverability? It was a good thing she was a string bean, she didn't have much trouble scooting through the obstacle course.

The waitress set the wine down in front of her and without trying to hide her irritation, waited for her to inspect the glass for any telltale lipstick kisses or sticky fingerprints. When she found none, just as she hadn't with the first drink, she laid a twenty dollar bill on the tray.

Faces of some of the pain-in-the-ass customers who gave her grief during her own waitress days were still pretty vivid. The same ones who hadn't taken enough money out of the bank to leave a dollar tip. She waved the change away.

"Keep it, you may need it to buy your way back to the bar."

"Hey, thanks. They're remodeling, things are going to be cramped for a while."

The waitress made her way back. Amanda took a sip of the Rhine wine and seltzer. It was a little early for wine, but her stomach was growling, and coffee only made it worse. As soon as she and Bob got to the Bahamas, she was going off her diet.

Talent for Deception

She made her fifth survey of the lounge, trying to look like a bored, disinterested traveler, while she looked for anyone who seemed out of place. Someone looking, like she was looking.

The waitress was chatting with the bartender. They were quite a pair. She was a string bean with a tiny swell in her belly, like maybe she swallowed a whole anchovy, and the bartender was a heavy duty weightlifter. He wasn't able to uncurl his arms far enough to place a drink down in front of a customer without leaning over. Every minute or so, he had to reassure himself that his zipper was up, and Sir Jolly Time was still inside the gate.

Most of the customers were businessmen, reading the *Wall Street Journal* or the sports pages of their local papers. There were a few women either traveling together or reunited with friends or relatives. A couple of college-age kids were having a chug-a-lug contest. No one looked threatening or unduly curious.

She was about to check the entrance again when a chain reaction told her she needn't bother, Dina Dmitri Coleman had arrived. All heads had turned toward the entrance.

Watching her approach, Amanda's brow gathered. It had been over a week since Gabby insisted on leaving the safety of the Ryan household. She had helped Gabby get her affairs straightened out and get her house ready to put on the market.

In her opinion, Dina Dmitri Coleman was still too thin. Her coppery black hair was pulled back into a French twist making her appear even more gaunt. The green eyes were still unwilling to show, or share, the depth of the pain behind them. Amanda had been wrong about Dina, she was *shtarke*. Tough.

"How're you doing, Gabby?"

"Good. And you?"

"Also good." She motioned to the waitress for another Rhine wine and held up a coffee cup.

"Sold the house."

292

"Wow! Less than a week's time. Congratulations. You're lucky."

"I don't think it was luck. I suspect the buyers were friends of yours or Bob's."

"Couldn't have been mine. My friends, with you being the exception, send telegrams when they buy a sample bottle of Dom Pérignon. Besides, they don't venture that far out of the City."

"Then they were friends of Bob's?"

"He didn't mention anything to me about any of his friends buying a house. He would have told me." She lowered her eyes. Nope, her nose hadn't grown. "What time is your flight out?"

"Eleven. Which gives me enough time for one cup of coffee."

"Nervous?"

"Not really nervous…a little anxious, maybe. Been a long time. I haven't called anyone, so no one's expecting me. Don't know if they'll recognize me, or me them."

"Uh-uh. I know one person who'll recognize you. Travis McGee."

"I don't know any Travis McGee."

"John D. MacDonald character. Read a lot of his books during my down times. First time I saw Jake Tanner in your hospital room, that's who he reminded me of. Looks the part. A knight in rusty armor. If I'd been you, I never would have left Hid'n Oaks without him. Nice to see a man who doesn't do a thing to hide his gentleness. Who isn't embarrassed by it. Lot of men don't realize it's a strength, not a weakness."

"Amanda, Jake's a friend. An old, dear friend." The clock on the wall said she had about ten more minutes. Without being conscious of it, she looked over at the entrance.

"You expecting someone?"

"Can't help it. I miss seeing them, being able to touch them. I miss hearing them laugh."

"You're not going to cry."

"Nope. The tears are over. There's anger, but someday, soon I hope, that will be over, too. Right now, I have to center on Leslie and Andy. I need them as much as they need me."

Amanda hoped her eyes weren't bulging out as far as it felt they were. She knew it was probably unkind. Kids do change, but the only frame of reference she had of Leslie was on the day of Dina's wedding. It was still hard to imagine that kid needing anyone. Kids did grow up, learn to be nice. She hoped that was true, for Dina's sake.

They both looked up at the clock on the wall at the same time and smiled.

"Ten-fifteen. I have to go, Amanda. Thanks for everything, and thank Bob for me. I'll call when things are settled."

They said their teary goodbyes, embraced one last time, and went their separate ways.

As Amanda exited the restaurant, a chauffeur-driven Cadillac pulled up alongside the curb and the back door immediately opened. A hand reached out to her, she took it and slid in beside her husband, giving him a peck on the check.

"Bob, tell me you have someone on that flight with her."

"Just dropped off Simmons at the airport; he should be sitting at the gate by now, waiting to board. Relax. I don't want an uptight wife vacationing on Paradise Island with me."

"I won't be uptight. How do the Callahans like the new house?"

"Love it. Loved it more when Dina dropped the price by fifteen thousand. It was a bargain before, now they're ecstatic."

"I'm just happy to have her out of here, back home where she'll be safe—if she isn't followed. I almost asked her to fly down to the Bahamas with the kids after the reading of the will, but she has too much on her mind. You think she'll be all right there in Hid'n Oaks?"

"Simmons will take care of her. He has his instructions. I told him to stay there for three months—if nothing shows, it should be okay for her to be on her own. He has the number in the Bahamas. If some-thing does come up, he'll call."

"I can't understand it. Nobody has any idea of who or why."

"We'll find him, sweetheart. It takes time. By the way, *we* bought a house in Hawaii this morning. Should be spending Christmas there."

"Hawaii! That's too far away."

"Amanda, Christmas is five months from now. If we have to, we can always fly Dina in and she and the kids can stay until we find out who it is and take care of it."

She kissed his hand. "So who needs Travis McGee?" She laughed at the puzzled look on his face. "Never mind."

CHAPTER THIRTY-NINE

It was going to be a real blister of a day. It felt like the sun was laying over everything, sucking up energy. Leslie felt as though she had been locked up in a closet with a thousand-watt bulb burning. Some ambitious soul was mowing the lawn across the way.

She was positively sweltering, and Jake wasn't helping. His presence alone stoked up her temperature by at least fifty degrees. Was he so dense that he couldn't see he was in her danger zone? He was putting a maddening strain on her patience. Patience was not a virtue. It was a stupid, superfluous show of politeness.

When he finally agreed to let her move back into her own home, she had been inches away from throwing him out of her house. What was his problem, anyway. In two weeks, she was going to be eighteen. Legally an adult.

It was fun having Jake convince her to at least let Andy stay with him and Phil until Dina came home for the reading of the will and stuff. Mr. Smartass didn't have a clue that agreeing to do that was the easiest concession she ever had to make. She wanted the pest out of her hair.

By the time she got Jake out the door, she was almost too tired to continue her search for a copy of the will, insurance papers, anything that would tell her how much she was worth. There had to be some legal document somewhere in the damn house.

She was convinced that probate was invented to drive people out of their minds. She checked everywhere, trying to guess what could be in the will. Were any guardians appointed? Not that she had to worry, she was almost an adult. Maybe Madame Zero would take Andy back to New York with her.

She rummaged through dresser drawers and closets. Through all the cabinets, even the books in the den.

To save herself from having to do it twice, while she was looking for the papers in her mother's jewelry boxes, she sorted out all the diamonds, pearls, rubies and emeralds and arranged them in separate piles. Her mother never was very organized, she threw everything together. Leslie placed the separated jewels into the boxes she brought in from her room.

Her father's chest of cufflinks and tie pins were all neatly arranged. She lifted the false bottom and looked underneath. Nothing. She replaced the tray. Andy could have most of the cufflinks and tie pins. She set aside a pair of gold cufflinks for Tony.

She was going to tackle the cellar next when the doorbell rang. Thinking it was the warden coming back again, she swore under her breath all the way to the front door.

It wasn't Jake. It was Tony. Before she could stop him, he kissed her, then took her in his arms.

"Ran into Jake…he said you were going to stay here by yourself. You shouldn't be here by yourself, c'mon home with me. My folks would love to have you."

"No. I just want to stay here by myself. My Aunt Dina is coming in a few days, and I want things straightened up. In good order."

"Tell me what needs to be done. I'll give you a hand."

"No, Tony, please, I'd rather be alone. I prefer to do this by myself."

"Okay, okay. Then I may as well get back to the station. But if you need me for anything, call me."

Jesus! She had forgotten about the Lincoln sitting in the parking lot of the Minneapolis airport.

"What time do you have to be at the station?"

298

"Not until five, but if there's nothing you want me to do, I can call my dad—"

"Oh, there is something you can for me…and for you."

He picked his watch up off the floor. Four-thirty. Plenty of time to shower and change. His work clothes were in the truck.

He rolled over and kissed Leslie's forehead. She moaned and snuggled up to him. He had only meant to comfort her, but things got out of hand real quick, as usual.

She had her arm around his neck and began massaging his thigh, working her way up. He began massaging her breast, working his way down. He couldn't tell whose breathing was heavier.

"Ready?"

"You kidding?"

Paul's black Lincoln Continental pulled into the Dmitri driveway and Dina stepped out. She went around to the trunk and lifted her suitcases out and set them down. For a few minutes she stood there taking it all in. The house, the landscape. It was the same, and different too. Like life. And people.

She walked up to the house and was about to ring the bell when a blast of music coming from inside told her no one could possibly hear it. She tried the door. It was open.

The two naked bodies in front of the fireplace turned to face the intruding sunlight and the woman in the doorway. Tony made a quick grab for his pants. Leslie merely leaned back on her propped elbows and nodded. Dina nodded slightly and walked on through to the kitchen.

"Jesus! Who was that?" He was hopping on one foot, frantically trying to get his right foot into a pant leg. He fell on the floor. "Les…turn the stereo off! I told you it was too loud." He saw his life turning into Technicolor shit with stereophonic sound. Big time.

Leslie gave him a look of disgust. He was acting like some kid caught with his hand in the cookie jar.

"*That* was my Aunt Dina. Relax. This is *my* house now. She is *my* guest."

"You said she wasn't going to be here until the day after tomorrow, or later."

"Well chicken, she obviously must have taken a plane, or maybe a broom. Don't sweat it. If you're worried about what she might think, forget it. I could tell you something about her that would curl your hair."

He had his pants and shirt on. "Jeez, Les. You just going to lay there? Get up and get dressed before she comes back in here."

She stood up, making no effort to cover herself. "First I'm going upstairs and take a shower, make myself more *presentable*."

"What the hell am I supposed to do? Go in and introduce myself? Hi, I'm the guy that just screwed your niece…"

"Don't be a jerk! Go in and have a cup of coffee with her, tell her we're engaged if it makes you feel better."

"I feel kinda foolish, not to mention scared."

"No one's going to haul you off to jail. We're two consenting adults."

"In case you *forgot*—you're not eighteen yet. I *am* an adult and I could be slapped with—"

"Get off it. I'm going upstairs to take a shower. Do what you want, chicken. I won't be long."

"Les? Did you mean that? About being engaged? Or were you just saying that?"

"'Course I meant it. Now go on into the kitchen and introduce yourself." She was tempted to stay and see the show, see how he handled it, but she had to have a shower.

He watched her walk all the way to the top of the stairs, then turned toward the kitchen door. With the enthusiasm of a condemned man walking to his final doom, Tony placed his clammy hands on the door to the kitchen. His fingers looked like hush puppies sticking out of a frying pan. His throat was tighter than a frozen bearing. He took a deep breath, gently pushed the door open and stepped into the kitchen.

She was standing next to the window facing the patio. He cleared his throat, building up the courage to speak.

When she turned to face him, he was unable to say a word. Gorgeous women always made him feel self-conscious.

"Hello. I'm Dina Coleman. Leslie is my niece."

He took the extended hand. Her hand was soft, her shake firm. There was a warmth in her smile that made him feel less threatened. Her voice didn't sound outraged. With luck, she wouldn't call the sheriff. Not yet.

"Hi, I'm Tony. Tony Williams. Leslie's fiancé. Can I get you a cup of coffee or something?" He felt like an ass playing the host, in the house she grew up in.

"Coffee would be nice. Black."

They were halfway through their coffee when Leslie walked in, brushed her aunt's cheek with a kiss and busied herself with pouring a cup of coffee.

Her presence didn't interfere in the least with their conversation, they carried on as if she were invisible. Tony was rambling on about his body shop, while Dina sat there listening like she was actually interested. What a fraud. Leslie gave her aunt a more thoughtful assessment.

Madame Zero was dressed in what she probably considered casual cool. A cocoa brown skirt, cream blouse and brown loafer-type shoes. A bit passé, but she probably thought it was *in*.

Something about her bothered Leslie. She couldn't quite grasp what it was that was so annoying. It was more than having Tony practically drooling over her.

She sat down at the end of the table, growing more irritated by the minute. Tony was making a complete ass of himself. He was getting on her nerves. He was acting like some asinine high school kid with a crush. It wasn't that she was *jealous*. It was insulting, especially since he had just made mad passionate love to her not more than twenty minutes ago. Twice. And here he was acting all glassy-eyed over an old broad more than twice his age. Madame Zero. Yeah. That *was* a perfect description for her. Madame Zero.

To her further frustration, she suspected that Dina, for some reason, could be trouble. Nothing real major, but there was definitely something there to watch.

"Excuse me, *Aunt* Dina, I almost forgot, we're invited to the Tanners for dinner tonight. You *do* remember Jake? And Phil?"

"Yes, I remember them very well. Where's Andy?"

"He's over at the Tanners'. Dinner's at seven sharp."

"I can pick you ladies up and..." Tony felt Leslie's eyes boring into him. "Uh, Jake invited me when I ran into him."

Leslie's head snapped away from Dina, back to Tony. "I thought you had to work tonight, and what about my father's car? Weren't you going to drive to the airport and pick up the Lincoln?"

"That won't be necessary." Dina laid the keys on the table. "I picked it up, when I came through Minneapolis. If you two don't mind, I'd like to shower and change clothes."

"Fine. Tony can get your suitcases out of the car. You can stay in this bedroom in here, off the kitchen. It was my mother and father's."

Tony felt the heat of her glare on the back of his neck all the way out to the car. When he got back with Dina's luggage, Leslie's mood hadn't improved. Her eyebrow was arched and she was drumming her fingers on the counter. He ignored her and started to take the suitcases into the bedroom.

"Hey, Romeo, she's getting ready to take a shower, leave the luggage here in the kitchen."

He had a sudden urge to split before it all hit the fan. He hurried out to his truck, Leslie wasn't far behind him.

"Are you some kind of jerk or what? I could barf." She wanted to strangle him.

"What are you talking about?"

"That *act* of yours. All that *golly, gee whiz* bull—I thought you were going to crawl up her ass. You'd better run home and change your shorts, they must be all wet."

"She's your *aunt*, for Pete's sake." He risked a smile. "I was just trying to make a good impression. Don't tell me you're jealous?"

"*Jealous*? Of her? Get serious. Don't talk like an *ass*. It was just a bad scene is all. Seeing you make a total gaga ass of yourself. *Jealous!* Get real. She's old enough to be your *mother*. In fact, she's probably older than your mother. Maybe that's your problem. Maybe you're a closet motherf—"

"Knock it off! I know this is a bad time for you and all, but don't ever say that, not to me. *Ever.*"

"I'm sorry. I didn't mean anything by it. I'm doing the best I can to cope with things as it is. Trying to keep my mind busy so I won't fall apart."

"I'm sorry, honey."

"Will I see you at Tanners'?"

"You want me to be there?"

"Sure. We'll take my dad's car. And, Tony? I'm going to make it your present from me, soon as the papers are transferred."

"I can't take it."

"Oh, yes you can. What am I going to do with it? I have my 'vette."

"We'll talk later. See you."

As Dina stepped out of the shower and reached for a towel she felt Leslie's presence in the doorway. When she looked over, Leslie was standing there, appraising her, with a rather hostile look on her face.

Despite her inclination to be critical, Leslie had to hand it to her aunt. Dina was in fairly good shape for an old broad. She wasn't as thin as she looked in her loose-fitting clothes. Her body was firm and well-conditioned, considering what she'd been through. Watching Dina slip into a pink bra and panties, Leslie found it amusing that Dina seemed uncomfortable with an audience. It almost made up for Tony's stupid display of fascination.

"Is there something urgent that you wanted?"

Determined not to show she was still seething over it, Leslie shrugged and walked over to the bed, looked down into Dina's suitcase and lifted out a dullish brown dress and a gray blouse. Words weren't necessary, her actions said it all, but she wanted to voice how she felt about Madame Zero's taste.

"Expensive glad rags, but drab. Who designed them, Rasputin? Well, I suppose at your age you prefer the understated look. But you really should have more color."

Dina smiled. "We all have our individual tastes."

"I suppose." She wanted to lay into her about Carl and Peter so bad it was hurting to hold back. Some inner instinct told her to hold back, that it would be premature to let loose now. But, on the other hand, what would it hurt to be candid?

"Well? Aren't you going to lay your middle-class morality on me about what you walked in on? Oh, that's right, you're the more liberal-minded Dmitri."

"You're nearly eighteen, an adult. People have different ways of handling stress. And pain. If I did have anything to say, it wouldn't have cut any ice anyway, would it?"

"Cut any ice? Wow, are we hip. No, it wouldn't. This is *my* house now. And you're a *guest*."

304

"You haven't answered my question. Did you come rushing in here for a specific reason?"

The question sounded more like a disinterested comment than a question. Leslie watched her step into a pair of pale gray slacks, then choose a turquoise blouse to give the outfit contrast. Although she thought it a becoming choice, she saw no reason to tell Dina it was.

"Leslie, is there something urgent you need to speak with me about?"

"No."

"I have to say you're holding up remarkably well, under the circumstances."

Leslie wasn't sure if she heard a note of sarcasm or not. Looking at Dina, she didn't detect anything to confirm it. In fact, there was nothing to read. Dina's face was as blank as an empty frame. She concluded Madame Zero, like Peter Pan, suffered from a severe case of tunnel vision, taking everything at face value.

"Thank you, but...I'm...not as together as I seem. I'm running on the Dmitri stiff upper lip, but *inside* I...I feel like I'm running around screaming..." When in a tight spot, stammer.

"Would you like to sit down and talk about it?"

"No. Not now, Aunt Dina. I have to run into town, take care of some errands. Say! I know what. Why don't you give *Uncle* Jake a jingle, let him know you're here. Bet he'll be over here in a flash. Well, I gotta run. See you around six."

On the way out to her car she felt nettled. Weirdly annoyed. Enough so that it was disturbing. It wasn't that Madame Zero posed any threat, Dina simply bugged her. It wasn't like she was doing it intentionally. Or was she?

Dina walked into the kitchen and poured herself a cup of coffee. It still felt strange, yet familiar at the same time, sitting in this kitchen with long-ago childhood memories. She reached above her head, lifted the phone off the wall and dialed a familiar number.

"Hello."

"Hello, Phil."

"Dina! Where are you? Need someone to pick you up?"

"No, I'm at the house. I have Paul's car. How are you?"

"Me? I'm okay. Bones do some complaining now and then but I can't. I'm walking, talking and I can still think. Jake and Andy are out fishing. Andy's been having a rough time of it, and Jake thought fishing would help get his mind off things. He's looking forward to seeing his aunt though. We all are."

"I'm looking forward to seeing all of you. I understand we're having dinner with you. It isn't too much trouble, is it?"

"Trouble? You kidding? What are you doing now? How about coming over for some coffee?"

"Can't right now, Phil. I want to run over and see Sam Olsen, then stop by the yard."

"Oh, okay. Sure. Say hi to the Olsens' for me. See you later then."

"Bye."

Driving through town Dina thought about something she'd read about people who had out of body experiences. She wondered if it was anything like what she was feeling now. Like a stranger in what used to be her hometown. She passed buildings that weren't here before and she was unable to recognize some of the ones that were here, buildings she probably went in thousands of times. The town had grown quite a bit.

The further into town she drove, the more aware she became that she was being looked at as much as she was looking. How many of the faces were once familiar? She smiled. Of course she was being stared at. She was driving Paul's car. It was only natural people were curious about who was behind the wheel.

She drove on through the town, turned down the first road after the new service station and went about half a mile. Her uncle, Sam Olsen, was sitting in a rocking chair on his front porch. He waved when she pulled into the driveway.

They spent two hours together.

CHAPTER FORTY

JOE MICHAELS SIGNED THE REGISTER, PICKED UP HIS KEY AND AMBLED OUT the door. As soon as he was gone, Peter spun the ledger around to take a closer look at it. Something about Joe Michaels didn't jive. He tried too hard to come off folksy, country-bumpkinish, talking about varmints and vittles like he was visiting the set of *The Beverly Hillbillies*. Peter doubted he was what he claimed, a fisherman. Mr. Michaels probably didn't know a bass from a walleye, or a blue gill from a crappie. He had traces of an eastern accent. Hotshot city boy. Peter thought about checking him out to see if hotshot even know how to bait a hook.

Late that night, Joe Michaels received a call from Bob Ryan's brother, Al.

"Seen him?"

"Not yet. Got in late. I'll have more time tomorrow.

"Okay. I'll be there in a couple days. Don't do or say anything makes you conspicuous."

"Who me? I'm just a country boy at heart. I eat this stuff up."

"Don't be cuter than you can help, Simmons. Adios."

"Michaels, Al. Joe Michaels. Remember the next time you call. See ya later."

* * *

Dinner at the Tanners was worse than Leslie expected it would be. The boys, all four of them, fawned over Madame Zero as though she were Princess Grace. Jake was more attentive than twins. Phil was making a boring ass of himself with his incessant, inane anecdotes about Mike and the glories of yesteryear. Andy was pathetic. At times he got so close to her, they could both be wearing her dress.

Tony was the worst. Making a fool of himself, jumping up in anticipation of any possible wants and needs Madame Zero might have. He was behaving like an idiot. For what? There wasn't anything, not one thing, exceptional about her. Leslie's cheeks were almost numb from smiling. Her ass cheeks were already numb from sitting in one spot so long.

It was getting unbearable, seeing them all act like the four stooges. Jesters, performing for the old broad. She *was* a zero, they were all zeroes. They were all grossly *sickening*.

Every one of them was an utter bore. An idea slowly made its way inside her circle of attention. Here she was sitting, bored out of her gourd while she could be taking advantage of a great opportunity. The chance to be the eye of a hidden camera, taking everything in, unobserved herself. Was she in a coma? It was a perfect opportunity to see if she could detect what it was about Madame Zero that sent off the bad vibes she was getting.

It didn't take long for her to become totally engrossed in her subject. It wasn't as though she had any real flair. Off the top, she would say Madame Zero was either guileless or maybe dense. On the other hand, maybe she was simply just *good* at the game? Better than anyone else she'd run across. It was hard to tell. She seemed so...simple.

As exposed as she was to all that New York sophistication, it seemed to have eluded her. Not that her present audience could tell, they were mesmerized by her. Why? She was no spellbinder. What they could possibly find so fascinating about her was a mystery. She had about as much sex appeal as mildew. She wasn't even ordinary.

Some people, she supposed, would think she had a certain class, but nothing exceptional. Her taste in clothes wasn't understated, it was nondescript. Dull, like her. Agonizingly dull.

The last of Leslie's patience seeped away. Weary of it all, she made several attempts to signal Tony to rescue her, take her out of here. But it was all in vain. He was so wrapped up in the good old days of the three bores he missed all the signals.

What did she need a plausible excuse for? She wanted out. Now.

She was about to stretch and yawn when Dina saved her the trouble by announcing it was time for them to leave. First Leslie had been grateful, then peeved. What right did Madame Zero have deciding when it was time for her to do anything? She yawned, just to let everyone know it was her decision as much as Dina's.

"Oh, excuse me. I guess I'm really exhausted. Tony? I'll ride with you."

"Can't, Les. Promised my dad I'd be back at the station tonight to finish tuning up Gertie's car. Her and Gus are going to the Cities tomorrow morning."

He did the best he could to avoid looking at her, knew she'd be wearing her witch face she was getting so good at. He quickly shook hands with everyone and was out the door before Leslie had time to decide whether or not she'd walk him out to his truck. She pretended to barely notice that he was gone.

What she did notice was Jake's arm around Dina's waist, not in a possessive way, exactly. More relaxed. Comfortable. For two people who hadn't seen each other for quite a few years, it didn't take them long to get back to square one.

She made it a point to mumble a good night and a thanks for dinner before walking outside.

Jake, with his arm still around Dina's waist, said he'd walk them all out to the car.

Dina paused long enough to kiss Phil on the cheek. "Good night, Phil. Thanks for dinner." Andy walked up to Phil and thanked him for taking care of him and having him over for dinner. Then he turned to Jake. "Thanks, Uncle Jake, for…you know…hanging out with me."

With his free arm, Jake pulled Andy to his side and hugged him. "Thank you. My pleasure, Andy. I appreciated the company."

Andy's smile dropped away as soon as he walked outside and saw the frosty look on Leslie's face. She yanked him by the arm, pulling him to get as much distance as she could away from Dina.

With a good thirty feet between them, she started in on Andy, about what a wimpy puppet he was, competing for his "auntie's" attention, looking up at her with stupid cow eyes, wrapping himself around precious Auntie Dina's finger.

It was the wrong approach. Andy got angry and snapped back. "You turn sunshine into rain. You're such a spoil head."

"Oh, you think so? And that's spoil sport, not head. You and me are all we have. All that's left. We have to stick together. Watch out for each other, you know, watch each other's back."

"We've got Aunt Dina."

"Wise up. Use your head. You think she's going to stick around after the reading of the will?"

It was the first time he had spent almost a full day not thinking about his mom and dad being dead. Now she had spoiled it. He hid his face from her. He didn't want her to see him cry, she'd only make him feel worse by making fun of him.

"Well? Do you? She'll be out of here like smoke." She turned to check on the lovebirds. They had stopped walking and were just standing and talking.

"Why should she? We're all she's got now, too." He hadn't even thought about what would happen to them. He was trying hard not to believe her.

"I'll be eighteen soon, it doesn't matter all that much to me, but *you* could end up in a foster home."

"A foster home." It sounded funny. He started to laugh.

"You think it's funny? It's no joke. We'll see how funny you think it is when you're in an orphanage or some foster home with mean people. Neither one of them is something to laugh about. I'll read you Oliver Twist, see if you can laugh then."

"I bet Aunt Dina will stay. We're family."

"Family? Family doesn't mean anything to her. *Your* Auntie Dina doesn't give a damn about us. *I* have to look out for us, protect you. Get it straight. We're the only family we got, you and me. To her, we're just unwanted problems. And believe me, Aunt Dina doesn't have much use for any unwanted problems. I'll explain later. I'll tell you why Dad and Mom didn't have much to do with her all those years."

She was scaring him. And he was getting worried. He did like his Aunt Dina, so did Uncle Jake and Phil. He could tell they liked her a lot. He wanted to tell Leslie she was wrong, but maybe she knew something he didn't. He didn't want to think about it now. He didn't want to think about his mom or his dad, or what Leslie was saying. He just wanted things to be the way they were. He wished Leslie would just shut up. Go away—no, not go away, just be quiet.

"Andy, are you listening to me?"

"I don't want to talk about it."

"Oh, really. Well, we're going to talk later."

Immediately he began planning how he was going to escape up to his bedroom and lock his bedroom door as soon as he got home.

Jake and Dina were standing beside the same oak tree the Three Musketeers once tried to make into their private castle.

The evening had been pleasant. One that Jake had enjoyed more than he thought he should. Nice dinner, pleasant conversation, and happy, fond memories. Dear friends spending time together with people they cared about.

A thought drifted in. As soon as it did, Jake tried pushing it away, but it insisted on being acknowledged. There didn't seem to be a choice. Looking at Dina, he knew Ben Coleman had been good for Dina, probably better than he would have been. It was all right there in her face.

He took her hand. "Dina, I'm sorry about Ben and your boy. And Paul and Karen."

"I'm sorry too, Jake. For you. You lost two very dear friends. You and Paul were like brothers."

"Yeah. We were."

"Thank you for making my homecoming easy. I had a very pleasant evening. It may sound trite, but believe me, it isn't." They began walking toward the car, then Dina paused. "Jake, I'm concerned about Andy. He's so young and his heart is so tender, like Karen's."

"That it is. But he is a Dmitri, you know. He'll make it."

By the time they reached the car, Leslie and Andy were in the back seat, waiting. Jake opened the door and Dina slid in. "Dina, I have to drive to the Cities tomorrow on business. I should be back around four o'clock. Need anything before then, give Phil a call. Good night." He leaned inside the car window. "Good night, kids."

Andy ran up the stairs to his room as soon as got inside the house. Leslie wasn't far behind him. She was in no mood to get stuck with any family chats with Madame Zero.

As she passed Andy's door, she heard the lock click and smiled to herself, thinking it would be good for him to stew overnight. Tomorrow was soon enough to have their little chat.

Dina had all intentions of taking a shower and climbing into bed, maybe reading a few pages of a book and hopefully slipping into a good night's sleep. Instead, she gave in to an almost forgotten habit, sitting down on the sofa to catch the late news on TV. By the third commercial, she was asleep.

Sometime in the early hours of the morning she awoke with a start, immediately aware that her subconscious had put on her on the alert. She lay very still, listening, trying to get a sense of what it was that had triggered the alarm. Slowly her eyes adjusted to the dark. The television was off…had she woke up during the night and turned it off? She was trying to think clearly about it when she made out a shape, sitting at the end of the couch. It was then she heard the stifled sobs. It was Andy.

"Andy? Are you okay?"

He inched closer to her and she put her arm around him. She saw the struggle he was having to keep in the tears, could see his throat working, trying to cut off his emotions. She took him in her arms. He hugged her closer.

"It's okay to cry, Andy. We all need to let the pain and anger out. No one is going to think you're a baby because your heart aches."

"Why? Why…did God let it happen! Why?"

"God doesn't make accidents happen. They just happen."

"Do you think if they didn't go to New York…"

"Your mother and father came to New York because they cared about me. Just as I came here because I care about you and Leslie. I love you. I wanted to be with you. We're family."

He believed his aunt. She did care. He didn't know why, but he was sad and he felt better at the same time. Relieved to hear it was okay to cry, that he didn't have to hold the tears in. Soon he was crying harder than he had ever cried before. Then he stopped abruptly and looked over at the stairs, half expecting to see Leslie there. But she wasn't. He sighed.

"Leslie said you were going to leave right after the reading of the will. That I might have to go into a foster home." He was being a ratfink. Leslie was going to be mad if she found out. But Leslie did not always tell the truth. And he had to know.

"Leslie made a mistake. You're not going to any foster home."

315

"I'm not? You promise?"

"I promise. Leslie's upset. We're all upset. Always remember Andy, we're family. The Dmitris stick together."

"That's what my dad always said. But if that's true, how come you never came to visit us for all these years?"

Dina hugged him closer. "I feel like having a cup of coffee. How about you, want some cookies and milk?"

He looked over at her, undecided about asking his question again. His face broke into a sheepish grin. "I am kinda hungry." He followed her into the kitchen.

Despite a gallant effort, Andy wasn't able to chomp down more than eight cookies and drink two glasses of milk. He had fallen asleep at the table.

Dina woke him up. He was too groggy to make it on his own so she put her arm around him and walked him into the living room. There was no way he was going to be able to make it up the stairs, and she couldn't carry him so she led him over to the sofa. She covered him with the afghan that was spread over the back of the sofa.

With Andy's head in her lap and her feet up on the cocktail table, she listened to house sounds and sifted through her thoughts. Andy found her sleeve and tightened his fist around it, the way Ben Jr. used to do, making sure he'd wake up if she moved out of reach.

The sounds of the house were altogether different than she remembered. Her eyelids began drooping and she felt herself floating down a familiar path that led her to where her husband and son were waiting. Only this visit was different, they were joined by her mother and father, then Paul and Karen.

The reunion was cut short: everyone disappeared behind the explosion in the Catskills, as it came crashing into her dream. Out of nowhere a sentry appeared and drove away the nightmare, pulling her inside a safer place. The sentry stayed until she fell into a deep, peaceful sleep. The first she'd had in a long, long time.

CHAPTER FORTY-ONE

It was nine-thirty when Leslie came down the stairs and saw the two of them sleeping on the sofa, like Mutt and Jeff. Andy was practically in Madame Zero's lap. With a burglar's stealth, she quietly crept past them and out the door to her car. Hoping Tony might be able to sneak away for breakfast, she drove to the station.

Tony's truck wasn't there and she didn't see him around so she drove past the station, down a block where she could make a U-turn and headed out to the yard.

Jim Olsen was standing inside the gate and he motioned for her to pull over to the side.

"What?"

"Sorry Les, premises are out of bounds to you, per your Aunt Dina."

Unable to speak or contain her rage, she threw her purse in the car and jumped back inside. Seething, she floored the accelerator and turned onto the highway.

Leslie always drove as if she were half an hour behind schedule. It had nothing to do with punctuality, she loved speed. Now she drove as if she were two days late.

Anger had dissolved all reason. She was fed up with playing for time, of being extra cautious, of forcing smiles, or worrying about possible snags and obstacles. Sweetsy-poo time was over. Screw appearances. Madame Zero had a lot of damn gall.

Leslie wasn't going to waste one more minute on strategy or

technique. Who the hell did she think she was? Come prancing in, trying to take charge. It was the last goddamn straw. Madame Zero was going out on her ass *tonight*.

She pulled up next to her father's Lincoln and stormed into the house, purposely slamming the door as hard as she could. A message to Madame Zero. Trouble was coming her way and she was going get a heavy dose.

"*Dina!* Where the *hell* are you? I want to talk to you *now!*"

Dina appeared in the doorway of the den. "In here."

Leslie brushed past her. Without thinking, out of habit she sat in her usual chair instead of the chair behind the desk. The chair that symbolized the power position. She realized her gaffe too late, and Dina was already sitting in it. She stayed where she was, not wanting to reveal the importance she attached to it. How significant was it now anyway? The chair, the house were all hers. She could afford to be a gracious hostess, allow Madame Zero to sit in it.

"I want to know what the hell's going on? I drove out to the yard and Jim Olsen says you told him I'm not allowed on the premises. He said those were your instructions. What kind of bullshit is this? I'm *not allowed* on my own property? The yard, the construction business, everything is mine, including this house. So where do you come off giving orders that my property is off limits to me? What is it with you? Are you playing the prodigal mother returning to the old homestead to claim her bastard son? You think you can cut him in for a share of what's mine? If you do, think *again*. I want you out of here tonight!" She was aware her face was probably firehouse red, and that Dina wasn't saying one damn word, just sitting there looking so goddamn calm. Expressionless. Leslie stopped to think. And stare.

For a long time they looked at one another, measuring. There was nothing readable in Dina's face. She looked at Leslie as if she hadn't heard a word.

318

When she spoke, her voice was soft and very calm. "Are you finished?"

Something inside Leslie erupted and hostility glistened in her eyes. "Finished? No, I'm not! I'm just getting started—"

"No, you're not. You are finished. I want you to pay close attention to what I'm going to say. I recognize deception, and you, Leslie, have a real talent for it—you're no novice, but you haven't graduated yet."

There was a stiletto sharpness in Dina's voice that cut through the air and caught Leslie by surprise. She felt the hairs on her arms and neck rise and it struck her like a pinched nerve, paralyzing her. Now she knew why Madame Zero had given her such bad vibes. Dina was something she had not encountered before: a formidable player. How could she have missed it? As Leslie glared into the uncompromising green eyes a voice inside tauntingly told her she had missed it by being overconfident.

Leslie knew she had made a costly mistake. A goddamned king-sized blunder. She had underestimated Madame Zero. Her head wasn't made of cottage cheese after all. Her brain cells thrived on a bed of ice, right next to her nerves. Leslie just sat in the chair, like an obedient child, listening to her better judgment warning her not to provoke her aunt any further. She wanted to think she was playing it smart, but she also suspected that some of what she was feeling was fear. And she didn't like it.

"I'm going to tell you what I've done, and what I'm going to do. I'll dispense with the tedious legal terminology, the deeper aspects, and give you a brief summary. You will not be allowed on any business property, unless accompanied by me. The yard, the construction company, everything including this house, belongs to me."

"Don't give me that bull—my father told me, promised me, that the company, everything, was going to be mine." Even to her, her voice lacked its usual conviction, its spellbinding quality she worked so hard to master.

"All yours? What about Andy? Your father and I had a long talk while he and your mother were with me in New York." She saw Leslie's mouth start to open.

"Be still. When I'm finished you can say what you want. Your grandfather left everything to me before he died. That was before your father returned from Korea. Why your father never asked me to change or transfer the businesses or anything else is immaterial. Only one thing was important, we were family. Trusted each other."

Leslie's face hung in disbelief. "You...*can't be serious.* All these years? That airhead has been telling me all this was going to be mine! You're *lying!*"

"Why would I? Believe me, I can and will show you a copy of your grandfather's will so you can read it yourself."

She *knew.* She knew Madame Zero was telling the truth. "All right. Cut the bullshit. Tell me what you think is mine. Exactly mine."

"Your car, your clothes...oh, and this." Dina opened the desk drawer and removed a key, placing it on the desk on top of the ledgers from the offices.

Leslie's eyes stared at the tape-smudged safety deposit key, but she couldn't believe it was hers. She opened her mouth but not a word would come out. She swallowed hard. Again. And again.

She was fighting for control, this was no time to go berserk. She concentrated as hard as she could to keep her cool, to keep her voice in control. To speak as calmly and evenly as Madame Zero. But when she was able to speak, her voice was two octaves higher than normal. *"You goddamn snoop!* How dare you! You have no right—going into my room, through my things. I'm going to call the sheriff." It was an empty threat, she knew it. Worse than that, she knew Dina knew.

Dina reached for the phone, picked it up, and placed it in front of her. "Be my guest."

"How? How did you find my key?" She made no move to pick up the phone.

"I was a narc's wife. You'd be surprised at the places people hide things. Incidentally, save yourself a trip to the bank, you won't find anything." It wasn't necessary for Leslie to know that Andy had told her about his sister spending so much time in her bathroom, always fiddling around with the tissue holder.

Struggling not to cry, Leslie worked at gathering some semblance of control.

"That money is mine. I insist you give it back to me."

"*Your* money?" Dina's right eyebrow arched. "Don't be absurd. You're not in any position to demand anything, or to bargain. You do, however, have a few options."

"Oh, goody. I'm all ears." *Absurd?*

"First, I'll tell you what I am not going to do. I am not going to press charges. I'll *overlook* your poor judgment. Don't misunderstand my motives. Your two redeeming factors are that you are my brother's daughter and my parents' granddaughter. Family. These are your options: Stay here. If you attend college, I will pay your tuition and necessary expenses and give you an allowance that, I'm sure, will seem penurious by your standards, but it will be adequate. Working your way through college is not a choice. As ethically dehydrated as you are, you'd bankrupt your employers and very likely wind up behind bars. However, it is only fair to explain the conditions of this option. I will take more than a casual interest in not only your scholastic achievements, but also your extracurricular activities. You will have to prove to me you are doing your best, not only academically, but also that you are exerting yourself to improve your character. You can live here or on campus. A word of advice, don't try to con me, *ever*. It would be the second biggest mistake of your life. There is one other option. You could marry Tony."

"Hmm. I pass. Any other…*options?*" The sarcasm came easily and Leslie made no attempt to apologize. Tact was out. If nothing else, she wanted Madame Zero to know she wasn't intimidated by her. She was not going to see her shaking in her shoes, or anywhere else.

"One. You can take your clothes and your car, and drive away."

What Leslie wanted, more than anything, was to vent the fury festering inside her. But first she wanted to think it out, how best to do that. She respected clout. For now, Madame Zero had all the power. *For now.* Her mind zipped through her so-called options, which were nothing more than thinly veiled threats. Who was she kidding?

She wasn't going to leave, not now. She'd be a fool. All the money she'd worked so hard to get was here. Dina was what? In her forties? As her father always said, the Dmitris didn't have a good track record for longevity. Dina did *look* disgustingly healthy, but then so had Leslie's mother and father. Health wasn't everything.

She made a quick guesstimate about how long Madame Zero had left. Twenty years, tops. When she did go, where was it all going to go? Not to some stranger. No matter what she said, the bottom line, by her own admission, was family first. She was too old to have any more kids. Peter posed no threat. Not any serious threat. Madame Zero wouldn't dare claim him now. Not in front of the whole town.

A light shone, drawing her focus back to a seed her mother had tried to implant. Brilliant. Coming from her mother of all people! Who would have guessed? What did it take? Eight years? If nothing else came up in the meantime, if nothing happened to Madame Zero, Leslie could do the eight years. What did shrinks make? Sixty-five, one hundred dollars an hour? In eight hours she'd be taking in close to eight hundred dollars a day, maybe more. Probably be bored out of her gourd, but with that kind of bread she could tolerate it *until* something better came up.

"I'll go to college."

"You want more time to think it over?"

"No. If I leave, I have zilch. If I stay and *cooperate*, I'll have all the comforts of home. Which, from the way you paint it, is going to be a little like hell with air conditioning."

Dina shrugged her shoulders slightly. "That's a fairly accurate description."

"I'll stay. Don't want to miss out on the rosy picture of *life at home with you* that you so graciously painted for me."

"You made a quick decision. I hope for your sake it's not a hasty one. Have you thought about what your major will be?"

"As a matter of fact, I had a discussion once or twice with my mother about something I've been seriously thinking about for some time. I'm thinking about psychiatry." She liked the sound of it. The more she thought about it the more it stoked her imagination. *A goddamn license to probe.* To discover people's secrets, all those lovely deep, dark secrets. Wealthy nuts getting all their problems and secrets off their gold-laden chests. Institutions were out. It had to be strictly private practice. Eight or ten years was a small sacrifice to pay when weighing it against all the lovely benefits.

"Impressive choice. But then I'm sure you know that. You could make a very good one, *if* you set your mind to it."

Leslie thought she detected a slight note of contempt in Madame Zero's voice, but she swallowed her resentment and tried not to show she picked up on it.

"Aunt Dina, I want you to know that I'm grateful for your giving me a break. I'm not proud of the way I've behaved, all the way around. I'm not proud of the things I've done. I guess part of it is being spoiled. That, and part is my rebellious nature. You must know how it is, you obviously had trouble accepting the Dmitri puritanism, I mean with what went on between you and Carl."

"We're not discussing me."

Dina's face remained blank, although her eyes did flash for a second. They didn't like what Leslie said. It was the first sign that something could get under her skin. Victory seemed closer. If she was on a roll, now would be the time to shake Madame Zero up, make her lose her composure. Make her lose her goddamn control.

"I know that. But you must see *similarities* in our natures. Except for your unusual taste in men. Which is kind of weird."

"No, Leslie. We are not similar. Not at all."

"You don't think so? Well, I do think I need to mention that when Mom and Dad were in New York with you, while Jake stayed with Andy and me, Jake was after me to get it on, if you know what I mean."

"Oh, I know what you mean. You should have left well enough alone. I know Jake's not a child molester. Stop playing games. If you have anything more to say, say it. I have some errands to run and I don't have the time nor the patience for this foolishness."

Foolishness? Child molester! Who the hell did she think she was dealing with? Some stupid kid?

"I don't want to hear anything more about what you have to say about anyone. Look at me when I'm talking to you."

Leslie stared into the menacing green eyes and she knew it was imperative that Dina never suspect what was on her mind. What was really on her mind.

"Keep this foremost in your mind. I'm not your father, nor your mother. You are family, that's a fact. But I'm warning you, I won't put up with bad behavior, and I will not put up with criminal behavior. Tell you what you can do. I want you to think of yourself as a parolee, with a very intolerant parole officer, who is hard-pressed to tolerate you. You could make a very strong case for abortion."

Unprepared for the sting of the words, all Leslie could do was call on every bit of her will power to keep a smile on her face, to ward off the tears she felt were going to break out. Why, she didn't know. What did she care what Madame Zero thought or said? "Okeydoke. I have a date with Tony so, if you don't mind, I—"

"I don't. Don't let me keep you. I'll see you later this evening, at dinner."

Leslie nodded, choking down a compulsion to tell her there was no way she'd be home for dinner. But she wasn't able to. She hurried out of the room, then leaned against the wall to calm herself. She had to be cool. Collected. She pushed herself away from the wall, quietly strolled out the door and into her car. What she wanted to do was drive out of town. Far, far away. But not without what was rightfully hers. What she needed was a plan. She started the car, floored the accelerator and headed for town.

CHAPTER FORTY-TWO

DESPITE THE FATIGUE ROLLING OVER HER, AND EVERY MUSCLE IN HER BODY serving notice it was ready to revolt, a faint smile appeared on Dina's mouth. The war wasn't going to be easy, it was going to be fought in inches. Yet she saw a glimmer of hope. No guarantees, of course, but a lot of possibilities. Leslie had accepted the challenge.

Ledgers firmly cradled in her arm, she picked up her purse, grabbed her jacket, went out to the car and drove straight to the lumberyard.

After she locked the ledgers in the safe, she walked across the yard, over to Paul's shop.

There were a few unfinished pieces in various stages, including the bottom half of a beautiful oak hutch and a hickory desk without drawers. She switched off the light.

She went back to the yard office to make one last check and was about to switch the light off when out of the corner of her right eye she caught sight of a pair of shoes protruding out from the shadows.

"Mrs. Coleman, it's Peter. I...have to talk to you. I didn't want...to bother you...at home..."

The cover of the shadows didn't keep her from noticing that something about his face didn't look right. She walked over to him and gently took his hand and led him into the light. His face was badly bruised and swollen.

"What happened to you?"

His first impulse was to tell her it was none of her damn business, but he didn't care anymore. "A little difference of opinion with…my father."

"Do you think you can make it out to the car? I'll drive you to the clinic. You'd better have a doctor look at your face. Can you feel your nose?" She was holding him by the arm.

He tried pulling his arm away from her, but to his surprise she had a strong grip for a middle-aged woman. Maybe it was just him. He was weak. It was dumb, giving in to impulses. He shouldn't have come out here. Not tonight. He was getting kinda dizzy. Her grip was firm. Unyielding.

"Peter, I'm taking you to the clinic. You're swaying. You can barely stand up, you're going to fall flat on your face."

He started to pull away again, but his head was getting light and fuzzy. On top of that, he was feeling nauseous. God, he didn't want to be sick in front of her. He let her walk him to the car.

"Is your face the only place he hit you?"

"No…yeah…no. I don't know." He wasn't about to tell her that Carl had kicked him in the nuts. Gonads came to him, but he was too sore to care.

Dina hadn't heard any car pull into the lot. "How did you get out here?"

He wanted to laugh. Who did she think she was, his mother? "I got a ride part way…walked the rest."

She opened the car door and helped him in. When she reached the gate, she knew he must have jumped the fence to get in, she remembered locking it.

"Did you fall when you came over the fence?"

"How tall…do I look? What's with all the questions? I came out here…to ask you…a few…" He was getting dizzy again.

"Because if you pass out I want to be able to tell Dr. Grant the extent of your injuries. You could be bleeding internally."

"No! I'm not going to the clinic. And if you try to take me, I'll jump out of the car."

"You're too weak to move your feet, much less do any jumping."

"Wanna...bet? *I mean it.*"

"Fine, then I'm driving you home with me."

He didn't want to go there either but it was better than the clinic or the resort. "Okay."

Usually a very cautious driver, Dina drove as fast as the road would allow.

"Peter? Don't fall asleep. Talk to me. About anything that comes to your mind." Which was it? Was it a child or an adult you were supposed to keep awake if there was a possibility of a concussion? She felt old resentments resurface as if they had been waiting behind a curtain. How many times were circumstances going to protect the cretin? If Peter refused to go to the clinic, there would be no report filed. Meaning Carl wouldn't be charged with assault and battery. Having Dr. Grant come out to the house ensured that a report would be filed. Carl wasn't going to get off the hook, not this time.

"I feel sick. I have to know—the scholarship—you set that up, didn't you?"

"Yes." Her voice was so low he had to strain to hear it. He stared at her and nodded.

"I knew it. I'm going to pay you back, every dime. I wasn't going to accept it at first, but then I figured I'd be foolish not to."

"You don't owe me anything. And you're right. It would have been foolish to turn it down."

"I do owe you. Tell me...I have to know...why did my mother give me to Carl? Martha told me Karen is my mother. He raped her, didn't he?"

That Martha knew about Karen jolted her and left her uncertain. Speechless. What could she say?

"If you're thinking up a story, forget it. I need to know the truth."

"Do you really want the truth?"

"Let's put it this way, I've been *protected* long enough, don't you think? Hasn't done a whole lot for me."

Making instantaneous evaluations had never been something she liked doing. This was tougher, since she didn't know Peter very well. Everyone deserved the truth, but this truth? Who was the best judge of what he could take? He was demanding to be told.

"It seems you've given this a lot of thought. Hearing the truth is hard."

"I don't expect it to set me free and I'm not so dumb I don't think it'll hurt. But I have to know."

"Yes, Carl raped Karen. But it wasn't Karen's, your mother's, idea to have Carl adopt you, it was mine. I wasn't thinking what life would be like for you growing up. My main concern was my family. What was best for my father, brother and Karen. I've always known Martha to be a warm, loving person. A gentle soul who wanted a child of her own. Decisions don't work out for everyone. Perhaps if I had been wiser, I wouldn't have had as much false confidence. When we're young, some of us see only the part of the picture that pertains to us. I'm sorry, Peter, that the decisions that were made didn't work out for you." She could feel Peter staring at her. At least he was awake. "How long has Martha known about Karen?"

"I don't know. She didn't say. I think she's known for a couple of years. I'm getting dizzy again...I think..."

He passed out. She wasn't going to waste time pulling over and trying to revive him, the house was less than five minutes away. She pushed down on the accelerator.

It was a relief to see Tony's truck in the drive. She honked the horn and Tony came out.

Together, they carried him inside and laid him on the sofa. As

330

soon as he was settled, Dina phoned Dr. Grant and asked him to drive out to the house. He promised to be there shortly.

Leslie stood in the living room scowling. First at Peter, then at Dina. "I might have known that sooner or later you'd bring the bastard here, now that your legitimate kid is gone. You've got your nerve! You read me the riot act, tell me I have to live like Sally Shit the Ragpicker, so you can—"

The slap was a total shock. And it stung. Bad. No one had ever dared to raise a hand to her. She covered her face with her hand to protect it in case Dina tried to hit her again. She was beginning to understand why Madame Zero kept her cool. For the simple reason the woman was nutso. Mean. No, she was ruthless.

"Don't open your mouth again. Go sit in that chair, stay out of the way. Out of my way."

Leslie had to take three deep breaths to regain her composure. Madame Zero was talking to her like she was some little five-year-old kid. Some pesky kid. An *insignificant* piece of furniture that needed to be shoved out of the way.

Tony quickly and quietly led her to the other side of the room. While she was being led, she glowered at Dina, then Peter, then included Tony.

"Where's Andy?" Dina directed the question to Leslie. It lacked her usual softness.

Before Leslie had a chance to answer, Tony jumped in and explained that Andy was over at the Tanners' for dinner with Phil.

Leslie, incensed over Tony's attitude, shot him a look that was filled with rage. It enraged her more when he chose to ignore it. When the time was right, she was going to tell them all they could go to hell. But not yet. She recited to herself that discretion was the better part of valor.

A few minutes later, when Dr. Grant arrived and began to examine Peter, Leslie slowly circled her way over to the sofa.

Talent for Deception

It irked her the way Madame Zero hovered over her little bastard.

Watching her circle, Dina was reminded of that shark in Florida. Before she got to the sofa, Dina intercepted her, grabbed her by the arm and led her out to the kitchen.

"Stay in here until Dr. Grant is through."

Dina returned to the living room just as the doctor was writing out a prescription. "Oh, there you are, Dina. There's nothing broken. Kids get into scraps like this from time to time. I'd like to see the other guy. He'll be all right in a day or two. Here's a prescription for something to ease the discomfort." He laid the prescription on the table.

Dina followed the doctor to the door. "This wasn't a scrap. Carl Anderson did that. I want it reported."

"Of course." He had tried to minimize Peter's bruises. He thought he was being diplomatic, protecting a good boy. Keeping him out of trouble. What Dina told him shed a different light on things. He assured her that he would write out a full report.

"I suggest Peter get complete rest for a few days and not do anything strenuous for a day or two. If he tries, I'm pretty sure his body will refuse anyway." He picked up his bag and started for the door.

"I'll walk you out."

"Oh, well, good. By the way, welcome home, stranger."

"Thank you."

When she opened the door he put his hand on her shoulder. "It is good seeing you again. And don't worry, I'll take care of the report. Good night, Dina."

She was about to walk him to his car when she heard the phone. She said a quick good night and hurried back into the house.

Tony had already picked it up and was holding it out to her.

"Hello."

"Hi. Would you consider having a drink and dinner with a weary old sailor? Or a cup of coffee?"

"Jake. When did you get back?"

"Just walked in the door. If you're thinking of an excuse, Phil and Andy had dinner already and are now having a go at thick malts and popcorn. I'm sure Leslie and Tony have something planned that doesn't include you or me. So what do you say?"

She wasn't hungry, she was exhausted. Leaving Peter alone was out of the question. "I'll have to take a rain check."

He correctly assumed the hesitation was reluctance. Before she had a chance he said, "I'll be there in half an hour." He hung up before she had a chance to say anything.

"No, Jake, don't hang up." She heard the click of the phone and thought about calling him back. Instead, she sighed and hung up, too.

CHAPTER FORTY-THREE

IF ANYONE DESERVED CREDIT FOR SUPREME EFFORT, LESLIE FELT SHE WAS A shoo-in. She bet no one ever accused Dina of overreacting, but Leslie outdid her. She had a choke hold on her temper, holding back all and any objections she had. She kept her mouth shut about Peter spending the night, or nights. Who knew how long he was going to hang around?

She pulled Tony out of the house and insisted that he take her into town to grab a bite to eat. He was about to protest, but one look at her glacier eyes cut him off.

Before showering, Dina gave Peter one more check. He was resting peacefully. Looking down at him, she could still see him as a baby. He was a good baby. Didn't fuss much and he smiled a lot. So far, she hadn't seen him smile. She felt bad that his life had been less than he deserved. Tomorrow she would ask that he keep the fact that he and Leslie were more than cousins to himself. If Dina had to explain why, she would. Might be better for him to know that Leslie would use it against him if she saw some advantage in doing so. More ammunition for her to conjure up her schemes.

Dina leaned over and brushed a lock of his hair away from his eyes. It was then she realized her hand was still smarting from the slap. Striking Leslie was inexcusable, just as the remark about abortion was unnecessarily cruel. She was disappointed with herself for losing her temper. However, she believed a few swats on Leslie's behind while she was younger might have helped her realize there were limitations to other people's tolerance. It worked for Ben Jr. But Leslie was Paul and Karen's daughter, not hers.

She sighed. What she needed was a long, hot soak in a tub, but there wasn't time. She settled for a short, hot shower.

CHAPTER FORTY-FOUR

IN THE PARKING LOT OF ANDERSON'S RESORT TWO MEN SAT IN A DUSTY dark sedan watching Carl move around in the office. Simmons sat behind the wheel. His passenger, Al Ryan, commented on how well the guy in the Catskills and Carl's buddy in Canada had described him.

Simmons lifted his chin in the direction of the neon sign. "He'll be putting on the No Vacancy sign soon and locking up."

Al lifted out the magnum from its holster, checked the magazine, gave the silencer a couple of twists, and returned it to its home under his arm.

"What's been going on?"

Simmons let out a disgusted laugh through his toothpick. "Our boy's had a busy night. First he beat hell out of the kid. After the kid took off, he started in on the wife. She's in the back bedroom up at the house."

Al kept his eyes on the office. "Seems like I'm doing more than a couple people a favor. Who else is around?"

"Everyone is over at some shindig in town. Some big dance going on." He would have gone, too, if he hadn't had to pick up Al. He loved that shit-kicking music, dancing and mixing with people who didn't have any idea of who he was, or what he did for a living.

"*Shindig*? What you been doing with your time? Learning how to speak hayseed?"

"Ha-ha. I can only fish for so long. Long enough to make my

get-away vacation look legit. I hate fish. They remind me of snakes. All the time I was cleaning 'em, Anderson was telling me how good the fishing is up at Rainy Lake, a place he goes to now and then to see a friend of his. They also like to go up to someplace in the Adirondacks when they can."

"Rainy Lake, huh? Try Lake Simcoe. Doesn't make any dif, Carl won't be fishing in any lake after tonight."

Simmons irritated him, but Al had to admit that without his help he might still be looking for the dynamite man. Not that he had much choice. His brother Bob and Simmons went back a long way and Bob trusted Simmons probably as much as he trusted Al. It was Simmons who introduced Bob to Amanda. Bob was grateful and Al would be grateful, too.

"How's the widow?"

"She's fine. Took a trip out to the yard. Figured as long as I kept my eye on Anderson, she'd be okay. She's a good-looking babe. She came back with the Anderson kid."

"She'd better be okay. And knock off with the babe talk."

"Hey, don't get touchy. Just an observation is all."

The lights went out in the office and the No Vacancy sign went on. A few minutes later Carl came out of the office and walked up the hill to the house.

Simmons handed Al a set of keys. "When it's done, there's a blue boat at the end of the pier. Here's a flashlight. Cruising speed, it'll take you maybe ten minutes to get across, over to that place that looks like a beached ship. There's a road out back of it that leads to the stone quarry. I'll meet you back of the house and drive us to the stone quarry. Got a 'copter there for us."

Al broke out in a sweat. "You mean one of those whirlybird things?"

"Yep."

"Who's flying it?"

338

"I am."

"Christ! You got a license? I don't care. I'm not getting in one of those, not at night. Not with you."

"Well, well. Get a load of Mr. Cool. Don't worry, I won't let you fall out."

"Goddamn it! No one said anything about a...'copter." Al had difficulty getting the word out. He hated anything higher than a curb. "Maybe you should just go by yourself, I'll find my own way out."

"No can do. Let me put it this way—I got explicit instructions from your brother, Bob, and Amanda. I don't leave without you."

"What if something goes haywire? I'm not there in an hour, take off. Not a good idea for you sticking around with a copter, you'll stand out..."

Simmons was smiling as he scooted out of the car. "I'll see you on the other side, pard. Gotta mosey now. Time for me to say my see-yas to the guests in the cabin next to mine, make sure they know I left. When you see me pull out of the drive, he's all yours."

Al slid out on the opposite side of the car and closed the door without making a sound. Staying in the shadows he made his way up to the house. He sat down next to a tree and waited for the sedan to pull out. It was a long fifteen minutes. When it did pull away, he waited a few extra minutes after the tail lights disappeared.

He made his way up to the back of the house. He was below the bedroom window where the wife was. There was a radio on, or it might be a phonograph. No air conditioner.

Reluctantly, he swung up into the tree and looked inside. The woman was on the bed, in a fetal position. As far as he could tell she was breathing, but it wasn't coming easy. His eyes went on through the door and down the hall. He didn't see anything, no shadows moving around.

The sound of a motor turning over startled him and his head

spun around, down to the lake. Swearing under his breath, he carefully lowered himself down out of the tree. As soon as his feet were on the ground, he broke into a jogging trot. Wasn't smart to go any faster, he didn't need to fall on his ass or break a leg.

He could see the running lights of the boat moving away from shore. He swore again. It had to be Carl. And he had to be in the damn blue boat because there was no boat at the end of the pier now.

Al ran along the shoreline, foam almost to his ankles, looking for anything that would be light and fast. He shoved the nearest boat out into the water and hopped in. He heard a motor sputter and die. He rowed harder and almost tipped the boat over. Then he heard the motor start up again. He muttered "son of a bitch" as he rowed.

CHAPTER FORTY-FIVE

PETER'S EYES TOOK A WOBBLY LOOK AROUND THE ROOM. A BELL FAR OFF IN the distance woke him out of a deep sleep. He was about to get up when Dina came into the room and told him to lie down and stay where he was. "I'll get it; it's probably Jake."

When she opened the door, Jake was standing at the end of the porch, looking up at the sky. "Will you look at those stars."

She walked over to him and looked. He watched the moonlight dance across her face. It wasn't planned, he hadn't even thought about it. Before he knew it, his lips were on hers, and once they were there the valves of suppression blew away and he was kissing her harder. He thought he heard a crack, felt her jerk in his arms.

His first concern was he'd gotten so carried away he went and cracked one of her ribs, but as soon as he eased away she slumped in his arms, and then he saw the Alice in Wonderland look in her eyes. His smile withered. He didn't have to look at his wet hands, he knew what they were covered with—blood.

"Dina! Oh Jesus, NO!"

A voice from somewhere behind them broke the awful stillness.

"Told her. Told her someday she'd get what was coming to her. Always sticking her goddamn nose in where it didn't belong. She always was a troublesome bitch."

Jake wanted to twist around to where Carl's voice was coming from, but to do that, he wouldn't be able to shield Dina. He craned his neck.

Talent for Deception

He estimated Carl was no more than forty feet to his left. He was swaying, the rifle was still in a firing position. Afraid to risk antagonizing him, he didn't say a word. He had two choices, either lay Dina down on the porch and make a try for him, or risk making a run for the house and getting shot in the back. He chose the house.

He braced himself and started to move toward the door, waiting for bullets to rip his back. He heard two consecutive spits and leaned into the fieldstone. He heard Carl groan, and turned and saw him stumble and fall to the ground. Then he heard someone running. Whoever it was ran down toward the lake.

Jake didn't wait any longer, he carried Dina into the house and laid her down on the floor of the foyer. Peter was there, and handed him a blanket.

"I called for an ambulance, they're going to try to locate Dr. Grant, he was here not long ago. I don't think it was long...I'm kinda fuzzy."

Jake gently placed the blanket over Dina. "Jesus! So much blood." He was about to grab her up in his arms and drive her to the hospital himself when Dr. Grant pulled in the driveway. The ambulance was right behind him.

Jake and Peter stepped aside immediately. Jake asked Peter if he knew where Leslie was.

"With Tony, I think they went to the Norseman's."

After Jake and Dr. Grant left in the ambulance with Dina, Peter went out to wait for the sheriff. He looked down at the man who was supposed to be his father, and felt nothing.

After the sheriff came with the coroner and took Carl away, Peter went back into the house to lay down. He felt better, but tired. He was going to call Martha, but he fell asleep.

At the hospital, Jake paced the floor going in one direction, Leslie paced in the opposite. Tony sat and watched them without saying a word.

Jake sat down beside him, praying harder than he had in his life for Dina to pull through. Leslie wasn't sure what to do. She didn't want her aunt to die, not like this. On the other hand, life was going to be as rosy as mud if Dina didn't die.

CHAPTER FORTY-SIX

THE SHERIFF CAME DOWN THE HALLWAY WITH A DEPUTY AND STOPPED TO talk to Dr. Grant about an anonymous caller telling him to go check on the wife at Anderson's Resort. The deputy wheeled Martha into the emergency room.

Dr. Grant mumbled that Carl had quite a night for himself. Martha had a broken arm, two broken ribs and some very nasty contusions on her face. Luckily, Peter didn't have any broken bones.

The sheriff was taking notes as Dr. Grant went through the damages.

Dr. Grant stopped to ask the sheriff a question. "Any clues as to who shot Carl?"

"Nope. To tell the truth, seeing Martha, and hearing what he'd done to Peter, I don't care if we never find him. That's between you and me."

Dr. Grant left the sheriff and walked into the waiting room, joined by Dr. Meyer, who had operated on Dina. From the beaming smiles, Leslie knew she wasn't going to get her money back, wasn't going to be leaving town, and life wasn't going to be beautiful for some time.

Dr. Grant shook Jake's hand and put his arm around Leslie. It took everything she had not to pull away. She wanted to stuff his arm up his ass.

"Dina's going to be fine. She's lost quite a bit of blood, but the bullet missed all the vital organs. She's one lucky lady." He took

Jake's arm and led him aside. "Jake, take that look off your face. She's fine."

"I have to see her. Five seconds."

"Don't you trust me? She's in recovery. She won't know you, much less—"

"I don't care. Five seconds. I have to see her."

"Okay. Five minutes. No more."

Jake didn't expect her to look like she did earlier, but he wasn't prepared to see her looking so lifelessly pale. His throat was parched and raw. He reached out to touch her hand. It was warm; she had to be alive.

Her eyes opened slightly and she smiled drowsily. "That was...some kiss."

He squinted away the tears and kissed her hand. "I love you, Dina. I always have, always will. You're not going to remember what I'm saying but we have a lifetime and I'm going to repeat it often. Every day."

She was already back in the arms of Morpheus. He leaned over her and listened. Satisfied that she was breathing, just sleeping, he gave her a peck on the cheek and went back to the waiting room.

He put his arm around Leslie. "Dina's okay. Let's go home."

"Uh, Tony and I can drop you off, then I have to go home and take care of our houseguest. All right if Andy stays with you and Phil tonight?"

"Sure."

She wanted to get back home, fast. Peter was going to be the owner of Anderson's Resort. Martha was older than Dina and probably not in the best of shape.

They dropped Jake off and headed for the Dmitri Place. Leslie's mind hummed with activity trying to figure a way to get rid of Tony as soon as they got home. It was better to invite him in for a cup of coffee and then send him on his way. He could keep Peter occupied while she improvised some sort of plan.

While she was making the coffee, Tony stayed in the living room with Peter. She brought three cups on a tray and poured them all a cup of coffee.

Peter normally didn't drink coffee but since she went through the trouble he didn't want to refuse. He already had enough guilt on his plate. He knew he should feel worse about Carl, but all he could identify was relief. Martha was the one he cared about. Tony assured him she was going to be okay. He tried to imagine a thousand times what kind of life she had before Carl...how did it compare? She never complained about how he treated her. He did know he wanted something more, something better, out of life for himself. And for Martha. Maybe now she'd have it. He was a better man than Carl. He'd take care of her.

Tony handed him a cup of coffee. "Here you go."

"Thanks." He and Tony had never had any real conversations before, until tonight. Never said more than "hi" whenever they ran into each other. Thinking about Tony now, Peter decided he liked him very much. Tony and Leslie made a nice looking couple. For a time he didn't know what to do, when he thought he and Connie might be related. His spirits took a 180 degree turn when he found out they weren't. That the girl sitting next to Tony was his half-sister.

Without being too conspicuous he looked his half-sister over. He had always thought she was beautiful. Like...their mother. He tried to find some similarity between them, but there wasn't any that he could see. He didn't like to even think it, but if he looked like anyone, it was Carl.

Tony's interruption into his thoughts was more of a rescue.

"Guess I'll be taking off. Good night, Pete." They shook hands and Tony went straight for the door. Leslie offered to walk him to the car and he declined the offer with what Peter thought was like a cat

347

jumping off the couch before it got yelled at. Leslie gave him a kiss and he mumbled something to her and was out the door. Peter felt pretty sure from the way he read it that Tony was glad to be on his way out and away from Leslie.

Peter was experiencing a weird sense of accomplishment. He was inside the Dmitri Place. Sitting on the couch in the same house his mother lived in. He didn't notice right away that Leslie had resumed her role as the gracious hostess. She had poured out another cup of coffee for him and started fluffing up his pillow. He didn't want to be rude, but he didn't want any more coffee. He was tired and getting drowsy.

"Pete, I'm sorry I acted like such a spoiled brat. It was a shock to me, finding out who you were, and, well, I guess maybe I was sort of jealous, being territorial. I shouldn't have said some of the things I did. About my aunt and your father. I've had a pretty rough time of it. It's awful what loss and grief makes us do sometimes. But it does bring about a better understanding, forces us to reach out to one another." She put her hand on his shoulder. "I can relate to you. You can identify with me, too. We're family. Cousins." How much time would it take? There wasn't much doubt in her mind that Madame Zero would probably be up, on her feet, in a week. Which meant Leslie couldn't afford to drag her heels. Still, it wasn't a good idea to rush him either.

Peter took her hand and held it in his. *Family*. It had a real nice ring to it. If only she knew *how nice* it was.

"Pete? I hate to bring this up...at a time like this, but you do have to think about it sooner or later. Are you going to college? If you are, you'll need someone to look after the resort. I mean Martha will need help. I'll help in any way I can. Fact is, I could manage it for you. We could be partners. I have all the experience—"

"Really, Les? You'd do that for me? Or should I say to me? No thanks. I can think of more satisfying ways of getting screwed."

348

The sweetness in her face vanished, replaced by the meanest look he had ever seen on a girl.

"You know, this family is going downhill fast, *real* fast. It was an honest, sincere offer, but if you don't want my help, it's no skin off my nose. Think about this. Who else do you have? You think that mother of yours is going to help you? Ask yourself where she's been for the past, what? nineteen years? You think she's going to reach out and bring you into the family fold? Get serious. As for Martha, she's already old as the hills and with the pounding your father gave her she'll need—"

"My mother *can't* bring me into the family fold. Anyway it's a dead issue. Martha, *my mother,* and I will manage the resort with Connie's help. We'll make out okay." He didn't feel it was any business of hers, but he no longer wanted to be a lawyer. Still, having knowledge of law would be a huge asset for a businessman. He made an on-the-spot decision, he would go on to college. And he'd study law, but he would also take business courses.

To settle the argument he was having with his conscience, he wanted to toss a coin, heads he'd tell Leslie that they were much closer than cousins, tails he'd keep his mouth shut. But he couldn't do it. Maybe someday they could become friends, and you didn't intentionally hurt your friends. One look at her told him it wasn't possible, you had to be able to trust your friends.

"I thought your ambition was to be a lawyer. At least that's what the grapevine says."

"Guess the grapevine doesn't know everything." He was slowly beginning to realize something. He liked Hid'n Oaks. "I like it here. It's a nice place to live. Things are different now. I want to stay."

"Is that so? My intuition tells me things are going to be painfully different around here. And far too soon. If Madame…if Dina heals as fast as I think she will, you may wind up being *flower girl* for your mother when she and Jake—"

Talent for Deception

"Ah, sweet Leslie. You have the charm and personality of a cobra. Personally, I think it'd be great if Jake had someone nice like Dina." Now that there was a body to go along with the person he'd heard about for so many years, he liked her. He believed all the things Martha said about her.

"Hey, I'm only telling it like it is. Truth hurts? Look I'll probably have to get along with you, but that doesn't mean I have to kiss your ass. You're nothing but a wimpy toad. You know who you remind me of? My ma. You're so...*what the hell are you laughing at?*"

"Nothing. Nothing at all. I must be delirious."

"You're a real space case, you know that? A kook. Tell you what, you hang in there, I may be able to help you in about eight or nine years. You are a real leaker. Strictly a candidate for a rubber room. I'm going to bed. If you need anything, the kitchen's in there and the bathroom's off the den over there."

"Good night, Les. Sweet dreams, *cuz*."

CHAPTER FORTY-SEVEN

AT SEVEN IN THE MORNING A LONG DISTANCE CALL CAME INTO THE HOSPItal, requesting information on the status of Dina Coleman. When told the information could not be given over the phone, the caller's request became a demand, then a threat. The nurse referred the rude, awful woman calling herself Amanda Ryan to Dr. Grant. After Dr. Grant told Mrs. Ryan that Mrs. Coleman's condition had been upgraded, her disposition improved remarkably.

Amanda informed the doctor she would be calling every day until she was assured Mrs. Coleman's condition was excellent, then hung up.

Flowers were delivered to the hospital signed "Love, Bob and Amanda." Get well cards were delivered without a return address.

CHAPTER FORTY-EIGHT

FOR THE FIRST TWO DAYS THAT PHIL AND JAKE VISITED DINA, PHIL STOPPED in Martha's room to look in on her before he left the hospital. The third day, Phil looked in on Dina and spent two hours visiting Martha, assuring her the resort was doing fine, that Pete and Connie were doing a good job running it, that they had things under control. He told her that Peter got a deferment, and she didn't have to worry about a thing except getting well.

After Martha and Dina were released, Phil dropped in at the resort every morning at 9:00 a.m. with sweet rolls and coffee—so, he explained to Jake, Martha didn't have to fuss.

On his fifth visit, Phil finally worked up enough courage to ask Martha to keep him company for the rest of their lives. When Martha said she'd be honored, he wasn't sure he heard right and asked her again. As soon as he left the house, he raced his car over to the yard office.

When he got there, Dina was scanning a pile of papers. She pushed them aside as soon as she saw his face, it was as red as a Christmas ribbon and he was extremely worked up about something. Her first thought was dangerously high blood pressure.

"Dina, I'm giving notice. Now that you're feeling okay, and you and Jake are handling everything with no problems, and Pete's helping out—"

"Phil, you don't have to explain anything. We've all appreciated how you've been here for us for more years than you probably should have been. And I want to thank you for taking care of things while I was recuperating." She motioned to the chair next to hers. "Sit down and calm down. You look like you're going to blow a gasket or something. Are you feeling okay? I'll get you a glass of water."

"No. I'm fine. Couldn't be better. And you don't have to thank me, I wouldn't have been happier anywhere else. I'll always be here for you. You know how I felt about Mike and your mom. And you and Paul. Loved all of you, and loved the job."

"I know that. And I hope you know that all of us loved you back."

"Oh hell! I might as well spill the beans. Dina, you're looking at one heck of a happy man. I asked Martha to keep me company for the rest of our lives. You know, marry me." He shook his head as if he was still trying to believe it. And his eyes were glistening. "Know what she said? She said she'd be honored. Can you beat that? Honored."

Dina got up from her chair, kissed his cheek and put her arms around him. "And why not? You're the best catch within a thousand miles. This is certainly the best news I've have in a long time. You know I wish you and Martha all the happiness you can possibly hold, and then some."

Their embrace was interrupted by the ringing of the telephone. Phil smiled and mouthed a 'see you later' as he backed out the door.

"Good afternoon, Dmitri's Lumber, how may I help you?" Dina pulled out two Kleenex tissues from the box on her desk.

"Hi, Gabby." The whispered greeting promptly returned the smile to Dina's face as she recognized Amanda's voice. Amanda didn't give her a chance to offer any response, she cut Dina off. "You know who this is, don't say my name. I just thought you'd like to know, your family can rest in peace. The man who killed them paid with his life."

"How do you know this?"

354

"That's not important. I don't know all the details, but it's been verified by sources I trust. Believe me, I know it's true. Take care, Gab. We love you."

Again, before Dina had a chance to respond, the line went dead. Her emotions were muddled, but one thing that stood clear was the eerie premonition that the words she'd just heard from Amanda would be the last.

For a long time after she hung up the phone, Amanda stood on the balcony and stared out at the ocean. She wasn't aware that her husband had joined her until he took her hand in his and kissed it.

"How did she take it? Think she believed you?"

"Oh, she believed me all right. She's not the only one with a talent for deception."

"What?"

"Dina once told me she had a talent for deception when she needed it. Well, you're looking at the master…make that mistress."

"Uh-uh. One would think you'd remember you're Mrs. Ryan by now." He pulled her over to him and hugged her. "Do you think you should have told her it was Carl?"

"No, I don't. What for? So she could feel guilty the rest of her life? Wondering if it was her or Paul he was after? That the miserable creep wiped out most of her family just to get to her? I don't think so."

He took her in his arms. "How would you like to go to Switzerland next month? We can look around, maybe find ourselves one of those chalets."

"Sure, why not?"

One week later, Dina received a postcard from Hawaii. The message on the back read: *Hi, Having a wonderful time in paradise. Take care. Live, Gabby. Don't let that silver get tarnished. Be happy. Ever in our hearts, always in our thoughts. Love, Amanda & Bob.* The way it was written reinforced the premonition she had when Amanda had called her. She knew this card would be the last communication she would ever have from Amanda.

The door opened behind her and Jake walked in. "Hi. Just talked to Peter. He told me about your offer. It was nice of you."

"I'm glad he accepted."

"It was a good thing to do, Dina. He's walking on air as it is with Connie, but the furniture shop was a real bonus."

"He's earned it. And I'm depending on him to teach Andy the trade."

"Kinda funny, the way things worked out. Pete always liked working construction, building things. And now he's willing to admit he likes working with wood. If nothing else we have to give Carl credit for that. If we overlook how he went about it, he did teach Pete everything he knew about carpentry. Mike always said Carl was one of the best around these parts."

"Okay, I guess that qualifies as a redeeming attribute. I'll concede to that much." A broad grin took away any thoughts of Carl. "Have I got good news for you! You are acquiring an aunt."

"Martha?"

Her grin widened and she nodded. "Of course, who else?"

"That's really swell news. About time Phil got his feet wet. How about we call and ask them out to dinner to celebrate?"

"I think they'd rather celebrate by themselves."

"Well, I'm famished. How about I take you and Andy out for dinner at the Norseman's?"

"Andy's staying over with Peter and Connie—Peter's teaching Andy all about carving tools. Leslie and Tony are going to a movie. So, Mr. Tanner, this is a chance for me to see if it's true that food is the way to a man's heart. I'm going to make dinner for you."

"Lady, you don't have to go through the trouble, mine's been in your pocket since puberty. And you can get rid of that look of dismay. I know you need time and I won't press. I just want to remind you how I feel. I've waited a long time; I can wait a while longer."

"I do love you, Jake, but I do need more time. Let's just take things a day at a time."

"Good enough for me."

* * *

Six months later, two days after Dina and Jake were married, Leslie received notification that in the event of Nadine Dmitri Tanner's death, all Dmitri property and business holdings were to be divided equally between Andrew Dmitri and Peter Anderson, and she would receive $10,000 per year. The screams heard on campus, coming out of Leslie's dormitory, attracted quite an audience. Half the bets were on the screams coming from someone who flunked finals, the other half was on some babe who just found out she was pregnant. It was a tie.